UPON A BLOODSTAINED LAND

A MASON COLLINS CRIME THRILLER 6

JOHN A. CONNELL

NAILHEAD PUBLISHING

UPON A BLOODSTAINED LAND

The bow of the freighter pitched up as it crested another wave, then shuddered as it slammed into a trough. The hull groaned upon the impact as if in its final throes of agony, something you don't want to hear when you hate boats and have a fear of open water. I was following the third mate through the short corridor serving the galley and crew's quarters and had to hold myself up by pushing off the wall. This while trying not to vomit at his feet.

He went first through the hatch leading amidships and to the exterior. We were immediately hit with a blast of wind and driving rain, blinding me for a moment as we stepped onto the deck. I had to squint, limiting my vision to my hands as I hung on to the safety lines.

I was getting soaked despite the raincoat the third mate had provided me. "Are we going far?" I yelled over the crashing seas.

"The body's belowdecks. The hatch isn't much further."

As I pulled myself along or braced against the pitching deck, I had to avoid people huddled together in groups and soaked to the bone.

"Why aren't these people below?"

The third mate glanced back at me as if I'd asked a ridiculous question. "You'll see once we're down there."

The freighter, named by its crew as the *Magen David*, was a vintage World War I steamer built in Sweden and now owned by a Greek shipping company. The crew consisted mostly of American Jews who'd served in the navy or merchant marines. Earl Rosten, the third mate and my current guide, was no more than twenty-five, though he'd seen plenty of action in the Atlantic during the war as a merchant marine. How the crew got ahold of a Greek freighter was something no one could—or was willing to —explain.

On board were 1,345 Jewish refugees, all hoping to get to Mandatory Palestine, though everyone on the ship called it Eretz Israel, or Land of Israel. The initial group of sixty or so that I'd helped smuggle to Naples and onto this ship had been joined by the additional passengers at two other ports in Italy. I'd volunteered to come along despite my fears. And not for the first time since the beginning of the voyage, I wondered if I'd lost my marbles.

I had a travel pass and visa for entering Palestine from my friend Mike Forester in the army's Counter Intelligence Corps, meaning I could have found a flight or taken passage on a passenger liner, but I felt compassion for the people I'd helped pass through Italy and had chosen to accompany them. Then and there, I promised myself to have my head examined.

To control the nausea, I kept my eyes on Rosten's feet and the safety lines, but as I stepped over another cringing passenger, curiosity got the better of me. I looked out at the waves lashing the ship. It was late afternoon, but the heavy clouds made it seem as if night had already fallen. Between the roiling clouds and the heaving sea, the dread of drowning gripped at my chest. I froze when another wave rose above the ship. It smashed against the hull, sending a wall of water onto the deck and flipping me off my feet.

Rosten rushed over and helped me to stand. That was when I saw a warship a half mile away. It appeared to be paralleling our course, and I pointed it out to him.

Rosten nodded and yelled near my ear, "She's been there for a while now. A British cruiser. Legally, they can't intercept us out here. They'll wait until we're inside Palestinian territorial waters."

I glanced once more at the cruiser. Like everyone on board, I'd hoped we might elude the British patrols and make it to Palestine unmolested, but that no longer seemed to be an option.

Rosten continued on, and I followed. A few yards further, he turned the handle—or dog, as the sailors called it—and opened the metal hatch, then ushered me inside.

As we climbed down the ladder, I got my first inkling of why a few hundred passengers were enduring the elements, even risking their lives, to remain on deck. Foul air assaulted my nostrils. The heat and lack of oxygen made it hard to breathe. Like on deck, we had to step around people huddling on the steps, many with their faces raised toward the hatch as if doing so would bring them fresh air and relief.

We reached Hold Two. Instead of a large open space for cargo, wooden bunks stacked eight high had been installed to accommodate the passengers. We moved down the narrow aisle between the rows of bunks. Most of the passengers suffered in silence, but there were a few who wailed in frustration or despair. Two men held down another man who fought to free himself while screaming for them to let him go on deck. Some people we passed peppered Rosten with desperate questions like, "When will the storm stop?" or "When are we going to get there?" but he and I ignored their pleadings and continued.

We passed through another hatch at the far end and entered what I assumed was Hold Three. It was a similar situation— another spacious hold filled to the brim with people and bunks. More crying, more questions. The passengers had boarded with excited anticipation, but now, with no food left and little water, and being holed up in the stinking bowels of the ship, they'd turned despondent and sour. I felt guilty for being among the few who bunked in the crew's quarters. The quarters were crammed, too, but there was ventilation and a chance to escape to the outside.

"Some crew and volunteers have tried to organize shifts for the passengers," Rosten said. "Everyone is divided into groups and allowed to go on deck for a few hours. Then they're herded back down to make room for another group. It's a pretty rotten job, forcing people back down to this hellhole. Fights have broken out. People scream or plead. Now this storm…"

Normally peaceful people had descended into rage and violence. Getting to Palestine would not come soon enough.

Rosten led me through an open hatch that accessed a ladder leading downward. The thrumming sound of the ship's engines and a wall of dense, hot air met me within the first few steps. I could feel the vibration of the engine and the shuddering hull through my shoes. The ship's groans were louder and now sounded like a wounded elephant.

"That sound ain't good," Rosten said. "Could be a weak hull weld."

"A weak what?" I asked, my voice rising an octave. "What if that weld goes?"

We reached the bottom of the ladder and stepped into a passageway. Rosten let me clear him, then he turned around and started climbing back up the steps.

"Whoa, where are you going?"

"I'm going to talk to the captain. Maybe we should slow down in this storm." He pointed down the corridor. "Just keep going that way. They're waiting for you."

Rosten hurried up the steps, leaving me to navigate this new level of Dante's inferno. The passageway was like a metal cage laced with pipes and electrical conduit. Dim bulbs were sparsely placed and flickered. The engine room thrummed just one level below. The smells of oil and diesel filled the air and threatened to squeeze out what was left of the oxygen.

I went about fifty feet before noticing four men in the dim light. They had formed a circle and were staring at something on the flooring.

A man broke off from the group and approached me. He was about thirty, with a handsome face only marred by a light scar that ran down his cheek to his chin. His name was Arie Feldman, someone I had linked up with in Italy and helped smuggle the refugees to Naples and then to this rust bucket of a ship. Our relationship had started out pretty rocky, but we'd grown to respect each other. I figured participating in the killing of a few Nazis would do that.

The ship pitched upward, forcing me to hold on to a metal conduit to keep from falling. The bow plunged into a wave, and the whole deck vibrated.

"You couldn't just let me puke in my quarters?" I said as Feldman walked up to me. "You wanted to make sure I got the full experience."

"And here I thought you were a tough guy."

"Not when it comes to drowning." I pointed my chin toward the group and the weeping woman. "I heard there was a dead male passenger. Is that why you asked me down here?"

Feldman nodded. "It's one of the crewmen. Dan Moritz."

I knew Moritz. He was a big, burly guy who'd been a Marine in the Pacific, and despite experiencing the horrors of Okinawa, he was a sweet kid and had a kind word for everyone. I paused to mourn his passing as I gripped a pipe to brace against another impact.

"We could use your expertise as an ex-cop," Feldman said.

"He didn't die of natural causes or an accident?"

"I wouldn't have called for you if he had."

I ignored the terse remark; he and Moritz had become close,

and the loss was sure to have affected him, too. I motioned for him to lead the way.

As we approached the group, Feldman said, "These men found him. We haven't touched the body because, well, you'll see why."

The group of men parted to let me through, revealing the victim. Moritz lay on his back with his legs bent under him as if he'd been dead before collapsing to the metal flooring. Someone had sliced his throat open from ear to ear. A mass of blood stained his shirt and had pooled on the metal decking.

I knelt next to Moritz and touched his cheek with the back of my hand. "He's still warm, and the blood looks fresh. It probably happened not long before you found the body."

I looked up at the men and studied their faces, their expressions. Any one of them could be a suspect. But none of them looked guilty. They glanced at each other and their surroundings as if afraid that the killer might still be lurking nearby.

I pulled back Moritz's peacoat and felt around for any signs of additional wounds. His hands and face showed no sign of a struggle, leading me to guess he'd been completely surprised by the attack. It took skill, strength, and speed to slice a man's throat open that wide without a struggle. And the killer knew opening both veins in the neck would cause him to pass out almost immediately and bleed out within seconds.

"There's not much else I can tell without the tools to dust for prints, and you guys managed to tromp all over the scene." I looked up at Feldman. "I'm still not sure what you expected I could—" I stopped. "You could have just asked one of the doctors on board to give you an opinion. I'm your American non-Jew cover for the British police."

Feldman looked away for a moment, then returned his gaze to me. "They'll listen to you when you tell them no one here did this."

"I don't know that."

"Mason, we all loved Daniel."

"If I were a police detective, I'd have held you all for questioning."

As I stood, the ship shuddered as the deck tilted up, sending everyone to the floor. A muffled explosion came from the engine room, then a metallic ripping was followed by the roar of rushing water. The crew in the engine room cried out, then the lights flickered and died.

In complete darkness, I heard grunts off to my left. One man next to me cried out in pain. Then another did the same. I reached out my hands to get my bearings and pulled myself to my feet. My eyes instinctively widened in an attempt to see what was going on.

The lights flickered, then came on again. I only had a moment to see a man in black pants and a sweater standing in front of me. He seemed as surprised as I was and kicked me jujitsu-style in the chest with his heavy boot. It knocked the breath out of me. I fell back when the ship tilted to one side, and lay there while trying to recover my ability to breathe. The roar of the water continued, and the crew was yelling out commands and banging hammers. Then I became aware of the ship listing at a steeper angle. A primal fear wrapped its icy fingers around my heart.

2

I shot to my feet and saw the assailant dashing for the ladder to access the upper decks. I glanced toward the other crewmen to see if they needed aid. One crewman held his stomach and staggered to his feet. Another was still out cold.

Feldman had both hands on his throat as he choked for air. I started to rush for him, but he waved me off. "Get him," he said through his spasming throat. "He ... bomb."

I raced down the passageway. Above me, passengers were screaming and yelling. I leapt up the ladder, ignoring the throbbing pain in my chest and the quivering in my lungs. Inside the hold, passengers had been separated like the wake left by the ship. Some yelled curses at the man cutting through the crowd. Some were in a panic over the noise of the bomb and the listing ship.

As I got about halfway across Hold Three, the assailant passed through into Hold Two. Then the passengers seemed to take the man running and me pursuing him as a signal to panic. Like the rolling waves of the sea, a couple hundred passengers surged toward Hold Two's hatch. I found myself fighting my way forward, while those behind me were pushing. Some of the slower passengers fell. Screams grew louder.

If I didn't do something fast, the bomber would get away, and people would get hurt. I pulled out my .45 and fired twice overhead. The booming of the gun caused people to cry out and scatter. Many covered their ears and cowered. I couldn't guess how many of these people had been harassed or chased or shot at by the Nazis.

I now had a clear path. I jumped through the hatch to Hold Two and faced the same situation with panic gripping the passengers. But I didn't have to fire the .45; holding it over my head and yelling for people to get out of the way was enough. I was gaining on the man, as he was having a tough time crawling over panicked passengers who were fighting to climb the ladder.

I hit the bottom rungs just as he shoved his way out the hatch and onto the main deck. People saw my gun and jumped off the ladder or cowered to the sides, making it easier for me to get to the top. On the deck, I caught a glimpse of the bomber heading toward the stern.

It was a mystery where he hoped to hide on a ship, confined and crowded, but he ran like he had a destination. People huddled on the deck cried out and scattered. He shoved the slow ones aside, rounded the bridge castle, and raced down the narrow deck between the castle and the railings. I poured on the speed and hit the same narrow deck seconds behind him.

He was waiting at the far corner, where the deck widened again and provided access to the rear holds. I saw his pistol aiming at me just before he fired. The bullet zipped past me as I dived for the deck. Lying on my stomach, I fired, hitting the bulkhead near his head.

He took off again, and I jumped to my feet and pursued him. At the corner, I stopped and aimed. I had a clear shot.

"Stop," I yelled. "Hands up."

The man turned as he ran and fired at me. I put one round in him. He tumbled to the decking. I came out from behind the bridge bulkhead with my pistol aimed at him.

I took two steps toward him. A woman growled to my right. Before I could turn to see who it was, the woman kicked my gun hand at the wrist with such force that I lost control of the weapon. It clattered to the decking. In rapid succession, she landed a blow to my throat then a punch to my solar plexus.

My throat locked. Fire radiated from my lower stomach, forcing me to hunch over. She got in several more strikes to my head, and I fell on my back.

She stood a few feet from me and withdrew a nine-inch knife from her jacket. She advanced while I tried to crawl backward on my elbows. She had a crazed look in her eyes. Her face was twisted in fury.

She lunged, but I managed to deflect her by kicking up at her chest. She slammed against the railing, only to launch herself for another lunge with her knife.

The yells and footsteps of several people came up from behind me. The woman looked up, fear and panic on her face this time. She shot me one more fiery glare as if memorizing my face for a future killing, and she tore down the deck.

Still prone, I watched, stunned, as she leapt over the railing to the sea below. Several men ran past me in pursuit. Someone knelt next to me. It was Feldman.

"Are you all right?" he asked.

I nodded, and with his help, I got to my feet. Feldman offered his shoulder, and we walked over to where the woman had jumped. I figured we'd see her in the last moments before she sank below the stormy water, but she surprised me again.

She was already aboard a motorboat that was speeding away from the ship at top speed.

~

BY THE TIME THE WOMAN ASSAILANT'S MOTORBOAT HAD disappeared into the darkness. I had recovered from both attacks. My throat and chest throbbed, but the pain was tolerable.

"Do you have any idea who they were?" I asked Feldman.

"I know as much as you do. Did you get a good look at the woman, at least?"

"Enough," I said and had to hold on to the railing as the ship swung wildly in a different direction.

The deck was not pitching as bad as before. The water had calmed slightly, and the waves were not quite as menacing. But the ship still listed at a frightening angle, and without the engine to control it, the rolling waves buffeted the hull, causing us to drift sideways to the south.

"You think we're going to sink?" I asked.

"If that's the case, it's been nice knowing you," Feldman said.

"Well, that's not comforting at all."

"Find a nurse if you want comfort."

We were all on edge, so I let that comment go and motioned toward the male assailant's body crumpled on the deck. "Let's take a look at our bomber."

We walked across the tilted deck and wedged our way through the people surrounding the man. Someone had already turned him on his back. Rain dropped on eyes frozen in death. The round from my gun had entered his side and must have bounced around considerably before exiting his left breast.

He was maybe thirty, muscular and lean, with bronze-colored skin and a close-cropped beard.

"Arab?" I asked Feldman.

He shrugged. "I forgot to ask him."

I knelt at the body and searched his clothes. I found a small knife and a couple of tools but nothing else. "I figured he wouldn't be carrying an ID. But not even a ticket stub or a pack of matches."

"An untrained bomber might be careless with carrying stuff

that might identify him," Feldman said. "This man was obviously a professional."

I looked up at Feldman. "Know that from experience, do you?" I smiled to show I was kidding. It was something to take the edge off my own fear of drowning, but Feldman didn't find anything amusing about the comment.

Another wave hit the hull and made the ship tilt even more. I went down on all fours to keep steady. Many of the surrounding passengers cried out. The ship righted again to the same shallow angle.

A young woman holding a baby grabbed onto Feldman's arm. "You must do something. Everyone is terrified of sinking. Please. My baby."

Feldman tried to reassure her that the ship was okay. She didn't look any more convinced than I was. Her pleading prompted others around her to fire desperate questions at Feldman.

"Everyone calm down," Feldman yelled. "The ship has run into some trouble, but she's still seaworthy. And panicking will only make things worse. Please, everyone, go below. The decks must remain clear for crew to manage the ship."

As the crowd slowly dispersed, I noticed that the British warship was closer now on what seemed to be an intercept course. Someone on the warship's deck was flashing a signal lamp at our ship, and our ship was responding. I missed most of the Morse code message from the other ship except "for a tow."

I hit Feldman's shoulder to get his attention and pointed toward the destroyer. "Our radio must be out. It looks like the captain called for a tow."

I expected to see relief on my companion's face, but he looked dejected and continued to persuade the passengers to leave some space. There wasn't much else I could do. My stomach started heaving again from the ship's uncontrolled movement, so I headed amidships and to the bridge hatch to get to my quarters.

At the hatch, Rosten and three crewmen burst out of the passageway.

"They got the leak in the engine room under control," Rosten said to me as he ran by. "We're going to clear the foredeck to accept a tow from that destroyer."

I watched the group run toward the bow. In the distance, the eastern horizon was clear of clouds, revealing a pink-and-blue sky tinted by the setting sun. My shoulders and neck muscles began to release some of their tension. We might get out of this yet.

The relief allowed my thoughts to turn to the woman who attacked me. She seemed like more than a partner in crime. Did I shoot a relation of hers or her lover? She was obviously a skilled killer. Who was she working for?

I saw nothing but hate in her eyes when she attacked, and I had the unsettling feeling she wasn't done with me.

3

I inched my way through the dense crowd of passengers on the main deck, made more challenging by the backpack hanging from my shoulders—the same backpack with which I had slogged through Italy. Anyone able to walk or stand had come up from the bowels of the ship to watch as we approached Haifa. Some prayed or talked excitedly at the sight of Eretz Israel, though most knew their time in the land of their dreams would be short-lived. The Brits had sent over some food and water, along with the message that everyone would be loaded onto another ship bound for the refugee camp on Cyprus.

I spotted Feldman standing at the starboard rail. With some gentle prodding, I made my way to him. He looked melancholy as he stared at the harbor.

The destroyer had begun to tow our ship at about six p.m. the evening before, and now it was after ten the following morning. We had endured another two hours of the storm, but then the sea calmed, and most people collapsed from exhaustion. The sun was now out, and it felt good on my face. The temperature was around fifty degrees, but that seemed balmy after the cold storm, not to mention the winter in Austria and the snowy mountains of Italy I'd left only weeks ago.

"These people have come such a long distance, only to be sent to another refugee camp on Cyprus," Feldman said.

"You and David got them this far. You should be proud of that. I'm betting they'll make it to Eretz Israel eventually."

Feldman gave me a weak smile.

"Speaking of David, where is he?" I asked. "I haven't seen him since we got on board."

I was referring to David Hazan, Feldman's partner in Italy. I'd run into them both in the Brenner Pass while they were hunting Nazi war criminals. I linked up with them later—really, they saved my butt—to help smuggle a convoy of Jewish displaced persons to Naples and onto this ship.

Feldman shrugged. "He's been hanging out with his friends."

"I thought you and he were close."

"I thought we were, too, but that changed when he got involved with those other blokes."

"Hotheads like him?"

Feldman glanced at me with a piercing look, which gave me the impression that my smart remark had come close to the truth. He fell silent, and I decided to let him volunteer more information in his own time.

I looked out at Haifa. The city faced northward at the end of a point of land that formed a hook-shaped bay. The white three- and four-story buildings were clustered around the shoreline or clung to the sloping limestone hills that began a few hundred yards east of the shore. Stubby pines and olive trees stood among the brush that covered the hillsides. The harbor was delineated by the breakwater with one half of the port dominated by British warships and the other half by freighters. But our destination appeared to be a separate port constructed away from the principal one. There, at least a dozen rusty freighters and passenger ships were crammed together, with the port's limits surrounded by high chain-link fence and guarded by a company-sized contingent of soldiers and police.

"To answer your question," Feldman began, "David and I were both members of Haganah—well, I'm still a member, but not David. Not anymore."

"And what is Haganah?"

"It's the defense forces wing of the Jewish Agency for Palestine. The agency represents all Jews in Palestine and organizes the immigration of Jews from Europe to Eretz Israel."

"Defense forces? Isn't that just a polite way of saying it's a paramilitary organization?"

"Call it what you like. We started by defending Jews from Arab attacks. The agency's policy toward the British was one of restraint, which angered a lot of members. Some split from Haganah and formed groups that are far more militant. Irgun and Lehi."

"And David joined one of those groups?"

Feldman nodded. "The Irgun. Extremists who think the only solution to the problem is violence. To use any means necessary to force the British to leave Palestine. David tried to recruit me, but I believe the task of forming a Jewish state requires far more than just committing violence. We haven't spoken since."

"What sort of operations does the Haganah perform?"

"When I enlisted in the Jewish Brigade and went to fight the Nazis in Italy, restraint *was* the agency's policy. That has changed since I went away. The British continue to refuse to increase the legal immigration of Jews, so we're determined to fight the system." He turned to me with his index finger extended. "But I still don't think the solution is bombing British institutions or killing British soldiers. The Haganah has even tried to clamp down on Irgun and Lehi, but that has simply put a wider divide between us."

"So you only go after Arabs?"

Feldman turned to me and raised his voice. "We defend our

people against any sort of aggression. Jews have a right to form their own state. A small slice of land where we can have self-determination and self-rule, where Judaism was born and thrived for thousands of years. A place where a future Hitler or Stalin can't create policies of extermination."

Feldman was getting angry over a subject I knew little about. I was all for the Jews carving out a homeland, but I also wondered if the Arabs on the same land would end up getting the short end of the stick.

"It's odd that David hasn't shown his face around here," I said. "Especially since someone tried to sink the ship. Even if you guys don't see eye to eye anymore, what's the purpose of staying out of sight?"

"You'd have to ask David."

"Ask me what?" a voice said behind us.

We both turned to see Hazan standing a few feet from us. Feldman tensed as if getting ready for a fight, which seemed to give Hazan a perverse delight, because he smirked like a playground bully. He and I had nearly come to blows on a couple of occasions, but by the time we reached Naples, I'd come to respect Hazan, as I believed he had for me. That apparently changed once we boarded. Now he exuded an air of outright hostility.

"Why have you and your buddies stayed out of sight with all the problems on the ship?" I asked.

"We deemed the crew competent enough to manage on their own."

"Help calming the passengers would have been welcome," Feldman said.

"Calm them for what? To stand by while the British take control of the ship?"

"Would you rather have seen the ship drift in the storm and sink?" I said.

Hazan only responded with a murderous glare.

Earlier, I had one of the artists on board draw a sketch of the dead bomber to use in a quick canvass of the passengers. I pulled it out and held it up to Hazan. "Did you ever see this guy, or do you know who he is?"

He gave the sketch a cursory glance. "Why are you asking me?"

"It's a simple question," I said. "He planted the bomb and tried to sink the ship. He had a woman accomplice on board who was trained in combat techniques. It doesn't make sense that they'd risk everything just to plant a bomb on a refugee ship. If you have any information, I'd like to hear it."

Hazan's nostrils flared. "I'm not answerable to you."

"Damn, David. I'm not the one you have to worry about. The Brits are going to be curious about the bombing and the shoot-out, and I don't want to be left holding the bag."

"As far as the Brits are concerned, the only good Jew is a dead one."

"You can tell that to the authorities when we dock."

Hazan took a step forward and gritted his teeth. "I advise you to get out of Palestine as soon as you can. Before you become a target."

He stormed off, pushing his way through the crowd. I turned and stepped up to the railing. Feldman joined me. The crew on the foredeck had released the towline, and the destroyer was turning away, allowing two tugboats to intercept our ship and guide it to the secured docks.

"Hazan has become intolerable," Feldman said. "It makes me sad to see him like this. But he's right: you shouldn't stay too long. I think all hell's going to break loose sooner rather than later. Your President Truman and the UN have gotten involved, pushing an unrealistic partition plan that is going to create more problems than it solves. The British are digging in their heels, and the Arabs are sharpening their knives."

"And I'm guessing your group, Irgun, and Lehi are amassing weapons and building bombs."

Feldman bristled and opened his mouth to say something, but he stopped and looked at the port. "I'm afraid so."

"All I plan to do is find my sweetheart and get her out of here. She's as hardheaded as I am, so that's going to be easier said than done."

"Five months pregnant and staying in Jerusalem," Feldman said. "You should do whatever you can to convince her to leave."

"*If* she's still in Jerusalem."

The tugboats were making quick work of getting the ship to the docks. Now came the painstaking maneuvers of pushing it the last few yards. Twenty British military policemen were waiting dockside. A system of chain-link fences had been installed to herd the passengers from the ship through a check-point and on to a convoy of trucks standing by to take them to another ship.

"Do the Brits know that you're Haganah?"

He shook his head. "I was recruited shortly after we were deployed in Italy."

"Then it's off to Cyprus for you?"

"No, I am *Yishuv*, a Jew born in Palestine, and have all my papers. I plan to see my mother in Jaffa for a few hours before going on to Jerusalem. If you need anything, I'll be staying at a sixth-floor apartment across from the Yeshurun Synagogue on King George Street. Can you remember that?"

I nodded. "I'll remember."

The ship was nestled up to the dock. The crew tossed mooring lines to the men on the dock, and the ship was lashed in place. The military police and other uniformed officials positioned themselves near the gangway being lowered to the dock. The passengers, anxious to get to dry land, pushed and shoved to be among the first to disembark. Some of the crew tried to form organized lines and let the women with children get off first, but most of the passengers had lost any sense of decorum. The prospect of hot food and potable water was too much to hold them back.

"I better help before someone gets hurt," Feldman said. He held out his hand, and I shook it. "Thank you for all you've done. I hope all the best for you."

"Likewise, Arie. Keep your head down out there."

"You too. Remember, get out as soon as you can."

Feldman left the railing and started pleading for calm to the crowd as he wedged his way toward the gangway. I remained where I was; I knew the British police would want a word with me on the shooting. I watched the crowd and recognized a few who had been on the convoy with me in Italy. A few gave me faint smiles. But most of their faces, once so full of hope and optimism on the trip down the Brenner Pass, were now filled with exhaustion and gritty determination.

People had to carry their suitcases on their heads, while parents clung to their children. I only knew a little bit of what those people had gone through to get to this point. It grieved me to know that they were to be herded onto another ship, only to be forced into another overcrowded camp almost two hundred miles away.

It took more than thirty minutes for the majority of passengers to disembark. Feldman was one of the last, and he waved good-bye to me as he descended the gangway. The sick and feeble, some ambulatory, some on stretchers, were the next to disembark, followed by several British MPs and crewmen who carried stretchers burdened by the dozen who had died during the voyage.

Finally, the only people left were the crew, me, and the dead bomber, who lay on a stretcher covered with a blanket. As much as I needed food and water—and to get off this infernal ship—I figured it was better to answer for my actions before disembarking. Below, Feldman talked with a couple of military police officers and pointed up to me. Then he was escorted away to be interrogated.

Two squads of British MPs came on deck and fanned out to secure the ship. The sergeant in charge went up to the captain and crew members and began asking questions. Two plainclothes men boarded and came up to me.

"Detective Inspector Barnes," the older man said to me. He was a head shorter than me and was at least ten years my senior. His expression was calm, though his eyes probed mine.

I introduced myself, and to deflect some suspicion, I told them I was a former police detective in the States and former CID investigator for the army. I offered to show him my papers, but he kept his hands clasped behind his back.

Barnes motioned toward the corpse on the stretcher. "Is that your handiwork?"

"I pursued him after he set off the bomb. He fired off several shots, and I fired back to defend myself."

"Several witnesses corroborate that," the detective inspector said, then narrowed his eyes. "Did you know the man?"

"If you're wondering if this was some kind of deal gone wrong, or we were conspirators, the answer is no. He planted a bomb and tried to get away. What you should be investigating is the woman with him. She must have had extensive training in demolition and fighting techniques to be with this guy. And she actually got away."

Barnes checked that his younger partner was writing everything down. I could tell he'd lost interest, and I figured he didn't care one way or the other if one of the Jewish passengers on an illegal refugee ship fell victim to foul play; he'd been sent here to ask enough questions to write up a report to satisfy his superiors. He removed a small notepad from his pocket and held it out to me. "Name, reason for your visit, and where you'll be staying."

I didn't know where I'd end up staying, so I wrote down the address of the Imperial Hotel, where Laura supposedly had a room. I handed him the notepad, and he scanned it with as much interest as the interview.

"One of my colleagues will be in touch," Barnes said and ordered me to get off the ship.

I gladly complied and descended the gangway. A Brit cop directed me to follow everyone else through the maze of chain-link fencing. At a gate with two alternate paths, a couple of MPs checked identity papers. Those with displaced persons IDs were directed to go left, while those few with residency cards or travel passes were directed to the right, including myself. I imagined Feldman and Hazan, and some Hazan's Irgun buddies, had been directed to go in the same direction, but I didn't see them if they had.

A handful of passengers and I were herded into a small enclosure and waited our turn to approach a sergeant's kiosk. One passenger was pulled out of line. He protested, but the MPs ignored his pleas and dragged him off to another holding pen. The crew was told to wait in another enclosure, and then it was my turn.

I showed the sergeant the travel and entry passes that my friend at the army's Counter Intelligence Corps, Mike Forester, had given me. The sergeant scrutinized the papers and then looked up at me with furrowed brows. He asked me the usual questions—the purpose of my trip and how long I planned to stay. I told him to see my girlfriend and didn't know how long.

"Why on earth did you come here on that ship?" the sergeant asked. "There are better ways to get here, you know."

"Someone told me it was the *Queen Mary*."

The sergeant sneered and thrust my papers out for me to take them. I did and walked through the final gate to freedom. I looked back at the system of enclosures. The vast majority of passengers were being ushered into a larger space and assembled into lines to board awaiting trucks. I continued to look for Feldman or Hazan but still didn't see them.

I turned to face the busy port. Buses, cars, British Army vehicles, and men riding donkeys all passed along the main street serving the length of the harbor. Dockworkers pushed dollies full of crates or loaded trucks. What really caught my attention were the various men standing or sitting at strategic positions. They all pretended to be loiterers or businessmen taking in the sea air but were most likely intelligence agents for the British, the Jewish factions, and the Arabs.

It seemed like I'd be running a gauntlet of hostile agents just to exit the harbor. That made me wonder what awaited me in the powder keg that was Jerusalem. I had a sinking feeling that the torturous voyage across the Mediterranean would wind up being the easy part.

4

I was sure I picked up a couple of tails while dodging traffic to cross the boulevard to get to a taxi stand. I was met with a swarm of mostly Arab cab drivers trying to persuade me to take their taxi, but I ignored them and decided to take the lead car, where the driver stood patiently by his cab. We both got in, and I asked him to take me to the train station.

"I advise not taking the train, sir," the cab driver said in British English tinted with an Arab accent. "Not safe. The bombings, you see."

"The bus station, then."

The driver pulled out onto the boulevard. I looked behind me and saw two taxis pull out a moment later. I chuckled to myself at their awkward way of tailing a subject. If they weren't careful, they'd run into each other.

The cab took a route north, paralleling the harbor and skirting the western edge of the city. British soldiers were everywhere, standing guard or patrolling in armored vehicles. There was a sour odor of an old fire in the air just as we passed an oil refinery at the northern end of the harbor. Several of the immense storage tanks were blackened and torn open by explosions, with ejected debris forming a circle of destruction around them. A few nearby cars and a small building were nothing but burned-out shells.

"The Irgun, sir," the driver said. "They have bombed many things. That is why there are so many soldiers around the port. It took several days for the fire to burn out."

I grunted a response and thought of Hazan and his buddies huddled on the ship, planning their next terrorist attack. I checked behind me and saw the two taxis still following us.

The driver glanced at me in his rearview mirror, then his gaze shifted to watch what was unfolding outside the back window. "Do you want me to lose them?"

"Not worth it. I'll be out of this town soon. Besides, I'm not anyone of value to them."

"American?"

I nodded.

"The buses are very irregular and are stopped frequently by the British to search the passengers. I can take you wherever you want to go."

"How do I know you're not working for them?" I said and pointed my thumb at the back window.

The driver let out a hearty laugh. "You will not do well in this country if you start to believe everyone is spying on you."

"What if I told you I want to go to Jerusalem?"

"I have the time, if you have the money."

I was aching to get to Laura, and the taxi seemed to be the quickest and safest way, at least according to my Arab driver.

"Name your price," I said.

"Two hundred British pounds."

I slid forward in my seat and got close to his ear. "That's more than a Brit soldier makes in a year. Try again."

"A hundred pounds?"

I continued to stare at him.

"Fifty?"

"Take me to the bus station. I don't like to ride with chiselers."

"Twenty pounds," he yelled out.

I sat back in my seat and said, "Jerusalem. The Imperial Hotel."

~

WE WERE NEARING JERUSALEM, AND I WAS ANXIOUS TO SEE THE city. I leaned forward in my seat and watched the landscape unfold outside the taxicab's front windshield. I couldn't wait to see Laura, but I was also looking forward to visiting one of the legendary cities of the world. I didn't practice a religion, but I'd been brought up Catholic, and my grandmother filled me with images of Jesus, the Apostles, and the Holy City itself.

We'd been traveling for more than three hours, a longer journey than the ninety miles should have been. There were herds of sheep to avoid or slow travelers on donkeys that made us crawl along, but mostly it was due to the system of British checkpoints. At each, they searched us, the car, and my backpack. The Brits were tense and vigilant, with their fingers on the triggers of their STEN submachine guns or revolvers. A couple of times, I had to use my U.S. Army pass from the CIC to prevent a wary guard from confiscating my .45 pistol.

After leaving Haifa and the coast, we'd climbed into a landscape of dry, undulating hills dotted with brush, the monotony only broken up by random stands of scrawny pine and oak trees or dusty settlements and villages. The two taxis that started following us at the port gave up once we were well away from the urban sprawl. But we'd picked up a black sedan a few miles outside of town that was still tailing us. The driver of that car kept a good distance and stopped at the checkpoints as we did, though he seemed to get through them with little trouble.

We crested another hill, and the driver, who had introduced

himself as Hassan, gestured with his free hand toward the windshield. "Jerusalem, sir."

The city was draped upon shallow hills and surrounded by higher ones. There were domes and towers rising above the cityscape, and then the distinctive ancient crenulated stone walls of the Old City. Modern buildings of brick and stone, villas, and houses spread out from the old center to the west and north. East of the Old City, the Mount of Olives rose above the ancient walls, where palms, olive trees, and cypress trees dotted the three peaks of a low mountain ridge.

A pity the beauty belied the hostility plaguing the land. To drive home that point, we passed the burned-out carcasses of several cars, and in the distance, a column of black smoke rose above the next hill.

Several British Army Humber armored cars and Bedford trucks charging in the opposite direction forced the driver to the side.

The driver growled at them in Arabic, then he hit the accelerator as he got back onto the asphalt, spinning the tires and throwing up gravel.

"Has it been tough living under the British?" I asked him.

He said nothing for a few moments as we approached the city limits.

He took a deep breath and said, "I am sorry, sir, for my anger. My brother died in one of their prisons. I will never forgive them."

"Why did they put him in prison?"

"For defending our homeland from the Jewish dogs."

I sat back in my seat. I wasn't about to get into it with the driver. Who was right about it being their land? I'd read a little history of the region on the ship between bouts of seasickness. Palestine had been settled and conquered too many times for me to count: the Tribes of Israel, the Canaanites, the Egyptians, Assyrians, Babylonians, Persians, Romans, and the Muslims, with shorter occupations by the Christian Crusaders and the Ottomans, just to name the major players. The Jews could claim to have been there for over three thousand years, and the Arabs well north of a thousand. The land, revered by three major religions, was a bloodstained patch of desert soaked by countless centuries of upheaval and violence, and likely remain so for countless years to come. I was anxious to see it. At the same time, I couldn't wait to get out.

Over the next rise and at the fringe of the city proper, we came upon the source of the column of smoke. A Humber armored car lay on its side and in flames. A team was attacking it with fire extinguishers while a uniformed crew loaded the limp body of a soldier into the back of their ambulance.

A British MP checkpoint blocked the traffic with their armored vehicles about fifty yards from the burning Humber. Guards had their STENs trained on three men in Western-style clothes with their hands in the air. None of them looked to be over twenty-five, and appeared European, leading me to think they were Jewish.

On the opposite side of the road, a group of six men with baggy trousers and scarves on their heads, who I presumed were Arabs, were being held near a troop transport truck.

Hassan uttered what sounded like curses in Arabic when a guard waved him to a stop. The guard came up to the window. He ordered us both out, and we were patted down. Then two guards took the driver in one direction, and me in another. The driver was shoved into the same group as the other Arab detainees. He protested while gesticulating wildly.

A corporal stood in front of me and nodded for his companion to start searching the car.

"My driver hasn't done anything wrong," I said to the corporal, adding, "at least for the last couple of hours. He picked me up in Haifa, and I paid him to bring me here."

"He'll be questioned. If he doesn't give us any trouble, we'll let him go."

The corporal looked to be no more than twenty-five and had blond hair, blue eyes, and pinkish skin that looked more burned than tanned. He asked for my papers, which I handed over to him.

He scrutinized my travel pass and entry documents, then looked up in surprise. "A Yank?" He held up the CIC entry pass for me to see. "Are you working on behalf of the American army?"

I shook my head. "A friend in army intelligence arranged it. I did him a favor. And I wanted to see Jerusalem, so here I am."

"You certainly picked the wrong time to do it."

"That's what everyone keeps telling me."

"You're lucky you didn't pass through here earlier," he said and nodded toward the three captives dressed in civilian clothes. "Those Jews set a mine in the road and blew up that Humber."

"They look like a bunch of kids."

"Old enough to plant a mine and kill two of our soldiers."

Over the corporal's shoulder, I saw that the other Arab detainees were harassing Hassan.

I pointed that out to the corporal. "Those men are giving my driver a hard time."

The corporal glanced over at the group and turned back to me. "Probably from different factions, or their families have a blood feud. If they could ever get over their petty tribal differences and unite, they'd be a lot more dangerous."

"That's all very interesting, but I'd appreciate it if you got him away from them."

He eyed me a moment, then said, "Stay here." He turned around and told one of his fellow guards to take Hassan over by a Jeep.

One of the guards pulled my backpack out of the rear seat and put it on the ground. It took a moment for him to find the pistol, and he held it up for the corporal, along with my Ka-Bar knife, brass knuckles, and binoculars.

The corporal turned to me. "Are those yours?"

I shrugged. "You never know what kind of trouble you'll be getting into these days." When the corporal showed he didn't find that amusing, I said, "I've had them since I was an investigator with the U.S. Criminal Investigation Division in Munich." I figured it wouldn't hurt to declare myself a fellow military cop, even if I was just a former one.

He raised one eyebrow at me. "I hope you weren't planning on doing any investigating in British territory."

"Nope, but with all the violence going on around here, one can't be too careful."

The corporal grunted and said to the soldier, "Put them back, Private. We won't go taking the Yank's things."

Someone cried out in fury to my right. I turned just in time to see one of the Jewish arrestees throw an elbow into a guard's stomach next to him. The guard bent over in pain.

The man spun around and grabbed the guard's Webley pistol. He aimed it at the corporal, but before he could pull the trigger, a quick-thinking guard came up from behind, grabbed the man's shooting arm, and raised it in the air. The gun went off just as two other guards joined in and wrestled the man to the ground.

The would-be assailant cried out in fury and struggled to get free. One of the guards struck him on the head with his truncheon, and the man became limp.

I turned back to the corporal, who continued to stare at the unconscious man. "You okay?"

The corporal finally tore his eyes away to look at me. "Unfortunately, this isn't the first time a gun's been pointed at me. Both the Jews and Arabs have people who want nothing more than to kill us."

"And none of them wear a uniform. At least we had that fighting the Germans."

"It does take its toll."

There wasn't much to say in response to that. They were fighting an invisible enemy, without an achievable goal or strategic objective, nothing to say you won a battle, let alone the war.

He seemed to snap out of it and pointed toward the taxi. "You can retrieve your rucksack. Sorry, but we're going to demand your driver return to Haifa. You can find a bus stop about a mile from here."

I went over to Hassan. The soldier detaining him tensed, so I showed him the money in my hand. "Just paying my driver what I owe him."

The soldier relaxed, and I approached Hassan. I handed him twenty-five pounds. I thanked him and told him there was an extra five in there for his trouble.

"An honorable man," Hassan said. "That is a rarity. Almost as rare as justice for Palestinian Arabs."

I said nothing and went to retrieve my backpack by the taxi. I then stopped in front of the corporal and held out my hand. He shook it.

"Good luck to you, soldier," I said.

"You, too, and watch how you go."

Normally, I'd have taken that as just a polite expression, but after what I just witnessed, I took it for everything it implied. I turned on my heels and headed for the center of the city.

5

I t was a pleasant day, so I decided to walk to town from the checkpoint. It had the added benefit of making my tail from Haifa work a little harder. His black sedan cruised past me on the road. I couldn't get a good look at his face due to the reflection on the windshield, and he turned away from me as he came up alongside, but the silhouette was definitely masculine. He had angular facial features, a large mustache, and he wore a gray suit topped by a black fedora.

I followed Jaffa Road through the modern section of the city. The closer I got to the city center, the older the buildings. Recently constructed office buildings and apartments gave way to those built by the British after kicking out the Turks at the end of the First World War, then finally those built in the 1800s, when the city grew out of its walled confines and began to spread.

Like Haifa, there was a mix of cars, buses, men leading donkeys and camels laden with bundles or crates, the younger crowd on bicycles, or women on foot with oversized bundles on their heads. Most of the people were easy to distinguish between Arab and Jew, the former with head scarves and flowing clothes while the latter wore European-style suits and dresses. However, some of the men were indistinguishable, and I caught myself scanning their faces for signs of danger. I chuckled: it appeared I'd already become overly suspicious in the span of a day.

Somewhere along the way, the man in the gray suit and fedora had picked up my trail and now dogged my movements on foot. He was good at his job, because it was tough keeping track of him. It was only my training as a cop and intelligence officer that helped me detect him on several occasions. While his face remained obscure, I could still pick him out of a crowd. He was trim, athletic even, with black hair graying at the temples and an equally black-and-gray mustache.

I had to ask for directions to Laura's hotel several times. That led me to the Jaffa Gate, one of the entrances to the old walled city. I didn't know what I expected, but there wasn't much of a gate. Just a wide gap in the ancient walls, where cars and small trucks dodged the throngs of pedestrians. I felt a thrill walking the streets where people had tread for thousands of years—a big leap from growing up in Ohio.

My heart thumped in my chest when I came up to the New Imperial Hotel just yards inside the Old City from the gate, though what they did with the Old Imperial Hotel was anybody's guess. I wasn't sure if my heart rate was from the excitement or nerves, probably a little bit of both. The turn-of-the-century building was three stories high and about as broad, with high-relief stone columns and windows framed in ancient Greek motifs, making it appear like a squarish Greek temple. There were men in sport coats and brimmed hats on every corner, and they watched my progress with seeming interest.

I looked back the way I'd come to see if I was still being followed, but either the man had given up or he was watching me from a concealed position. I passed through the hotel's double doors and followed a short hallway to the lobby. The space retained its turn-of-the-century décor, with dark mahogany trim and golden cherubs. Tourists, businessmen, and British Army officers circulated in the lounge area, taking advantage of the ceiling fans and the breeze coming from the open windows. Before approaching the reception desk, I scanned the men and women chatting, sipping drinks, or reading newspapers. After registering their faces, their positions, and their attitudes, I stepped over to the receptionist.

The man's smile was so wide that it made his tarboosh hat rise up on his head. "Welcome to Jerusalem, sir. And all the way from America."

"How did you know I was American?"

He tapped his right eye. "The eye knows. I can spot an American from a great distance. You walk in like you own the hotel, but you are not as pompous as a British man, and you are not as angry as a Jew."

"Your eye could be useful in another line of work."

He chortled as if he took my meaning. "How may I help you, sir?"

"I'm looking for Laura Talbot. She's supposed to be staying here. She probably checked in a little over a month ago."

The receptionist furrowed his brow as if trying to recall a guest by that name. He then checked his register book, licking his forefinger and flipping pages, stopping and studying several pages, scanning each one with his forefinger as a guide. He shook his head. "I see no one by that name, sir."

"Try McKinnon, then."

His smile drooped as he repeated the process. He shook his head again. "No, no one under that name, either. Are you sure of the dates?"

"Just sometime in early March."

"I checked from the end of February to the end of March. Perhaps she has moved on."

My heart sank even as a burning spread across my chest. I felt despondent and angry at the same time. The woman was maddening, but I ached to see her. Especially when she was going on five months pregnant with our child. I suppressed the urge to grab the register book out of his hands to see for myself. Instead, I asked, "I don't suppose you know where she might have gone?"

He shrugged while flashing a fake sympathetic smile.

"Maybe she left a note. My name's Mason Collins."

With an impatient sigh, he stepped over to a basket next to the mailboxes for the rooms. With his back still turned, he said, "No. I'm afraid nothing is here for you."

I didn't wait for him to return to the counter or watch for any suspicious activity in the lounge area. I marched out of the lobby, burst through the entrance door, and stood in the busy street. Pedestrians filed around me, and I pondered what I should do next. As I got my anger under control, a kernel of worry began to grow in my stomach—maybe she left the hotel because she was in danger. She had taken a refugee ship, like I had, to write an article on the hardships and perils of Jewish immigration to Palestine. Maybe the Associated Press had an office here. Or one of the newspaper offices might know where she was.

As I pondered this, I noticed the man in the gray suit slip into a little store selling newspapers and tobacco. With quick strides, I advanced on the shop and pushed through the door. Surprised and confused, I stopped a few feet inside. An old man in black was at the counter buying cigarettes from an Arab vendor. A woman perused the magazines. But the man who'd been following me was nowhere to be seen.

I asked the vendor and the two customers if they'd seen a man in a gray suit come into the shop. They all claimed to have not seen him. While that didn't seem possible, I didn't press it. My respect for the man in the gray suit rose, as did my unease.

∾

AFTER ASKING AROUND ON THE STREETS, I WAS TOLD ABOUT A local watering hole for foreign journalists no more than a half mile from the Jaffa Gate. A ten-minute walk put me within sight of the old Palace Hotel. According to a couple of Brit soldiers, the hotel had been open only a few years before shutting down and being converted into a British administration building. Well guarded, it made for a secure place for the journalists to gather. Not to mention the opportunity to get plastered.

The U-shaped building was on Mamilla Street and bounded by a pond and an ancient-looking cemetery on the north side. The architect apparently couldn't make up his mind on the design and created a weird mix of Greek, Renaissance, and Arabic elements. The front entrance on the bend of the U was guarded by a squad of soldiers behind sandbags and barbed wire. In fact, the short street on the south side of the hotel was filled with soldiers and army vehicles. Not for the first time, the heavy army presence reminded me of my time in occupied Germany. No wonder the journalists felt they could unwind here without having to watch their backs.

I stopped at the intersection across from the hotel, and instead of heading straight for the entrance, I crossed Mamilla Street and stopped at the edge of the park. Pretending to be lost, I scanned the area. Sure enough, I spotted the guy who'd been following me since the Jaffa Gate. He was lighting a cigarette and facing away from me as if stalling, waiting for me to continue.

I wasn't too concerned. As far as I could tell, he was only observing my movements. I was curious about him and who he was working for, but my priority was getting information on Laura's whereabouts. I crossed the street again and headed for the sandbagged entrance.

The guards tensed up as I approached but then relaxed when I spoke to them in American English. "I hear this is a good place to get a drink."

A corporal scrutinized my papers, then said I could go in. Just inside the door, I was faced with another four guards. One of them asked to have a look in my backpack.

"Why don't I just leave it with you fellas," I said, and I repeated the same thing I'd told the corporal at the checkpoint, that I'd had the weapons stashed inside since I was a U.S. Army investigator. "The only thing I need is my wallet to buy a few drinks."

The guard looked to a sergeant behind a desk, who studied me for a second, then nodded his approval. "It will be in my possession until you leave, sir."

I thanked them and stepped out of the short foyer. Before me was an immense open lobby, all marble—the columns, flooring, and the staircase to the upper floors. Uniformed officers and clerks, both men and women, sat at desks or went about their duties. From my left, I heard the kind of laughter that almost always accompanied the consumption of alcohol. I passed through the lobby and entered a bar with paneled walls and a long mahogany counter. Tables and chairs filled the large space, and patrons in officers' uniforms or business attire lined the bar or sat at the twenty-odd tables. Then I spotted a table of six dressed in rumpled suits. They looked the opposite of the tidy bureaucrats and army personnel. There was one woman among them in a beige jacket and pleated pants.

"Sorry to interrupt," I said, and the table fell silent. "I'm looking for a fellow reporter. Her name is Laura McKinnon or Talbot. I think she's here doing an article for the Associated Press."

They all looked at me with suspicion and remained silent.

"If you couldn't tell already by my accent, I'm an American. My name is Mason Collins. Laura and I were together for a while, and she wrote me about a month ago, telling me she would be here and staying at the New Imperial. But according to the reception desk, she never checked in."

The six reporters exchanged looks. The woman and a younger man appeared nervous.

"Look, I'm not a spy or an agent for any government. I just got into Haifa this morning."

Their continued silence made my heart beat faster, both out of anger and apprehension. I leaned on the table with balled fists, causing the two guys on either side of me to slide away. "You all may think you're protecting her, or you don't want to get involved, but what about protecting your own? I'm a former intelligence officer and cop. I can tell by your faces that you're hiding something from me. If you think she's in danger, I'm someone who has the training to help. She's the love of my life, and I'll make it very unpleasant for anyone who stands in my way. Do you understand?"

Most looked at anything but my eyes. The guy on my right tried a defiant expression, but it just looked smug, and it pissed me off. I stood, grabbed the man's beer, took a big gulp, and slammed it back on the table.

"To hell with all of you," I said and walked away.

6

The desk sergeant handed me the backpack, and I was out the door.

I got past the exterior guards when a woman said, "Mr. Collins?"

I turned to see the woman reporter from the table standing at attention with her hands clasped at her waist. She was short and had to look up at me. She looked to be about forty, had fair skin, sandy-blond hair, pale blue eyes, and the build of an aging gymnast—a few extra pounds were layered on her muscular form. The glasses perched on the end of her nose only accentuated her intense look. There was a no-nonsense air about her that I liked.

"I know Laura," she said with a British accent. She glanced at the hotel entrance, presumably to see if any of her colleagues were watching.

"Do you know where she is?"

The reporter shook her head. "But I know how to reach her."

"Is she in trouble?"

"She claims her concealment is just a precaution, but I suspect it's more than that."

"Sounds like Laura. Where can I find her?"

"Well, that's the thing. She doesn't want to be found."

The reporter shifted her weight when she said that and glanced away, making me think she wasn't telling me everything.

I was about to press her when she said, "Laura worked out a signal so that I can let her know I want to get in touch. Then she contacts me with a time and place. It's all very cloak and dagger, if you ask me."

She looked back at the entrance again and then took my arm to lead me across the street and into a stand of cypress trees at the edge of the ancient cemetery.

"Prying eyes," she said. She held out her hand. "Evelyn Atkinson. The *Guardian* newspaper."

I shook her hand, which she returned with a single jerk. She held herself rigid and continued to give me a no-nonsense expression. I figured that was her default strategy after suffering the usual chauvinist attitudes or sexual innuendos she encountered in her line of work. That behavior reminded me of Laura's, her coolness under fire brought on by her experiences with the same loutish behavior.

"How do I know you're sincere?" Atkinson asked.

"The best I can do is tell you we fell in love in Munich. I was an army criminal investigator, and she was doing a piece about the black markets. We were together for a few months. We were both too bullheaded to make it last, and we went our own ways. Then she married a Brit by the name of Richard Talbot. He was murdered, and she's been trying to find her way ever since. I never stopped loving her. And here we are."

Atkinson thought a moment, then said, "I'll leave the signal for her. I have to go get some work done, so I'll do it on the way back. But there's no guarantee she'll respond in a timely fashion. Do you have a place to stay?"

I shook my head. "I haven't had the chance."

She looked me up and down. I had on the same battered

leather jacket, stained khaki trousers, and threadbare sweater I'd worn on the ship. "You might try the Stratford Hotel. They cater to patrons who, shall we say, are faced with particular circumstances."

"You mean, they'll take a shady drifter for the right amount of money."

"Exactly," she said. "Speaking of drifting, the authorities have put martial law into effect because Jewish terrorists machine-gunned and set off a bomb at an officer's club. They killed twelve. You shouldn't go out after ten this evening."

"I knew things were tense, but not as serious as that."

"You should see the King David Hotel just south of here. The entire south wing is gone. There might be a worse time ahead, but I shudder to think of it." Her serious expression turned friendly. "Come on. I'll take you part of the way."

I followed Atkinson northwest on Jaffa Road and away from the Old City. The area had restaurants and cafés and clothing stores. We conversed along the way, she asking me about how I got here, where I came from, and what I was doing in Italy. Her curiosity and ability to pry without being pushy must have made her a good reporter. I liked her frankness, and it was refreshing to be around someone who exhibited no bravado and didn't preach to me about a cause.

"What kind of story are you investigating?" I asked.

"Life of the everyday British soldier. Half of them came from fighting Jerry to this without much of a rest. The other half are just boys thrown into this cauldron. The Arabs resent them, and the Jews hate them."

"I saw a little bit of that on the way here. It's tough when you don't know where your enemy is coming from."

"I get the feeling you're someone who's comfortable in troublesome situations."

"Maybe I used to be that guy. I don't know anymore. Especially with Laura being pregnant—"

Atkinson stopped in her tracks and turned to me. "Laura is pregnant?"

"You didn't know? By my guess, it happened a little over four months ago."

"It happened," she said, parroting me with a sly smile. "Sounds like it wasn't expected." When I hesitated, she waved her hand to let me off the hook. "That doesn't matter now. She shouldn't be in a place like this. Get her out of here as soon as you can."

"That's my goal, but easier said than done."

She gave me a knowing nod, then narrowed her eyes as she stared at me. "I'm going to take a chance."

"What chance would that be?"

She tilted her head toward a small street on my right. "Come on."

I followed her, and we entered an area with a maze of narrow streets. There were cramped cafés and a couple of cinemas. One was showing a Hitchcock film and the other a western with Henry Fonda. I hadn't seen a movie in two years. I had some catching up to do on life.

"So you knew where to find her all along," I said.

"I wasn't sure I could trust you. Anyone can make up a charming story. But you seem sincere, so I'm going to take a leap of faith."

"The way those other reporters clammed up at the hotel, I got the idea that she's in the kind of trouble no one wants anything to do with. Is she? I know Laura will have her version, but I want to hear yours."

"Between us—and I mean you keep it to yourself—I think she's playing a dangerous game. But that's all I'm going to say on the subject. The rest is between you and her."

We stopped at an intersection of three streets, two just wide enough to walk side by side. She nodded toward the one in the middle. "Third door on the left. It's a tiny hotel. Inside, ask for Mr. Hammersmith."

I looked at her to see if she was joking.

Atkinson raised an eyebrow and shrugged. "Amateurish, but she means well. Be patient with her. I think she's worth it."

We shook hands. I thanked her, and she wished me luck.

I watched her walk away for a moment, then turned my attention to the surrounding area. The gray-suited man was nowhere to be seen. Maybe he'd given up, but I doubted it. No one else stood out as suspicious.

Instead of seeking out the hotel, I craved a cigarette at that moment. I lit one up and puffed away, still unwilling to move. I guess I was—despite my excitement—nervous about seeing Laura. We'd clashed as much as we'd seen eye to eye, and I had no idea what to expect now that our future included a child.

I chastised myself for being a coward, threw the cigarette to the ground, and headed toward the hotel.

7

Vendors had wooden signs and product displays outside their establishments, and diners sat at outside tables, making the narrow street even more so. I came across the third door on the left, as instructed. If it were a functioning hotel, there wasn't a sign of it, and the three-story structure was in serious need of repair.

I stepped inside a dark lobby the size of a small bedroom. There was just enough space for me between a table and the counter. The man I assumed to be the receptionist was in his early twenties and a hundred thirty pounds, soaking wet. He wore a rumpled white shirt and a yarmulke on top of auburn hair.

The young man seemed surprised to see anyone coming through the door and reluctantly stepped up to the counter.

"I'm looking for Mr. Hammersmith," I said, feeling ridiculous saying it.

The receptionist sucked in his breath and looked at me with wide eyes.

"Do you speak English?" I asked.

He squinted as if he didn't understand.

"*Sprechen Sie Deutsch?*"

I didn't think his eyes could get any wider, but I was proven wrong. I wasn't sure if he was surprised at my change in language or because I looked like a German. This was not going well.

"*Ich suche Herr Hammersmith.*"

He blinked but that was it. I guessed it dawned on him a moment later, because he got out from behind the counter and waved for me to follow him. We entered a short, dark hallway and passed a closet crammed with cleaning equipment, then went up some back stairs to the third floor. The boards groaned under our feet, which I figured would be a good way to warn her of anyone coming. At the top, my companion pointed to a door at the end of the hallway. I waited for him to disappear down the stairs before I headed for the door.

As I approached it, my heart started pounding. Just as I raised my hand to knock, the door flew open. Laura and I both froze for a moment. She was as beautiful as always, though there were circles under her eyes, and her hair was unkempt, her clothes ruffled.

"Yeah," she said, "you look like hell, too." She smiled and charged into my arms.

We held each other for a moment. She felt soft and warm, and though she obviously hadn't bathed for a few days, she smelled great to me.

She broke the embrace and pulled me into the room. As she shut the door, I dropped my backpack to the floor and took off my fedora. She turned and leapt into my arms again. She kissed me with a kind of force that comes with relief. I returned the kiss with the same aggressiveness. The action filled me with passion, and I became aroused.

She pushed me back and took in several deep breaths. "Not so fast. I haven't bathed or shaved in days."

I stepped toward her. "That's not going to bother me."

She put a hand on my chest to stop me. "It does me. And you smell like a latrine."

"Well, then, let's not waste any time. We check into a nice hotel with a giant tub, and we can pick up where we left off."

Her smile faded a bit. "I can't."

I looked around at her sparse room. Aside from her typewriter and papers everywhere, there wasn't much besides the ratty furniture. "I didn't think you picked this place for the view. But whatever got you into a tight spot, we can get out of here. Tonight even. I've got enough dough that we can fly... well, anywhere but here."

"I can't leave now that—"

"Yes, you can," I said a little too forcefully. I took a breath to calm down. "Laura, you're five months pregnant."

"I knew you'd use—" She stopped and took a deep breath. More calmly, she said, "I'm the one who's pregnant, and I'm the one who decides what's right for me and the baby."

"My point is, even if you weren't pregnant, this place is a powder keg ready to go off. I've been to some dicey places, but this one had me jumpy the moment I stepped off the boat. And look at you, hiding out in a dive, where someone has to use a codename to see you."

She put a hand on her hip. "How did you find me, anyway?"

"Evelyn Atkinson."

"You move fast, don't you?"

"When it comes to finding you, yeah."

Her body relaxed when I said that, and she cooed, then walked up to me and wrapped her arms around me. "We always seem to get off on the wrong foot, don't we? You came to me across the Mediterranean, like I asked, and I'm acting like a bore."

"I would have gotten here sooner, but I helped some friends get a boatload of refugees at least part of the way to Palestine."

She held me at arm's length and scanned my face as if she'd

mistaken me for someone else. "Is it possible that you've gotten a little altruistic between now and Vienna?"

"If you're trying to change the subject, it's not going to work. We need to get out of here. It doesn't matter what you're working on. It can't be worth your life."

"It might be worth several other people's lives if I leave."

"I'm listening."

She turned away and moved toward the single window covered by a yellowed blind. "Oh, you're listening," she said in a mocking tone. "I don't need your approval."

"That is partly my child. I think I have a say in your and the baby's safety."

Laura stopped at the window and kept her back to me. This was not how I wanted this to go, but I knew it was a distinct possibility. Our passion was always intense, but we were both stubborn and driven. I still loved her intensely, and I wanted to make it work.

"Look, let me help," I said.

She remained silent for a moment longer, then said, "I'm sorry. I've been afraid of what becoming a mother might mean for my life. Maybe I wanted to dive off the deep end one more time to make up for it."

"Is somebody threatening you?"

She turned to face me. "No one's come after me, if that's what you mean. At least, not yet."

"Why don't you start from the beginning?"

"I've been writing a story about two opposing villages north of Jerusalem, one Arab and one Jew. A shallow valley with a ravine is all that separates them. I spent time with each, getting to know the people. Well, mostly the women and children in the Palestinian village. The Arab men would have nothing to do with me. The Jewish men may not be comfortable around me, but they heard that I'd been on a refugee ship from Naples and were more interested in me telling their story than objecting to me being there."

"Sounds pretty benign so far."

"And it was at first. Then I noticed the Palestinian women getting skittish about being in my presence. Then, one day, a group of men physically removed me from the village. It was terrifying, but they didn't do anything more than yell at me to leave and shove me."

I was seething at this point, partly for Laura's rough treatment but also for her recklessness. I pushed down my anger and asked, "Since then, have you seen any of those men or received threats from them?"

She shook her head. "That's not what has me scared. A few minutes after the men left me at the bottom of the valley, a young Palestinian woman from the village approached me. She was out of her mind with fear that someone would see her with me, but she was more afraid of what might happen to her family and the others in the village. She said there were men and some women who came to the village to hide. They're members of a clandestine militant group called the Black Hand."

"The Black Hand? That sounds appropriately menacing. Did she tell you why they are there and what their intentions are?"

"She only knew they planned to do terrible things and that I should leave the valley. Apparently, I saw them, and now I'm in danger."

"Did she tell you anything about the group's plans?"

She shook her head.

"Have you told this to anyone?"

"I warned the leaders in the Jewish settlement to be on the lookout," Laura said and stopped. She clasped her hands and seemed to shrink where she stood. "A couple of the Jewish settlers found the Palestinian woman's body in the ravine the next day. She'd been tortured and strangled. I got so scared that I went to Evelyn for help. She's the one who arranged this place for me to stay."

"How long ago was that?"

"Coming up on a week now."

"You haven't gone to the British authorities?"

She shook her head again. "I'm afraid to make a move out of here. Saul, the man who runs this hotel, gets me food. You met his son, Yosef, downstairs."

"The Brits should be informed about this. They might be able to round up the group before they do any harm."

"We could try, but it's been over a week, and all we have is the word of a Palestinian woman who is now dead. Plus, we have nothing specific to report. I have no idea who is a member of the group and who is simply a villager."

I lifted my backpack off the floor, opened it, and removed my .45.

"What are you planning to do?"

I popped a loaded magazine into the gun. "I'm going to the Brit authorities."

"With a loaded gun?"

"No," I said and held it out for her. "This is for you."

"Won't you need it?"

"I'll be fine, but I'd never forgive myself if anything ever happened to you."

She took it reluctantly.

"Don't let anyone in but me. Okay?"

I fished my brass knuckles and Ka-Bar knife out of the pack. I pocketed the brass knuckles and slipped the knife into its sheath and attached that to my belt.

"You'll want to try the King David Hotel first," Laura said.

"I thought it had been bombed."

"The south wing, yes. But the rest is intact. They made it into a fortress and put several administrative offices in there."

She gave me directions. I nodded and started to go.

"Mason, wait," Laura said.

I stopped and turned to her. She was on the edge of tears as she ran into my arms, kissed me, then put her head on my chest. "Take care of yourself. I can be a real heel, but it's just because I'm scared."

We kissed again with passion.

I broke the embrace and held her at arm's length. "We'll get this taken care of, then get to a nice hotel. And I mean run, not walk."

She gave me a half smile. "That would be nice." The smile seemed genuine, but her body was wound so tight that she seemed to have shrunk.

I'd never seen her like that. I turned and left before I was tempted to stay.

8

Out on the streets again, I took the same route back toward the Palace Hotel. I did the occasional check for my earlier tail but didn't detect him or any other suspicious individuals. About halfway down Jaffa Road, I took a right fork onto a narrow street, which I figured would take me straight to the Mamilla Pool. Shortly before getting to the pool, the road narrowed even more. Shop display stands and outside restaurant tables created a bottleneck for pedestrians. Just as I got in the middle of the bottleneck, two British Army MPs began following me. A moment later, a police sergeant in his bobby helmet and a plain-clothed man stood in my way.

Their serious expressions told me they weren't there to chat, and I wondered if they knew about my escape from justice back in Austria. I looked for a way to beat a hasty retreat, but then the two MPs came up behind me and grabbed my arms. Resisting them was a bad idea, so I let them lead me up to the two men in front. The civilian-dressed man appeared to be in charge, as the broad-shouldered sergeant stood slightly behind him. He was in his forties, barrel-chested, and sported a thin mustache. He was dressed in a rumpled tan suit, black tie, and a gray fedora that had seen better days.

The sergeant patted me down and found the knife and brass knuckles.

The man in charge raised an eyebrow at the sight of the weapons and peered at me down the bridge of his nose. "Mason Collins?"

"Yes, and who are you?"

"This is Sergeant Mills, and I'm Detective Chief Inspector Gilman of the CID. That's Criminal Investigation Department to you. Would you come with us, please?"

"Why?"

"That's not something to discuss here. And I'm afraid you have no choice in the matter."

"I was coming to you guys, anyway," I said. "So you don't need the two goons to escort me."

"It's just a precaution," the inspector said and nodded at the two MPs.

The two men clamped down on my arms and forced me forward. The inspector and the sergeant walked several paces ahead of us.

"No need for the rough stuff, boys," I said. "I'm going quietly."

They ignored me and continued to half lift me off my feet and drag me along the street. Maybe they didn't like Americans, or they were putting on a show for the inspector. Whatever the reason, I kept my temper down to a simmer and played along.

As we passed near the Palace Hotel, I glanced at the entrance to see if Atkinson might be there to witness me being taken into custody and let Laura know I hadn't skipped town. But the guards in front of the hotel were the only ones to watch me being led down a single-lane street not far from the Jaffa Gate. I was ushered toward the back of a nondescript, three-story building. There were armored vehicles and machine gun posts, and dozens of soldiers and policemen around the building.

Once inside, it became clear we were in the principal police station. Just like any police station around the world, phones rang and typewriters clacked as cops interviewed arrestees or witnesses, policemen and MPs wandered around or drank coffee and smoked cigarettes in groups. A police station was still one of my favorite places to be, except that—once again—I wasn't the cop but the arrestee.

I was led up a flight of stairs and to a door. My two police ushers peeled off, leaving me with the sergeant and inspector.

"Leave the backpack out here with me," Sergeant Mills said. "You can have it and your weapons when you're done."

Gilman opened the door and walked in. I followed him and found myself in a cluttered office with another man dressed in a tailored blue suit sitting behind the desk. I found it interesting that a portrait of Winston Churchill hung on the wall instead of the current prime minister, Attlee. The windows looked out onto a corner of the Old City and the thick, stone walls that defined it. They were open to let in the cool, spring air and the sounds of passing traffic.

I sat, as instructed, in one of the two stuffed chairs in the middle of the room. DCI Gilman stood off to one side of the large desk in deference to the man sitting behind it.

"This is CID Superintendent Wetherbee," Gilman said.

The superintendent said nothing as he lit his pipe with bony fingers and manicured nails. The man looked to be approaching sixty, with a sinewy frame and graying beard and mustache. His thin face was wrinkled from too much time in the sun. Once he got his pipe going, he said, "It might surprise you that we have a rather interesting dossier on you, Mr. Collins."

He eyed me, making my stomach churn; they brought me there to send me back to the Brit police in Austria. I said nothing; defending myself to these men would fall on deaf ears, especially since one of the charges against me was for beating a British officer.

"I can tell by your expression, you know what we're talking about," Wetherbee said.

"Look, before you send me back, I need to make sure that my fiancée is protected and escorted out of the country," I said, exaggerating Laura's and my status. "She's in danger for what she saw and, potentially, what she knows."

"We'll get to your ... fiancée, do you call her?"

"Laura Talbot," Inspector Gilman said to me, more as a statement than a question.

I must have betrayed my surprise, because Gilman chuckled and said, "We've been aware of her presence and her work in the area."

"Are you also aware that she may have accidently witnessed members of a group called the Black Hand hiding out in the Palestinian village not far from here?"

Gilman and Wetherbee exchanged a look. I couldn't tell much from their expressions, though I figured it was news they hadn't expected.

Wetherbee turned his attention back to me. "The Black Hand disbanded in 1935 when we killed the leader, al-Qassam."

"Did you eliminate everyone in the organization?" I asked.

"No, but we haven't heard any references to that group for close to ten years."

"Maybe some of the remaining members reformed under the same name."

Gilman and Wetherbee exchanged another look. "It's possible," Wetherbee said and nodded to Gilman.

"That kind of information is exactly why we brought you here," Gilman said.

"I don't follow."

"We know about you and your friend in the American CIC conspiring to present false documents in order for you to escape from one of our facilities in Austria. We know the Austrian police issued a warrant for your arrest for murder in Vienna, and the Italian and British authorities want you for the same crimes in Italy."

He paused and stared at me with a smug smile. I figured the pause was to give that time to sink in. Which it did.

"This is some kind of shakedown, isn't it?" I said.

"If you mean blackmail," Wetherbee said, "then, yes."

They both seemed to be enjoying my predicament. Their smirks didn't bother me as much as knowing what their expressions meant: whatever they had in mind for me, it was going to be a doozy.

I said, "By the looks on your faces, maybe I'd be better off going back to your prison in Graz."

"Oh, not Graz," Gilman said. "No, we were thinking more of our charming facility in Khartoum. That's in Sudan, by the way."

It didn't take much imagination to conjure up the horrors of doing time in a British prison in the deserts of Sudan. "You can't throw me into prison if I haven't been convicted of any crime."

"This is not a civil criminal matter but a military one, Mr. Collins," Wetherbee said. "I have no doubt that your military would do something similar if warranted. We could hold you there while you await trial or extradition to Italy or Austria, or if your government decides to intervene. God knows how long any of that might take."

Gilman and Wetherbee fell silent and continued to stare at me. They were trying to make me squirm and doing a good job of it.

"The CIC is keeping tabs on me, so you couldn't get away with it."

It was a feeble retort. They knew it, and I knew it. Even if they couldn't send me off to a Sudanese prison, they could still make things tough on me in the meantime. They were holding all the cards. I was at their mercy.

I slumped in my chair. "What do you want me to do?"

Gilman rubbed his hands together. "Ah, I knew we could come to an understanding."

"Before I agree to anything, I want you guys to assure me that my fiancée will be protected and given assistance to travel wherever she wants."

"Getting out the country is her idea or yours?" Gilman asked.

"She's scared enough to agree … I think."

"If she hasn't done anything wrong or doesn't want to go, we are in no position to force her. We have enough bad press as it is."

"We'll see what we can do," Wetherbee said. "We'll certainly do our best to protect her. But she has to stay away from that Palestinian village."

"We will investigate her claims," Gilman said and looked to Wetherbee for his agreement.

Wetherbee nodded, and Gilman continued. "What can you tell us about the incident on the ship, the *Magen David*?"

I told him about being asked to consult on the murder of a crew member, the subsequent explosion, my pursuit of the male bomber, and the woman who attacked me and made a daring escape. "I'm sure the pair worked as a team. Possibly related or lovers. I'm guessing the bomber got trapped shortly before setting off the bomb, then used the chaos and blackout caused by the explosion to make a run for it."

"And you happened to be carrying your pistol when that happened," Gilman said.

He was trying to keep me off guard with that statement. I didn't begrudge him; I'd do the same thing when questioning a witness. "After years of being a cop and an army investigator, I got in the habit of wearing one when called to a crime scene."

"It's a pity this bomber couldn't have been detained for questioning," the chief inspector said.

"He was shooting at me. I gave him a warning. Either he was going to shoot me, or I was going to shoot him."

"Can you describe the woman with him?"

"Athletic and muscled. Maybe thirty, with curly, dark brown hair and brown eyes. Five foot six. Attractive. Caucasian, though sort of Greek- or Italian-looking, with high cheekbones and long nose and chin."

Gilman looked at Wetherbee again as if asking whether the boss wanted to take it from there.

The superintendent said, "A woman with a similar description has recently come to our attention. Based on what scant information we have, we believe she's a Syrian operative. She's suspected of assassinating several of our officers as well as a couple of leaders in the Jewish Agency."

"If she is the same person, I can tell you she's been well trained. She nearly incapacitated me and almost got her knife in me. If it wasn't for several men coming to the rescue, I wouldn't be talking to you right now. She jumped forty feet into rough seas and got on a motorboat like a seasoned commando."

Wetherbee grunted as he puffed on his pipe.

"What about the bomber?" I asked. "Do you guys have anything on him?"

"Nothing so far," Wetherbee said, though by a change in his tone, I suspected he was not telling me the whole truth. "Now, on to what we expect from you. There are several items on the agenda."

A moment of silence fell on the room while the superintendent relit his pipe. I figured the pause was a way of asserting his control over the situation. I ignored him and concentrated on a fly buzzing around the superintendent's head. The traffic noise from the street grew louder as a convoy of armored vehicles rolled by spewing exhaust into the room.

Wetherbee got his pipe going again and took several puffs. He stood and came around his desk, sat on the corner, and smiled as if we were old pals. "We know you partnered with Arie Feldman and David Hazan in Italy, and that you accompanied them on the Jewish refugee ship out of Naples."

Their knowledge of the two men's identities was unsettling but not surprising. I had a good idea of what was coming next, and I didn't like it.

Wetherbee continued. "We want you to continue those associations."

"Meaning you want me to spy on them," I said.

"I could try to put it more delicately, but in essence, that's correct."

"They're not friends of mine, and I'm not a Jew. What makes you think I could get close enough to learn anything?"

"You were an intelligence agent and an investigator," Gilman said. "I understand you infiltrated a dangerous black-market gang in Garmisch and posed as a businessman in Austria to get to the head of an organized crime syndicate. I'm sure you can tap into those skills and devise a plan."

"You fellas know a lot more than you could learn on your own. Who gave you that information?"

Neither of them answered. I probed their faces and saw looks of amusement as if enjoying a spot of irony.

"It was Mike Forester of the CIC, wasn't it?" I said.

"He said he sent you here to do some investigating on behalf of your army's CIC. That you were to investigate any Soviet meddling in particular. When we told him of our idea of enlisting you, he was quite cooperative. Especially after we explained our knowledge of his and your ..." He paused. "Misadventures."

There went my one hope to get out of my present predicament by getting Forester to bail me out once again. Now that that was gone, I felt trapped.

Wetherbee stood, prompting Gilman to approach me. That was a signal. They wanted to wrap things up, then do the same to me with a big bow tied around my neck and throw me to the wolves.

Wetherbee held out his hand. "We expect frequent reports and signs of progress, Mr. Collins. And if you do glean any information on the identity or whereabouts of the woman assassin, pass that along as well."

I stood, but I didn't take up the offer to shake either of their hands. Declining the pleasantries didn't seem to bother them; they were enjoying themselves too much.

"I or one of our operatives will contact you," Gilman said. "I'm sure I don't have to mention that it would be unwise to come here."

"What about your promise to protect Mrs. Talbot?" I asked, though it still felt uncomfortable to utter her married name.

"We will hold up our end of the bargain," Gilman said.

"I'm guessing you know where she lives."

"Of course," Gilman said.

"Of course," I said, deflated.

Gilman stepped over to the door, opened it, and leaned out to say something to the sergeant waiting in the hall.

Sergeant Mills came in with handcuffs in his hand. "Extend your hands, if you please."

"What's this?" I asked.

"We can't have anyone thinking you were in here gossiping with officers in the CID, now can we?" Gilman said. "Too many prying eyes. The sergeant will see that you're escorted to the detention barracks as if you've been arrested. You'll be released under cover of darkness."

Mills cuffed me and nodded for me to follow him. As I got to the door, Wetherbee said, "Oh, and Mr. Collins, we want you to avoid any contact with Mrs. Talbot for the moment."

I said nothing and walked away. I had no intention of following that directive.

9

I stood in the doorway of a small grocery store diagonally across from Laura's hotel. The store was on a perpendicular street and situated close to the three-way intersection. My wrist-watch was no longer in sync with the real time, but I figured it was around nine thirty p.m., as the restaurants and bars were hurrying along their last customers in order to close before the ten p.m. curfew.

After DCI Gilman and Superintendent Wetherbee put the screws to me, two police escorts took me from the central police station to the detention barracks and held me there until night-fall. The idea was to let me slip away under cover of darkness to avoid anyone suspecting I was now a British police asset. But then word got around the detention center that I'd put a Brit officer in the hospital in Austria, and the courteous treatment turned nasty. The sergeant in charge unceremoniously kicked me out. At least they returned my backpack with all my weapons and the box of ammunition.

I immediately made my way to Laura's, despite the DCI's warning to stay away. I'd used the darkness and a circuitous route to shake off any tails and arrived at my present location an hour ago to scope out the area. DCI Gilman's promise of protection turned out to be a couple of plainclothes detective inspectors sitting in a car in front of the building. Getting past them wouldn't be a problem. It was the frequent police and army patrols circulating at random intervals that could make things difficult.

I did one more scan to check for any suspicious lingerers and stepped out of the doorway. I crossed the street at a quick pace. The sharp angle of the two streets kept me from view of the inspectors. At the corner, I peered down the hotel's street. The inspectors' car faced the other way, but I still had to cross behind. I listened for footsteps or approaching traffic. All was quiet. I bent low and hustled across the street, holding my breath in hope that I wasn't spotted. Staying low, I stopped at a six-foot-high wooden barrier that closed off the alley between the hotel and a small clothing shop.

A Jeep came charging down the road. With no time to lose, I hurdled myself over the fencing and had to roll to keep from breaking an ankle. When the Jeep passed, I moved to the end of the alley. It opened up onto a small, square, graveled area hemmed in by the surrounding buildings. A man was yelling at someone from a neighboring apartment building. A baby cried. A radio played Benny Goodman's "All the Cats Joined In." The song echoed in the confined space and brought back memories of dancing with Laura. I looked up to where Laura's apartment would be and saw a faint glow coming from the yellowed shades covering the two rear windows.

I found a rear entrance to the hotel and was about to fish out my lock-picking tools from my backpack when I froze. The back door stood ajar. I resisted the urge to burst in and charge up the stairs. I had no idea if the owner or his son had simply been careless or if someone had gained access. If it was the latter, the question was who. Maybe the police. But my instincts told me to get out my Ka-Bar and brass knuckles.

I tucked the pack behind a trash can, slipped the brass knuckles onto my left hand, and pulled out my Ka-Bar knife. I would have preferred my .45, but I was glad I'd left it with Laura. I pushed open the door. The hinges let out a short creak. There was scant light in the courtyard but even less in the short hallway.

Regardless of the potential danger, I had to move fast. It could already be too late.

At the end of the hallway, I looked around the corner to check the reception desk. My heart slammed into high gear when I saw the owner's son, Yosef, lying on his back behind the counter with his neck opened from ear to ear.

I bounded up the stairs, two steps at a time. In my panic, I abandoned stealth for speed. I reached the third floor and rushed for Laura's door at the end of the hallway. The only light came from the street and barely pierced the blackness. I reached for the doorknob.

I felt more than heard movement, like a disturbance of air around me. A split second later there came a slight rustling of fabric. I spun around just in time to see a figure dressed in black charging me with a large knife poised to strike.

With my body braced and my feet firmly planted, I brought up my knife. The attacker jumped and whirled, using the momentum to kick the Ka-Bar from my hand and swipe their blade at my throat. I lunged to the left, but the blade still sliced through my leather jacket and shirt. A searing pain burned my shoulder and left arm.

The attacker kicked me in the ribs and whirled for another swipe with the knife. This time I was ready for the maneuver and caught the attacker's wrist just above the knife. I used their momentum to throw the assailant against the wall.

The impact caused the attacker to cry out. A woman's voice. It had to be the woman from the ship!

She recovered in an instant and kicked again and hit me in

the chest. I still had her knife hand trapped, but after a potent kick struck my stomach, I lost control of her wrist.

My lungs seized, but my fury won out over my need to breathe.

The woman growled as she charged with the knife straight out. Not her best move. I caught her knife hand with my right, pushed it safely away, and struck her with the brass knuckles on my left.

She recoiled from the blow and lost her knife. A hit to the jaw with the brass knuckles usually rendered an assailant unconscious, and while I'm sure I did some heavy damage, she simply spun out of my grasp like an Olympic gymnast and coiled for another assault.

With deafening explosions, several bullets blew through the door from inside Laura's room. The angry buzz of the bullets rocketed past my torso. I ducked away from the door. My assailant did the same on the other side.

The presence of the powerful weapon seemed to be enough of a deterrent. The assassin shot me a fiery glare and sprinted down the hall. Without hesitating, she leapt out the open window at the other end.

I rushed up to the window and looked out. She was already bounding across several rooftops, and she disappeared into the darkness.

"Mason!"

Laura was standing in her doorway holding my .45 pistol. She let out a soft yelp and ran toward me. We collided in the middle of the hallway and held each other. She gasped as she tried to control her fear.

"Come on," I said. "Let's get you inside."

"Where were you?"

I waited to answer her until we got into the room, and I closed the door.

"The cops picked me up."

She looked up at me in surprise. "What? Why?"

I slowly took the pistol from her hand and placed it on the nightstand. "It's going to be too long to explain, but the short version is they have me over a barrel and want me to spy for them. In exchange, I demanded that they protect you. There are two flatfoots that are doing nothing but sitting in a car outside your building."

"How do they have you over a barrel? Who are you supposed to be spying on?"

"I'll explain once we get out of here."

Laura held me tighter and looked at the door. "Was that woman here to kill me?"

"I don't know."

"What do you mean—" Laura stopped. "You're bleeding." She pulled open my jacket enough to see the minor knife wound. "She must be pretty good. She almost got you."

"Yes, she did."

Laura pulled a towel off a rack by the sink, opened my shirt, and pressed the towel against the wound.

"She's as fast and agile as I've seen and took a beating without slowing her down. We tangled on the ship when I shot her accomplice. She went into a rage, which makes me think I'd shot her lover. That's why I don't know if she was after you or waiting to ambush me."

"Do you think she's with the Black Hand?"

"I don't know that either." I gestured toward her closet. "Come on, get packing. You can't stay here."

"Doesn't look too bad," she said as she checked the wound. "Still, you should get it looked at." She seemed to be nursing the wound longer than she needed, which I figured meant she was reluctant to leave my side.

I gently urged her toward the closet. "Shooting off that cannon will bring the police. I'd like to leave before they get here."

She went to the armoire and started to gather her things. While she did that, I ripped a towel and tied a piece around the gash on my arm. I picked up the .45 from the nightstand, checked the magazine and safety, then belted it. I stepped back out into the hallway and found my knife and the assailant's. All seemed to be quiet.

I went back inside. "No one's bothered to come out of their rooms to see what was going on."

"There are only two other rooms with occupants, and I never see them," Laura said and spotted the assailant's knife in my hand.

She glanced at the door again. "Just before you got here, I heard someone check the other doors on the floor. I didn't dare look to see who it was. I locked the door and barricaded it with a chair."

"Then she knew the building's address, but not your exact room."

She stiffened for a moment and silently went back to packing her suitcase. She finished and latched it closed. "You said there are two cops stationed in front of the building. Did you tell the police where I was?"

"They already knew when they brought me into the station."

"Maybe there's someone on the force who gave the assassin my location," she said, raising her voice.

"Laura, that doesn't matter right this moment. We have to get out of here now."

"Where? If they can find me here, they can find me anywhere."

"We'll hole up somewhere until I can get you on a ship to Italy or France."

"A ship? Me? No. I'm not going without you."

"You can't stay in Palestine. And the Brits aren't going to let me leave." I told her about the accusations against me in Austria and Italy and about Gilman and Wetherbee's threats to clap me in irons and send me to a hellhole of a prison if I didn't comply with their demands.

"Then I'll make a big stink," Laura said as she jammed more things in her suitcase. "I'll go to the press about them threatening to detain an American citizen against his will."

A commotion from the street was loud enough to come through the closed door. I rushed down the hallway and peered out the window. A police squad car and an army Jeep were parked in front of the hotel. Two policemen and three soldiers were looking into the inspectors' car and calling out orders. The two policemen went to the hotel's entrance and pounded on the door.

I raced back to Laura's room. "We've got to go now. The police are here."

"I haven't finished packing, and my papers—"

She didn't finish because I grabbed up the suitcase along with her coat, latched onto her hand, and dragged her down the hallway.

"My papers," she hissed.

"We'll come back for them."

The pounding continued. We moved down the hall as quietly and quickly as we could. We hit the second floor, and I led us down the hall and away from the stairs.

"Where are you going?" Laura whispered.

Below, the door exploded open. The two cops shouted. No doubt they'd found the murdered boy.

I ran up to the last room and put my shoulder into the door. The lock gave way, and the door flew open. It was dark and silent. The apartment's layout was the same as Laura's, a square room with a bed, living room/dining room and tiny kitchen area. The bed had only a bare mattress. No one was staying there.

I went directly to one of the two windows. I opened it and climbed out onto the small balcony that faced the interior court-yard. It was just ten feet to the ground, and I negotiated that easily enough. Footsteps sounded on the stairs. Laura didn't hesitate to follow me, climbing over the railing and dropping down while clinging onto the lower rung, then I took some of her weight when she jumped the last few feet.

I grabbed my backpack from behind the trash can, and we rushed across the courtyard to the rear entrance of a building facing the opposite street. I kicked it open and hurried down the short hallway to the front entrance. Fortunately, no one was around. We exited the building. I took a chance and turned right.

"Now what?" Laura asked as we moved down the street.

"We look up a friend of mine. At least, I hope he's still my friend."

10

I found the door easily enough; the occupant was the only one who didn't have their name on the mailboxes in the lobby for the sixth floor. It was 11:35 p.m. according to Laura's wristwatch, and we hadn't heard a sound coming up the building's six flights of stairs. I knocked quietly and hoped he was home.

It took a couple of agonizing moments before I heard rustling behind the door. I imagined the occupant getting his pistol ready and debating whether to open it or not.

"It's a friend," I said.

The door opened, and Feldman stared at me and Laura for a second with wide eyes. He said nothing as he popped his head out the doorway, looked both ways, then pulled us inside.

He closed the door quietly and turned to us. "What are you doing here?"

"Hello," Laura said.

He formed a smile over his worried face. "Is this the woman you spoke about?"

"This is Laura McKin—" I stopped myself. "Talbot."

Laura smiled at me, then turned to Feldman. "Once we get to

know each other better, you're going to have to tell me exactly what he said about me."

"All good, I assure you," Feldman said. "And congratulations on the child. Excuse me for not acknowledging you, but these are stressful times." He looked at me, my backpack, then Laura's suitcase in my hand. "Are you two leaving?"

"Not exactly."

He motioned for us to follow him to the living room. We moved out of the foyer and stood by the sofa and chairs. Feldman went over to a cabinet. "Can I get you two a drink?"

"Thanks, we both could use one," Laura said. "Something with a good kick would be nice."

While Feldman poured scotch into three glasses, I pulled off my pack and put it next to Laura's suitcase. I sat on the edge of the sofa and let out a sigh of relief. Laura was too nervous to sit and paced the room. Feldman came back with the drinks and handed them to us. He then sat in one of the chairs facing the sofa.

"Now, what can I help you with?"

"We need a place to stay for a few days while I try to figure out how to get Laura out of the country."

"I'm not leaving without you," Laura said in a sharp tone.

We glared at each other until Feldman said, "I'm afraid that's impossible. This evening at least. I'm expecting someone important to come by."

"A special friend?" I asked.

"A girl? No, not in that way," Feldman said defensively.

"Arie, we're desperate. How about just for one night?"

"Another night, perhaps."

A silence fell between us. Feldman glanced from me to Laura and seemed to pick up on our rattled nerves.

"Does she know?" he asked me.

I shook my head.

"What don't I know?" Laura asked, looking at both of us.

"If I tell you, I don't want it to be as a reporter," Feldman said.

"By that preamble, you're either Haganah or Irgun," Laura said.

"How did—" Feldman stopped as if remembering me telling him about Laura's sharp mind. "Haganah."

"I was hoping it wasn't Irgun or Lehi," she said. "They are the true fanatics."

Feldman crossed his arms. "I wouldn't go that far."

Laura gave Feldman the look of a disappointed teacher. "Lehi tried to make a deal with Hitler; they would help the Nazis fight against the British in the Middle East and promised to set up a totalitarian government—"

Feldman interrupted. "In exchange, Nazi Germany would send all Jews in Europe to Eretz Israel."

She clucked her tongue and waved away Feldman's statement. "That wasn't going to happen. And when the news started coming back about the Nazi atrocities, instead of admitting they were wrong, Lehi proposed to set up a Stalinist-style regime instead."

"That's all in the past," Feldman said.

"That was only a few years ago. Do you think people really change that quickly? Their dream is still to set up a totalitarian state, and they believe the Jews are the master race. That the Arabs are only worthy to be slaves. Sounds like another regime we've had to deal with recently, doesn't it?"

Feldman fell silent and glared at the wall in defiance.

"Why are you defending them?" I asked Feldman. "On the ship, you told me how angry you were about them vowing to kill Brits."

"I don't agree with either group's philosophy. It still hurts to think of David joining Irgun."

I explained to Laura who David Hazan was.

Feldman sighed and said, "Nevertheless, since I've been away for a while, someone from Haganah is supposed to vet me to make sure I'm okay to join the local group. And I'm expecting that someone to come by tonight."

"And it'd look bad to be with two American goyim," Laura said.

"All of Palestine is on the brink. The Brits, the Jews, and the Arabs. Suspicions are rampant. Loyalties are being questioned constantly."

I got in Feldman's eyeline. "We need your help, Arie. I wouldn't be asking this if I saw another way, and you said that if I needed anything to come to you."

"If you stay out of sight when the Haganah operative comes, then I'm fine with you staying here. But you came here to hide, and I'd like to know why."

"The woman who was with the bomber on the ship was waiting for me at Laura's apartment."

Feldman raised an eyebrow in surprise. "Did she get away?"

I held up my thumb and forefinger. "And came this close to cutting my throat. Even after nearly breaking her jaw, the only thing that scared her off was Laura blasting through the door with my .45."

"It wasn't exactly heroic," Laura said. "I shot at the door because I was scared to death." She put her hands on my jacket. "That reminds me," she said and coaxed off my coat to examine the wound.

"Aside from almost plugging me with holes, it did the trick," I said. "Then the woman got away by jumping out a window and bounding over the rooftops with the agility of a cat."

Feldman studied me while unconsciously spinning the liquid in his glass. "You didn't go to the police?"

"It's complicated."

"We have all night," Feldman said.

"Do you have any bandages?" Laura asked Feldman.

"In the bathroom," Feldman said.

Laura and I followed Feldman down a short hallway, passing

two bedrooms before entering the bathroom. I was happy for the distraction because I was unsure how much to tell Feldman, at least how much of the truth.

Laura sat me on the toilet lid while Feldman found some medical supplies in a closet. She untied the towel around the wound, took what she needed from Feldman, and leaned in close to clean the wound. I could smell her and felt her breath on my wet arm. The proximity aroused me, and I had a hard time resisting the urge to pull her into my arms. She must have sensed this, because she looked at me like a mom warning a kid not to stick his hand in the cookie jar.

Feldman handed her more supplies and sat on the edge of the bathtub.

"You should get some stitches," Laura said to me.

"A tighter bandage will have to do."

She snatched the glass of whiskey from my hand and poured it on the wound.

It stung like fury, but my anger focused on the wasted whiskey. "I was drinking that."

While Laura wrapped gauze around the wound, she glanced at Feldman, who looked impatient for answers. "For me," Laura said, "I went into hiding because I may have witnessed some people who, according to a Palestinian woman I'd become friendly with, are members of the Black Hand."

Feldman leaned forward and looked intently at Laura. "Black Hand? Are you sure?"

"That's what the woman said. She was terrified. The next day, some men from the neighboring kibbutz found her body. She'd been tortured and killed."

"I thought the Black Hand ceased to exist when al-Qassam was killed," Feldman said.

Laura finished securing the bandage. "Could be that someone else decided to pick up where he left off."

"This is important news," Feldman said. "I'm glad you brought me this information."

"I think the woman assassin was at my apartment to kill us both."

"Then it's imperative that you get out of Palestine as soon as possible," Feldman said and looked at me. "And you, too."

"Well, here's the problem with that: the police grabbed me up this afternoon and took me to the superintendent for the CID."

"I don't like where this is going."

"You shouldn't. They know who I am, and that I'm under suspicion of murder in Vienna and in Italy. They know that a friend of mine with the army's CIC helped me escape one of their jails for beating a Brit officer enough to put him in the hospital. They're threatening to put me in a prison in Sudan if I don't work for them."

Feldman jumped to his feet. "You came here, of all places, even when the police know who you are?"

"Arie, they know about you and David. They know or suspect we worked together to take out some Nazis."

Feldman hissed and turned in place, sloshing his drink in the process.

I kept my voice calm and said, "I don't think they have too many particulars, but they know we partnered up in Italy, and while they didn't say it, I think they have some idea of your association with Haganah."

"They want you to spy on us," Feldman said. "And you agreed."

"Yes, to keep me from going to Sudan and guaranteeing protection for Laura, although that didn't happen. But I—"

Feldman growled in anger. "How dare you come here asking for my help. Get out."

"Arie," Laura said, "Mason just told you what they want. Do you think he would spy on you and your colleagues after admitting it?"

I stood to look Feldman in the eye. "We just need a place for the evening, while I work out how to get Laura out of the country. Then I'll disappear and fabricate intel to keep them happy."

Laura stood and clenched her fists. "I told you I'm not going without you. We can sneak out."

"The only way out is by sea," Feldman said. "Or through Egypt, Syria, Jordan, or Lebanon. All of which are not about to welcome you with open arms. And that's if Mason could even slip past the British checkpoints and naval blockades."

I turned to Laura. "And he didn't mention that the Arab militant groups could be searching for you. We can get you out, but I have to stay."

"For how long? And who's to say if and when you've satisfied the police? They might keep you indefinitely."

She had a point, and I didn't have a good answer. We all fell silent a moment while Laura finished wrapping gauze around the wound and cinching it tight.

"I see getting you out is to both our advantages," Feldman said. "Stay here for the night. If the vetting goes well and I'm allowed to join, then I might be able to use Haganah's resources to help you slip away."

"How?" Laura asked. "You just finished telling us the dangers for Mason if he tries to leave."

"I can't tell you how yet, but Haganah has a network of smuggling routes. Something you or I couldn't manage on our own. In the meantime, I can arrange to have you stay at a kibbutz where my sister lives. It's not far from here, and I'm sure the community will agree to shelter you once I explain your circumstances and what you've done for the *aliyah*."

Laura silently implored me with her eyes. I tried to see all the angles. There was still a great deal of risk. We could be caught by the British police or captured by Arab militants, or worse, gunned down if things went south or we got caught in a crossfire. And if we made it out in one piece, I'd still have the Brits chasing after me. And there was a good chance I'd ruffle feathers of some in the U.S. intelligence agencies, including Mike Forester …

I took Laura's hand. "We'll do it."

There was a knock at the front door. We all turned toward the hallway.

"It's him," Feldman said. "You two need to get into the bedroom."

We all rushed to the living room. Laura grabbed her suitcase, and I got my backpack. Feldman told us to get into the spare bedroom on the right. Laura and I rushed down the hall. I closed the door just as I heard Feldman welcome someone at the front door.

The room was spartan, with a double bed, a small dresser, and a nightstand. We stuffed our suitcase and backpack in the closet and stood near a single door to a balcony just big enough for two people. We listened to the muffled talking from the living room. They spoke in Hebrew, but I could tell Feldman was talking nervously, with the visitor's voice responding in a calm yet cold manner.

"It sounds like they aren't friends," Laura whispered.

"Like Arie said. Everyone in this town is jumpy."

The voices seemed to be getting closer.

Laura pointed toward the hallway. "If he's checking out the apartment, he's definitely going to wonder about the only closed door in the hallway."

I turned and gently opened the door to the balcony and motioned for Laura to step onto it. I was right behind her. I pulled the curtain closed as best I could before closing the balcony door. There was just enough room for us to huddle close together. The balcony was at the rear of the building, which was perched on a hill. The property fell sharply away to Mamilla Park. No one could see us, and it felt like we were alone, hovering above the city. It was breezy with a chilling wind. Laura shivered and put her arms around me for warmth.

We held each other tighter when the door opened. Through the narrow gap in the curtains, Feldman came into view. He used his hands to sweep the room. His voice was muffled, but I could tell he was in a tense conversation. Feldman's gaze remained fixed on the doorway, and moments later he moved in that direction. The door then closed with some force. I assumed that was to let us know that they had moved on.

"We'd better stay where we are," I said in a quiet voice.

Laura looked up at me. Maybe it was the danger of being caught or the events in the last hour, but whatever the cause, I could feel a yearning, the chasm between us falling away. It burned in me and radiated from her.

Laura took my face in her hands and pulled me in. We kissed deeply and didn't stop. It had been so long since we had embraced with so much passion that it took us over. Without the fear of peering eyes, we lowered each other's trousers, and she lifted her legs and wrapped them around my waist. I turned and rested her onto the railing.

We made love with abandon, without making a sound except for our heavy breathing, with only the stars as witnesses.

11

Traffic was dense and creeping along, and though it was only around ten in the morning, it was already hot. No matter which road Feldman took, there were traffic jams, drivers honking horns, and car exhaust choking off the available oxygen. I figured the police and army had thrown up roadblocks and checkpoints throughout the city.

Feldman was driving a taxi he'd borrowed from a friend. Laura and I sat in the back as "passengers." He was getting nervous about the delay, sticking his head out the window and honking his horn.

I was concerned but still enjoying the warming aftereffects of making love with Laura then sleeping next to her in a soft bed. It'd been a long time for either. That and a long shower all brought my energy back to normal. I think Laura was feeling something similar, as she sat close to me and sported a contented smile. The chance of getting out of there and going home together—wherever that ended up being—had lifted her spirits.

The plan was for Feldman to take us to a kibbutz north of the city. We were to make contact with someone there, who would escort us along a smuggling route into Lebanon. The rest of the details were left purposefully vague.

Feldman kept nervously drumming the steering wheel. "I told you stopping to get Laura's papers was a bad idea."

"I can't leave them there," Laura said. "There's too much information for prying eyes to find."

"This wasn't part of the deal," Feldman said. "I could have slipped out of the city using secondary roads."

I looked out the rear window. Cars were backed up for at least two blocks on a major street called Julian's Way. It was too late to get out of the snarled traffic. To keep Feldman's mind on the task, I said, "I'm glad the meeting with the Haganah contact went well. What's next for you?"

Feldman looked at us in the rearview mirror as if debating what to say.

"I'm not going to tell the police anything," I said. "Plus, we're on our way out of here. At least I hope we are."

"It's good you two are getting out now," Feldman said. "Haganah has decided to reactivate the Palmach."

"What is Palmach?" Laura asked.

"If the Haganah is the security wing of the Jewish Agency, Palmach is the covert military strike force."

"You guys are planning to step up your attacks," I said. "Just what you said you wouldn't do."

"War is coming. And sooner than I thought. With the British looking for a way out and the UN debating the partition, war is brewing between us and the Arabs. It's inevitable, and we're surrounded by an ocean of Arabs. We have to be prepared. Because of my experience, I was selected to train new recruits for Palmach. We're split up into squads and train at many of the kibbutzim." His intense expression melted into a smile. "And I requested to train at my sister's kibbutz, Kiryat Anavim."

While Feldman talked, we crept closer and closer to a British checkpoint. From what I could see past the long line of cars, this one looked to have been hastily put in place.

"This doesn't look good," Feldman said. "They must be searching for someone or something."

"Even if they know who you are," I said, "you haven't done anything to be on their radar. And the most I've done is disobey an order to stay away from Laura."

I didn't necessarily believe my own words. I said them to keep Laura calm.

A handful of British police performed the checks while a dozen heavily armed soldiers manned two opposing stacks of sandbags, each equipped with a Bren machine gun. The policemen and soldiers looked grim and vigilant. Something was going on.

Feldman started to sink in his seat as we got within two cars of the checkpoint. Laura fished her passport and visa out of her purse. I did the same, pulling them out of my backpack. The .45 pistol jammed in my belt suddenly felt like a jagged rock at the small of my back.

The policemen took their time examining IDs and searching the cars. We were next in line and anxious to get going, but then the three passengers ahead of us were asked to get out of the car. They looked Arab by their dress and stood near their car as two policemen went through the interior and trunk.

The Arab man protested with hand gestures while a woman and young girl tried to calm him down. A male pedestrian tried to bypass them, only to be stopped by two other policemen, which then halted the line of pedestrians waiting to clear the checkpoint.

On the opposite side of the barrier, the traffic and waiting pedestrians were also being held up by the two altercations blocking both lanes. On the other side of the checkpoint, a group of pedestrians, a man and two women, were also confronting the police. The man was elderly and doing most of the arguing. The lead woman was young and striking, like a model in a magazine. Despite standing passively by, she still got more attention from the soldiers than the old man did. The second woman suddenly disappeared from view behind one of the sandbag barriers. I found that odd, and my attention was drawn to her. She moved gracefully, like an athlete, and wore a headscarf and sunglasses that obscured most of her face, though I could still see enough to notice that she was young and attractive.

Feldman struck the steering wheel and growled in frustration, bringing me back to our present dilemma. Finally, a soldier persuaded the male driver to get back into his car and advance through the barrier. The backlog on both sides began to flow, and Feldman eased the car up to the awaiting policemen.

We handed over our IDs and waited. The pedestrians from the other side began to pass, and I watched the mostly Arab crowd come past our car. The woman I'd noticed with the head-scarf and sunglasses was in the midst of a crowd, and I watched as something about her tickled my brain …

"Mr. Collins?" someone said at my window. "Please look at me."

I turned to see a guard was leaning down and peering in my window with my passport open to the picture page. While he studied my face and the photo, my mind searched for the reason the hairs on the back of my neck were standing up. As soon as the guard straightened and moved away, it came to me.

The woman wore combat-style boots under a long, ankle-length dress. Then her lips, the way she moved. The blackened bruise on her right jaw!

"It's the woman assassin!" I said and leapt out of the car.

As I ran back the way we'd come, I heard Laura and a policeman yell for me to stop. I ignored them. I would get my hands on the woman no matter what. The logjam of people and cars forced me to dodge in and out of the crowds as I tried to peer past their heads. It was a two-lane street with narrow sidewalks, and I felt sure I could spot her. People barked at me as I pushed past them, or cars honked when I jumped out into the street to get around the dense crowds.

I came across the first side street and stopped to check for my quarry. Nothing. I pushed on and picked up the pace. A block later, the street emptied out onto a wide square, with five streets branching off in different directions. The place was dense with people and cars.

I came to a halt. There was no sign of the woman, no one running to get away. I'd lost her.

I immediately turned and jogged back toward the checkpoint. Feldman's car came into sight when I went around a curve. It was about thirty yards distant. Both Feldman and Laura were still there. Feldman had been pulled aside to the opposite gun emplacement, where a constable appeared to be questioning him. Laura was standing between the body of the car and her open door, waving for me to hurry up.

A ball of fire, smoke, and flying debris enveloped the car. The boom and blast hit me a split second later, knocking me off my feet. Stunned, my ears ringing, I clambered to my feet. I cried out. "Laura!"

My voice was muffled and blended with the screams of those around me. I ran unsteadily toward the carnage. Feldman's car was on fire along with the one behind it. Bodies were sprawled on the pavement. Others staggered aimlessly, bloody, clothes torn. The sandbag emplacement on the left was gone. Cops and soldiers lay on the ground.

I found Laura beside the car, crumpled on the pavement. I crashed to my knees and gently turned her over. Her face was bloody, her hair burned. She was limp, and her eyes were closed. She seemed lifeless when I lifted her to me. I felt for a pulse. It was faint and slow.

"Help! I need help!"

12

The blazing light of sunset streamed through the large windows and assaulted my eyes, but I was numb to any pain. The shock of the blast had given way to the paralysis of heartache and rage. I sat in the waiting room in the surgery wing, which resembled any you might find in a larger-sized hospital in the world. This one was sparkling clean, immaculately maintained, with long banks of modern windows along the hallway just outside the room.

I didn't know how long I'd been in that same position on the wooden bench—I had no desire to even turn my head to look at the wall clock—but I was sure many hours had passed.

I'd ridden over in the ambulance with Laura to the Italian Hospital north of the Old City. I had no idea why the sprawling complex was named that, except the exterior looked like a Renaissance church and tower flanked by twin Florentine palaces. A nurse had removed the bits of glass and metal from my face and neck while I constantly demanded any word about Laura's condition. I was only told that she was in surgery and would be there for a considerable amount of time.

I called Laura's parents in Massachusetts shortly after I got there. Her mother had answered. I'd never met or spoken to her before, but from her icy tone, I could tell she wasn't a fan of mine. She broke down when I told her the bad news and accused me of being responsible for putting her in danger. Listening to her sob was gut-wrenching. She finally got herself under control and said she would get there as soon as possible. Her father was in Quebec for a biochemistry conference and would follow. I hung up the phone and found it hard to move.

A sympathetic nurse had escorted me to this room, and there I sat. My backpack and Laura's suitcase lay on the floor beside me. Being in the trunk, they'd survived the blast, and I had someone get them before the fire spread. Without those IDs, we would both be in deeper water. That is, if she survived. That thought caused another wave of rage and anguish.

I hadn't seen Feldman after the blast; I was too fixated on Laura at the time. He had been standing by the left sandbag emplacement. That position might have saved him from injury, even saved his life. Then again, maybe not. I'd seen too many victims near his position to think that was a sure thing. We were not close friends, but I cared about him, and my mind was plagued with images of him dead or dying. Maybe he'd been just far enough away and protected by the car. Maybe he was being treated at another hospital.

Soldiers and officers passed by the waiting room windows, some in uniform and others dressed in medical gowns with bandages or on stretchers. The British had taken over the hospital in 1917 to care for their military personnel, and I took some comfort knowing that the doctors and nurses here were well trained in battle wounds like Laura's. The best I could figure, she ended up here because the closer hospitals' emergency rooms were already full of victims.

Images leading up to the bomb and the moments right after kept rolling around in my head. I analyzed each moment, the faces that had passed by the barrier and Feldman's car. The woman assassin was at the forefront, and I replayed each of her movements.

My thoughts were interrupted when Feldman appeared in the waiting room window. He spotted me and continued to the entrance. He wore a green gown, though his heavy boots looked comical poking out from the bottom of the gown. A bandage was wrapped around his head, and his left eye was bloodred and circled by a black bruise. His arm was in a sling. He walked slowly and grimaced with each step.

"I thought I'd find you here," Feldman said and let out a heavy sigh as he sat.

Seeing Feldman lifted my spirits enough to give him a weak smile. "I'm glad to see you're in one piece."

"Multiple pieces," he said and raised the arm in the sling.

"Broken?"

"No, just dislocated. I think it hurt more when they put it back in place. But who's counting? And you?"

"Cuts and bruises."

"What's the news on Laura?"

The question made my stomach twist into a knot. "I don't know yet. She's still in surgery."

"I could offer you a platitude, like she's a strong woman, but I won't. A bomb doesn't care."

My stomach made knots upon knots with that statement. "You were better off spouting the platitude."

Feldman nodded and looked away.

"Don't worry about it," I said. "You caught me feeling sorry for myself. But I've decided the cure for that is plotting my revenge."

We sat in silence for a moment. A pack of nurses and a doctor rushed by pushing a stretcher with another soldier lying bloody and motionless.

While I watched the grim parade, I said, "I was trying to figure out how that woman managed to plant a bomb so quickly and without being noticed. And without blowing herself up."

"I could see her tossing a grenade, but not planting something the size of that bomb," Feldman said.

"And if she was going after Laura and me, why not plant it closer to the car?"

Feldman shook his head as he continued to look away. "Maybe she was hoping to do double duty—get you guys and take out a few soldiers and police at the same time."

That sounded plausible, but a lot of questions still brewed in my mind. And I intended to extract the answers out of her one way or another.

A man dressed in surgical clothing and a mask pulled down to his chin popped his head in the doorway. He spotted me and came toward the bench. Every nerve fired, and my heart shot into high gear. I got to my feet and was glad Feldman stood next to me. I wanted to ask the question, but my mouth was suddenly too dry to vocalize the words.

"I'm Dr. Blake, the chief surgeon. Mrs. Talbot is out of surgery. She suffered severe brain trauma. Massive hemorrhaging, which was putting pressure on the brain. We managed to stop the bleeding, but she's not out of the woods yet."

"Can I see her?"

"Not yet, but it shouldn't be long. I'll send someone out to get you. But you have to know that her appearance may alarm you."

"I don't care."

Dr. Blake stared into my eyes for a moment. "You also must know that she's been unresponsive."

"What do you mean?"

"She could come around at any time, but there's also the possibility she might not."

"You mean like a coma?"

"It's too early to tell," Blake said. "Some people take a while to recover from the anesthesia." He put up his hands to keep me calm. "We'll be monitoring her and will make sure she gets the best care.

But, in large part, it's up to her." His face turned from stolid to sympathetic. "There's one more thing that you need to know. The extreme trauma caused her to lose her baby. I'm sorry, Mr. Collins."

The weight of anguish caused me to drop onto the bench. Feldman sat beside me. He was saying something, but I didn't hear the words. An emptiness enveloped me, but most of my sadness was for Laura. She would be devastated, and it might just erase any will for her to get better.

That was, if she survived.

～

A NURSE LED ME TO WHAT WAS PROBABLY THE WARD'S WAITING room before they crammed three beds in there. Each was separated by curtains on foldable stands. According to her, there were so many soldiers and policemen coming out of surgery that they'd run out of regular rooms. The patients in the other beds were behind curtains and remained deathly still and quiet. The only noise came from the hushed tones of the nurses and the shuffle of their soft shoes. The nurse led me to the first bed. She pulled back the curtain and let me pass.

Only a small portion of Laura's head was visible. What wasn't covered in bandages was red, purple, and swollen, including her right eye. I could only imagine the other gashes and wounds covered up by the blanket. I'd seen plenty of wounds and their aftermath during the war, but the sight of her lying there, motionless and battered, made my legs turn to rubber. My chest constricted, nearly cutting off my breathing.

I put my hand on her arm tucked underneath the sheets. "Laura, it's Mason. I'm here."

I was hoping hearing my voice might get her to stir or open her eyes, but she showed no reaction. "Has she shown any sign that she'll be waking up soon?" I asked the nurse.

She shook her head and came in closer. "She has a good pulse. All her vitals are doing fine."

"It's just the trauma to her brain."

She nodded, and I looked back at Laura. As she lay there, the IV steadily dripping blood plasma into her, rage began to fill the void that had crippled me in the aftermath. It burned my brain and pumped adrenaline into my veins. She'd lost—we'd lost—the baby, and there was nothing I could do for her. It tore at me and made me feel helpless. I had only one outlet left to make things better.

I thanked the nurse and marched out of there.

I knew what I had to do, and there was no time to waste.

13

I stood at a distance from the blast area to see if I could spot anything or anyone suspicious. It was a long shot, but criminals sometimes visit the scene of their crime to gloat or get perverse satisfaction at the carnage. The assassin didn't fit that MO, but I scanned the area anyway. I also did this for my protection; I'd given my backpack and gun to Feldman for safekeeping, leaving me vulnerable to attack. Feldman tried to stop me from going, but I guess the look in my eyes was enough for him to back off and stand by waiting for any word about Laura's condition.

The site was surrounded by a phalanx of policemen and illuminated by portable lights. The sandbag emplacements were gone and replaced by police barriers to prevent any traffic or pedestrians from using that section of the road.

I pulled out my CIC travel papers and headed straight for the police barricade. "Agent Collins with the U.S. Counter Intelligence Corps. I'd like have a look at the crime scene."

A corporal glanced at my document and gave me a look of exasperation. "That's worthless, chum. Do you think we're that stupid? Get out of here."

"Look, I'm working with your CID—"

"I said shove off before I have you arrested."

"Is there a problem, Constable?" a voice said.

DCI Gilman stood behind the policeman with a grim look on his face. "It's all right, Corporal. Let him through."

The cop glared at me as he pulled back the barrier. Gilman's expression remained dour, though a self-satisfied smile poked through as I got closer. "So good to see you, Mr. Collins. I rather thought you were, how do you Americans say it? On the lam?"

"I changed my mind."

"I'm glad. That saved us the effort of tracking you down and sending you to Sudan." His smile faded. "I'm sorry to hear about Mrs. Talbot. I trust she's getting proper care."

"She's in good hands."

"Good," Gilman said with little sincerity behind it. "Now you can explain what happened to the two detectives we stationed outside Mrs. Talbot's hotel."

"Explain what? They were in their car the last time I saw them. They weren't paying attention, because I was able to slip past them."

"They weren't paying attention because someone cut their throats. One appeared to have been taken by surprise. The other put up a brief fight before he, too, was murdered."

The news left me stunned. It explained why there were so many policemen at Laura's hotel. When I noticed Gilman's look of suspicion, I growled, "It wasn't me."

"I'm not accusing you. Yet. I was asking for an explanation."

"Yeah, I went back to see Laura. But there was a surprise waiting for me." I told him about finding the hotel owner's son murdered and the assassin waiting in the shadows to attack me. About how she almost got the better of me and that the combination of getting in one good hit with my brass knuckles and Laura firing the pistol scared her off. "She jumped out a window without hesitation and ran across the rooftops to get away."

Gilman stared at me in silence. He was trying to unnerve me to keep me off balance. I would do the same with a suspect.

"You know I didn't do it," I said. "And you've got to realize that the assassin did. She's got to be stopped."

Gilman let out a noncommittal grunt and gestured toward the epicenter of the blast. "I assume you came to examine the scene." As we walked toward the spot, Gilman said, "I take it you suspect the same assassin also set off this bomb."

"I saw her pass our car just before the blast. The thing is, she couldn't have been working alone."

Gilman said nothing as we approached Feldman's car, now a burned-out shell. Sounds and images of the blast rolled through my head, and the pain in my chest swelled when I saw the blackened concrete and the debris radiating out from a distinct center. But instead of the bomb's epicenter being next to the car, a crater in the concrete showed it was located where the sandbag emplacement used to be.

Shredded cloth and sand from the bags were spread out in a wide circle. Remnants of uniforms, blood, and bits of tissue formed a ring closer to the radius of the blast. Broken glass from the surrounding buildings was everywhere.

"We lost six soldiers," Gilman said. "Two were only identified by process of elimination. And we lost three policemen further out from the epicenter. Some were just boys. Others had families."

"That is tragic, but you seem to be forgetting the civilian victims."

He looked away. It was the first time I saw him flummoxed. "A tragedy, of course."

"Of course."

I knelt to examine the area around the crater. Among the detritus, I picked up a fragment of aluminum with yellow paper stuck to it. "Looks like part of a blasting cap."

"To set off an RDX compound, I'd imagine," Gilman said.

"Any traces of a fuse or wire?"

"We found traces of wire, but not enough to determine if it was used to set off the blasting cap. The alternative is a fuse, but I can't imagine any of the soldiers missing a burning fuse at their feet."

"There was a heated argument going on at the barricade, a lot of confusion."

Gilman pointed upward. "My guess is the bomber was on that rooftop with a twist-handle blasting machine."

I looked to the roof of the building in front of us. The first floor was scorched by the blast, and most of the windows were broken. The person setting it off would have had to plant the explosives ahead of time and conceal a wire that ran up to the roof. Neither the fuse nor a wire scenario seemed possible to pull off undetected.

"I saw the assassin duck behind the barrier for a moment, then pass right in front it. Maybe she activated a timer."

"It could be you're so sure it was this woman that you're ignoring the other possibility."

The question left me feeling like the rug had been pulled out from under me. I came for answers, but now I had more questions.

"I see by your troubled look that you haven't considered anything else," Gilman said.

"You're saying that me seeing that woman was just a coincidence?" I shook my head. "I don't buy it."

"Consider this: she followed you and happened to be there when another party set off the bomb. If she's working with a militant Arab network, then she may have gotten word of your direction and guessed your location. There are only so many main roads leading out of the city."

"What are you getting at?"

"Bombing British military and police installations and checkpoints are almost all the work of the Jewish militant groups. The

Arabs mostly target Jewish shops and institutions. I want you to consider that the assassin's appearance was a coincidence and that it is most likely Irgun or Lehi that's responsible for the carnage."

"Is this to convince me to keep spying for you?"

"Why not look at it as a cooperative effort. You've already done well by making contact with Mr. Feldman. You continue your work for us while simultaneously searching for the bomber."

"You're talking as if I have a choice."

"Your cooperation also ensures that Mrs. Talbot continues to receive the very best of care at the Italian Hospital. A *British* military hospital," Gilman said, emphasizing that the hospital was under British control.

I balled my fists but resisted throttling the man. Attacking a policeman would land me in jail or a good beating, or both. "You bastard. You're using Laura as a bargaining chip. That's why your men took Laura to that hospital."

My threatening move had garnered the attention of several police guards. Gilman waved them off and turned to me. "If you want what's best for her, you'll remain in Palestine and do what's required of you."

14

Feldman was sitting in the chair by Laura's bed when I entered. He'd nodded off, his head tilted back and his mouth hanging open. I stepped quietly up to Laura's bed and put my hand on her arm. Laura was in the exact position as when I left. The only thing the nurse could tell me was that her vital signs were steady though she was still unresponsive. They had tried several tests, and all the indications were that she was in a deep state of unconsciousness. The nurse had hesitated to say the word *coma*. Instead she said that time would tell, and she avoided any speculation about whether Laura would stay that way or if she'd ever wake up at all.

A nurse entered the room and went over to another patient's bed at the other end. The noise must have alerted Feldman, because he sat up and rubbed his eyes.

"Thank you for watching over her," I said.

"Did you discover anything useful?"

"I went to the site of the bomb."

Feldman stopped in mid-stretch. He stood out of the chair and came around the bed to face me. "That place must be crawling with cops," he said in a hushed voice.

"It was. DCI Gilman was there, and I requested permission to inspect the crime scene."

Feldman tried to maintain a neutral expression, but his face told the story: he went from alarm to anger to suspicion. "And he let you?"

"On the condition that I continue to spy on you and get whatever information I can on Irgun and Lehi."

"If word gets out about what you're doing, you're dead. Then they'll be looking at me. Guilt by association, and I'll be next. I hope whatever you found is worth it."

"They think the assassin and the Black Hand are responsible," I said, lying. I felt a twinge of guilt about doing so, but I would do anything within my power to get the information I wanted, and obfuscation was my strategy for the moment.

Feldman seemed to relax at that news, and more than I expected. Meaning he was still not in the inner circle of trusted operatives and might have suspicions of his own.

"That makes sense since the woman was there at the exact time," he said.

"And that's why I'll do everything in my power to track her down. But I need help."

"I'll do what I can, of course. The problem is that I'll be pretty busy training recruits at the kibbutz."

"Then make some introductions for me."

"In Haganah?" Feldman said with surprise. "The last thing you want to do is bring attention to yourself with them. They have experts in intelligence, and rest assured, they'll be looking at you hard. It would be only a matter of time before they'd learn of your pact with the police."

Feldman had raised his voice. I pointed to the hallway so as not to wake any of the other patients. We took a few steps past the door and stopped.

"Go to someone you trust and tell them what I've told you," I said in a hushed tone. "That I've been coerced by the police to be their spy. That I'm offering to give the police false intel and will pass on anything to them that I can get my hands on."

"Coerced is the key word here. You've been compromised. That makes you a liability. In their minds, the smart thing would be to kill you and be done with it. And I don't want to follow you to the grave, so figure out another way to get what you want."

Feldman walked into the room, grabbed his things, and marched down the corridor without saying another word.

I went back into the room and sat in the chair Feldman had occupied. My backpack sat on the floor next to me, and I lifted it to my lap to make sure my .45 was still there. While doing this, the light from the hallway dimmed for a minute, prompting me to look up. I wasn't sure whether to go for my gun or smile.

Hazan had just walked into the room. He wore his typical gloomy look when he nodded a silent greeting at me, but his expression turned tender when he looked at Laura. It puzzled me that he seemed to take an interest in her; the man had never met her. And I began to wonder if guilt was his motivation for coming.

I stood and stepped over to him with my hand extended. He shook it, and an unspoken truce passed between us.

"Did you have any trouble getting past security?" I asked.

"I told them I was her doctor before the bombing. I spouted some medical mumbo jumbo at them, and they let me through." When I returned a puzzled look, he said, "I was studying to be a doctor before the war." He tilted his head toward Laura. "How is she?"

"Likely in a coma. The blast chewed her up pretty bad, and she had a lot of bleeding on her brain. I think her standing between the car and the car door was the only thing that saved her life."

Hazan nodded, and his attention turned back to Laura. "And the child?"

I shook my head. "She lost it."

"I'm sorry," he said, and a slight whimsical smile passed his lips. "The entire three weeks before we could board the ship, you wouldn't stop talking about her and being a father. I started to think I knew her."

I said nothing. I still had no clue why he'd come, and I hoped my silence might get him to talk.

"Any idea who planted the bomb?" he asked.

I told him the same lie I'd given Feldman about suspecting it was the Black Hand, though I left out the part where I'd gotten this supposed information from DCI Gilman. I then described Laura's and my encounter with the assassin, the same woman who was on the ship when the bomb went off below decks.

"I didn't think the Black Hand were still around," Hazan said.

"Laura may have witnessed a group of militants in a Palestinian village. A woman from the village warned her that she could be in danger and claimed that the group's members belonged to the Black Hand. The woman was found murdered the next day."

"Where is this village?"

"I don't know. She only told me it's north of Jerusalem."

Hazan's gaze drifted to a spot on the wall as if running through his mind all the possible sites.

I saw an opportunity to get into good graces with Hazan and, by default, his organization. "How about I try to find out and forward the information on to you?"

"What was she doing in that village in the first place?"

"Just some preliminary legwork for a book," I said, lying again. "She kept all her research in her head for safety reasons. I don't know why she'd do such a thing, but that was her way of working."

Hazan showed his disappointment.

"I could sniff around," I said. "I imagine knowing if this group is real and a threat would be important."

He eyed me with suspicion. "Are you playing me?"

"Look, if the rumors are true about the Black Hand setting off that bomb, then I'm going to find out who, one way or another. I could use the help, but I'll do this on my own."

"I suppose you offered the same deal to Arie."

"I'm willing to use any source available." I pointed toward Laura. "David, that bomb put her in a coma and killed my unborn child."

Hazan shifted his gaze from me to Laura. I could tell he was ruminating. Finally, he said, "I'll see what I can do. Give me a couple of days."

"How can I find you?"

"You don't. If I have anything for you, I'll be at the Church of All Nations on Mount Olive. Thursday afternoon."

"I'll be there."

He glanced at the room one more time and said, "Sorry again for your loss. And I hope your lady friend gets better." He turned and walked away.

I was taking a real chance deceiving Hazan and, by extension, Irgun. It was like poking a stick in the lions' cage, then stepping inside. And I knew Hazan wouldn't just sleep on it. He'd contact his Irgun buddies to investigate me and tear the town apart looking for clues to the existence of the Black Hand.

One place I knew Hazan or one of his fellow militants would search first was Laura's hotel room. I had to get there before they did.

I looked in on Laura one more time and kissed her exposed cheek. I slipped on my backpack, wedged my .45 in my belt, and headed for the door. I stopped and turned to look at her again. I hated having to leave her, but I had to do something, and making her better was not in my wheelhouse. Forcing myself to put one foot in front of the other was the only way I could tear myself away from her bedside and leave.

15

The entrance to Laura's hotel was cordoned off by a painted sawhorse with "Police" stenciled on the crossbar. It was past midnight, and the streets were empty. The car where the detective inspectors had been murdered was gone, and I was surprised there wasn't some kind of police presence in the vicinity.

I stood in the same place as last time, within the darkened doorway of a shop. Before venturing out, I scanned the other doorways and rooftops for any sign of surveillance, or the assassin lying in wait. Nothing stirred. I emerged from the shadows and hurried across the street, all the while listening intently for any sound of movement.

I bounded over the wooden fence, slipped down the alleyway, and peeked around the corner to make sure the courtyard was empty. Like the night before, the only signs of life came from the other buildings. The police had neglected to put a barrier at the back door and didn't bother to lock it.

There were no lights on in the building, and I imagined the few tenants living there had decided to leave after the disruption. I used my cigarette lighter as a torch and moved down the dark hallway. In the minuscule front lobby, there was a large blood-stain behind the receptionist counter where the owner's son had bled out.

I turned to the stairs and listened. All was quiet. I pulled out the .45 from my belt and disengaged the safety. The cement steps muffled my footsteps as I climbed. My heart pounding was the only sound. I scanned the first-floor landing with my pistol out in front. I was taking no chances, checking every corner and my rear, any place in the darkness where an assailant could lie in wait.

As I rounded the second-floor landing, I heard a muted rustling coming from the third floor. I stopped to try to identify the sound and from where it was coming. It had to be Laura's room. With light steps, I mounted the last flight of stairs until my head was just above the level of the floor. The door to Laura's room was ajar, and a light leaked through the gap.

Before going any farther, I looked behind me and through the balusters to make sure no one was lurking in the shadows. I then took long strides toward Laura's room. At the door jamb, I stopped and peered inside. There was nothing visible within the narrow angle. I brought the gun up near my face and slipped into the room. The person's back was to me, and they were rummaging through papers Laura had stacked on a small desk with her typewriter.

I'd expected the police or someone from Haganah or the Black Hand, not the reporter I met yesterday.

"Hello, Evelyn."

Atkinson spun around and let out a yelp of surprise. "Good God, you gave me a fright."

I tucked my gun into my belt at the small of my back. "What are you doing here?"

A look of guilt crossed her face, and she glanced at the papers spread out on the desk. Her expression turned defiant. "I could ask you the same thing."

"My guess, it's for the same reason."

"To collect her papers?"

I nodded. "No one can find out what she was up to."

Her expression turned sad as she peered into my eyes. "How is she?"

"Not good," I said and found my throat tightening. "She's still unresponsive. The shock to her brain probably put her in a coma."

Tears welled in her eyes. "And the child?"

I shook my head. I choked back my tears; I had a job to do.

"I'm so sorry. Poor Laura."

Atkinson took a step toward me but stopped when I took a half step back. If she embraced me, I would have broken down right there, and I needed to stay focused.

"I'm going to find out who did it, Evelyn."

"I want to help."

"I'm going to be playing a dangerous game. I don't want you to get sucked into the quagmire."

"I'm sure you're a good investigator, but I have access to resources that you don't. Plus, I speak Arabic and Hebrew. I'm not going to charge into a shoot-out with you, but you could use an extra pair of eyes and legs."

"Why? What do you get out of this?"

She looked like she'd just been slapped, and I regretted my tone.

She said, "I don't intend to turn this into a story, if that's what you're worried about. Laura means a lot to me. I may not have the same relationship to her as you do, but I'm mad as hell, and I'll do whatever I can to see those bastards get what they deserve."

"Those bastards could be an Arab militant group called the Black Hand. They have a woman assassin on their side who is extremely dangerous. Both Laura and I had a very close encounter with her last night. The point is, they'd cut your throat without a second's hesitation."

"What makes you think it's them?"

"I saw the same woman pass by a police barricade just before the bomb went off. But after I examined the blast site, I'm not so sure."

"Bombing the police and military is more Irgun's or Lehi's methods."

"I'll be looking into them, too. And that's another reason why this could be dangerous. If any one of them thinks you or I are getting too nosy, they'll cut us down."

Atkinson glared down her nose at me and somehow appeared taller. "All the same, I'm going to look into things with or without your approval. I know Laura can be a stubborn woman, but it's nothing compared to me."

I suppressed a smile; I now understood why the two of them had become friends. "All right. I could use someone on my side."

"I'm glad you've come to your senses," Atkinson said and turned back to the papers on the desk. She scanned the pile, then started gathering them. "I think I've found everything Laura was working on for her articles."

"We should get out of here. We don't want to be here when someone from the police or one of the groups shows up."

"I'll take them back to my flat."

"I need them to find out all the places Laura visited."

"Then we'll look them over together."

While Atkinson gathered up Laura's papers, I surveyed the rest of the room for anything that might be a clue. I checked for discarded ticket stubs, receipts, anything having to do with her movements.

She didn't have time to pack everything, and I found some clothes, some of her makeup, and other personal items scattered about. My heart felt like it had burst in my chest when I found a small stack of photographs under the bed. There was one of us together at Christmas in Munich and another of just me smiling at her—a smile I imagined I hadn't made since that time. There were a couple of photos of her deceased husband, Richard Talbot, and one of her parents. Then came a thick bundle of photos and a box of negatives bound by string. I leafed through the photos. They appeared to have been taken during her stay here, as there were photos of several villages and compounds that I assumed were kibbutzim. Then portraits and group photos of Arab women and Jewish men and women.

I found a large woven shoulder bag and put everything inside. By that time, Atkinson signaled she was ready. I took the lead, and we exited the hotel by the rear door. To Mrs. Atkinson's credit, she didn't question why I took her across the courtyard and through the broken door of the building to the back. And she said nothing as we went down the short hallway and out onto the street where I had us go left.

"It's to the right, Mr. Collins."

"I'd like to see something before we go."

Call it instinct, call it premonition, or just chalk it up to knowing the depths of the dark heart of man, but when we went around to the three-way intersection and came in view of the front entrance to the hotel, I saw a figure move the police barricade. The man turned just enough for me to make out his face.

David Hazan entered the hotel, armed with a flashlight and a gun.

I wasn't surprised, but I did regret having to add his name to my nascent list of suspects.

ATKINSON LIVED ON THE SECOND FLOOR OF AN ELEGANT BUILDING in what appeared to be a wealthy area of the city, near a concert hall and a couple of blocks north of Street of the Prophets. But while the building was neoclassical, Atkinson's furnishings were not. Modern minimalist furniture, and art of colorful squiggles and geometric shapes graced the walls.

The orange light of sunrise streamed through the windows. We sat on the floor as we went through Laura's handwritten notes, typed pages, and a notebook filled with diary entries. I'd napped for a couple of hours on the floor of her living room while leaning against a lounge chair. I had no idea if Atkinson had done the same, but now we were back at it.

She had put on a record that played a type of music I hadn't heard before: snappy drums, running bass, and wailing incongruous trumpet, the whole thing wrapped in a jumping beat that was at once familiar and completely foreign.

"You keep looking over to the record player," Atkinson said. "You don't like the music?"

"I don't know. I've never heard anything like it."

"You've been away from the States too long."

I didn't know why that remark rubbed me the wrong way, but I only answered with, "Maybe."

"That's Dizzy Gillespie, one of your American chaps, playing bebop. A new type of jazz. He's a genius. My husband would have hated it. As a matter of fact, he detested most things I hold dear. And he certainly hated the idea of me being a reporter."

"You're divorced?"

"You shouldn't ask a British person such forward questions."

"Being direct saves a lot of time."

She smiled at me. "He was colonel in the army. He died at El-Alamein."

"I'm sorry."

"Thanks," she said and took a puff of her cigarette. "Ours was an arranged marriage. What was proper for our families. I was a rebel, so my father forced me to marry a staid English gentleman with family connections. Oh, I was sad my husband died, but I took to my freedom with relish and moved here to be far away from his and my family's influence."

She went back to Laura's papers and fell quiet. She was done talking, which I figured meant she preferred to leave that part of her life behind.

I leafed through Laura's diary, being careful not to dwell on anything that was personal and only looked at entries that had to do with her activities, particularly the several villages and kibbutzim she'd visited around Jerusalem and Jaffa. I wrote down every place she'd visited and the number of times she mentioned each.

After I tallied up the list, I said, "The village and kibbutz that she mentions the most are a Palestinian village of Alal and a kibbutz called Avida. They're both about twelve miles north of here on the road to Ramallah."

"I'm familiar with the Avida kibbutz," Atkinson said. "And there is a Palestinian village on an opposing hill."

Atkinson shuffled through the pile of typewritten pages until she found what she was looking for. She held it up and studied the page through the glasses perched on the end of her nose. "Here she talks about meeting the women in the village Alal. And one woman in particular named Fatima. Unfortunately, that's a pretty common name. She describes the two settlements and the people, and their reactions of her presence, particularly the hostility from the Arab men."

She read out loud more of Laura's notes, mostly what I'd already heard: the hostile reception, the woman's claims, and her being found dead the next day. I let her continue while I examined the photographs one more time. Laura had marked each photograph on the back with the name of the village or kibbutz or the individual and location. I separated out the ones marked Alal and began to look at them closely.

There were several with the face of a young woman in a headscarf and a dowdy dress with the name Fatima written on the back. She wore a shy smile. Her sunbaked skin and refrained expression told a story of hardship, though her piercing eyes gave me the impression of intelligence and worldliness. I looked at several of her portraits and felt sad for her brutal death. Then, the last photograph of her made me freeze.

Over her shoulder and in the near distance were several people looking at the camera, a mix of men and women. They were small in the frame, and their faces lacked definition, but I could tell that none of them appeared happy about being photographed, and one woman was attempting to cover her face. She wore a headscarf and shawl, and her fingers had reached her chin when Laura clicked the shutter. But I recognized her all the same: it was the beautiful woman who had been with the assassin at the checkpoint.

I handed the photo to Atkinson. "In the background. That woman was with the woman assassin I saw at the bombing, the same one who attacked me on the ship and at Laura's hotel."

"Are you sure? It's not very clear."

"I'm sure," I said and shifted through the others. I found another one with a group of women arm in arm and smiling. But what struck me was the group of men behind the women. They were small in the frame, but their faces were reasonably clear. The men sat or stood near one of the one-story buildings and frowned at Laura.

"Here's one of a group of men," I said and handed that to Atkinson.

"She kept the negatives, so I could get these enlarged. Maybe the faces will be clearer."

"Make several copies if you can. Also, do you know a sketch artist? I could try describing the assassin accurately enough to get a decent likeness."

"I can arrange something."

I took back the photo of the men and studied it. The details were fuzzy, but I could see that a couple of them had rifles slung over their shoulders. "Now I know which village to target," I said.

"You're just going to walk in there? A green-eyed, blond-haired American?"

"Indeed, I am."

"Uninvited. Not knowing who's who or if this woman's companion—or the assassin—is there? At best, you're going to get thrown out on your bum. At worst, your throat slit."

She had a point. My rage urged me to charge ahead, but experience told me that I should arm myself with intelligence and not just my .45.

Atkinson rifled through the handwritten notes and found what she was looking for. "I came across this earlier. I didn't have any context, but now that I know the village in question, this is what Laura wrote: *While I was accompanying a group of women down the hill to gather water, I noticed dust rising from the road linking the highway located about a hundred yards from where I stood. It surprised me to see a British military vehicle driving toward the village. The other women didn't seem to be alarmed, bringing me to the conclusion that this wasn't the first time a military vehicle had approached the village. The car stopped before entering, and a single man in uniform got out. He was too far away to discern his rank, but I could clearly see that he was a police officer. A lone officer walking into a village populated with rather belligerent Palestinian men would have been a dangerous act, but this man walked up the main road as if confident that he would be welcome. I regret not having been closer to clearly see his face or rank. I asked the women about the policeman, but they either didn't know him or weren't going to tell me.*"

Atkinson lowered the paper and looked at me. "Peculiar, to say the least. Of course, there could be any number of mundane reasons why he was there, but it's definitely something to look into."

She was correct again, and as much as I disliked it, I knew what my next move would have to be.

16

There was a flurry of activity on the second-floor corridor at the central police station. Apparently, there had been an attempted robbery at Barclays Bank in the early hours of the morning. One constable had been killed, but they'd managed to nab two members of Irgun. This I'd overheard in all the excitement while waiting to see DCI Gilman since nine a.m. I hoped it wasn't Hazan, as I had plans for him, and they didn't include him being put in jail. Just off to my left, there was a display of framed portraits of policemen and their names hanging on the wall, with a gold-lettered title of "To Our Brave Men Who Lost their Lives in the Line of Duty." The collection took up a good ten feet of space. Maybe eighty photos, but I didn't count them all.

"Mr. Collins," Gilman said from the doorway of his office.

I got up and followed him inside. It was the first time in his office, and I was surprised at the variety of books he had lining one wall, from philosophy to classic novels to decorative arts. He had papers and files everywhere, photos of places and people in uniform or civilian clothes. The only space on the wall left pristine was the large portrait of King George VI and a much smaller portrait of Britain's prime minister, Clement Attlee.

"I didn't expect you so soon," Gilman said as he sat behind his cluttered desk. "And you were instructed not to come here."

"I didn't want to wait around for you or someone else to contact me."

"You already have something for me?"

I sat opposite him in a plush leather chair. "I've made contact with my two friends. They're not going to make it easy to get inside, but I'm working on it."

He gave me a nod, but his mind was elsewhere as he shuffled through some papers on his desk. "A couple of my inspectors went by your fiancée's hotel room." His eyes drifted up to me and paused, probably to test my reaction. When I gave him a neutral expression, he said, "It had been ransacked."

That part surprised me, and I guess it showed.

"I see it wasn't you," he said.

"And what were your boys doing there? Planning to do the same thing?"

"We know she was traveling and doing extensive research for a newspaper article. Where are those papers, Mr. Collins?"

"I don't know. She told me she kept them in a safe place in case the CID decided to stop by."

"And where is that?"

"She didn't tell me. We were on our way to retrieve them when that bomb went off."

"I find that hard to believe."

"Believe what you want. I'd like to get my hands on them, too. There might be a clue in there that could lead me to the bomber."

"Lead the proper authorities to the bomber, you mean to say."

"I'd be happy to share them, if I knew where they were."

Gilman raised his eyebrows in a skeptical look. "I hope you're not holding back information. If we find out that's the case, I could make things very difficult for you."

"That goes without saying."

Gilman continued to study my face as if searching for the truth.

To change the subject, I said, "I saw the wall of photos out there for the fallen policemen."

"Yes. That was started twenty years ago. But a third of those are from just the last couple of years after the war. What's your point?"

"I was thinking about your men involved in the blast yesterday. How are the ones who were wounded? Six, weren't there?"

"I've found you don't indulge in small talk, so why are you asking?"

"If any are in any condition to talk, I'd like to ask them a couple of questions."

"You must know that can't happen. If anyone is going to question them, it will be me and my detective inspectors."

"How about I just sit in? I might think of something your DIs wouldn't. After all, I had a front-row seat at the event."

To my surprise, he said, "We'll look into it. Perhaps, once we have had a chance with the interviews, and if they're up to it, then you might have a go."

"I'd also like to look over what you have on suspected Jewish and Arabic militants."

"And what do you hope to accomplish by doing that?"

"If I'm going to get chummy with Haganah or Irgun, it would help to know some of the most wanted to watch out for. And I want everything you have on the Arab groups because I'm interested in the woman assassin. She's here for more than just killing me or Mrs. Talbot."

He nodded again. "I'll arrange it. But none of the records leaves the premises. You can take notes, request copies of select photos, and that is all."

"Your wish is my command."

Gilman told me to wait out in the hall while he found an officer to take me to another office. Moments later he returned with a constable, who he introduced as Sergeant Bennington. Gilman said nothing further and went into his office. Without a word, Bennington escorted me to a door down the hall. He unlocked it and waved for me to enter. The room contained a long table with six chairs and little else.

"Have a seat, sir," the constable said. "I'll be back directly."

I did so and waited. The constable came back a couple minutes later with an assistant, and they placed two cartons in front of me.

"DCI Gilman has given you one hour," he said. "I'll be back at precisely that time to escort you out. And he insists that I check that you aren't trying to carry any documents out of the building."

"Trust is in short supply around here."

"Yes, sir," he said dryly.

"Will it be possible to get some copies of the photos of suspects?"

"Set aside those most important to you, and I'll have copies made," Bennington said and left.

There were a little more than eighty files. I was sure there were more that they weren't about to let me see, but it was a start. I settled in and began to survey the documents. The folders of Jewish suspects were grouped by militant organizations, Haganah, Irgun, and Lehi.

The Haganah files had a sizable directory of known members, but only a dozen or so had been put on a watch list. It was Palmach, Haganah's strike force, where more members had made the list of suspects for bombings of railways and bridges before pulling back on operations a year earlier.

For the Irgun, they only provided me with files that had little concrete information on the secretive group, aside from the members being considered dangerous terrorists and "most wanted." With estimates of between one and two thousand members, the investigators posited that the organization's discipline was as sophisticated as any that they'd ever studied. That most members were expected to maintain their civilian lives, making it difficult to determine identities. The ones they did include for me were already dead or in prison.

For Lehi, or the Stern Gang as the cops seemed to call them, they had a decent list of suspects and known offenders. The catalogue of offenses was extensive: assassination, attacking police and military installations, sending letter bombs to British officials, or simply opening fire on soldiers. But actual intelligence on the group was thin. The list of dead or executed was longer than those thought to be still active and alive, whereabouts unknown.

I noted some names from each organization and set aside photos of suspects that I wanted the police to copy for me.

Next, I turned to the Arab groups. What surprised me was that the police had even less information on them. The reports stated that the Arabs were only loosely organized. The few charismatic leaders who had created a united front had been killed or gone into exile. Tribal rivalries and competing factions didn't allow any cohesion. The last major threat had occurred during an Arab revolt in the mid-1930s, and British reprisals had weakened and effectively disarmed them. But indications were that small, clandestine militias existed, which, according to one analyst, were gathering to fight the inevitable war with the Jews once the British decided to leave.

On paper, the Black Hand had ceased to exist, but the flocks of Arabs inspired by the dead leader, Izz ad-Din al-Qassam, were determined to follow in his footsteps or use his legacy to inspire potential fighters and terrorists. I figured the current group by that name had used that tactic to recruit its members. Whether that was why the woman assassin had joined, I didn't know, but her presence made me think they had something sinister planned and were not going to wait around until the British decided to pull up stakes.

There were two other Arab groups mentioned in the reports, the Organization for Holy Struggle, and a militia group called al-Najjada, but police intelligence provided more speculation than facts, and even fewer names aside from the founders who were prominent members of Palestinian society.

I sat back in my chair after closing the last file. A whole lot of nothing. At least little that I could use. Any one of the groups could be responsible for the bombing. I had some faces to go with names, but only key figures, not much on the rank and file. The ones who would carry out an attack. The ones I wanted to see pay for what they did to Laura and my child.

It looked like I was going to have to get into the dirt and dig.

17

I t was past two p.m. when I stepped into Laura's hospital room. I was hoping to find her awake, but she was in the exact same position as the last time I'd left. I was surprised to see Atkinson in the chair next to her bed reading a book. I nodded to her and went over to Laura's other side to look down on her. My chest constricted when I saw that her face was more swollen and redder than it was yesterday. I took comfort that her breathing seemed normal, and she looked peaceful in her sleep.

"The doctor was by a little while ago," Atkinson said. "Not much change, but that's also good news. Her body is healing. The swelling should go down in a couple of days."

Her arms were outside the blanket, and I put my hand on hers. I talked to her in my mind, telling her that I had to go, to forgive me for not remaining by her side, that I couldn't rest until I found out who did this to her. I squeezed her hand, hoping my message might somehow flow from me to her and convey my love. I then turned around and walked out.

"Wait a minute," Atkinson said behind me. "Where are you going?"

"Out."

She came up behind me as I marched down the hallway. "You're going to that village, aren't you?"

"That's none of your concern."

She zipped in front of me, forcing me to stop. "You're not going to get anywhere alone. Except maybe to the morgue."

I tried to go around her, but she slid over to stop me again. "Can you speak Arabic?"

"I can get my point across in other ways."

"Don't be a fool. I can help. We go there together. We pose as …" She paused to think. "I don't know. We go as UN representatives. American and British."

It wasn't a half-bad idea. Still, I shook my head and tried again to get around her. She blocked me.

"Evelyn, I don't want to lose my temper."

"I promised Laura that I'd make sure you stayed out of trouble. She knew that if anything happened to her, you'd tear the place apart to find whoever harmed her. She said that your bull-headed stubbornness and primal need to be a hero would likely get you killed one day, but she was adamant that you wouldn't do it on her account."

"You've only just met me. How would you know she was talking about me?"

She put her hands on her hips. "Do you really have to ask me that question?"

We squared off like two gunfighters. I had to admire her determination. She was right about not speaking the language, and my tendency to go off half-cocked. I'd lost my cold reasoning when it came to Laura. And I could use a partner, especially one as bold and resourceful as Atkinson.

"Do you have a car?" I asked.

"I suppose you were planning to get there on foot?"

After I returned an impatient glare, she said, "It's parked a couple of blocks away."

"Then let's go," I said and followed her down the stairs. I

picked up my backpack that I'd left with the sergeant in charge, and we exited the building.

Atkinson crossed the street despite the passing cars. I followed suit, and we headed south, toward Jaffa Street.

"What did you learn from your visit to the police station?" she asked.

"That their intelligence is pretty thin. Although I get the feeling they're holding out on me. Or at least Gilman is."

"Anything on the Black Hand?"

"Nothing after around 1936. I'm guessing the group in the Alal village is just using that name to get recruits."

Atkinson made an abrupt turn down an alley between a small hotel and an Italian restaurant. We reached a courtyard of gravel and walked up to a battered 1930s Vauxhall. Underneath a month's worth of dirt and dust, the silver paint had faded almost to white from years of sun and blowing sand. The doors creaked when we opened them, and my seat felt like there was nothing between the tattered leather covering and metal springs.

"You sure this thing is going to make it up the hill to that village?" I asked.

"Best way to travel without gaining attention," Atkinson said.

She started the engine and pulled out of the alley without bothering to look if another car was coming. Then she zoomed up the street while holding a cigarette with one hand.

"I'm not surprised you didn't get much on the Arabs," she said. "The Arab revolt in the late thirties went on for a few years and only stopped with the beginning of World War Two. They didn't have much of a chance going up against the British. It cost them dearly in men and resources."

I grunted and pulled out the photograph of the woman who had turned her head away from the camera, the one I had seen with the assassin. "Women assassins have to be a rarity, especially for Muslims."

Atkinson chortled, forcing cigarette smoke out of her nostrils.

"There are plenty of Jewish young women with Palmach. For the right reasons, women can be just as determined and brave as men."

"I'm not talking about soldiers. The woman I encountered is a trained killer, not an impassioned fighter defending her family and homeland. I looked into her eyes and saw a merciless fighter. She's not here for a cause, or for family or village."

"You got all that from looking into her eyes?"

"I've fought enough adversaries eye to eye. You start to get a gut feeling about your opponent."

"And what about the other woman? The one in your photograph?"

"They work together is my guess."

"Two deadly assassins? That's a frightful thought."

I shook my head. "I think our assassin does her killings alone. Maybe this other woman is her companion or relative of some kind."

"The pretty companion could be a member of the village, and she asked the assassin to come."

I had to brace myself using the dashboard when Atkinson braked hard for a sharp turn. "Whatever the reason," I said. "I'm beginning to suspect that the two women, the group, are in that village for a specific purpose."

"Now you're scaring me."

"Good."

We left the city and wound our way through dusty switchbacks. We rehearsed our cover story, what we would say, and our objectives. On the western horizon, black clouds roiled, darkening the distant hills. We passed small settlements, some surrounded by plowed fields prepared for planting in an otherwise sparse landscape.

We were on the road to Ramallah, though there was little traffic aside from an occasional truck, army vehicle, or men riding donkeys or camels. Then, a mile or so away, three men in long headscarves of black and white sat on horses on a hill. They were motionless, and though it was too far away to tell for sure, they appeared to have rifles slung on their backs. It reminded me of a western film, where the passing cowboys observed Indians watching their every move.

"Have there been incidents of snipers covering this road?"

"Most certainly, though this section has been pretty quiet lately. Another reason to have a shabby car—less of an obvious target."

That gave me little comfort. I thought back to the incident while coming to Jerusalem and the soldiers under the constant threat of trigger-happy civilians or planted bombs. And I thought of Laura, carelessly venturing into this hostile place. I loved her and fretted over her struggle between life and death, but my anger flared when I thought of her taking such risks.

"Sometimes I wonder if Laura has a death wish," I said.

"Nonsense. Don't be so hard on her. She told me about the dangerous assignments she went on during the war. I did my share, and I found such situations invigorating. So much so that regular assignments became somewhat of a bore. I think she did this because she saw what becoming a mother would mean. That she'd have to back away from danger. This was her last hurrah."

Which begged the question: If she survived and found out she was childless, would she go after dangerous assignments again? I struggled with dark thoughts: perhaps, not only had I lost a child, but Laura as well.

"Snap out of it," Atkinson said and pointed to a cluster of single and two-story buildings perched on a hill. "Alal."

Beyond Alal and splayed on another hill to the west had to be the kibbutz, Avida. There, newer buildings were huddled together above what appeared to be vineyards clutching the slopes.

Atkinson turned off the paved road and onto a dirt one. The car bounced as it rolled over endless ruts and kicked up a cloud of dust that surely warned of our approach. As the car struggled up the hill, I watched for any suspicious activity.

The road led directly to what seemed to be the main street. Atkinson stopped just shy of the entrance to the village. The street wiggled farther up the hill to a domed structure of white stucco that I assumed was the local mosque. No one moved on the street; no one came out to greet us or shoo us away. Neither were there any animals, including within the primitive sheep pen constructed just outside the town's limits.

Maybe it was because the storm was coming. The storm clouds were close now, darkening an already somber sky and stirring up a wind that swirled between the buildings.

"What do you think?" Atkinson asked.

"I don't see any signs of a struggle, so either they're all huddled in their houses or they've gone."

I grabbed the backpack out of the back seat and pulled out my .45 and Ka-Bar knife.

"We're just two UN officials on a fact-finding mission, not robbing a bank," Atkinson said.

"We're in Indian country now, Mrs. Atkinson."

18

A tkinson started to say something else, but I got out of the car before she had a chance. I leaned over and looked into the car. "Wait here until I know what's going on."

She ignored my suggestion and stepped out of the car. I had to squint to keep the sand out of my eyes. Atkinson held on to her cap and lifted her scarf to her nose and mouth. I tucked my .45 behind my back, slipped the Ka-Bar into my boot, and signaled that I was ready. She peered at me over the edge of her scarf with a hint of trepidation in her eyes, then she started walking.

We joined at the front of the car and moved slowly down the main street. Most of the buildings were made of stone, some exposed, some covered in stucco, some looked ancient. They were all square with flat roofs, arched windows, and thick wooden doors.

"We can't just start knocking," Atkinson said.

At random, I picked the second building on the left and rapped on the door. Atkinson huffed her displeasure behind me. I ignored it and knocked again.

I looked at Atkinson expectantly, and she called out something in Arabic. I got "UN" out of the jumble of words, meaning she was going off the script we'd devised before arriving.

Nothing but silence from inside. I tried the knob, much to Atkinson's objections, but it was firmly locked.

I moved to the next door on our right, and we repeated the process. The first drops of rain began to fall.

"Are we going to do this at every residence?" Atkinson said, looking up at the sky.

"I thought all Brits carried an umbrella."

"And I thought all Yanks wore cowboy hats," she said in an irritated tone. "Even if I did, it wouldn't do much good in this wind."

I decided to skip a few doors and attack one farther down on our left. I knocked, then noticed the door was ajar. I stepped to one side and gently pushed Atkinson to get behind me. I shoved the door open and knocked.

The interior was dark and silent.

Atkinson recited her UN routine in Arabic to the empty space.

I put my hand on the handle of my pistol and took a step into the room. "Hello?" I said in a friendly tone.

We both went deeper into the room and stopped to wait for our eyes to adjust. The scents of cooking oil and cumin were pungent in the dim light. The shadows receded, revealing a living room with a kitchen to one side. Cabinets had been left open. The couple of shelves stood partially empty. Bits of food had been left on a round table to the side of the kitchen. I touched a bit of unleavened bread. It was stale but couldn't have been there for more than a couple of days.

"Looks like everyone left," Atkinson said.

I grunted an agreement and continued to scan the area. "It looks like they were in a hurry and took only what they could carry."

We made a cursory search of the rest of the house, which

didn't consist of much, just two bedrooms and an outhouse a few feet from the back of the house. Like the living room/kitchen, the bedrooms showed signs of hastily gathering a few items and leaving the rest.

With the rain falling sparsely in big drops, we picked another house a few doors down. No one came after several knocks, and I looked questioningly at Atkinson. She shrugged, and I moved to the side as before and tried the knob. The door opened with a creak. We took a couple of steps inside, and as before, the room showed signs of a quick abandonment.

Atkinson sucked in her breath and pointed at the floor ahead of where I stood. A dark liquid the size of a dinner plate had puddled in the middle of the living room floor. Two jagged lines of the same liquid ran from the puddle toward the front door.

I stepped over it, squatted, dipped my finger in the liquid, and brought it up to examine it in the light from the doorway. "Blood," I said in a hushed voice. I stood and pulled out my pistol. "Get behind the door."

I moved quietly to a short hallway serving two doors. Both were open, so I positioned myself to glance in each without becoming a target. The disheveled bedrooms were empty.

The floor creaked above me just one time, then all fell silent again. Atkinson must have heard it, because she rushed up to my side for protection. She followed right behind me as I moved to a concrete staircase.

"You should stay here," I whispered to Atkinson.

She shook her head and tilted her chin toward the second floor.

"Then stay behind me."

We moved up the steps. Only our shoes on the accumulated dust made any sound. Just before the last step, I clicked off the .45's safety. At the landing, a short return wall opened up on each side, which I figured were two rooms. Remaining behind the return wall, I peered into the room on the right. The sheets had been torn off the simple mattress on the floor, and a scattering of children's clothes lay in front of a dresser.

I did the same cautious routine for the room on the left. A tiny window let in very little light, but I could make out the silhouette of a man sitting slumped on a wood-framed bed in the far corner. He kept still despite my presence.

Atkinson peeked over my shoulder. She said something in Arabic to the man. He slowly lifted his head and looked at us. He said nothing as Atkinson stepped deeper into the room.

I lowered my pistol and came in behind Atkinson. Now that I was closer, his features became more visible. The man's face was grooved with age, and his skin was dark mahogany from decades in the sun. In contrast to his skin, his feathery gray hair and week-old beard seemed to glisten in the muted daylight. His feet curled unnaturally, and a cane was propped on a chair at the foot of the bed.

Atkinson knelt in front of him and asked him something in Arabic. His hollow eyes filled with tears as he stared at her. Finally, he responded. I didn't understand the words, but I could hear the anguish in his voice. They started to converse, Atkinson keeping her sentences short, her voice soft.

While they did this, I walked over to the window and peered out through the film of dirt. The street remained quiet, and the threat of a downpour appeared to have abated. I fished out Laura's photograph of the woman turning her head and gave it to Atkinson.

She said something in Arabic as she held the photograph for him to see. They went on for a few moments until the man started to cry. Atkinson looked up at me. I wordlessly told her she could stop the interview.

Atkinson said, "*Shukran*," which I knew as the Arabic word for "thank you." She stood and tilted her head toward the door. I followed her out and down the stairs. We stopped in the living room.

"I assume the blood isn't his," I said.

"It's his grandson's. He stayed behind to take care of him while the rest of the family fled the village."

"Where is the grandson now? Is he dead?"

"The old man said he was upstairs, sleeping, when he heard shouting and a scuffle. By the time he came down, the grandson was gone, and his blood was on the floor. He assumed the worst. He went out onto the streets to look for him but got frightened and went back upstairs. He stayed there waiting for his turn to die, but no one ever came."

"He doesn't know who did this?"

Atkinson shook her head. "The villagers were told that the Jews were coming to kill them all, and that's why most of the people left."

"Does he know where they fled to?"

"He said the interlopers—which I assume he means the Black Hand—came to every house in the village to warn them and take them to a safe place. That's all I got out of him before he broke down."

"Did you get the sense that he was telling the truth?"

"I don't see what he'd get out of lying."

If I hadn't seen the man, I might have questioned her logic, but he seemed sincere to me. "Did he know the woman in the picture?"

"His eyesight isn't so good, and neither is the picture, but he thinks her name is Rana Dawoud al-Katib. Her family came to this village from Syria when her father, Dawoud, was a boy. He started to give me the entire lineage, but I changed the subject. Then I asked him about a possible woman companion, and he said a cousin from Syria came here just a few days ago. All he knew was her given name of Nadia."

"Not a lot, but it's more than we had before," I said and headed for the door. "We better move on. I don't want to stay here any longer than we have to."

"You'll not hear an objection from me. This village gives me the flutters."

We exited the house and turned left to proceed up the sloping main street. The dark clouds remained, though the rain was sparse, as if most of it evaporated long before it reached the ground. A drop would hit the dirt and bounce up to form a ball of mud that was tossed about by the wind. We checked a number of other houses, but all were empty and free of blood.

Shortly before reaching the mosque, we came upon a building that was easily twice the size of the other houses. I stopped near the front entrance, prompting Atkinson to do the same.

"The village palace?" I asked.

"Probably the school or community center. Or both."

"Shall we?"

"If you promise me this is the last one. The farther we go, the more frightened I become."

"I promise this is the last one, but I'd be happy to walk you back to the car and do this on my own."

She moved toward the door. "Let's just get this over with."

I caught up to her and got around in front. I readied my pistol, and we used the wall as protection before I pushed the double doors open. A faint odor reached my nose. Not rot but the smell of death all the same, like meat left out too long. "Maybe you should stay here."

She grabbed my arm and nervously looked around. "Not on your life."

I raised my gun and slowly entered. Atkinson squeezed my arm as she followed me inside. We were in a hallway of concrete painted a light blue and embellished with Arabic script in black. There were two doors on each side, with a single door at the far end next to a staircase leading to the second floor.

We proceeded down the hallway, repeating the routine of finding protection before pushing open a door. The first two rooms appeared to be classrooms. A few items had been taken out of a closet or removed from the wall. We both sighed from relief when there were no signs of bodies or blood. The last two rooms lacked much furniture besides a series of closets and an old phonograph on a table.

The closer we got to the end of the hallway and the final door, the stronger the odor. I put my hand on the doorknob, and Atkinson drew in a long breath. This time, I didn't bother hiding behind the return wall and shoved the door open.

Atkinson let out a sigh of anguish at the sight of ten bodies lined up on the floor. They were all adults, men and women, lying facedown with a single bullet wound in the head, execution style.

I went over to the bodies, while Atkinson stayed near the door. I leaned over to check each victim for a pulse just in case one had miraculously survived. None had. The bodies were cool to the touch, at about room temperature, with some rigor mortis present in the legs and upper arms.

As I stood, Atkinson let out a yelp of alarm. I spun around while bringing my .45 up. I stopped.

Four men had slipped into the room while we concentrated on the victims. They all had STEN submachine guns, two of which were trained on me.

19

A wiry man with a scraggly beard said something to me I didn't understand. I was so surprised to hear Hebrew and not Arabic that I hesitated. He barked at me again.

"He wants you to drop your weapon," Atkinson said to me.

I extended my hands and slowly lowered the pistol to the floor. When I straightened, four more men filed into the room. Even more were gathered in the hallway or searching the other rooms.

A tall, thin man stepped forward and had that posture of the man in charge. "You speak English."

"American," I said.

"What are you two doing here?"

"I could ask you the same question."

He bristled at my remark. "I'll ask you again, and I expect an answer this time."

"We wanted to ask the villagers a few questions," Atkinson said.

"The village was empty when we got here," I said. "We came upon these people just a few minutes ago. Do you or your men have anything to do with this?" I asked and gestured toward the line of victims.

The leader glared at me, and those eyes told me he'd seen far more violence than his youthful face belied. I'd seen the same eyes on soldiers who had just been kids and then gone through the meatgrinder. That made him potentially trigger-happy, which put Atkinson and me in a bad spot. Cooperation would be the only way out of the situation.

"Let me rephrase the question," I said. "Do you know who might have killed these people?"

The leader said something to one of his companions and tilted his head at me. Two armed guys about the same age as the leader marched over. One retrieved my .45 from the floor while the other frisked me and found the Ka-Bar in my boot. They stowed them, grabbed my arms, and pulled me past the leader and out into the hallway. Two others followed close behind with Atkinson, and we were led out of the community center and across the street.

To my surprise, we were taken into the mosque. From my short time in Morocco, I'd learned that it was forbidden for non-Muslims to enter, but inside the mosque was a squad of men relaxing as they smoked cigarettes and chatted. They stood around an older man with a thick mustache who sat on a folding chair in the middle of the space.

The conversations stopped when the men holding Atkinson and me stopped a short distance away from the mustached man. The young leader went up to talk to him. A few moments later, the man with the mustache signaled for us to be brought closer. They did as ordered, then released us and backed away.

The man took his time loading his pipe and lighting it while we stood there. Once he got his pipe going, he said in accented English, "We were quite surprised to find an American man and a British woman in this village. My second told me your reasons, but I would like to know what you intended to ask the villagers."

I debated what and how much to say to the leader of a group who, I had to assume, was a good candidate for my list of suspects behind the bombing.

Atkinson stepped in front of me. "This man volunteered to help European Jews come to Eretz Israel. He was on board the *Magen David*, the ship that was crippled by a bomb less than a week ago. He's the one who shot the bomber before he could escape."

I saw where she was going with this, a clever way of getting around admitting our investigation into the bombing that injured Laura.

"The man who set off the bomb had a partner," I said. "A woman. A highly trained assassin. In fact, she tried to kill me and my fiancée. We came here hoping to track her down. I traced her to this village and suspect she's a member of a group who call themselves the Black Hand."

The mustached man continued to stare at me and said nothing. I could tell he was considering the veracity of our story. "A foolish thing to do, walking into the lion's den," he said and puffed on his pipe as if considering what we had told him.

Finally, he said, "You can call me Mordechai." Then he added, "We also heard of this Black Hand group and that they were rumored to be here."

"It looks like they knew you were coming," I said. "But I don't see them killing their own people."

I watched for any reaction, but Mordechai revealed nothing. He looked at Atkinson and asked, "Who are you?"

"A friend of my fiancée," I said.

The commander looked at both of us. "Do you always answer each other's questions?"

Atkinson tittered theatrically and said, "An old habit of ours."

Mordechai looked skeptical and said something to one of his other companions in Hebrew. Atkinson looked at me nervously out of the corner of her eye. The man stepped forward and produced a small cloth pouch.

Mordechai opened the pouch and removed some documents. He held them up for us to see. "We retrieved these from your car. Your automobile registration, Mrs. Evelyn Atkinson." He pulled out a small card. "Your identification as a correspondent for the *Guardian* newspaper." He handed the pouch back to his companion. "A reporter," he said as if it were an accusation. Then to me, "Are you a reporter, too?"

I shook my head. "An ex-cop. My last employer was the U.S. Army."

"You are far from America."

"My fiancée is also a reporter. She was doing an article about everyday life in the kibbutzim." I told him about missing Laura in Italy and deciding to hop on the *Magen David* to help out some friends with Jewish refugees trying to get to Palestine.

"And who are these friends?"

"Arie Feldman and David Hazan."

I saw a flicker of recognition when mentioning their names. He grunted and said, "I don't like reporters, and I don't trust policemen, ex or not. And I know that you two aren't telling me everything." He studied us and puffed on his pipe. "I don't feel you are a threat, but you have seen our faces. That is a security risk. You will come with us."

He nodded to his men, who came forward, grabbed our arms.

"Unhand me," Atkinson said as they pulled her away.

"We're not going to reveal who you are," I said as we were being hauled toward the exit.

Mordechai ignored us and turned to his men. I was tempted to fight back, but even if I could escape, I wouldn't leave Atkinson. When we got to the street, I stopped resisting, prompting Atkinson to do the same. But I wasn't about to let them hold us for too long. I would find their weak spot and exploit it.

No one was going to keep me from finding the people responsible for killing my child and putting Laura in the hospital.

No one.

20

O dors of turned earth and aging wood seeped through the hood over my head. At the village, Atkinson and I had been put in a small van and taken for a ride that lasted about thirty minutes before reaching our present location. I had tried to keep track of the vehicle's turns and the smells and sounds of our surroundings, but there weren't enough clues to get a fix on our position.

We were led across a large open space and down some stairs to wherever we were now. Someone pulled off the hood. They did the same for Atkinson. As they untied our hands, I looked to see if she was okay and expected her to look frightened, but her face only expressed anger and determination. I had to admire her control, as we had no idea what fate awaited us.

One of the men pointed to chairs situated around a metal table. "Please."

"No thanks, I'll stand," I said.

"Me too. My backside needs a rest after that bumpy van ride."

"Please, please," the man said, pointing to the chairs, which probably was the extent of his English.

Atkinson snapped at him in Hebrew. The man threw up his

hands in exasperation and left with the others. He closed the door, and a heavy lock was slid in place. By the sound of the footsteps, two of the four climbed the stairs, leaving two others to stand guard.

I looked around the room. We were in a small space with earthen walls and a wooden floor. Crates and burlap sacks had been piled in two corners, which I assumed contained some kind of produce.

"Do you have any idea where we are?" Atkinson asked.

"I was hoping you'd know."

"Not a clue."

"We're about thirty minutes from the village, so there's that. By the speeds we were going, maybe forty miles. We didn't pass through any urban areas to speak of, so nowhere near Jerusalem."

"Okay, so forty miles east, west, or north," she said and rubbed her forehead in frustration. "I don't see how that's useful."

"Good to know if we have to hoof it back to the city."

Atkinson groaned and rubbed her forehead again. She went over to the chair and sat.

"Headache?" I asked.

"I'm officially diagnosing my condition as a Mason Collins."

"Sorry you insisted on coming along?"

"No. I'm sorry we didn't get out of there as soon as we knew the village was abandoned."

Footsteps on the cement steps had us turning toward the door. A key rattled in the lock, and the door swung open. Mordechai came in and stepped aside to let David Hazan enter. Neither of them looked happy to be there, but unhappy was Hazan's usual MO.

Hazan kept his gaze on the wall behind me while Mordechai reversed direction and exited. The commander left the door open, and the guards followed the man upstairs. I couldn't tell if that was a good sign or a bad one.

"Why did they drag you in here?" I asked.

He jerked his head my way and glared. "Why did you bring me in on this reckless scheme of yours? They're now questioning my loyalty and discretion."

"They wanted to know why a non-Jewish American would be on the *Magen David*. I told them it was to help some friends bring the refugees to Palestine. They insisted on names. I didn't have much of a choice but to give them yours and Arie's. How could that hurt your reputation?"

"Any gentile connection is a point of vulnerability. You were supposed to pass any information on to me, and I would see if the leadership would offer you any assistance."

"It seems to me I've already helped by passing on what I knew to you. How else would they know about the Black Hand?"

"You should have stayed away."

"You know I'm not going to do that."

Hazan pointed at Atkinson. "And bringing a British reporter to that village is your way of tracking down the bomber?"

"I have a name, you know," Atkinson said.

"They told me who you are," Hazan said to her.

"I'll be discreet, if that's what you and your compatriots are worried about," Atkinson said.

"We can't be sure of that," Hazan said.

"You know who I am, and it probably wouldn't take much to find out where I live. So why would I dare to report on you or your group? I don't know any of your colleagues' names, besides yours, and I would never compromise a friend of Mason's."

David and I said at the same time, "We're not friends."

She gave us both a bemused look. "I'll take your word for it."

A silence passed between the three of us.

"What now?" I asked.

"I was brought here to vouch for you."

"And?"

Hazan clenched his teeth and stared at the wall. "Believe me, I'm tempted to renounce you."

He clammed up while his jaw muscles worked overtime. I didn't know if he fell silent to make us sweat, or he genuinely debated leaving us in a lurch. Atkinson and I kept our eyes on him and waited for him to say more.

Finally, I said, "To sweeten the deal, I'll tell you what we found out."

Hazan shifted his gaze to me, which I took for his assent.

"The woman on the ship, who was the bomber's companion, is Syrian. We only got a first name of Nadia. I believe she was staying with a cousin living in the village by the name of Rana Dawoud al-Katib. But here's the real scoop: the Black Hand knew your buddies were coming to the village."

"Did you say this to—" He stopped, as if remembering to use the commander's alias. "To Mordechai?"

"I did."

"How do you know all this?" he asked.

I opened my mouth to answer, but Atkinson interrupted me.

"We ran into an old man fleeing the village. He told us members of the Black Hand warned the villagers that Jews were coming and that they would take them someplace safe."

"I figured they all left maybe two days ago," I said. "Except, of course, the ones executed in the community center. The best I could tell by the state of the bodies, they'd been killed between twelve and twenty-four hours ago. What I couldn't determine is who's responsible."

"It seems obvious," Hazan snapped back.

"I don't know. Does it?"

Atkinson stepped in between us and said to Hazan in her best diplomatic fashion, "What Mason is trying to say is that, while the Black Hand seems likely to be the perpetrators, without evidence it would be premature to come to any conclusions."

Hazan continued to stare at me and said, "I know what Mason is trying to say. But our group had nothing to do with those killings. We weren't even sure we had the correct village."

Atkinson sighed with exasperation. "You two are behaving like little boys, comparing your willies to see whose is the biggest."

The remark made me smile. "Can't say that I've ever done that."

"I was speaking metaphorically, you nit."

That made Hazan chuckle, which was something I'd rarely seen him do.

"I'm not joking," Atkinson said to both of us. To Hazan, she said, "You and your group have your work cut out for you to find the Black Hand and, you," she said to me, "you have Laura to look out for."

Hearing that brought back the pain in my chest. It was no longer amusing.

"I'm supposed to determine whether you can go or remain," Hazan said. "But if I recommend that you can leave, I am responsible for anything you do once you're free. Anything or anyone you've seen here or at the village must not be divulged to anyone else. Certainly not the police or fodder for a newspaper. Doing so will not only bring terrible consequences for you but also for me. Do I have your word?"

Atkinson nodded and pledged to remain silent.

Hazan and Atkinson looked at me expectantly. I wanted to say that I would never stop looking for the perpetrators. That I hoped he and the Irgun might still help me find who's responsible for the death of my child and putting my fiancée in the hospital. But the prudent thing was to swallow those words and get the hell out of there. "I have nothing to gain from revealing what I know."

"Then you are free to go."

21

M y nerves were in high gear as Atkinson and I walked down the sidewalk toward the hospital. We'd been gone more than eight hours, and it was approaching ten p.m. Being away from Laura for that long had left me anxious.

After a circuitous route in the Irgun's van with hoods on our heads, a driver dropped us off in the middle of nowhere. Fortunately, someone had driven Atkinson's car from the village to the same location. My backpack and weapons had been placed in the back seat.

The driver took off before we could ask him where we were, but we managed to find our way back to Jerusalem, and Atkinson parked her car in the same lot. She hadn't said much on the drive back, and now she walked beside me with her head down and her shoulders pulled into her chest.

"We're lucky they didn't hold us indefinitely," Atkinson finally said. "Or worse."

"I have to say, you did a good job of staying calm under fire."

"Someone had to with all the testosterone wafting around in there."

I felt more than heard someone behind us. I turned my head

to look back and saw a man in Arab garb about fifty yards to our rear. He used a long staff as he walked leisurely and didn't flinch when I spotted him. How long had he been there? Was he just out for a stroll, or was he following us? More concerning was that he resembled the man who had followed me the first day I arrived in Jerusalem—at least from what I could tell in the darkness.

At the next intersection we turned left, with another two blocks to go before reaching the hospital.

"What is it?" Atkinson asked in a hushed tone.

"Nothing," I said to dissuade her from looking back.

We covered the two blocks and were about to cross a busy boulevard when I checked for the man. He was gone.

Atkinson glanced back and said, "Jumping at shadows, are we?"

"It's called being vigilant."

Atkinson grunted, and we hurried across the street. We passed through the security screen and took the stairs to the third floor. The hallways were quiet, with only an occasional nurse circulating between rooms.

As we approached Laura's room, I steeled myself against the worst. I didn't breathe again until I saw that she was still there and alive. But from what I could tell, she hadn't moved an inch. I went up to her side and held her hand. It was warm and soft, but lifeless. I held back the urge to break down or scream at the heavens.

Atkinson seemed more disturbed by my behavior than Laura's condition. She barely looked at me. "I'll go see if I can find the doctor," she said and left.

The nurses had changed the bandaging again and left more of her face exposed. The swelling and bruising had receded a bit, making Laura look pale and drawn. Her eyes were sunken, and black circles had formed around them. I was not a religious man, but I prayed Laura would survive her injuries and the loss of the child.

Overwhelmed and exhausted, I pulled the chair up close to the bed and sat with my head on the mattress next to her hand. I'd nearly dozed off when I heard the shuffling of fabric and the soft clump of crutches on the linoleum. I straightened and was surprised to see a man standing a few feet from the bed. He was in a hospital gown with bandages around his head.

He looked to be no more than twenty-five, with handsome features. He held himself up with the help of his crutches, a cast encasing his ankle and foot.

I said hello. He said nothing as he stared at Laura.

"Were you wounded in the same bomb blast?" I asked.

He looked at me and nodded. "I remember seeing this lady by the car when the bomb went off. She was lovely, standing there. The next minute, I'm flat on my stomach and unable to move. I looked over to where she'd been a second ago, but she was on the ground, too, and covered in blood. I tried to get up to go to her. I wanted to help. But I guess I fainted when I tried to stand."

"Have you visited her here before?"

He nodded. "At night. I can't sleep. I just relive the explosion over and over and see my mates torn to pieces. And I see her."

"Her name is Laura," I said in a soft voice.

"Are you her husband?"

I shook my head. "We were trying to get out of the city. Maybe get married."

He turned his gaze to Laura for a moment, then started to negotiate a pivot with his crutches. "Well, I guess I'd better go."

"You can stay if you like." I got up and started to push the chair over to him. "Take a load off."

"No thanks."

"Well, since you're here, could I ask you a few questions? I'm trying to find out who was responsible for the bomb. Anything you remember might help."

"I figure the police are doing that. Looking for the bomber, that is."

"I'm sure they are, but they only have so many investigators and too many bombings. I've got one purpose, and I won't stop until I find who's responsible."

The boy's face tightened in anger. "If you find out who, you'll kill them?"

I nodded.

"What do you want to know?"

I tiptoed over to another chair and placed it close to mine. He muttered a thanks and eased himself onto the chair. I rotated mine a few degrees toward him and sat.

"What's your name, by the way?" I asked him.

"Gerald."

"Mine's Mason. I was a detective before the war and an army investigator during. I'm telling you this so you know I'm not just a guy off the street. I know what I'm doing."

"Good to know."

"Did you notice anything unusual before the blast?" I asked. "Any minor detail might help."

Gerald's gaze lost focus as he stared at the curtain dividing the beds. "It's always tense when we set up a checkpoint. Everyone's on alert. So you could say that time was no different from any other. But then, just before the bomb went off, things really got dodgy when that Arab started protesting the search of his car. That got everyone else agitated. When traffic and pedestrians started moving again, the situation seemed to ease."

"What about the people? Particularly the ones on foot? Anything unusual?"

Gerald glanced at me before turning his gaze to the room. "The pedestrians started to cross. A few protests, but nothing out of the ordinary." He looked at me as if remembering something. "There was a man in a suit and tarboosh across the street. He was staring at something on my side of the road. Really intense. Not at me. Maybe a person who was passing. I only say that because his eyes seemed fixed on something moving. He acted suspicious enough for me to think about asking one of the constables to check him out, but then the bomb went off."

Sweat had beaded on Gerald's forehead. His face widened as if in fright or pain. I didn't want to push him, but it was probably the only time I'd have the chance to ask him any questions.

"Have you told anyone else about what you saw?" I asked him.

He shook his head.

"I know asking you these questions brings up bad memories—"

He looked at me. "If it helps get those bastards, I'm fine with going on."

Atkinson stopped at the doorway and saw Gerald. She said nothing and signaled that she'd be waiting out in the hall.

"Can you describe this man across the street?" I asked Gerald.

"I'm not sure," he said with a wavering voice.

"Take your time."

"Have you got a fag?"

I fished a pack of cigarettes out of my jacket. I gave him one and took one for myself. I lit them both, and he took a puff with a shaking hand.

The smoke and the act seemed to calm him a bit, and he said, "He had an average build. White or light-skinned Arab. About five eleven. Maybe twelve stone. Black-and-gray hair and mustache."

That last detail got my heart beating fast. Could it have been the same man who had tailed me? I wanted to think so, only because that would mean I had a chance to catch him if he dared to tail me again.

"Is there anything else you recall about the man? Big or small nose, eyes far apart or deep set, scars."

"I was too far away to see much in the way of details. Normal features, nothing stood out. That's the best I can say, I'm afraid."

If it was the same guy tailing me on several occasions, he was always too far away from me to discern more than Gerald had described.

"The man didn't signal someone or have a device in his hand, like a small blasting machine?"

"No, he was just standing there."

"Anything else you'd like to add?"

Gerald shook his head in a way that told me he didn't want to go any further into his nightmare.

"Do you think some of the other soldiers or policemen in the ward might agree to talk to me?"

He fidgeted in his chair and felt for his crutches. "I'll ask around. But I ought to be getting back. The nurses don't like me wandering around."

"They can be tough. I know from personal experience."

"In the war?"

I nodded. "Six weeks after spending time in several Nazi POW camps."

"How did you ever get over the experience?"

"You don't. It just gets a little easier over time."

Gerald took up his crutches and hoisted himself up to his feet. I stood, and we shook hands. I thanked him and wished him luck, and he hobbled off. How many times had I seen boy soldiers battered by war? The politicians and brass make policy, and the common soldier always pays the price.

22

A tkinson and I walked down Street of the Prophets. Though it was only two lanes, it was a fairly busy east-west route from the Old City's Damascus Gate to the western suburbs. We'd already been stopped and questioned twice by military patrols after leaving the hospital. My American papers and Atkinson's reporter credentials were enough to allow us to continue, but it was getting annoying, and we still had blocks to go before reaching the street leading to Atkinson's apartment.

"Let's get off the busy street," Atkinson said. "I know an alternate route. I don't use it much, but it'll get us there quicker."

She turned right onto a single-lane road that gently curved to the left. We were hemmed in by stone walls, and there were no streetlights.

"I see why you avoid going this way. I can barely see what's ahead."

"Don't worry, I'll protect you," she said in an exaggerated tone. "We'll be there in ten minutes."

I didn't find her teasing particularly funny; the streets were too dangerous, especially after midnight. As we continued, I pulled the backpack off my shoulders and rifled through it to find my .45. I also got out the brass knuckles and put them in my pocket, then shouldered my backpack.

"Did that soldier give you anything useful?" Atkinson asked.

"We'll talk about it once we get to your place. Right now, I want to stay alert."

We came up to a Y-intersection, with the other street taking a sharp right. We stuck to the main road that veered to the left. I glanced down the right fork. It appeared empty, though it fell off to darkness after a few yards.

I got the same sensation as before, that someone had started tailing us, presumably picking up our path at the Y-intersection. I kept pace with Atkinson, though I took lighter steps while I considered how to deal with our shadowy friend.

Barely above a whisper, I said to Atkinson, "If I stop, you just keep on going. Get back to the apartment."

Atkinson sucked in her breath, and her body tensed. But, to her credit, she remained silent and continued to move forward. I slowed my pace, clutched the brass knuckles in my left hand, and slipped them on my fingers. I would leave the gun nestled in my beltline. It was entirely possible that the person was out for a stroll. Plus, I wanted whoever was there to remain alive for questioning. If at all possible …

I spun around and charged into the darkness. I ran toward what I figured was the tail's approximate location, but after several strides, whoever had been there was gone. I slowed to a lope with all my senses on alert.

I heard quick footsteps in the distance, and I darted forward. Just steps onto the adjoining street I saw a flash of movement out of the corner of my eye. Two hands grabbed my head and left shoulder and skillfully threw me off balance.

Before I could recover, my assailant used my forward momentum to spin me, then pin me against a stone wall with my arm bent behind my back. I threw my head back, slamming the hard part of my skull into the assailant's face. He recoiled and lost control of my arm.

I spun around and saw that it was the mustached man who had been tailing me. I swung my brass-knuckled fist at his face. It clipped his chin, though he dodged out of the worst of the blow.

He yelped, and his tarboosh went flying. I kicked his legs out from under him. But he was up in a flash and delivered a series of judo moves that had me on the ground and pinned.

I attempted several moves to break his hold, but he knew exactly how to counter them.

"Hold on a minute, mate," the man said with a British accent. "I mean you no harm."

I struggled against his grasp in anger—a good deal of it directed at myself for failing to subdue the man.

Finally, I stopped resisting. I would wait for another opportunity. I also realized that, with his skill and me helpless, he could have snuffed out my life right then and there.

"There, that's better," he said.

"What do you want?" I asked between heaves of air.

"I imagine this is as good an opportunity to talk as any. I was hoping for a less confrontational encounter, however."

"You have a strange way of introducing yourself."

"I had wanted more time to make sure you were a man to be trusted. I'm guessing we share similar goals."

Intrigue overtook my anger. He must have sensed my change in attitude, because he loosened his grip.

"I would like to release you, if you agree to discuss things in a calm manner."

I nodded as much as the pavement would allow.

"I do have your pistol, so please keep that in mind," the man said.

He stood and offered his hand to help me up. I accepted and got to my feet. I brushed the dirt and sand off my cheek and clothes. Surprisingly, the man handed me back my .45. I felt like

I'd been twisted into a pretzel, but at least he had a small gash on his chin.

In the murky light, I couldn't see much detail in his face, but he did look to be a decade older than I was. That stung my pride a bit.

"You have some impressive moves," I said.

"You're not so bad yourself."

Atkinson stepped out of the shadows and said, "Now that you've admired each other's manly prowess, perhaps we can sojourn to my apartment."

The man bowed his head at her in a courtly manner. "Mrs. Atkinson."

She raised an eyebrow. "And you are?"

"You can call me Nicholas."

"I'm suitably curious," Atkinson said and made a gesture in the direction of her apartment. "Shall we?"

"Too much exposure," Nicholas said. "I prefer a more secluded spot." He gestured toward the opposite direction.

When we hesitated, he said, "I assure you, it's safe."

My curiosity outweighed my caution, and I suppose the same was true for Atkinson, because she made the first move. We followed Nicholas in silence, taking a circuitous route to avoid the main roads and the roving patrols. We ended up in an area directly north of the Italian Hospital and finally stopped at a decades-old Citroën sedan that had more dents than smooth areas.

The man went up to the passenger's rear door and opened it.

"Seems like everyone in this town drives a rusted old heap," I said.

Atkinson got in back, and I went around and sat in the front passenger's seat. Nicholas got behind the wheel. It took several tries to get the engine started, but it finally came to life, and our mystery man drove off.

Nicholas steered the car through several small streets. He

obviously knew where the patrols were circulating and the impromptu checkpoints, and we left the city behind.

Nicholas drove along the same Ramallah road that we had taken earlier, but he didn't go far before turning off onto a dirt road that cut between limestone hills. Not more than a mile later, he pulled onto a small dirt road carved up by wind and rain, which led to a box-shaped, single-story house.

He parked the car behind the building and out of sight of the road. He switched off the engine and said, "Welcome to my humble abode."

I couldn't resolve the man's high-brow British accent with the ramshackle house in the middle of nowhere. "Great place for a murderer's hideout."

"Same concept, different motive," Nicholas said.

"This better be worth it," Atkinson said, and she got out of the car.

Nicholas and I did the same, and we all walked up to a rear entrance. Once our host unlocked the door, we entered a single room with a kitchenette and a bed in the far corner. Aside from the weightlifting gear and a punching bag suspended from the ceiling, there was little in the way of furnishings or decorations. The kitchen was clean and void of utensils. I imagined if I looked in the cabinets, there wouldn't be any food either.

"I don't spend much time here, as you can tell," Nicholas said. "This is one of many of my bases of operation. But at least I do have a fully stocked bar." He walked over to a crate on a rickety table. "Anyone care for a drink? I have single malt, blended, Scottish, and for those without a modicum of taste or refinement, Irish."

"Whatever you're pouring," I said.

Atkinson said the same, and I studied the man as he removed a bottle and three glasses from the crate and carefully poured the liquid. He looked to be about forty and was lean and muscular. His skin was drawn tight and brown from years in the sun. As he came over with the glasses of whiskey, he moved with the swagger of an officer but with a power in his stride that said he'd spent the majority of his time soldiering in the field.

Nicholas handed us our drinks. "Since you came all this way, I poured a favorite of mine, a Talisker." He held up his glass and said, "Cheers."

We all took a sip. It was the best scotch I'd ever tasted, but I had the feeling all these niceties served a particular purpose. And time was ticking.

I tapped my watch. "We need to get down to business."

23

"Typically American, isn't he?" Nicholas asked Atkinson.

"I find it refreshing," Atkinson said.

Nicholas made a gesture toward a group of wooden chairs in the middle of the room. "Then shall we retire to the parlor?"

Once we all sat, I asked, "Who are you, and why have you been following me?"

"There's only so much I can tell you, but I can say that I'm with British intelligence."

"A clandestine branch, obviously," I said.

Nicholas nodded.

"So, why me?"

"At first, I was curious about the non-Jewish American who decided to come over on a Jewish refugee ship. There have been several foreign mercenaries or zealots coming here looking for profit or adventure. Shady financiers, gun runners. I needed to find out if you were one of those ... how shall we say, undesirables."

"If you've been following me since Haifa, then you know why I'm here."

"Yes, and I'm aware of Mrs. Talbot's activities. And by the way, I'm so sorry that she was gravely wounded."

"Then you must also know that my sole objective is to find who's responsible. Do you know anything about that?"

"We'll get to that in a moment. While I determined that you weren't a security threat, I discovered you came here with Arie Feldman and David Hazan. Also, I learned of your encounter with the bomber on the ship and his female companion—"

"You hoped I would lead you to leaders in the Irgun or Palmach, and maybe a lead on the companion," I said, finishing his sentence.

Nicholas only smiled and took a sip of his whiskey.

"You know I'm working with the police," I said.

"Are you?" Nicholas asked with an arch to his eyebrow. "Because I've seen little of that in the last few days."

"I've been trying to track down the bombers who did this," I said, pointing to the cuts on my face. "Maybe I just found him."

Nicholas gave a quizzical glance over the lip of his drinking glass. "I'm not sure I follow."

"I spoke to a witness, an injured soldier from the bombing. Odd thing is, he put you, or someone who closely matches your description, at the scene. Just before the bomb went off. He said you were acting suspiciously, and he almost called over his squad leader to investigate you."

Nicholas said nothing for a moment, which I figured was him taking the time to come up with a digestible answer. "Yes, I was there. But not in the capacity that you suspect."

"I'm listening."

"You're mistakenly under the impression that I'm obligated to answer you. But what I can tell you is that I was gathering intelligence on a person or persons who may be a threat."

"In other words, you were following someone who just happened to lead you to that spot before the bomb exploded."

"That's right."

"Is this person, or are these persons, likely the bombers?"

"I'm not at liberty to say."

I was about to lose my temper over his obfuscations, when he added, "What I can say is that I'm as interested in Nadia, the woman operative, as you are."

I was both surprised and excited to hear it. "What do you know?"

"Her full name is Nadia Chamberlin, though she goes by Nadia Yassin al-Katib."

"Chamberlin? She's British?" Atkinson said.

"Half. On her father's side. Her mother was Syrian, though Nadia was born in Iraq in 1919. What makes her so formidable is that she trained and served in the SOE. Special Operations Executive to you."

Atkinson said to me, "A secret organization conducting espionage and clandestine military operations during the war. Sort of like your OSS."

"Oh, hardly," Nicholas said and winked at her.

"Yes, I'm aware of what the SOE did during the war," I said.

Nicholas said, "Nadia was assigned to the Cairo branch and assisted during the North African and Italian campaigns."

"If she risked her life for king and country, what is she doing assassinating Brits?" I asked.

"After the war she became a killer for hire."

"If you knew all this, why didn't you take her prisoner the day of the bombing?"

"I was hoping she'd lead us to the group she's been associating with."

Atkinson said, "We can link her with this group who calls themselves the Black Hand, but nothing beyond that."

Nicholas showed no signs of surprise, or even curiosity.

He said, "Even if you discount the idea that a group of Muslim men would consider hiring a female, I don't see how this group could afford to pay for her services."

"Her cousin was a resident of the village where we believe Nadia was last seen," Atkinson said.

"You mean Alal," Nicholas said. "That was good intelligence work, you two narrowing down that location."

"It was a dead end," I said. "Now, how about you get to who might be responsible for the bombing."

"The bombing method and target point to Irgun or Lehi," Nicholas said.

"More dodging. What about me spotting Nadia moments before the blast?"

"I know you think it was Nadia, and possibly the Black Hand, but that kind of attack points to one of the Jewish groups. Regardless, we'd definitely like to get our hands on her. And that's where you come in."

"You seem to know a lot more about her than I do. I don't see how I could help."

"Whilst what happened to your fiancée is tragic, the fact that it has compelled you to remain in the country provided us an opportunity."

"In other words, I'm the bait."

"Crudely put, but accurate."

"Then you're going to have to stand in line. The police already have me out on a hook. But say I'm okay with being the bait, I want something in return."

"It's not like you're a hero who volunteered. We're simply taking advantage of your situation."

"I'm sure you want to find the perpetrators of the bombing that killed ten cops and soldiers. You pass on what intelligence you have and let me access some of your organization's resources, and I'll do the rest."

"Even if it turns out one of your friends is responsible?"

"I haven't ruled anyone out. That includes you, or *your* friends and colleagues."

I let him stew on that thought while watching his reactions.

As a good intelligence agent should, he betrayed nothing, but his silence spoke volumes.

Finally, he said, "You will only hear from me. If you have a request for information, you will run it through me. If you have a notion to come here, you won't find me. You will not try to contact me. I will make contact with you."

"That's a one-sided deal, with you holding all the cards," I said.

"Why did you bring us here and volunteer this information, Mr. Whatever-your-name-is?" Atkinson said. "You could have left us on that road. Yet you showed us one of your bases of operation and revealed your cover." Before Nicholas could answer, Atkinson answered her own question. "Because you actually need *our* help."

I'd respected Atkinson before for her intelligence and brashness, but now she had risen to the level of admiration.

Nicholas said, "Any contact could compromise my cover. Yes, your help could be valuable, but not at the expense of revealing my identity."

"Mason was an investigator and an intelligence officer. And I've been a journalist for twenty-odd years. We know how to keep secrets and protect sources."

Nicholas took a moment to finish his scotch. "There's a café next to the Ecce Homo Arch in the Muslim Quarter of the Old City. Meet me there at noon tomorrow. Now, I should get you back to the city."

24

The sun blazing in my eyes woke me up. For a moment, I forgot where I was, and for a brief, blissful moment, neither could I remember why. Then it all came flooding back. My stomach constricted, though there was nothing in there to churn; I hadn't eaten for almost twenty-four hours.

I stood out of the single bed in a small room with simple furnishings. I followed the scent of coffee to the kitchen. Atkinson was sitting at a round table, smoking a cigarette, with a cup of coffee and a plate of toast and jam in front of her.

"I was about to get you out of bed," Atkinson said.

"What time is it?"

"Almost ten."

I cursed under my breath. I had to pull myself together before heading out to meet Nicholas in the Old City.

"There's more coffee and bread for toast. There are also some sausages still in the pan."

I put together a plate, poured some coffee, and sat across from her. I figured she had just gotten up herself, as she was still wearing her bathrobe and her hair was unkempt. Nicholas had driven us home, arriving close to four a.m., and we'd gone straight to bed, vowing to review everything in the morning.

I needed food and coffee before talking and attacked my breakfast, devouring it in less than five minutes. I then joined her in smoking a cigarette. In younger years, I could have snapped back from sleep deprivation and starvation in a heartbeat, but now I required more time to start my engine.

"I must say," Atkinson began, "partnering with you is full of adventures. Though last night was more puzzling than hair-raising. Our Nicholas had an odd way of asking for help."

"He did it out of desperation or urgency."

"Urgency for what?"

"I don't know, but if I were working intelligence, I wouldn't drive someone all the way to my hideout and let them know that he or she was being used as bait. Let alone reveal my identity."

"Perhaps he felt he didn't have a choice once you went after him."

I shook my head. "He could have subdued both of us and left without a 'how do you do.'"

I got up and poured another cup of coffee and returned to the table. "I get the impression that something serious is going to happen. Nicholas and his agency are pulling out all the stops."

"And we're one of the stops."

"Seems that way."

Atkinson's gaze drifted to the ceiling as she puffed on her cigarette. "He didn't seem too concerned about the Black Hand group. He knew the name of the village, and that we'd tracked it down, but he volunteered nothing about the group."

"He's not going to give us everything. Only what he thinks is needed to recruit us as assets."

"Now we're intelligence assets and bait?"

"In a sense. He'll use us as long as we're useful to him."

"Chilling thought."

"Believe me, I know his game. As a former army intelligence

officer during the war, I once played it myself. We turn it around by using him. You must have used it, too, as a journalist, to pry a story from a source. Same concept; different rules."

"Then it's high time we go see our new friend."

IT TOOK US ONLY FIFTEEN MINUTES TO WALK FROM THE ITALIAN Hospital to the Old City. We'd stopped by to see Laura and check on her condition, and her lack of progress was weighing on my mind. We passed through the castle-like fortress of the Damascus Gate and entered the Muslim Quarter. We crossed a covered area filled with open markets of spices and produce, where merchants called out their wares to the passing crowds. The mix of Arabs, tourists, and patrolling cops reminded me of Tangier.

At the far end of the square, we turned onto a street that was barely wide enough for three to four people across. We had to dodge crowds and donkeys and groups of men gathered around cafés. While the scene reminded me of the Tangier's medina, the streets were far straighter, thanks to the Romans, who had a fondness for grid-patterned thoroughfares.

Despite my low spirits after visiting Laura, I felt a thrill walking these ancient passages. It was the first time I'd ventured deep into the Old City, and I found my imagination wandering instead of listening to what Atkinson was saying or thinking about what we were going to say to Nicholas. I even failed to notice Atkinson turning left off the bustling street.

"This way, Mason," she said behind me.

I turned back and followed her onto a quieter and narrower street.

"This is Via Dolorosa," Atkinson said. "The sorrowful way, way of suffering, or way of pain, depending on who you ask. Jesus supposedly came this way while carrying the cross to his crucifixion."

"If I were the superstitious type, I'd say this wouldn't be the optimal meeting place."

We passed fewer shops and people as we climbed the gentle slope of the land beneath the cobblestoned street.

Atkinson pointed to an arch half-embedded in a stone building. "The café must be here."

Indeed, a few steps later, we came upon a small entrance with a sign in Arabic. The only way I knew it was a café was by the cartoonish picture of a steaming cup of coffee depicted on a spot near the arched entrance. Like the other cafés, men were gathered outside, talking and smoking cigarettes. They stared at us as we approached but did nothing to stop us from entering.

Atkinson greeted the men in Arabic, and we passed the open door.

We had to pause a few steps into the room to let our eyes adjust to the darkness. Two small windows let in just enough light to illuminate the space, meant to keep the heat to a minimum during the long hot months. Ten small tables were dispersed around the surprisingly spacious room. The stucco on the walls was half gone, revealing stone. Ceiling fans had been hung from the low, vaulted ceiling.

The patrons turned to us for a moment, then went back to their conversations and coffee. In a far corner, Nicholas sat at a table behind a stone pillar. He was dressed in Palestinian robes and wore his distinctive tarboosh. He remained still as we approached, as if he didn't know us. He said nothing when we sat across from him.

A man with a bushy mustache emerged from the back room and came up to our table. Atkinson said something to the man in Arabic, and the man left.

"I ordered us two coffees," Atkinson said.

"Good," I said to Atkinson. Then to Nicholas, "But we didn't come here to drink coffee."

Nicholas replied by speaking Arabic to Atkinson. They

carried on a short conversation. While Atkinson spoke the language with a heavy British accent, Nicholas sounded just like any Arab on the street. I'd heard enough here and in Tangier to tell that much.

Sitting on the sidelines was beginning to annoy me.

Keeping my voice low, I said to Nicholas, "I understand you want to maintain your cover, but you asked us here. Now skip the Arabic prologue and get down to business."

"Touchy, isn't he?" Nicholas said to Atkinson.

"You don't know the half of it," Atkinson said.

I was about to protest when the man came back with two tiny cups of coffee. We fell silent as the cups were laid out on the table.

Once the man disappeared into the other room, I asked Nicholas, "Did you get approval to share information and resources?"

He nodded and plucked a cigarette from a silver case and lit it. "Ones that don't violate national security interests, of course."

"You didn't ask us here just to tell us that."

Nicholas played with an unlit cigarette, tapping one end, then flipping it over and tapping the other. I got the impression something was troubling him, and I gave him time to summon up the courage to say whatever he needed to tell us.

He lit the battered cigarette, took a puff, and lowered his hands to the table. He looked at his cigarette and said, "The Black Hand was spotted in Jaffa. Their exact location isn't known, but it's in one of the buildings near the Ottoman clock tower. That's just a block north of the old part of the city."

"Are you sure about this?" I asked.

"That's the word from one of our sources. Though I can't guarantee anything."

"Is the army or the police going to investigate?" Atkinson asked.

"They may have heard similar news from the same source, but

not from us."

"Why not?" I asked.

"I'm not at liberty to say."

"You keep saying *us*," Atkinson said. "What organization are you with, exactly?"

"I'm not at liberty to reveal that either," Nicholas said. "Not yet, anyway."

I paused to study Nicholas's face. His arrogant expression was gone, but he managed to return a nonchalant look, concealing anything going on behind his dark brown eyes.

"Either you're using us to get more intel, or this is some kind of ploy," I said.

Nicholas fidgeted in his chair. "I don't follow you."

"You figure I can't ignore the intel. I'll have to go. Either this is your way of using me as an asset or it's entrapment."

Nicholas seemed unruffled by my suspicions, which I found revealing if not a little unsettling.

"It's not me you have to worry about," he said.

Atkinson and I exchanged a look. There was apprehension in her eyes, which matched what was going on in my mind. Were we stepping into something more dangerous than we'd anticipated?

"Who should we worry about, then?" Atkinson asked.

"I'm not—"

"You're not at liberty to say," I said, interrupting Nicholas. "So far you've thrown crumbs in our path. Nothing concrete."

"I wish I could say something more substantial. If you haven't picked up what I'm trying to convey, it's to be very careful what you wish for. Go to Jaffa, don't go to Jaffa, it won't make much difference in the scheme of things. As a matter of fact, in my opinion, going there would be foolhardy. Chances are, you'll be killed, which won't accomplish a thing." He leaned forward and stared at me with piercing eyes. "I know, viscerally, you want to unleash holy hell on whoever put your fiancée in the hospital and deprived you of your unborn child, and you'll take down anyone in your path."

"Can you blame me?"

"No. But be smarter. Find the source and eliminate it. The periphery will wither and die."

"You keep beating around the bush. Why not give us something we can sink our teeth into?"

"Maybe later," Nicholas said. "Other things have to play out before I can go any deeper into what's going on. In the meantime, I recommend you dig deeper into your fiancée's notes." He held up his hands. "That's all I can say, which is more than I intended." He stubbed out his cigarette. "Now, I've lingered too long. We'll be in touch. And be very careful if you decide to go to Jaffa. The Arabs are feeling squeezed by the Jewish expansion and are at a boiling point. And the Irgun is vowing revenge after His Majesty's authorities executed four of their members a week or so ago. Jaffa is a likely target. As I said, be very careful." He stood. "We'll be in touch. That is, if you make it back in one piece. Cheerio." He left money on the table and walked out.

"You should listen to the man," Atkinson said. "The old city of Jaffa is a good place to hide. Winding, tightly packed streets and a sewer system that's easily accessible and perfect for moving around unnoticed. All that makes it difficult and dangerous."

"I *have* to go. And alone this time."

"I'm not going to argue with you, but I think that's a bad idea. And after Alal, you wouldn't catch me within ten miles of any location where there might be members of the Black Hand."

"It's settled then. I'll go scout Jaffa while you comb through Laura's papers again. See if you can figure out what Nicholas is talking about. Oh, and I'll need to borrow your car."

Atkinson fumbled through her purse, retrieved her car keys, and dropped them in front of me. "I'm just wondering how I'm going to tell Laura—when she wakes up, of course—that you were found with your throat cut in a dark alley in Jaffa."

25

The late afternoon sun streaked across the tops of the buildings on the other side of the street. In the shadows, I sat at a café sipping on my third cup of coffee and watched the foot, donkey, and camel traffic circulate on the wide street. Jaffa's shops, fruit and vegetable stands, cafés, and restaurants vied for attention. The Ottoman clock tower Nicholas had mentioned was a half block to my left, and I'd situated my chair so I could keep an eye on that area while still having a view of the street in front of me.

I'd already spent an hour at the café and two hours walking the old city. Like Jerusalem, Jaffa was an ancient place conquered and occupied by countless armies. The latest scars had been left by the British after they dynamited sections during the Arab riots a decade ago. The original fortifications had long disappeared, but the distinctive horseshoe-shaped boundary remained. Despite its small size, there was a lot of ground to cover, as the streets were cramped and wound aimlessly or dead-ended in rubble. I didn't expect to have much luck spotting Nadia, her cousin, or members of the Black Hand, though it did help to get the lay of the land in case I needed a quick escape.

I had Laura's photo of the village that showed a group of men in the background and included Nadia's cousin, Rana. I kept it in my lap and checked faces of the people who passed against those in the photograph. The Arabs seemed to outnumber the Jews by about two to one. I got a lot of suspicious stares, maybe because I didn't look like either. I figured they took me for British, and probably an undercover policeman. Despite trying to look like the man on the street, I knew I oozed cop, especially when scrutinizing passersby. Word had probably already gone out about my presence. That didn't do much for keeping a low profile, but it could work in my favor if it drew out one of my quarries.

A dangerous game, but I had my .45 under my jacket, my knife in my boot, and the brass knuckles in my pocket.

Someone came up to me from behind, and I spun around in my chair to see a young man, barely more than eighteen, stop a few feet from me.

"Good afternoon, sir," the boy said. "You need a guide? I'm a good guide. I can show you the famous sights of our beloved city."

"Not interested," I said and waved him away. He was the third such person to try this, and I was getting irritated.

Instead of leaving, he sat across from me. "There is many history here. I know. I can take you to such places."

"I said I'm not interested, and I didn't ask you to sit down. Take a hike, kid."

"You are not British," the boy said. "Where you from?"

"None of your business."

He smiled and shook his finger at me in excitement. "You are American, no? Do you know Betty Grable? I would like very much to know Betty Grable." He glanced somewhere across the street.

That's when I knew he was following someone's instruction to check on me. "Sure, Betty Grable's a friend of mine. What's your name? I'll tell her about you."

The boy froze; it wasn't supposed to go this way. He made another glance toward the opposite side of the street, then returned to me, and he made an exaggerated smile. "That's okay."

"That's okay, what? You don't want me to talk to Betty, or you don't want to give me your name?"

"Mohammed."

"Okay, Mohammed, let's go on that tour."

The boy seemed relieved that things were finally going his way. We stood, I slung the backpack on my back, and we headed for the heart of the Old City. I wasn't sure if this was an ambush to rob me or slit my throat, but I was determined to find out who was behind the ruse.

While Mohammed started yammering about the long history of the city, I remained vigilant. The kid seemed to know his stuff, but I couldn't verify any of it. I imagined that there wasn't much tourist business these days with the unrest, so he probably took up larceny as a side hustle.

He was up to Rome's dominance of the city when I noticed a man tailing us dressed in white baggy pants and a brown outer robe, with his knit skullcap worn low on his forehead. I followed Mohammed down a cramped street that curved sharply to the left a block later. Sure enough, the man made the same turn and had closed the gap to within fifty yards.

As soon as we entered the curve, I grabbed the collar of Mohammed's ragged sport coat and stopped him in his tracks. I whipped out the photo of the men in the village and shoved it in his face.

"Do you recognize anyone in this photo?"

The boy struggled against my grasp. "Let me go!"

"Is one of them following us?"

He cried out. I heard footsteps pounding up the street toward us, leaving me no time for more questions. I released him, and he ran back the way we'd come. I ducked into a doorway, slipped my brass knuckles on my right hand, and waited.

The guy rushed around the corner. I launched from the doorway to tackle him, but he was ready for me. It was as if he knew I'd laid a trap. We collided.

I attempted a kick to knock him off his feet, but he countered it. With each blow, he blocked. I had twenty pounds on him, but he was faster. Both of us landed a few hits, but none of them were very effective.

Then he got me in the stomach. I bent over, and he pulled out his knife. But that move caused him to drop his defenses. That split second gave me the opportunity I needed.

I swung my right fist with all my might. The brass knuckles connected with his jaw and neck. His throat locked up. His hands instinctively went to his neck, and he staggered backward.

Like a winded boxer, he wrapped his arms around me to keep me from delivering another hit. I grabbed onto his shirt to throw him off. The shirt gave way, and he jumped back, still unsteady on his feet.

I was on him and got in a series of hits. He'd taken serious punishment but remained standing. He lunged at me in desperation and latched onto me. We fell, him landing on his back with me on top of him. Even then, with his face bloody and the breath knocked out of him, he tried to stab me in the ribs. It took one last hit with the brass knuckles to get him to stop moving.

I yanked the knife out of his hand and threw it to the side. I seized his shoulders and lifted him to within inches of my face.

"Who are you? Are you a part of the Black Hand?"

He protested in Arabic and struggled to get out from under me, but he was too weak to resist against my weight.

I shook him and growled, "Answer me!"

The man just continued in Arabic. That was when I noticed the tattoos on his chest and arms where I'd torn his shirt. He had tattoos of a regimental crest, swallows, and a Christian cross with a crown of thorns on top of it.

"You're a Brit! What the hell are you doing? Who are you!"

I sat up while still straddling his chest and held the photo next to his cheek. Blood covered the man's face, and his features had already started to swell, but I could still recognize him in the group.

"What's a Brit doing with the Black Hand?"

He didn't answer. I searched his clothing for a wallet or ID, something that might identify him, but came up empty. I pulled out my Ka-Bar and put the point of the blade against his throat.

"Your bomb killed my unborn child and put my fiancée in a coma. If I don't get any answers, I'll cut them out of you."

His gaze jerked in my direction. He had a confused looked on his face, though he remained calm.

I pushed the tip into his skin, and a trickle of blood leaked from the wound. His stoic demeanor turned to fear.

"Where is the rest of your gang?" I asked.

"Go ahead and use the knife," he said with a British accent. "But you might want to think twice before you open me up." His eyes moved toward the street ahead of us.

I looked up. A crowd of Arabs had begun to gather. The woman looked horrified, but the men glared at me in anger.

The Brit said something loudly in Arabic, and the crowd surged forward. I jumped to my feet to defend myself. The knife in my hand made them stop just yards from me. They shook their fists and yelled.

Something struck me in the head and back. I spun around. Three middle-aged women were using their bundles as weapons. The blows weren't painful, but now I was surrounded, and the mob was growing.

I saw swift movement out of the corner of my eye and looked in that direction. My captive had made his escape. More blows came from the women, but I wouldn't fight them. The mob might become emboldened and attack, then the police would surely come.

I couldn't afford either. There was nothing left to do but make my escape.

I pulled out my pistol, though I kept it aimed at the ground. The crowd moved away while they continued to yell. I backed up, pushing past the angry women, then turned and marched away.

The crowd followed me for several yards, then, fortunately, they stopped, seemingly satisfied that they had saved the young man and were rid of the Anglo ruffian.

I got to the main street and headed for the clock tower. A short distance north of the square, the Jewish section they called Tel Aviv would begin. It wasn't necessarily safer; I had to figure that Irgun or Haganah spies already were aware of the incident. I had to get out of Jaffa before the entire city descended upon me.

26

I was within a block of Laura's hospital when the incident in Jaffa finally caught up with me. The police must have staked out the area to wait for me, because as soon as I was in sight, five cops came trotting in my direction.

No use in running. I stopped and raised my hands. I looked around to see if anyone was observing this from a distance. They searched me and removed my weapons. I was expecting handcuffs, but I was simply escorted to a waiting car and told to get in back.

DCI Gilman occupied the space behind the front passenger's seat. He waited until the constable had closed the door and the driver stepped out of the vehicle. "You created quite a stir in Jaffa today."

"I heard a rumor that the Black Hand was there. I went to check it out. A local Arab tried to rob me, and I fought back. The people in the neighborhood didn't appreciate me beating up a member of their community."

"Did you learn anything?"

"No."

"All that way on a rumor?" Gilman asked with a tone of sarcasm. "Who passed on that information to you?"

"I was sniffing around in the Arab quarter of the Old City and overheard it on the street."

Gilman raised an eyebrow and glared at me. "Mr. Collins, our threat still stands. You provide information, and we refrain from sending you prison for offenses against the United Kingdom. So far, you haven't been very useful."

"I made contact with Irgun and Haganah, but their security is so tight that they don't just avoid suspicious characters, they eliminate them. I have to go slow or wind up dead."

"No other names in those organizations, then?"

I shook my head.

"Anything on the Black Hand or your assassin?" Gilman asked.

I had to give him something, if only to stay out of prison. "Nothing on the group, but I found out the assassin goes by the name Nadia Yassin al-Katib. But her real surname seems to be Chamberlin."

I watched for Gilman's reaction. He showed genuine surprise at hearing an Anglo name.

"She's British?" he asked.

"Syrian mother and British father, and she was raised in Iraq."

He nodded. "It shouldn't be too hard to track down from her father's records."

"If you find out anything, pass it on to me. It could help."

Gilman seemed bemused by my request. "You are the giver of information, not the recipient. You are certainly not in any position to demand I do anything."

I said nothing. I had expected for him to tell me that they knew about my contact with Nicholas, or Atkinson's and my adventure in the village of Alal. Such titillating details would be too tempting to ignore. But either he was stringing me along, or he wasn't aware of them. Meaning there were limits to police intel.

"I'm not going to ask where you learned of her name," Gilman said. "You won't be truthful. Just so we understand each other. And I want you to remember that the care of your fiancée is at our discretion. Deviate from your directive, deceive us, misdirect, or hold back information, and there will be consequences."

I wanted to hit him right in that smug smile of his. Instead, I did nothing.

"You may go now, but I expect more frequent reports and improved progress."

"Next time put a little thought into choosing where to make contact. Someone from Irgun or Haganah could have spotted me being put in this car with you and put two and two together. You may have signed my death warrant."

I got out of the car before he could protest and headed for the hospital. The constables moved to stop me, but Gilman told them to let me go.

As I walked into the evening shadows, I kept my eyes and ears peeled for Irgun or Haganah spies, or worse, a squad of men lurking somewhere in order to nab me and take me somewhere for execution. I was now more vulnerable than ever, but I did get something out of the meeting with Gilman: the police and at least one faction of British intelligence were at odds. Things were being concealed. The Black Hand was far different than it appeared. Something was afoot, and it would end badly.

JUST STEPS FROM THE ENTRANCE TO LAURA'S HOSPITAL, A FLASH OF light illuminated the dark sky. I looked in the direction of the source, a sharp clap and a ground-shaking boom reached my ears a split second later.

A bomb had gone off somewhere south of my position. With

the sound delay, it was less than a mile. A secondary flash came right after it, throwing light on debris ejected into the air. The smaller bomb's blast arrived an instant later. Smoke and flames rose up above the city's skyline. The skin at the back of my neck shuddered as if being pricked with needles. A thin film of cold sweat formed on my forehead.

The police, who had escorted me to Gilman, rushed to their squad cars and motorcycles and raced off toward the bombing. Hospital staff and security guards came out of the entrance and stood by me, and we all looked toward the flames with dismay.

I looked down the street and found it odd that Gilman's car hadn't moved. It was only after a few moments passed that the driver made a U-turn in the road and proceeded in the opposite direction.

Three ambulances emerged from a side street, sirens blaring, and hurried off toward the destruction. Gilman's strange exit was something I would mull over later. But getting to Laura was more pressing, as there would soon be a new wave of victims pouring into the hospital.

The few security guards who had remained at their posts let me pass with a quick wave. The police stationed on the upper floors stood at the windows, trying to get a view of the bombing. Meanwhile, doctors, nurses, and orderlies darted about to make ready for the new patients.

Atkinson was at the window at the far end of Laura's room. I stopped in alarm. Laura lay on her side. I sucked in my breath and was at her side in two strides.

"Don't worry," Atkinson said behind me. "They nurses have to turn her to keep her from getting bedsores."

She came up to the opposite side of the bed. "There is some good news. According to one of the nurses, she opened her eyes, though only for a moment. She's made a couple of voluntary movements while we were out."

I pulled up the chair close to her bed and leaned in. "Laura, it's me. Mason. I'm here, darling."

She showed no reaction to the sound of my voice.

"Do you think she can hear me?" I asked Atkinson.

"I don't know. It can't hurt. But I'll give you the same caution the nurse gave me: her movements don't necessarily mean she's coming out of it."

I nodded as I stared at Laura's closed eyelids and found myself willing her to wake up.

Atkinson broke my concentration when she said, "That sounded like a serious explosion. It rattled the windows. I felt it in my feet."

A siren announced the first ambulance's return to the hospital.

"Once the victims pass through triage, it's going to get pretty busy up here," Atkinson said.

"I hope they keep giving Laura enough attention."

"Or they don't try to move her to another hospital."

"I just talked to DCI Gilman," I said, looking up at Atkinson. "As long as they think I'm doing what I can for them, he promised not to kick her out."

Atkinson glanced nervously at the door. "And?"

"I gave him something to nibble on."

"How did it go in Jaffa?"

"I'll tell you later. Not here."

Atkinson pulled a folded piece of paper out of her purse and held it out for me. "I went to the newspaper's sketch artist and had this done according to your description."

I unfolded the paper. Staring back at me was a decent likeness of Nadia. The square jaw was there. It ended in a prominent chin, and the aquiline nose, full lips, and furious eyes under thick eyebrows. All a good match.

"Not bad, though it could resemble a half million other women," I said.

"It might do the trick in a pinch."

We settled into our seats and traded off talking to Laura. We stuck to light conversation, though I was quickly running out of pleasantries. In the meantime, activity in the hallway rose to a frenzy. Nurses and orderlies rushed bomb victims to operating stations or parked gurneys in the hallway with groaning and bloody patients. Soon after, the orderlies started rolling gurneys into Laura's room. Some lay deathly still, while others writhed in pain and shock. The victims appeared to be a mix of soldiers, policemen, Jewish and Arab civilians all caught in the blast zone.

"Who did this?" Atkinson asked, more to herself. "It's barbaric."

"Whoever it was, it looks like they didn't pick a police or military target. There are as many civilians as police and soldiers."

"There are almost always civilians involved. They had to know that such a large bomb in a dense city would create so much collateral damage. I'm sure the first victims went to the Bikur Cholim Hospital, but that one must have filled up fast. So many people. It's an abomination."

Atkinson teared up as she watched the chaos outside the room.

"Why don't you go home and get some rest," I said. "I'm staying here tonight."

She shook her head and walked over to Laura. "We should turn her. I doubt anyone's going to be looking after her for some time."

I got up and helped turn Laura onto her back. We fixed the sheets, and Atkinson patted her lips with a damp cloth.

I figured it was safe to talk, as the pandemonium inside and outside the room would mask our conversation. "Jaffa created more questions than it answered," I said as we remained standing close to Laura's bed. "Some kid came up to me posing as a guide. I knew he was there to lure me somewhere, but it made me curious. I followed him into the old part of the city and was jumped by a man posing as an Arab."

"What do you mean posing?"

"We fought, and in the process, I ripped his shirt. Underneath, he had several tattoos, including one representing a British Army regiment. And then there was a Christian cross and a crown of thorns tattoos. He was dressed as an Arab but one hundred percent British."

Atkinson froze in place, either from shock or bewilderment. It took her a moment to get her mouth moving again. "One of the members of the Black Hand is a Brit? Are you sure it wasn't just a hoodlum trying to rob you?"

I plucked the photo out of my jacket pocket and held it up for her to see. "He matches one of the men in this photo. That man in Jaffa is the same one in Laura's photo, Evelyn."

Atkinson's gaze turned to a spot on the bedsheets. She shook her head. "I don't understand. Why would a British soldier join an Arab group? And why would the Arabs accept him?"

"My questions exactly. It doesn't make sense. Unless the Arab group is being sponsored or led by British commandos. The man —boy, really—had fighting skills he would only learn in elite forces."

Atkinson seemed deep in thought as she continued to stare at the bed. Finally, she looked up at me. "I went back through Laura's notes looking for anything that might answer what Nicholas was talking about. The only thing that stuck out was when Laura describes the strange visit to the village by what appeared to be a British police officer. Do you think …?"

"I don't know. Like you said, it doesn't make sense."

Maybe it didn't make sense because I didn't want it to. Not only would that expand the field of suspects, but it would make it far more dangerous. I was alone in a volatile land with no police or military support. In other words, I was in over my head.

"I want you to go home, gather up all of Laura's papers, pack a bag, and get the hell out of there. Go somewhere safe and stay there."

Atkinson's look of fear transformed to resolve. Without a word, she kissed Laura on the forehead, grabbed her coat and purse, and left.

For the first time that I could remember, I wanted to cut bait and run, dream up a plan to take Laura, get the hell out of there, and leave the place to the wolves.

27

The sun was cresting Mount of Olives when I stepped out of the hospital. I'd passed out while sitting next to Laura with my head on her arm. A nurse shook me awake and kicked me out. By that time, the ward was less crowded with gurneys and patients. Some patients had been treated and sent home, or they were placed in other wards, or they died, leaving the nurses time to administer to the other patients, including Laura.

Police and soldiers were everywhere, patrolling the streets or stopping pedestrians. As I walked back to Atkinson's apartment, I was questioned twice and told to stay out of the Old City, as martial law was in effect. There was little traffic and fewer pedestrians. Even the wind decided to stay off the streets of Jerusalem, and at 7:40 a.m., the day was already turning hot.

The odors of cooking food and coffee reached my nose halfway up the stairs to Atkinson's apartment, and I climbed the remaining steps two at a time. I must have knocked impatiently, because she yanked the door open, displayed a frown, and tossed a key at me.

"From now on, let yourself in," she said and made a beeline for the kitchen.

I followed her. "You were supposed to pack up your things and get out of town."

"I'm staying here and helping you and Laura. End of discussion."

I knew there was no use in arguing and went directly to the coffeepot. "What about Laura's papers?"

"Safely hidden away."

I poured a cup and said, "If I didn't know better, I would have thought the entire town is populated by police and soldiers."

She grunted and asked, "When's the last time you had anything to eat?"

"Aside from yesterday's breakfast, a couple of biscuits."

Atkinson got up from the table and went for the refrigerator. "You need to keep your strength up. I've got some eggs and sausage." She nodded toward the kitchen table. "Sit down before you fall down."

I did as I was told and watched her while my stomach growled. She was in her bathrobe and slippers. I found that I was comfortable around her. There was little delicacy to her movements, and she attacked the frying pan like she was just as likely to strangle it as to use it to fry eggs. She reminded me of my grandmother in many ways, her no-nonsense approach to everything. Once she finished and put the food in front of me, she stood over me with her hands on her hips. I felt like a little kid and enjoyed a nostalgic moment as I scarfed down the food. I made a promise that, if Laura and I lived through this, I would take us back to Ohio to see my grandmother.

Atkinson seemed satisfied that I would clean my plate, and she went into the living room. I joined her a moment later, and she motioned for me to follow her.

We went into the bedroom I was using, and I was shocked to see that she had created a board of photos and notes connected, and labels of suspects and possible allies.

"I know you detectives are fond of using this method. Since I couldn't sleep, I made this. I hope you don't mind that I used your room. That way, when you go to bed or get up, you might find inspiration."

She had several of Laura's photos and notes pinned up there, along with some I'd collected from the records room at the police station. In lieu of photographs, she had put up signs with Nicholas's and Gilman's names, along with a couple of newspaper clippings about the DCI and Police Superintendent Wetherbee. Labels of the Black Hand, Arab Higher Committee, Army of the Holy War, and al-Najjada for the Arab side, and the Jewish Agency, Haganah, Palmach, Irgun, and Lehi for the Jewish side. Then there was the police Criminal Investigation Department, MI5, MI6, and covert intelligence teams with a question mark, for the British.

A lot of names and organizations with, sadly, very few arrows linking them. It summed up what we were up against and what little we had to show for our efforts.

"Have you heard anything about last night's bombing on the news?" I asked.

She shook her head. "So far, no one's claimed responsibility. But it does resemble bombings done by Irgun or Lehi."

"That's what everyone says about the one that nearly killed Laura. But I'm not convinced."

Atkinson returned a noncommittal grunt.

"A strange thing happened after the bombing last night. All the police squad cars and motorcycles rushed toward the site, but DCI Gilman's car went in the opposite direction."

"You don't know his intention. It could have been for a number of reasons."

"Maybe, but the British connections in all this have me thinking. The Brit in Arab gear in Jaffa, who's also in one of Laura's photos, and Laura spotting a British officer arriving in the village. And what is Nicholas's story? I get the impression he and his group aren't on the same page as the rest of the British forces."

"More questions than answers."

I stepped into the living room, pulled on my jacket, and grabbed up my backpack.

"You just got back," Atkinson said, following me into the room. "Where are you going, now?"

"I can't sit around here, waiting for someone to show up with answers. I've got to shake some trees."

"Then I'm coming with you."

"No, not this time. I don't know if I'm walking into a hornet's nest or not."

I charged out the door before Atkinson could object.

THE KIRYAT ANAVIM KIBBUTZ LAY IN A DEPRESSION IN THE JUDEAN Hills and was bounded by dusty prominences on three sides, with the north butting up against high ground covered with stubby pine trees. The road curved up a rocky slope—usually difficult land to farm, but I passed vineyards and orchards before coming upon a complex of single-story buildings, two large processing plants, and a handful of storage sheds.

I parked Atkinson's car at the base of the settlement and got out. I stashed the backpack and my weapons in the trunk, then stood by the hood with my hand over my eyes to block the sun. I waited.

A large group of children gathered to look at me from a safe distance. The youngest ones smiled, seemingly excited to see a visitor, while the older ones regarded me warily. Four men with rifles eased the children aside and approached me. They descended the rocky path while remaining vigilant and stopped thirty feet from the car.

I greeted them with a "*Shalom*," one of the few words I'd picked up during the trek in Italy and the ship.

A middle-aged man, whom I took to be the leader, returned the greeting, then started talking in Hebrew.

I waved my hand. "That's all the Hebrew I've got."

"What do you want?" the leader asked in English with a thick accent.

"I'm a friend of Arie Feldman, and I wanted to say hi."

"We don't know this person," the leader said.

"Yamin," a man said behind the group.

The men parted, and Feldman stepped forward. He stared at me a moment, then motioned me forward. "Come on." He and the leader exchanged a few words in Hebrew. Whatever Feldman said caused the others to relax and disperse.

"It was very unwise to come here," Feldman said to me.

"I didn't have another choice. I need your help."

He pointed his index finger at me and hissed, "Not a word about working with the police."

We strolled up the path. There was a group of men and women digging a large hole. There were bags of concrete mix piled nearby.

"Wine cellar?" I asked facetiously.

Feldman smiled. "A bomb shelter. War will come. It's only a matter of time, and most of the kibbutzim are preparing. Trenches and barbwire fences are planned, but the British do not take kindly to us actually constructing such things."

"How is the training coming?"

"Good. The people are motivated. They'll get there."

We entered the complex. Feldman introduced me to a few of the residents, men and women. Once they heard of my help smuggling fellow refugees through Italy and accompanying them on the *Magen David*, they relaxed, and I seemed to be accepted.

"Where is your sister?" I asked. "I'd like to meet her."

"Unfortunately, she's working in our orange groves some distance from here."

In a circle of grass, two women were conducting an outdoor class for the children. Others worked in the vineyards or constructed more housing. They would look my way, then go back to what they were doing.

Feldman quickly guided me to a single-story rectangular building. Inside was a large space filled with cots separated by curtains. Clothes hung from lines suspended between walls at the far end. The occupants were elsewhere, leaving us alone.

Feldman stopped a few yards and turned to me. "What do you want?"

"Did you know about the bomb going off south of the Old City last night?"

"Is that why you came here? To ask that? It had nothing to do with us."

"No. I came here for help, Arie."

"Then you have a strange way of asking. And I heard about your escapade in Jaffa."

The door opened, and two men entered. They wore grim expressions as they came up to us. Feldman seemed to shrink, though he tried to maintain his aggressive stance. They were both older and had that walk that said they were in charge.

"Are you going to introduce me to your friends?" I asked Feldman.

"They are the leaders of the kibbutz. That's all you need to know."

"Then I can ask them about giving me some assistance."

The two other men remained silent. I didn't know whether this was a test of my usefulness or they were simply there to kill me. I went with the former and told them about Jaffa. How I'd heard from a source that the Black Hand was holed up there, and I went to see if I could ferret them out or question one of them. Keeping my eyes on Feldman, I recounted my encounter with one of them in the streets of the old part of town and discovered the man was a Brit, identified by his tattoos, and being in one of the photographs Laura had taken in the village of Alal. That he had to have been trained by one of the British commando units like the Special Operations Executive or Special Air Service.

"That's not the first clue I've uncovered of Brit involvement. Something's going on, and I want to find out what it is. I'm beginning to believe it leads back to the bombing that nearly killed Laura."

All three of them were stunned to silence. Feldman glanced at them as if asking what to do next.

"My name is Joshua," the oldest of the two leaders said. "There were Palestinians who joined the British Army during the war."

"Tattoos are *haram*," Feldman said to Joshua. "Tattoos are forbidden for Muslims as they are for Jews," he said to me for clarification.

"And I bet there were few if any Palestinians admitted into the commandos brigade, the SOE, or SAS," I said. "I'm sure there are light-skinned Arabs, but when I tore off his shirt, his skin was as pale as mine below the tan line."

"There are Brits and Arabs who have intermarried," Joshua said.

I nodded. "The woman assassin who attacked me and was involved in the bomb planted on the *Magen David* is half Syrian and half British. But my gut instinct tells me there's more to this than mixed offspring, and you guys are trying to find an excuse to explain it all away. Or are you holding out on me?"

I reached into my coat, which made the two leaders go for something underneath theirs, presumably weapons. When I slowly pulled out the photograph, the two stopped and removed their hands. I held it out for Feldman, who took it and showed it to the two men.

"You see the group of men behind the Arab woman? Second from the left. That's the guy I fought off yesterday."

Joshua shook his head. "I don't recognize—" He stopped when his eyes shifted to another spot on the photograph.

The other man saw it, too, and they exchanged looks.

"What is it?" I asked.

"The man you fought with is unknown to us, but we are familiar with the one standing next to him."

Feldman looked it and said, "Are you sure? He's wearing a *keffiyeh*."

"I'm sure," Joshua said. "During the war, we worked closely with British intelligence. This man, Frank Hadley, was an MI6 agent. Counterintelligence for North Africa and the Middle East bureau. He was a fanatic and hated the Nazis only slightly more than Jews. We were warned to steer clear of him, and we happily complied."

"What's he doing with the Black Hand?" Feldman asked more to himself.

"That's what I'd like to find out," I said. "What are any of them doing posing as Arabs? What are they up to? Who's leading them?"

"Can we keep this?" Joshua asked.

I nodded. "I have a couple more copies."

He pocketed the photo. "We will share what we have to help you, though as far as I know, we don't have anything current on this group. Our intelligence units are very good, but this news is surprising."

"It's unsettling is what it is," Feldman said.

Joshua glanced at his companion and turned back to me. "We offer this to you on the condition that you share what you have with us, naturally."

"Naturally," I said. "But I have to ask …" I glanced at Feldman, whose eyes widened with apprehension.

"Go on," Joshua said.

"You may or not know that the bombing at the checkpoint

three days ago put my fiancée in a coma and killed my unborn child."

"We had nothing to do with that bombing," Joshua said with anger in his voice.

"Who did, then?" I asked.

"We don't know."

"If you did, would you tell me?"

"It would depend."

"Meaning if it was Irgun, you wouldn't."

Joshua glanced at his partner again. "I mean it when I say we don't know."

"You have to understand why I won't stop until I find out."

"And you have to understand that you may die before that happens," Joshua said.

I had nothing to counter that and remained silent.

After a moment, Joshua said, "You are welcome to play with fire as long as it doesn't affect Haganah. Is that clear? If your continued search for the culprits affords you new intelligence, then we would be happy to receive such information. In exchange, we'll pass on what we learn about the bombing incident."

"Do you have anything on Nadia Chamberlin? She also goes by the name of Nadia Yassin al-Katib."

"This is the woman assassin?" the second leader asked.

I nodded. "I saw her the day of the checkpoint bombing, just moments before it went off. She could be the key to finding out what's going on with the Brits and the Black Hand."

"Do you have a photo of her?" Feldman asked.

"Only a sketch," I said and pulled out a folded piece of paper with Nadia's portrait. I handed it to Feldman. "It gives you a general idea of her appearance, but it's not the same as a good photograph."

Feldman passed the sketch to the two leaders, who both shook their heads.

Joshua said, "I'm afraid we don't know this individual. But we'd like to keep this as well. We can pass them on to our networks."

The looks in their eyes told me they were holding something back. I didn't expect them to spill everything, and demanding additional information at that moment might ruin the fragile alliance.

"Of course," I said. "I just hope your associates can come up with something quick. I have a feeling that whatever's being planned is going to happen sooner rather than later."

28

The police had thrown up roadblocks throughout Jerusalem, and every time I was held up for an ID check, it reminded me of the bombing at the checkpoint with Laura, and an additional knot would form in my stomach. Another cop patrol stopped me while walking from the parking lot back to Atkinson's apartment. I constantly checked for a tail and had to fight against the impression that there were eyes at every window. Foot and motor traffic had increased since that morning, but it was still less than usual.

I was in deep thought as I climbed the stairs to Atkinson's apartment, and it was only by chance that I noticed the door to her place was slightly ajar. I froze and visually checked the landing and hallway. No one lurked in the corners. The only sounds came from the street.

I lowered my backpack as quietly as I could, retrieved my pistol, and pulled back the slide to load a round. I got out a spare magazine and put that in my back pocket. The brass knuckles and knife had shifted to the bottom. Finding them would take too much time.

I hugged the wall with my .45 at the ready and listened. I

worried that I was too late, that whoever had broken in had already come and gone, leaving Atkinson dead on the floor.

Leading with the gun barrel, I advanced one slow step at a time. Using the doorjamb as cover, I kicked open the door. Still no sound from inside. I scanned the section of the room visible through the open doorway. Atkinson's books, knickknacks, even the pictures on the walls were tossed haphazardly on the floor.

There was little in the way of cover. A good ten feet of open space lay between the door and the furniture. Halfway into the room, the wall ended, with the dining room beyond. A good spot for someone to lie in wait. I had to figure there was more than one intruder, and the optimal place for a second shooter would be on the opposite side of the room and hidden by the open door.

I took aim and fired three rounds at the wall just a few inches from the dining room's doorframe.

Someone cried out in pain and pivoted around with his gun up. He fired several rounds at me, but they were off the mark. I hit him one more time in the chest, and he went down.

The wood of the door next to my head exploded from three rounds fired from somewhere on the opposite side of the room.

I squatted down, avoiding several more bullets. Within the same movement, I thrust myself into the room while aiming in the direction of the shots.

A man was standing near the front corner. He fired at me as I dropped to the floor. But his aim was too high. I fired at him over the back of a chair and saw a small chunk of his left shoulder splatter on the wall behind him.

He screamed in pain but managed to duck behind the chair. I took aim through the gap between the bottom of the chair and the floor. He lay there, holding his shoulder and grunting in pain.

I whistled, and he looked my way. With my gun pointed at his head, he dropped his gun and extended his fingers.

Staying low, I rushed over to him and threw his gun across the room. He appeared to be in shock from the wound. I lifted him to his feet by the lapels of his jacket, causing him to cry out in agony. I forced him forward, using him as a shield, and quickly cleared the rest of the apartment. Much to my relief, Atkinson was nowhere to be found.

I stopped the wounded man beside the dead one and forced him to lie on the floor, facedown. He grunted and huffed when I put a knee on his back.

The dead shooter's head was turned away from me, and I moved it to see his face. It was the guy I'd fought with in Jaffa. I searched his body for an ID, thinking he wouldn't be able to get through the constant police patrols without one, but again, he had nothing on him except for a key and a spare magazine for his Browning Hi-Power pistol—one of the favored pistols used by British commando units.

I tore open his shirt to get a closer look at his tattoos. What I'd thought was a regimental tattoo was the emblem for the Royal Marines. A former British commando for sure.

I turned the second shooter over onto his back. I'd seen that face before. I pulled out the photo and spotted the man standing with his buddies in the village. I held it near his face. "This is you, isn't it?"

He clamped his mouth shut and tried to look away.

I squeezed his wound, digging my fingers into the bullet hole. He screamed.

"You're Black Hand, aren't you?"

"I don't know what you're talking about."

I squeezed harder. He writhed as he groaned. I let off the pressure. "Are you Black Hand?"

"Yes!"

"Who recruited you and the others to pose as Arabs?"

I made the motions to squeeze his wound again, prompting him to yell, "Wait! Wait!"

"Who's behind this?"

"I don't know. My mate convinced me to join. I've never seen the leader. I swear. Please, I'll bleed out if you don't get me to a hospital."

"Maybe. If you answer my questions. What's your plan?"

He clamped his mouth shut and panted in anticipation of what was to come.

I accommodated him. I pressed down on his nose and mouth with my left hand and jammed my thumb into the wound and twisted. His muffled screams coincided with kicks. He tried swatting at my hands, but his damaged shoulder prevented him from doing much.

I kept up the pressure until he appeared to be on the brink of passing out. I removed my hand from his mouth and retracted my thumb.

"What is your plan? Why are you posing as Arabs?"

His eyes struggled to focus, and he formed a crooked smile. "You're too late, chum. Everything's in place."

I shook him, but the shock was taking over his consciousness. "What's in place. What is your group planning to do?"

"Light up the sky. What causes the greatest pain to your Jew friends. They won't know what hit them."

Heavy footsteps came racing up the stairs. A half dozen or more, by the sound of it.

"Police!" several yelled as they burst into the room with their guns aimed at me.

I dropped my .45 to the floor and raised my hands.

29

The interview room wasn't much bigger than a broom closet. There was the ubiquitous rectangular table bolted to the floor, three chairs, a caged lamp hanging from the ceiling, and a square mirror that I assumed was two-way for observation. A fan sat on the table, but it was motionless, leaving the room stiflingly hot.

I figured the heat and lack of oxygen was a way to wear me down. I'd already spent what I guessed was about two hours handcuffed to the table. Sweat poured down my face and back, but I was too wound up for the discomfort to get to me.

The door opened, letting in a brief wave of cool, fresh air before someone closed it. I faced opposite the door, and my gaze remained fixed on the mirror.

A plainclothes, middle-aged man came around the table.

"I'll only speak to DCI Gilman," I said.

The man sat with a huff and slammed a file on the table. "You get me. I'm Detective Inspector Bennett."

"Gilman."

Bennett leaned on the table and glared at me. "You're in a lot of trouble, boyo. Murderers don't get to dictate terms."

I said nothing.

"What were you doing at Mrs. Atkinson's apartment?"

"Gilman."

"Were you there to rob the place, and your chums turned on you?"

"Gilman."

"I advise you to cooperate, or it's the hangman's noose for you."

With each question or statement, I simply said, "Gilman." And each time I did that, the inspector got hotter under the collar. The heat in the room didn't help. I knew he might go on for some time, thinking at some point he could break me or apply some muscle to my torso. I didn't have time to wait him out.

"Are you deaf as well as dumb?" I said. "I bet they reached into the bottom of the barrel to get you."

Bennett's face turned red. He stood, stomped over to me, and slammed his ham of a fist into my jaw. My ears rang, and my head swam. Through my blurred vision, I could see him winding up for another blow.

"Inspector!" someone shouted from the door.

Bennett's roundhouse froze in mid-delivery.

"Leave immediately," the man behind me said.

I recognized the voice. It was Gilman. That seemed to make Bennett even more furious. He remained in the same position and glared at me, as if to say that he would get his revenge soon enough.

"Inspector Bennett!"

The inspector straightened and walked out of the room.

When the door closed, Gilman stuck his face in mine. "If I get the slightest hint that you're uncooperative with me, I'll put you in a room with Bennett, along with several other DIs, and throw away the key."

Satisfied by my silence, Gilman went around the table and sat. "Explain yourself."

"First, is Mrs. Atkinson all right?"

"I'm the one asking the questions. But I'll give you this one: yes, she's fine. She happened to be out at the time."

"Thanks. I've been staying with her. She's a good lady, and I'd hate to think something bad happened to her."

I glanced at the two-way mirror as I massaged my jaw.

"No one is listening, if that's what concerns you," Gilman said.

"Good. 'Cause this information is only for you."

"Where were you before the shooting?"

"I went to see a friend."

Gilman looked annoyed at the vagueness, but he continued. "And you went back to the apartment and found those two men?" Gilman asked.

"Yes. And they weren't there for a friendly chat. They had set up an ambush. Both shootings were in self-defense."

"What were they looking for?"

"The only thing I can think of is Laura's papers and photos."

Gilman raised his eyebrows. "This is the first I've heard you were in possession of potential evidence."

"The only bit that's relevant is about the Black Hand, which I passed on to you."

"You will turn those documents over to me."

"Okay, but you have to know that a lot of people want to get their hands on that stuff. It should be for your eyes only. I don't know who's involved."

"Involved in what?"

"I don't know. A conspiracy of some kind."

"A conspiracy? Perhaps the bombing gave *you* a concussion."

"Look, I know that three of the Black Hand are former British commandos. They're posing as Arabs for some reason. They tried to kill me, and they're after something in Laura's papers. Something Atkinson and I were unable to find."

Gilman drew something out of his tunic pocket and put it in

front of me. It was a blown-up version of the photograph I'd been carrying around of the Black Hand. "Point them out."

I tapped my index finger on one of them. "That's the guy who your constables found dead in the apartment. He attacked me in Jaffa—" I held up my hand to stop Gilman from asking. "I'll get to that in a moment." Gilman didn't protest, so I continued. "I saw Arie Feldman yesterday." I pointed to the next man in the photo. "One of his Haganah buddies recognized that guy and said he knew that man as British intelligence during the war." I moved my finger on the image. "And this one is who I wounded and, I assume, you have in custody."

Gilman stared at the photo. Blood had drained from his face.

"Now you see why I only wanted to speak to you," I said. "Have you gotten anything out of the wounded shooter?"

Gilman shook his head. "He's still in surgery. He lost a great deal of blood. I don't expect he'll be talking anytime soon." He leaned back and folded his hands in his lap. "You told me that, in Jaffa, the man only intended to rob you."

"I lied. I didn't know who to trust. And I still don't trust you."

"Understandable. But now you have no choice. Not if you want to avoid prison."

I told him about following the teenage "guide," only to be attacked by the now-dead Brit. That during the fight, I tore his shirt and spotted the Royal Marines tattoo along with one of the crucifix and crown of thorns. "He spoke only Arabic until I persuaded him with the tip of my knife. But once I was surrounded by an angry mob, I didn't have a chance to get anything else out of him."

"I assume the source who gave you the Black Hand's location also told you that your woman assassin is half British."

I said nothing.

Gilman smiled. "Protect your sources. Once a cop, always a cop, hey?"

I shrugged. "What about the bombing last night? Who's responsible?"

"Irgun is the most likely suspect."

"So, once again, you don't know."

"Often, if it's a civilian target, the Irgun will spread the word for civilians to avoid the area."

"But not this time."

Gilman shook his head.

"You said it was a civilian target. But I saw wounded police and soldiers at the Italian Hospital."

"It was an area with restaurants and bars. It's been known to happen, but Irgun usually goes after police and military installations, infrastructure. Not civilians."

"Then it could be some other entity."

Gilman rubbed his face and nodded.

"What are you going to do about this?"

"You must know this all sounds rather implausible. Nonetheless, I'll look into it."

"Whoever's behind this seems to have friends in high places, including the military or police. Or both. If I were you, I'd watch my back."

Gilman fell silent and lit a cigarette. He offered me one, and I took it. As he lit my cigarette, he tried to maintain a neutral expression, but I noticed a tick of worry cross his face. I took that as a good sign; he wouldn't be worried if he was involved. At least that was my thinking.

I wanted to ask him about driving off in the opposite direction from the bombing last night, but I'd leave that for another time. I needed to see what he might do with this new information. Either he'd turn around and pass it on, in which case my days were numbered, or he'd use the resources I didn't have to probe the halls of power.

Gilman exhaled a cloud of smoke and picked a piece of tobacco off the tip of his tongue. "I'm going to let you out on bail, but on a short leash, and until such time as the court summons you for a hearing. You know what I expect in return. See that you fulfill that obligation, or the Black Hand will be the least of your worries."

He tossed his spent cigarette onto the floor and stubbed it out. He rose and leaned on the table with both hands, getting close to me. "Oh, by the way," he said softly, "it was Wetherbee who ordered Mrs. Atkinson's apartment be searched. Follow your own advice and tread carefully out there."

He straightened and walked out of the room.

30

E velyn Atkinson was sitting by Laura when I entered the hospital room. She shot up from her chair and rushed over and hugged me. "Thank God, you're out. I'm scared, Mason." She released me and took a step back while avoiding looking at me. "Sorry. I was terrified when I went back to my apartment and saw everything tossed and blood on the floor."

"Don't worry about it. I needed that hug."

She gave me a quick smile and returned to the chair. That was when I noticed that Laura's eyes were open. I stepped up to the bed and bent over her, but her eyes didn't register my presence.

Atkinson said, "According to the nurse, she started doing that a few hours ago. She seemed to respond to my hand moving over her face, but then stopped."

"Did the nurse say she's getting better?"

"She said—rather dryly—that it merits cautious optimism, but that the movements could be involuntary. At least some part of her brain is on the mend."

"I'll take it as a good sign."

"I hope she recovers soon. The doctors say that the longer she's under, the more difficult it will be for her to get back to the way things were. The greater the danger of brain damage. By all means, you should be hopeful, but you also need to prepare yourself for … disappointment."

Atkinson tilted her head toward the rolling tray near Laura's bed. "Speaking of good or bad news, there's something on that table you might want to read."

I picked up the folded piece of paper. It was a Western Union telegram, with a sender's address of London, to the Italian Hospital and addressed to Laura. "*Darling I am coming. Father tied up in Quebec. Be there tomorrow evening. Mother.*"

"Have you ever met her parents?" Atkinson asked.

"No. The first time I talked to her mother was the day Laura was admitted. It was brief but long enough to hear the disappointment and hostility in her voice."

"Oh, stop whining. She'll be good for Laura."

I opened my mouth to argue, but Atkinson was right. Anything that could help Laura, I was all for, but her mother's presence would complicate things.

I got a chair from the hallway and placed it opposite Atkinson. I dropped my backpack on the floor and sat close to Laura.

"Were the police hard on you?" she asked.

"Tolerable enough." I made a motion to stand. "I need some coffee. Care to join me?"

We stood and walked out of the room. The cafeteria was on the ground floor. It was after nine p.m., but there were still a handful of people finishing dinner or having beverages. I got a cup of thick, black coffee, and Atkinson made a cup of tea. We found a quiet corner and sat.

We both lit up cigarettes and scanned the room for anyone too close for comfort.

Satisfied, I said, "Did they get the documents?"

"I hid them shortly after you left. I had an odd feeling they were vulnerable."

"I'm glad you listened to your odd feelings."

"They're tucked away in an unused portion of the boiler room in my building. I couldn't risk walking out with an armful of boxes."

"DCI Gilman is demanding that I hand them over."

"Gilman? How does he know about them?"

"Me," I said and held up my hand to stop her from scolding me. "He's the only reason I'm not behind bars. I had to confide in someone, so I told him that the intruders were after Laura's papers. I said I'd already passed anything important on to him, but he insisted. And apparently, someone else is very interested in them too. Gilman said Detective Superintendent Wetherbee ordered your apartment get tossed."

Atkinson's eyes widened in surprise. "How did he know where they were?"

"Beats me."

"Is there something we missed? Is there information in those papers that could implicate him?"

"All good questions. Gilman's going to sniff around to see what he can come up with inside the police force. One thing's for sure: the deeper we go, the more Brits pop up on the radar."

"I was scared before," Atkinson said. "But now I'm terrified."

AS WE WALKED BACK TO LAURA'S ROOM FROM THE CAFETERIA, I scanned the faces of those we passed in the hallways and nurses' stations, and I noticed that Atkinson was doing the same. I had no doubt there were informants working for all three sides, or even plants who might have taken the place of regular nurses and orderlies. Atkinson's nervousness emanated from her like a radiator.

"I wouldn't blame you if you called it quits," I said.

"You'd have to be out of your mind not to be at least a little frightened."

"I am out of my mind, and I'm terrified."

"Then don't ever patronize me like that again."

We walked into Laura's room. My heart kicked up to high gear when I saw a man in a tarboosh with almond-colored skin leaning over Laura. In two steps, I was on him. I grabbed him by the shoulders and slammed him against the wall. The man's tarboosh tumbled to the ground. His eyes were wide with fear. He wore a three-piece suit and glasses that were perched on his nose.

"What are doing? Who are you?"

"I was examining her. I meant no harm."

"Examining? Are you a doctor?"

"Yes," the man said, though I detected some hesitancy in speaking.

"I've never seen you on this floor," I said and looked to Atkinson.

"Neither have I," Atkinson said.

I pulled him away from the wall, then slammed him into it again. "Start talking."

"I came here with a message for you, but while I waited, I decided to check the patient."

I kept the man pinned but eased the pressure on his shoulders. "I'm listening."

"A ... a mutual friend would like to see you." He glanced toward the door as if afraid someone might be listening. "He met you at a café in the Old City."

As far as I knew, no one was aware of our meeting with Nicholas. That made me think the guy was legitimate, but I wasn't taking any chances. "You're taking us there." I released him.

"I'm to follow a specific set of instructions," the man said as he straightened his suit coat. "The man is very careful, and any deviation on my part will cost me dearly."

"Your instructions have just changed," I said and pointed toward the door.

I didn't relax until we passed through the gauntlet of security and exited the hospital. I'd half expected the doctor to plead for help from the guards, but he remained silent.

We followed the doctor to the left and up the hill. The street immediately narrowed, leaving just enough space for a single car to pass. Most of the two-story buildings' façades were of limestone, giving them an ancient look, though the majority were less than twenty years old. The street was dark and only lit from the windows of the houses and apartments.

"Do you work for Nicholas?" Atkinson asked the doctor.

"I've given aid to a few of his colleagues."

Which, to me, meant that he'd treated wounds off the record books and that Nicholas and his buddies had truly gone underground. And I wondered if that was a good thing or a bad one.

Ten minutes into our walk, the doctor stopped at an alleyway and pointed. "He said to go down that alley, and he will direct you from there."

Both sides were lined with junk, discarded car parts, and trashcans, and the only light came from the streetlamp behind us. A dark alley was a great place for an ambush.

31

I pulled the backpack off one shoulder, removed my .45, and said to the doctor, "You're coming with us."

"But that is against his wishes."

I belted the pistol. "His wish but my command." I pointed toward the alley.

He did what he was told, and I made sure he was in the lead. The doctor walked with cautious steps, and he rubbed his hands. He glanced from side to side as if expecting someone to come leaping out at him.

I laid my right hand on the pistol grip and watched for movement in the shadows.

Halfway down the alley, a shadow swept across us created by the streetlamp behind us. I spun around. A man in silhouette stood at the entrance to the alley.

"Mason!" Atkinson hissed.

I turned and saw another man stationed at the other end. Then a third man came into view behind him.

I pulled out my gun. At the same time, I pushed Atkinson and the doctor into the trash cans. "Get down."

The man behind us got off the first shot. The round splintered brick by my head. I dived in between two trash cans. Bullets struck the cans in front and behind and ricocheted around us like angry bees. The darkness was the only thing that kept the shooters from being more accurate. But it was just a matter of time before one of them found their target.

I fired at the man in the entrance to the alley. The sound was deafening in the narrow space. He ducked behind the stone wall. I turned and fired at the other two. They, too, dived behind the corners of the buildings.

I wouldn't be able to hold them off indefinitely. The two behind me fired to keep me pinned. I knew that was to give the solitary man cover to advance.

I took aim at where one of the two shooters poked his head out to fire then pulled back behind the building. I waited. He popped his head out. I fired. The big .45 round smashed into the limestone façade and splintered in his face.

That shooter grabbed his eyes and stumbled backward and behind the building.

The clang of metal in the trash can behind me was followed by a burning sensation in my side. It was like someone had stuck me with a hot poker.

I swung around to the single shooter. Emboldened by the cover fire from his partners, he was a few feet into the alley. I fired and must have hit him in the shoulder, because he cried out, dropped his pistol, and dived behind the building.

I turned back to the last man of the pair. We fired at the same time.

The bullet hit my pistol, and my hand felt like a hammer had smashed my fingers. I lost control of the gun. The remaining shooter took a few paces forward, aiming his pistol directly at me.

Then the man spun on his heels. A tall figure in silhouette popped out of nowhere, grabbed the shooter's head and twisted. The man collapsed to the ground.

The stranger came running up to us. I felt for my knife tucked in my boot, but I stopped when I recognized the athletic gait.

It was Nicholas.

I jumped to my feet. The numbness in my side turned to a burning pain, and I had a hard time keeping my balance. "Evelyn, are you all right?"

"No, I'm not all right!" she said as Nicholas helped her to stand. "But I'm not hurt."

While I retrieved my pistol, Nicholas helped the doctor. He held his head and was unsteady on his feet.

"I hit my head on the brick when I fell," the doctor said.

"Let's go as quick as we can," Nicholas said. "The police will descend on this place in moments."

My head spun, and Atkinson helped steady me.

"Are you hurt?" she asked.

"Just woozy."

We all moved toward the end of the alley. When we exited, I saw the man I'd blinded crumpled on the ground. His partner lay next to him. Both of their heads were twisted at odd angles, their necks snapped. Atkinson let out a soft yelp and held me tighter.

We turned left, then right, and followed a narrow street lined with stone walls and intersected by alleyways. As we began to descend a small hill, police sirens sounded in the near distance. That prompted us to increase our speed despite my vertigo and the doctor's wobbling gait.

Halfway down the hill, the road squeezed into a single lane with sidewalks a couple of feet wide, forcing us to rush down the middle of the road. If a police squad car approached, there was nowhere to hide.

Fortunately, we went only a few yards before Nicholas led us down a short flight of stairs to a door below street level. He pushed open the unlocked door, and we all filed into the dark interior.

Atkinson found a lamp and turned it on. We were in a small

square room with stone walls that had once been a cellar serving the single-story structure above us. A tiny kitchen sink sat in one corner, while a single-framed bed sat along the opposite wall. A toilet was situated in a back corner enclosed by a makeshift wall of spare timber and plywood.

Nicholas lowered the doctor to a ratty lounge chair facing an equally ratty sofa and a square wooden table with three chairs.

Atkinson sucked in her breath when she looked down at my shirt. Blood had soaked my left side. A chunk of my shirt was missing and exposed my bloody skin underneath.

"It's just a scratch," I said to her. "The trashcan absorbed most of the punch."

"Take off your shirt, and we'll clean it out," Atkinson said and went to the sink.

I sat on one of the wooden chairs around a small dining table. My head had stopped spinning, and pain around the wound had diminished to a dull throb.

Nicholas retrieved a case behind a curtain that covered some shelving. He returned to the doctor and began dabbing at the man's blood.

"I'm sorry for my ghastly appearance, madam," the doctor said to Atkinson.

"Nothing I haven't seen before. What's your name?"

"Amin Salameh," the doctor said through grunts as Nicholas put a new rag to his head.

Atkinson returned with a damp towel and scissors. She cut open the shirt and helped me remove it. "Good God," she said when seeing the numerous scars on my torso I'd acquired over the years.

"Every one of these has a little story," I said.

She grimaced. "Some other time." She began wiping blood from the wound. "The bullet grazed your rib cage. I don't think it broke anything, but you'll have some bruised ribs. And it needs to be stitched up."

"I'll take care of him once I'm done with Amin," Nicholas said. He stopped what he was doing. "But first things first."

Nicholas went over to the same curtain-covered shelves and pulled out a bottle of scotch along with three glasses. He poured the alcohol into the glasses and brought them over to Atkinson and me. "You need this as much as a bandage."

We clinked glasses and drank. I finished mine, and the alcohol immediately helped wash away the lingering shock. He poured another one for me and went back to tending to the doctor.

"At first, I thought it was you who'd set up that ambush," I said to Nicholas.

"And I had a passing thought that they were there for me. It wasn't until they started shooting that I realized they were after you."

"Well, you wanted us to be the bait."

"Yes, but it's not what I expected."

"What *did* you expect?"

Nicholas said nothing.

"Do you think they were Black Hand?" Atkinson asked.

"I didn't get a good look at them," Nicholas said.

"Neither did I," I said. "But if these guys were part of the Black Hand, they weren't trained in special forces."

"My thoughts exactly. They were essentially firing at each other from both ends of the alley. And luckily for you three, they weren't particularly good shots."

"Perhaps they were desperate, or not planning for Mason to shoot back," Atkinson said.

"That mistake just illustrates our point," Nicholas said.

Atkinson pressed the towel against my wound. "The question remains: Who were they? The one I saw on the ground was White."

Nicholas began shaving the doctor's hair around the gash on his head. "The one that got away was, too."

I caught Nicholas's eye and glanced at the doctor.

"We can speak freely in front of Amin," Nicholas said. "I trust him implicitly."

Salameh made a gesture with his hands. "Thank you, Nicholas."

"Do you think they were Irgun or Haganah?" Atkinson asked.

My head threatened to spin again, so I took another swig. "They've had better opportunities to kill us. And I don't see what that would accomplish."

"Then who else?" she asked, her voice rising an octave.

I hesitated to say it. I even hesitated to think it. "Assuming they weren't Black Hand operatives, probably hired guns or undercover cops."

Nicholas looked at me, and I returned his gaze—a shared moment of dread. The list of those who wanted Atkinson and me dead had just grown. I could tell Atkinson was disturbed by the idea, though she tried to hide it with a resolute expression.

"We have to assume that the hospital is being watched," I said. "That's the only place those shooters could have picked up our trail."

Salameh groaned as Nicholas began stitching up the gash at the back of his skull.

"Nothing for the pain?" Atkinson asked Salameh while cringing.

"Amin doesn't believe in pain medication," Nicholas said.

"This is the third time he has closed a wound for me," Salameh said.

Nicholas tied off the thread and dropped the needle into a metal tray. "He's stitched up his share of wounds for me." He grabbed up the first aid kit and came toward me. "Now, to take care of you."

The man had said that with such a self-satisfied smile on his face that I instinctively pushed back into my chair. He knelt on the floor to better examine the wound.

"I hate to waste good scotch—" Nicholas stopped and splashed the rest of his drink on the wound.

It stung like fire, but I wouldn't satisfy him with a grimace of pain.

"We'll have you fixed up in no time."

While Nicholas prepared the surgical needle and thread, I said, "The Black Hand members are British operatives. All ex-special forces. But you knew that, right?"

Instead of answering, Nicholas plunged the needle into my flesh.

"From that jab, I'll take that as a yes," I said. "But those shooters tonight weren't. The Black Hand has to be taking orders from someone. Who is it?"

Nicholas pulled the thread through and stuck me again. "I don't know, exactly."

My voice went an octave higher following that jab. "What does *exactly* mean?"

"Despite a majority in the U.K. wanting to back out of the troubles here, there are some in the government and military who don't want to give up a strategic position like Palestine. Especially after losing control of Transjordan and Iraq."

"Are you one of them?" Atkinson asked.

"No."

"Are you saying that those opposed to pulling out of Palestine are behind the Black Hand?"

"Among others."

"There's more than one?" Atkinson said with alarm.

"I don't know if there are other groups or if the Black Hand is comprised of individual cells. But they seem to have one goal, and that is to create chaos and incite violence between the British, Arabs, and Jews. Several UN delegates with the investigative committee on the partitioning of Palestine are coming. What they find out and report back to the UN body will determine what the UN's recommendation is for the Palestine issue."

"In other words, if it all blows up around them, partitioning could be off the table," I said.

"That's one goal. Right now, global sympathy for the Jews is high, but if it's seen that the Jewish groups—or it appears that the Jewish groups—are committing terrible acts of violence, then the British government would have little choice but to continue their presence here."

"The little bit I got out of the wounded Black Hand member—"

"Wait," Nicholas said, interrupting. "What wounded Black Hand member?"

I told Nicholas about returning to Atkinson's apartment and finding the place ransacked and two shooters waiting in ambush.

"What were they looking for?"

"They weren't looking for anything. They were there to kill me."

"Then who ransacked the apartment?"

"Detective Superintendent Wetherbee ordered the place to be searched."

"The CID?"

"One would assume," Atkinson said, "but it could have been someone Wetherbee paid to do the break-in. The point is, they were looking for something in Laura Talbot's papers. But for the life of me, I can't imagine what's in there that's so important."

"Something you've overlooked, obviously," Nicholas said and turned to me. "Did you get anything out of the wounded shooter?"

"The police showed up before I got much out of him. I did get him to admit he's part of the Black Hand. And when I pressed him even further, he said I was too late. Everything's in place. When I asked him their plan, he said, 'to light up the sky.' That Palestine, the Jews, won't know what hit them."

That stunned everyone to silence. Nicholas betrayed nothing of his thoughts and patiently finished applying a bandage to the fresh sutures on my torso. Finally, he said, "Then we have far less time than I thought. Reports are that *Palestinians* set off the bomb near the Old City."

"They weren't Palestinians," Salameh said. "I would know."

"Dr. Salameh is our lead man in Palestinian affairs," Nicholas said to Atkinson and me. "I suspect the bombing at the checkpoint was just a rehearsal for the Black Hand. The bombing near the Old City is the first in a series against Jews and Arabs. This is just the beginning."

Silence fell on the room again. A Jeep passed on the street above. Two people were having a lively discussion in Arabic that was playing out from a radio in the distance.

"What's next?" Atkinson asked.

"First we have to find a place to stay," I said to her. "Your apartment isn't safe."

"You two should stay here," Nicholas said. "At least for the night."

Atkinson looked at the single bed, then the toilet in the closet. "Out of the question."

"Madam, Salameh and I won't be staying. We have another place nearby. You'll just have to contend with Mr. Collins."

I looked at Atkinson, who didn't raise any objections to the arrangement. I nodded at Nicholas. "Evelyn and I will go get Laura's papers first thing. Then I want to have a chat with Wetherbee."

"And how do you propose to do that?" Atkinson said. "Ask the wrong question, and he'd sooner throw you in jail than tell you anything."

"I can be very persuasive."

Atkinson frowned at me as if she didn't like what she was hearing.

Nicholas packed up the first aid kit, then slipped on his jacket. "I'll be occupied most of the day, with a particularly interesting rendezvous with an asset by the Church of the Ascension on

Mount of Olives this afternoon. I'm hoping we can get a lead on this case. I should be back by nightfall and will come by here with any news."

He helped Salameh to his feet, and they headed for the door. He stopped as if remembering something, and he turned to us. "Those shooters in the alley may have simply been the first wave. They'll assume that we are somewhere in the vicinity. Even as we get closer to the truth, the circle around us is tightening. Good night and sweet dreams."

32

Atkinson and I stood against the exterior wall of her apartment building with our backs flat to the wall. A scraggly fir tree helped obscure us from view and put us in the shade from the morning sun.

Both of us studied the people and cars facing the front entrance. I pointed to a black sedan parked on the street, diagonally across from us. "There. The two guys with fedoras, trying to look like it's normal to sit in a hot car with nothing to do."

Atkinson leaned out to see. "Do you think your idea will work?"

"Let's see if we get our money's worth."

From down the street, three Palestinian men chattered among themselves as they came up the street. Their arms were burdened with bolts of cloth and leather goods.

"Get ready to make a run for it," I said.

The three merchants approached the two men in the sedan and stood in a line as they pretended to offer their wares for sale. They had effectively blocked the men's view of the apartment. The two men raised their voices, but the merchants persisted.

"Go!"

We dashed for the front entrance. I glanced to the side to see if the merchants were still there. They were, but the driver was trying to push them out of the way with his car door.

We got to the front entrance. Thankfully, it was unlocked, and we pushed through at full speed. I closed the door, then I looked out the side window. The two men in the sedan were shooing the men away as they peered at the front entrance. A moment later, they both got back in. We'd made it without being detected.

I quickly turned my attention to the interior. I had my gun, knife, and brass knuckles tucked away and ready if needed, but all seemed clear. We were in the lobby made of marble with brass trimmings. The staircase was across from us, also marble, and then an area to the left offered access to the courtyard.

I nodded toward the back of the building, and we moved swiftly to the basement door situated under the main staircase. Atkinson had her key at the ready. She unlocked it, and we slipped inside.

She flicked on the light. We were on a small landing, with concrete steps leading down. It smelled of dust that left a metallic taste in my mouth. The hum of an electrical circuit and the rush of water through pipes accompanied us as we descended the stairs.

At the bottom was a long hallway with wooden doors on either side. Numbers above indicated the storage room that matched each apartment.

Atkinson stopped and stared at an open door. The padlock had been cut and left on the floor.

"Is that yours?" I whispered.

She nodded.

I got out in front and led the way with my right hand resting on the handle of my pistol. We approached the open door and peered inside. I found a light switch to the left of the doorway and flicked it on.

Atkinson sucked in her breath at the sight of everything from old furniture to items on the shelves torn open and tossed into a heap.

"The bloody bastards," Atkinson hissed.

She started to go inside, but I held her back. "Another time. We should grab those papers and get out of here."

She groaned in frustration, switched off the light, and closed the door. She tried her best to make it look like the padlock was engaged, then shrugged at me when it just hung from the hasp.

"Come on, then," she said and moved forward.

We reached the end of the hall and stopped at a heavy door. Atkinson popped the latch, and we entered. I pulled it closed, while Atkinson yanked the cord to turn on the light.

We were in a rectangular room with a low ceiling that was crammed with water pipes and electrical conduits that converged from every floor of the building. At the far end stood the furnace and boiler with pipes heading out in several directions.

I followed Atkinson to a space behind the boiler and a recess in the stone wall. I stepped ahead of her and removed a carton from the recess.

"I'll get the bag," she said and reached in and pulled out a canvas bag. "That's everything."

We returned to the wooden door, opened it, and froze.

Hazan and two other Irgun men I recognized from the village stood in our way.

"We've been waiting for you," Hazan said.

"What do you want?" I asked.

"You know why we're here."

I put my hand at my back, near my pistol.

"I wouldn't do that," he said.

I slowly moved my hand to the front.

"Now, I'd like you to hand them over," Hazan said.

"There's nothing in these papers that concerns you."

"We'd like to see for ourselves. Your fiancée spent some time with two of our operatives. Both were killed during an attempted raid on an ammunition depot. Under very mysterious circumstances."

I took that to mean Irgun had executed them.

He continued. "They may have passed on sensitive information. Apparently, your fiancée can be very persuasive."

"Mrs. Atkinson and I have been over them a number of times, and not once was Irgun mentioned."

"If you had so many opportunities to review them, then you shouldn't mind sharing them with us. Once we're finished, we'll give them back."

"They're not leaving our hands," I said.

"You're in no position to make demands."

"How about we review them together? We have some new information that could help us look at everything with a new perspective."

Hazan glanced at his companions with a skeptical look in his eyes. "What information?"

"Something vital to your organization and Haganah. And potentially every Jew in Palestine."

He took a step toward us. "If it's that vital, we need to know."

"We get to review the material with you, and in exchange, we'll pass on what we know."

Hazan stared at me as if debating how much he could take me at my word. He shrugged. "I don't see the harm. And if the leadership decides you are too much of a liability, well, then we won't have to track you down."

Atkinson nudged me with her hand. I didn't have to ask why; she was as troubled as I was about being at the mercy of Irgun.

But the clock was ticking down, and it was time to jump off the cliff without a parachute.

33

It took two hours to get to the outskirts of Tel Aviv. One of Hazan's companions had driven a circuitous route on small roads over the brown hills, parched valleys, and then the orange groves that announced our proximity to the coast.

Hazan was in the back with us, and his other companion rode in front. Aside from Atkinson falling into her reporter routine and peppering Hazan with questions—which he refused to answer—we'd been mostly silent.

The contrast was striking between Tel Aviv's modern buildings and wide boulevards compared to its poorer and mostly Arabian neighbor of Jaffa to the south. Hazan broke his silence to tell us how Tel Aviv was begun by a small group of Jews who had built a community upon sand dunes and transformed it into a modern urban center in only four decades.

It was one of the few times I saw the man relax and even smile as he spoke. I still wanted to throttle him, but I understood what it meant to him to have a homeland and what it might take to hold on to it. I also wondered what the human cost would be in the coming months and years.

The driver pulled into a narrow street barely wide enough for the car. After passing several streets, it became apparent that we were in a tight grid of intersecting streets. Two intersections later, a man emerged from a two-story house and opened a garage door.

The driver pulled into the space and shut off the engine. We all got out and went around to the back corner, where the man escorted us through a door and into a sizable living room. All the furnishings were modern, with chrome and white leather. The kitchen had the latest appliances. Two children sat at the dining table, pencils in hand.

The man asked the children to do their homework in their bedroom. A middle-aged woman emerged from another part of the house and went into the kitchen. She wore a simple dress and a black scarf that concealed her hair. She didn't look at us or address us and prepared to make coffee.

Our host was middle-aged, and though he was no more than five foot nine, everything about him was oversized, from his facial features to his arms and his barrel-shaped chest. He waved his beefy hand toward the living room. "Please, sit. I'll be with you in a moment," he said in English with an American accent.

As if he knew what was about to happen, there was a knock at the door. He left our sight and came back with three other men, who were then followed by three more with bulges in their suit-coats. The armed men checked the room, then headed for the front door, presumably to stand guard. I figured there were more men stationed at strategic positions outside the house.

I recognized two of the three men they guarded, including the mustached leader, Mordechai, and his young, thin companion who had grilled us that day at the Palestinian village.

Mordechai gave me sly smile. "I had a very strong feeling we hadn't seen the last of you."

"Under the circumstances, I can't say I'm happy about it," I said.

The young, thin man scowled at Atkinson and me but said nothing. We all found places to sit in a circle. I laid the carton of Laura's notes next to Hazan, and Atkinson did the same with the canvas bag.

"We appreciate your cooperation," the man of the house said.

"Cooperation at gunpoint, more like it. But if it'll help, I'm fine with you looking at everything. We just want them back when you're finished."

"That depends," Hazan said. He passed the canvas bag to one of his companions, and he opened the carton. He started to hand out the files. "I thought we could save time by dividing up the material."

"I understand you have some information to pass on to us," Mordechai said.

It took me aback, and I wondered how he'd found out about my deal with Hazan made only a few hours earlier. "The Black Hand is not a group of Palestinian militants but British former special forces disguised as Palestinians. The woman assassin I'd asked you about was also a British operative during the war."

Everyone looked up from the papers they were examining.

"You know this how?" the host asked.

I told them about my encounter with the tattooed operative in Jaffa, and that he'd shown up again at Atkinson's apartment. That the other shooter with him said they would light up the sky and the Jews wouldn't know what hit them. And while I wouldn't name my source—meaning Nicholas—I told them about the faction of British men in positions of power wanting to disrupt the visit by the UN representatives. And that they wanted to make sure that global sentiment shifted away from the Jewish cause and compel Britain to maintain control of the region.

"And how do they propose to do that?" Mordechai asked.

"Set off bombs to make it look like your groups are guilty and get the Arabs to rise up. They'll choose the worst kind of targets and kill as many innocent people as possible. In all probability,

Black Hand was behind the bomb near the Old City two nights ago. According to my source, they're just getting started."

The Irgun men exchanged looks. The host and Mordechai spoke softly in Hebrew.

The host said, "For the purposes of this meeting, you may call me Ezra. Do you know where the Black Hand is now?"

"Jaffa was their last reported location, but after I encountered one of their men, I doubt they're still there. And if they set off the bomb outside the Old City, my best guess is that they're closer to Jerusalem."

"We believe they have split into several groups," Atkinson said.

Someone knocked on the door. I heard it being opened, and one of the guards talked to someone outside. A guard came into the room looking grim. He said something in Hebrew to Ezra. The others reacted in surprise.

"Haganah is here," Atkinson said to me, translating. "They want to talk."

Ezra said something to the bodyguard, then turned to us. "This man will escort you to another room. We ask you to wait patiently while we discuss the situation. I assure you, you are in no way considered prisoners in my home."

Atkinson and I stood and followed the guard across the living room. We had to pass the front door to access a hallway. I glanced at the door and had to force myself to keep going.

Feldman and Joshua—Feldman's superior from the kibbutz—stood just inside the doorway.

The guard led us down the short hallway to the second room on the right. He gestured for us to enter and closed the door behind us.

"Who was that man at the door?" Atkinson asked. "The one who you reacted to so strongly?"

"You noticed that?"

"Reporters can be as observant as detectives."

"His name is Arie Feldman. He's with Haganah. I'm not sure I could call him a friend, exactly, but I spent some time with Hazan and Arie in Italy and on the *Magen David*. We're certainly on friendlier terms than Hazan and me."

"He was with you and Laura when the bomb went off?"

"Yes, and he's the one I saw at the kibbutz. I asked for his and Haganah's help. But I think they had different plans."

Shouting from the other room prompted us to put our ears next to the door in hopes of overhearing. The shouting stopped, and even though they were speaking Hebrew, it was clear they continued a heated argument.

"It seems your Haganah friend followed us here from my apartment," Atkinson said, paraphrasing the conversation.

"The police, Irgun, Haganah. Was everyone watching your place?"

Atkinson put her finger to her lips to shush me. Usually, someone who reprimanded me like that would get a boot in their butt. But Atkinson was different, and it made me smile.

"Feldman and his companions know something consequential is brewing," Atkinson said, continuing to translate and paraphrase. "They don't want to be left in the dark." She then strained to hear and pressed her ear against the door. "Now they've moved farther away, or they're keeping their voices down."

She sucked in her breath and jumped back. A split second later I heard it too. Someone was approaching.

The door opened, and Feldman stood at the threshold. "You've certainly been busy." He glanced at Atkinson. "Who is this?"

Atkinson and I explained our relationship and connections to Laura. "I wouldn't have gotten this far without her," I said. "You can trust her. She's on our side."

"And what side is that?" Feldman asked.

"Is this some kind of test? I'm on my side, Mrs. Atkinson's side, and Laura's side. As long as Haganah and Irgun are moving in that same direction, then we're good."

"A pretty cheeky answer for someone who's at the mercy of Irgun."

"Do you want our help or not?"

A smile formed at the side of his mouth. "Direct, as always."

"What were you doing at Mrs. Atkinson's apartment? Trying to get the papers?"

"We didn't know your fiancée's papers were that important. We were there waiting for you. I assumed that was the best place to make contact." He motioned his head toward the living room. "They're waiting for us."

Atkinson and I followed Feldman down the hall and into the living room. The guards were gone, as was one of the two men who had come in with Mordechai. Mordechai's young companion had Laura's papers spread out on the dining room table and was taking photographs of each page and photo.

Our host, Ezra, sat on the sofa and had a handful of Laura's papers and photos spread out on the coffee table. "Please have a seat."

We took chairs opposite the sofa. Mordechai stood over his commander's shoulder, while Feldman and Hazan stood on opposite sides of the room.

Ezra tapped on a photo. It was one Laura had taken of two Palestinian women carrying burdens on their heads with two men standing outside a door in the background. His finger rested on one of the men, and he looked up at Mordechai. "Levi Weiss."

Mordechai seethed as he studied the photo.

Ezra slid the photo over to me. "That man was Irgun. We had suspected Levi was working for British intelligence as an informant, but it now appears he's with your Black Hand group."

I lifted the photograph and studied the man. Though his skin had been darkened by long exposure to the sun, he had European features, and his mustache appeared blond or light brown in the black-and-white photo. "He could be working for both of them."

Ezra eyed me for a minute, then continued. "How much he has revealed of our plans, our safe houses, or our operatives is anyone's guess. Very disturbing."

"We've dispatched our men to alert all concerned," Mordechai said. "We plan to use every resource we have to find this Black Hand gang."

"Speaking for Haganah, we plan to do the same," Joshua said.

Hazan came around the coffee table and bent low to examine another photograph. "That woman," he said, pointing to Nadia, the assassin. "I've seen her recently."

I blurted out, "Where?"

"Near the Italian Hospital, not two nights ago."

A current of electricity burned through me. "She's been casing the hospital? She's the skilled assassin I've told you about. Laura could be in danger."

"Call Moshe and get two men over there and give them a description of the woman," Ezra said to Hazan.

As Hazan left the room to use the phone, I said, "Tell them she's skilled and dangerous." I stood. "We've got to get back."

Atkinson stood and gathered her things.

"You are not going anywhere," Ezra said. "If you want the papers returned, you will wait until Emanuel has finished photographing everything. Then I'll have someone drive you back to Jerusalem." He looked at both of us over his reading glasses as if waiting for any objections. We both sat in silence.

Ezra continued. "You two have been most helpful to the Zionist cause whether that was your intention or not. For that, we are grateful."

Hazan hurried back into the room. His face was red with anger. "When I told Yitzchak about sending two men over to the

Italian Hospital, they had just learned that the British found the Palestinian villagers of Alal, all dead and dumped into a ravine near Ramallah. The police claim the evidence of the murders points to us and Lehi."

I shot to my feet. "Was that your people? Did Irgun massacre those people?"

"Sit down, Mr. Collins," Ezra said forcefully.

We glared at each other. Atkinson tapped my leg, and I looked down at her. She frowned and tilted her head toward the sofa. I sat while locking eyes with Ezra.

He said, "No, that was not us. I would—"

Interrupting, Hazan said, "Sir, I have to report that information is coming in of a bomb going off at the Kiryat Anavim kibbutz." When he finished, he looked at Feldman.

It was the kibbutz where I'd visited Feldman, where his sister lived and worked.

"Rachel!" Feldman cried out and ran for the door.

Ezra looked at me. "It has begun, hasn't it?"

I nodded.

"Select two men and go to the kibbutz," Ezra said to Hazan. "See what you can do to help and get as much information as you can."

Hazan nodded, glanced at me, then left.

"Emanuel, are you finished photographing everything?" Mordechai asked his companion.

"A couple more minutes," Emanuel said.

"Finish now and give the documents to Mr. Collins," Ezra said. "I need you and Mordechai to take our guests back to Jerusalem, then get with our intelligence there and track down the Black Hand."

Atkinson and I stood and waited for Joshua to gather up everything from the dining room table. He put as much as he could in the carton, and the rest went into the canvas bag. He brought them over to us.

Ezra stood and shook our hands. "Good luck in your endeavors. We will meet again, I'm sure. In the meantime, watch your backs very carefully."

34

It took two nerve-racking hours to get back to Jerusalem. Emanuel drove, with Mordechai in the front and Atkinson and me in the rear. Twice, someone came out onto the street to warn Emanuel of roadblocks ahead, as if the messengers knew exactly the path he would take to get into the city.

Emanuel pulled up a block away from the Italian Hospital.

Mordechai turned in his seat to face us. "I advise you to steer clear of Mrs. Atkinson's apartment."

"We have a secure place to stay," I said.

"And I don't have to tell you to avoid the hospital. At least not until our men can secure the area. Joshua and I will go check on them."

"Third floor, room eleven," I said.

Mordechai nodded. "We'll be in touch."

Atkinson and I got out of the car. We waited until Joshua pulled away before making an about-face and heading for the tangle of streets west of the hospital. While constantly checking for a tail, I led us in a circuitous route to Nicholas's safe house.

The British had lifted the lockdown for daytime hours, but it was dusk now, and few people were willing to brave the streets as night fell. We made it back to the safe house and slipped into the basement entrance without anyone noticing, but I didn't relax until I made sure we weren't being followed and was able to lock the door behind us.

It was close to seven p.m. We had the place to ourselves. I wasn't too concerned about Nicholas's absence, as he had stated he wouldn't return until nightfall. Atkinson already hand a drink in her hand and was laying out a pile of Laura's notes on the coffee table in front of the sofa.

She held up her glass. "There's more in the bottle, though I plan to empty it in the coming hours."

"No, thanks. I've got to go out."

"What? Mason, that's not a good idea."

"Now that you're safe—at least relatively safe—I have to see Laura."

"The Black Hand, the police, and God knows who else are surely watching for you to do something foolish like that."

A pointed my finger at her. "Stay here. Don't go after me. And if Nicholas shows up, tell him to stay put until I can make it back." I ignored Atkinson's protests, opened the door, and looked back at her. "Lock the door behind me."

She opened her mouth, but I pulled the door shut before she had a chance to say how stupid I was being. She'd be right, but I couldn't concentrate on anything other than Laura's safety.

I stuck to the shadows and calculated a way through the smaller streets to circle around behind the hospital. I didn't have a plan for how to get into the building unobserved. Getting there was the priority. I headed north for several blocks, then turned east. The sky above was still an inky blue as it held on to the final blush of daylight. The empty streets made it easier to watch for a tail and avoid any police patrols, though a lone man wandering the streets might raise suspicion.

When I figured I'd gone far enough east, I turned right and

caught a glimpse of the hospital's ornate tower that stood like a sentinel guarding an Italian Renaissance palace. A few more indirect turns brought me to the back of the north wing of the complex.

I stopped in the shadow of a doorway across the street and scanned the surrounding area. I was hoping that anyone observing the comings and goings would be around the front entrance. That seemed to be the case, as I couldn't spot anyone posted at the rear.

Headlights lit up the street as a five-ton truck pulled up to the back of the building and stopped. I took advantage of the sweeping headlights to check the shadows. All appeared clear. A large door in the center of the wing opened, and the truck reversed into the bay and stopped at the loading dock. The headlamps threw their light my way, forcing me to retract deeper into the doorway.

The driver switched off the motor and headlights. He climbed down from the cab and met a man dressed in blue coveralls. They walked toward the loading dock.

This was my chance. I hurried across the street and hoped I wasn't being observed by any lookouts I might have missed. I made it to the truck's cab door and watched as the two men climbed the steps up to the level of the dock. The driver opened the cargo door while the man in coveralls opened a door to the service area of the hospital.

The driver rolled a hamper out of the back and proceeded to push it inside.

I dashed up the steps and into the truck's cargo bed. A dozen hampers were lined up to be unloaded, and each had a label with different hospital names on them. A hasty survey revealed they all contained bed linens and kitchen supplies.

I hurried out of the cargo bed and got to the opposite side of the service doors just as the driver and the man in blue exited and headed for the truck. I slipped inside and took long, quick strides down the hallway and pushed through a set of swinging doors.

I had entered a large kitchen, where several women were washing up and arranging things for the next day. I slowed my pace and nodded to a woman who eyed me warily. A confident smile and a tip of my hat seemed to mollify her, and I exited the kitchen by a side door. I found myself in a short hallway with a series of administrative offices, then a large room storing surgical supplies, bed linens, and surgical gowns. Without missing a beat, I swiped a gown and cap off the shelves and went out into the hallway again.

A few steps down, I found an empty office, closed the door, and pulled on the gown. I tucked my fedora under the desk and donned the cap. There was a pair of reading glasses on the desk. I put them on the tip of my nose, only intending to make full use of them if I needed to. Back out in the hallway, I used a rear stairway to climb to the third floor.

Laura's room was up the hall and around the corner, just past the nurses' station. Nurses, orderlies, and staff delivering food bustled from room to room. I grabbed some papers off a table and kept my head down, as if reading a report. Keeping up a swift pace, I passed the nurses' station and rounded the corner.

Two men in street clothes stood down the hall from Laura's door. I stopped. I wasn't sure if they were cops, lookouts for the Black Hand, or Irgun. Regardless, I wanted to avoid a confrontation. Someone on the staff had left their food cart outside a room. I got behind it and pushed it, while keeping my head in the stolen papers.

The trick was to act like I belonged and give off an air of boredom. I could see legs, but nothing else, and those legs stiffened as I approached Laura's door. One of the men approached me. I kept going, but he stood in front of me and blocked my progress.

My gun still rested in my waistband, and I'd use it if it came to it.

The man asked me something in Hebrew. The two men were from Irgun.

I looked up at him with a cool expression. "Mordechai," was all I said.

He studied me for a moment, then tilted his head to let me pass. I parked the cart outside the door and went inside.

A flood of disbelief and joy hit me at the same time.

Laura was awake.

35

"Mason," Laura said and weakly raised her arms.

I ran over and embraced her. She wept in the crook of my shoulder. Her hold on me was tenuous, and her arms shook. Then she lost her grip, and I lowered her to the pillow.

She breathed heavily from the effort amid her sobs. "The baby."

"I know, darling."

She choked back her tears and tried to smile. Her hands caressed my face. "Did you find the ones who did this?"

"I'm getting close, but don't worry about that now. Use all your strength to get better. Okay?"

She nodded, and her eyes closed. I gently lifted her hands from my face and laid them on her chest.

"Well, look who's here," a woman said from the door.

I straightened and turned to see an elegantly dressed, middle-aged woman standing just inside the room. I felt I was looking at a version of Laura in thirty years. Even the striking blue eyes were the same, though they were spitting fire at me at that moment. With her hands on her hips, she took two steps forward and pointed her index finger at me like a weapon. "What kind of man leaves a woman alone in her greatest hour of need?"

"The one who's going to find the bastards who did this to her and make them pay." I was fairly certain of who she was, but I had to ask anyway. "Who are you?"

"I'm Grace McKinnon. Her mother. And it's a good thing I was here when she woke up. She would have had to hear the news of her miscarriage from a total stranger."

"You told her ..." I paused to get my anger under control. "You could have waited until she got better."

"It's not any business of yours, but she asked. She's a strong woman, and she would only tolerate the truth. And you have no right to question me."

"Mother," Laura said barely above a whisper.

Mrs. McKinnon strode over to her daughter and leaned over. "I'm sorry, dear, but these words had to be said." She turned to me. "I blame this on you."

"Ma'am, we were trying to get out of the country—"

"If she hadn't met you, she would still be with her husband, having a good life somewhere away from war zones. Your actions put her and Richard in danger in the first place." She opened her mouth to say something else—

"Mother, please."

Mrs. McKinnon closed her mouth but continued to send an icy glare my way. "As soon as she's able to travel, her father and I are taking her home and away from you. For good."

I said nothing in response. I refused to carry on an argument in front of Laura. Going with her mother was her choice to make, and I had to acknowledge that being under her parents' protection and care was probably the best thing for her to heal her body and her mind. Not to mention that I had little money, no prospects, and a questionable future, especially with multiple bull's-eyes on my back.

Mrs. McKinnon turned her attention to Laura. "I'm arranging

for a private room," she said loud enough for me to overhear. "Then I'm bringing in the best doctors to give you the best treatment. The level of care you've received so far is appalling."

"They're doing the best they can," Laura said. "There are just so many bombing victims ..." Her voice trailed off.

I braved Mrs. McKinnon's wrath and went to the other side of the bed. "You have to rest."

Laura's eyes popped open. "You're leaving?"

"I'll be back. You should rest now."

"You'd better. And rescue me from my mother."

Mrs. McKinnon hissed her displeasure, but she stepped away to give us a moment.

"I have some things to follow up on, and your mother will make sure you're taken care of."

Laura's eyes closed. I leaned over and kissed her on the cheek.

She opened her eyes halfway. "My notes."

"They're safe. Evelyn and I have them."

She shook her head weakly as she drifted off to sleep. "Maybe not all of them."

My stomach formed another knot when she fell asleep so profoundly that I had the impulse to check her for a pulse. I relaxed when I noticed her breathing was steady. I kissed her again, straightened, and looked at Mrs. McKinnon. "Do what you need to do to make her better. I won't interfere."

Mrs. McKinnon jerked her head in a curt nod, and I left the room.

Out in the hallway, I expected one of the Irgun guards to question me about the loud argument in the room after alluding to being there on Mordechai's direction. But they ignored me.

I went the same way I'd come but didn't bother hiding my face this time. The nurses and staff seemed too busy to notice. Even if they did, I wasn't aware: I was too occupied by the swirling emotions of Laura coming awake and her mother's threats of never allowing me to see her again. Then my thoughts turned to Laura telling me that I might not have all her papers. Were there more damning notes hidden somewhere? That might explain why everyone was so desperate to get their hands on them. Maybe the most important stuff was still hidden.

I took the back stairs down to the ground floor and used the same hallway. Halfway to the kitchen, a man emerged from one of the administrative offices and shut the door while stuffing something in his suit coat pocket. He stiffened and turned his head away when he saw me, then moved in the same direction toward the kitchen and the loading dock. At first, I didn't think much of it, but then that simple yet suspicious act triggered my detective's instincts, which made me look harder at him.

Then it hit me. It was the man Ezra had pointed out in one of Laura's photographs. Levi Weiss, the mustached man, and a former Irgun member working with the Black Hand. What was he doing in one of the offices of the hospital? And what did he stuff in his pocket?

I decided to see where he led me and slowed my pace, letting him put some distance between us. He might lead me back to a Black Hand hideout. But underestimating the man's countersurveillance skills would be a mistake. I would operate with the assumption that he was aware of my presence.

I ducked into the supply room to slip off the surgical gown and retrieve my fedora. At the doorway, I listened as his footsteps faded and the door to the kitchen opened. I stepped out again into the hallway and made it to the end. The door had stopped swinging when I got there, and I pushed through to see he'd already exited the kitchen.

The kitchen was down to two cleaners. They apparently couldn't care less about strangers passing through, and I made it to the exit without raising an eyebrow. The loading dock was empty. The loading dock doors were closed. The man was gone. A dim lightbulb illuminated enough of the area for me to find a single door. The man could have set a trap. I pulled my pistol from my waistband and pushed the door open just enough to slip outside.

My quarry had turned right and was heading for the Street of the Prophets. That was a busy thoroughfare, with plenty of traffic, which made me wonder what he was doing by going in that direction. Cop and military patrols used its east-west route at regular intervals.

Out of caution, I returned the pistol to my waistband and, instead, reached into the right pocket of my coat and slid my fingers into the holes of the brass knuckles. I lowered the brim of my hat and set off.

The man walked with an air of confidence even while his head moved from side to side as he kept a vigilant eye on his surroundings. He stopped at the curb of the wide avenue and waited for a few passing cars.

I knew he'd use the opportunity to check his rear, and I changed direction just as he glanced behind. He then dashed across the road and disappeared onto a dark side street. On the chance he watched for a tail following the same path, I cut diagonally through the hospital's grounds and crossed at a point farther down the road.

This cat-and-mouse game could only work for so long with a trained opponent. But I might not have another opportunity. I quickened my pace, crossed Street of the Prophets, where he wouldn't be able to spot me, then I jogged along the other side until I reached the entrance to the same side street.

I peered around the corner and saw him about sixty yards ahead and about to take a sharp curve. Just as he started to follow the curve, I moved forward, sticking to the same side of the street and skirting the stone walls that divided the properties of elegant houses.

As soon as he was out of sight, I surged forward and reached the point of the curve. The man was about forty yards in front of me when a car's headlights came up fast toward us from the opposite direction.

I flattened myself into the recess of an iron gate serving one of the walled estates. It was a cop car, but my quarry continued. Maybe he figured it was too late to duck out of sight. The car pulled up next to him. The man stopped, and the uniformed driver got out. The two men exchanged a few words. Both appeared relaxed, like they were sharing a social moment rather than a security check. They obviously knew each other, which was why the man hadn't gone for cover.

A second cop got out of the back. He was dressed in an officer's uniform. It was dark, and I was too far away to be sure, but the man appeared to be wearing the uniform of a high-ranking policeman. There was a short exchange. Nothing out of the ordinary.

With lightning speed, the officer pulled out his revolver and fired twice into the man's skull. An electrical shock blazed through me. I pushed my back against the iron gate as far as it would allow.

The two cops checked their surroundings, then they both got back inside the car. I put my hand on the butt of my pistol and watched as the car raced toward me. The driver neither slowed nor sped up as it passed. I looked at the back seat window, and there was just enough light to make out the passenger's face. It sent a chill up my spine.

Sitting in the back was CID Superintendent Wetherbee.

Once the cop car turned onto the main street, I headed for Street of the Prophets. Alerted by the gunshot, lights in several houses came on, though no one dared come out to see what had happened. I proceeded at a leisurely pace so as not attract attention and hoped I could get far enough away before the police arrived to investigate the shooting.

By the time I'd gotten a few blocks away, the cops did arrive, lights and sirens. Once I reached the street for Nicholas's apartment building, I could relax, and my thoughts turned to what had just occurred. If Weiss was a member of British intelligence, why did Wetherbee shoot him down in cold blood? And what was the man doing in an office at the hospital? Did he not follow orders? Were Wetherbee and his associates cleaning house? Who was next?

That last thought compelled me to increase my pace.

36

I fell back against the door to close it behind me. I took deep gulps of air, only then realizing that I'd forgotten to breathe half the time as I walked back from the scene of the shooting. Atkinson was still sitting in front of Laura's documents splayed out on the coffee table and floor.

"How's Laura?" Atkinson asked without looking up.

I made a beeline for the liquor cart and poured myself a copious amount of whiskey. Atkinson knew not to press me for questions until I'd managed to get in a few good swigs.

"She's awake," I said and felt a couple of hot tears fill my eyes. "She's still very weak, but at least she's out of the coma." For a moment, the warm glow of feeling her in my arms quelled images of the killing and all it implied.

Atkinson spun her head in my direction and stood up. "What? Tell me—" She charged over and gave me a hug. "That's such great news." She released me and stepped back. "Sorry, how very un-English of me."

I put my hands on her arms and tried to smile. "I'm happy, too. And relieved." I'd tried to sound cheerful, but it came out flat.

Atkinson moved to the cart. "This calls for a celebration." She poured a drink for herself and faced me. "You look rather dour. I would have thought you'd be ecstatic."

I took another swig. "Her mother was there."

"I take it that didn't go well."

"I could see where Laura got her looks, but also her hot temper."

"She blames you for everything that's happened to her daughter and thinks you're not nearly good enough for her."

"Something like that."

"Maybe she'll come around once you turn on that charm of yours." She snapped her fingers. "Oh, no, wait a minute, you're lacking in that department."

"She insists on taking Laura back home once she's well enough to travel."

Atkinson squinted her eyes at me. "You seem rattled. And not just from a row with the mother."

I finished my drink and poured another one. "I saw CID Superintendent Wetherbee gun down a man in cold blood."

"You what?"

"In the middle of the street, no less, like he had no fear of the repercussions."

I told her about being in the hospital and nearly running into Weiss, the man Ezra had pointed out in the photograph. That I followed him down a side street not far from Street of the Prophets and wanted to see if the man would lead me back to one of the Black Hand's hideouts, or maybe I could beat some information out of him. Then about the police car pulling up and two officers getting out. "Weiss knew Wetherbee. He didn't appear to suspect a thing. One moment they're having a conversation, and the next, bam."

"Do you think Wetherbee took justice into his own hands? Or was he eliminating any complications?"

"Your guess is as good as mine."

"How could they possibly know Weiss would be there at that exact moment?"

"The best I can come up with is that Weiss must have been very close to his hideout, so Wetherbee knew where to find him. But how he knew when is something I can't answer. And it doesn't matter. What's got me rattled is that the head of the CID could be involved in this bombing plot. There aren't too many men in this town I'd fear more as an enemy than him. A cold-blooded one at that."

Atkinson said nothing and took a drink of her whiskey, then she marched over to the sofa and pushed around the documents on the table.

The pendulum clock on the mantel chimed, announcing it was eleven p.m. That made me aware of the stillness in the apartment. "Where's Nicholas? He was supposed to be here by now."

"Not a word. I'm worried for him."

Now I was too. "He might have gotten tied up or moved on to another issue."

"More than likely," Atkinson said with little conviction.

I walked over and sat on the arm of the sofa. She picked up papers, then put them down as if she was having trouble focusing on any one thing.

"You should back out," I said. "It's getting too hot."

She glared at me. "When I commit to something, I see it to the end. No more talk of quitting."

She was scared, all right, and I admired her bravery. "Find anything new?"

"Not really. At least, not with what we have. There are several gaps in her notes. Then there are thoughts she expressed and then didn't finish. It's as if there are pages missing."

What Laura said to me now made sense. "When I told Laura that we had her notes, she said maybe not all of them."

Atkinson looked at me. "She said that? Are you sure she wasn't just delirious or confused?"

"She was lucid. Losing the baby was at the front of her mind, but concern for her notes wasn't far behind. She seemed genuinely afraid they might be in the wrong hands."

"She hid the more damning items in a secure place."

"Seems that way."

Atkinson stood as if a fearful thought prompted her to do so. "Do we have to go back there?"

"That's my plan, but you're staying here."

"Not on your life—"

Someone knocked on the door. Atkinson jumped, and I put my finger to my lips. I pulled out my pistol and turned off the lamp closest to me. Atkinson hit the switch on another lamp, putting us in near darkness.

The person knocked again.

I went to the door and listened.

"Mason? Mrs. Atkinson?" a man's voice whispered on the other side.

It was Dr. Salameh.

I whipped open the door, pulled him in, and shut it behind him. The doctor stiffened when he saw my gun.

"What are you doing here? Where's Nicholas?"

"He can't make it this evening."

"Why?"

"He's on an operation in Bethlehem."

"What kind of operation?"

Salameh held up his hands as if trying to hold back any more questions. "I only know it has something to do with the Black Hand."

"If it has to do with the Black Hand, then I want to be there."

"I advise against that."

"I insist. And you're going to take me."

Dr. Salameh's eyes widened in alarm. "He will be very angry. I cannot say what he might do if I take you, and you interfere."

"Let me worry about that."

"I'm going, too," Atkinson said.

"Too dangerous," I said.

"I might be scared out of my wits, but I'm not about to cower in a corner. I'm going."

"No."

Dr. Salameh tried to slip out the front door. I caught him by the shoulder and pulled him back in the room.

"Please, sir. I only came by to tell you that Nicholas was indisposed. I must go now."

"You can go home after you take us to wherever he is in Bethlehem." I leaned into his face and glowered. "I won't take no for an answer." I led him by his lapel into the middle of the room. I grabbed my backpack and pulled on my coat.

Atkinson had already donned hers.

"What do you think you're doing?" I asked her.

She came up to me and got in my face. "You don't want to get on my bad side. I'm going, and that's final."

"If you are determined to come, please hurry," Salameh said. "I parked out front. The car is blocking part of the road."

I studied Atkinson's eyes to check her nerves. I didn't like the idea of me going somewhere in the middle of the night on a mysterious mission with a man I barely knew, let alone her. "Then you'd better gin up your nerves. This could get interesting."

37

Salameh took a big northerly loop around Jerusalem before heading south along a low ridge overlooking sparse hills. Atkinson and I sat in back as if Salameh was our driver. With his white suit and tarboosh, he fit the part, which helped when we encountered a checkpoint north of Bethlehem. With Salameh's charm, Atkinson's press card, and my CIC papers, the guards waved us on with the usual warning about the dangers of venturing out at such an hour.

Bethlehem proper sat on a rocky hill—rocks seemed to be the largest commodity of the place: rock walls, buildings built of rock, rocks piled along the side of the road. From what I could see, the land was barren and treeless, and not for the first time I wondered why so many civilizations had chosen to live and die here over the centuries. Small buildings and single-story houses were packed in tight along the way as we climbed the winding road toward the center of town.

Salameh slowed when the bell tower of a church became visible. He pulled over and parked next to a two-story structure with arched windows that looked centuries old. A couple of blocks away was a large open plaza bounded on the south and west by more centuries-old buildings.

Atkinson pointed toward the plaza and a jumble of structures all haphazardly joined together. "That's the Church of the Nativity, built over the spot where Jesus was said to be born."

"It doesn't look like much," I said. "More like the remnants of an ancient fortress."

"It's fifteen hundred years old. What did you expect?"

"Something a little grander for the birthplace of Jesus."

"After so many wars and earthquakes, it's a wonder it's still standing."

Dr. Salameh still sat in the car as if he wasn't about to move.

"It's time to go, Doctor," I said.

Dr. Salameh let out a sigh and opened his car door. "Come with me."

Atkinson and I followed the doctor to the entrance of a three-story building. On each side was a small shop, though the central door opened to a long narrow hallway. At the end was a set of stairs, which we began to climb.

Salameh moved cautiously, prompting us to do the same. We'd made it to the second-floor landing when our guide stopped. He knocked on the wooden railing three times. The sound echoed in the enclosed space. A moment later, a single knock replied.

Salameh waved for us to continue, and we slowly mounted the last flight of stairs. Then I saw why he'd signaled our approach. A man stood at the top of the third floor. He looked odd, dressed as he was in a gray suit while wearing combat boots and holding a STEN submachine gun pointed at the ceiling. Despite his business attire, he looked ready to use his gun if he didn't like what he saw.

Atkinson drew in her breath when she saw the man. I stopped behind her and assessed the situation. Salameh had, unintentionally or not, already led us into an ambush once before. The guard looked calm, though that could change in an instant.

Salameh looked back at us, standing halfway up the stairs. "It's okay. This man is with Nicholas."

"And where is he?" I asked.

The man with the gun tilted his head toward a closed door to his right. He then aimed his weapon at the floor and stepped back to let us pass.

Atkinson and I reached the top of the stairs to join Salameh at the door the guard had indicated. I was getting impatient and knocked before the doctor had a chance. The door swung open, revealing another armed man in a suit and tie with a submachine gun. He glowered at me, then noticed Salameh.

"The American and the reporter," the man said to someone behind him.

"What the bloody hell?" Nicholas said from somewhere inside the room. "Let them in."

The man moved aside, and the three of us entered. We were in a sizeable living room. Though most of the furniture had been draped in sheets of cotton, I could tell by the gilded architectural details of the ceilings and moldings that the owners—previous or otherwise—were loaded.

Nicholas stood with another man peering at a large sheet of paper laid out on a carved mahogany dining table. They, too, were dressed in business clothes and combat boots. Their weapons, both submachine guns, were propped against a table leg.

Without looking up, Nicholas said, "Doctor, you disappoint me."

"I ... I just went by to tell them what you told me to say. But he insisted."

"Did he point a gun to your head?"

"That was my next option," I said.

"We demanded he take us to you," Atkinson said. "He isn't to blame."

Nicholas looked up but not at us. "Doctor, you can wait in the bedroom. One of my men will bring you some tea."

Dr. Salameh looked at the floor as he left the room.

Nicholas turned to me and forced a smile. "Since you two are here, you might as well help. We could use a sixth man. But, Mrs. Atkinson, this is no place for a reporter."

"I've been in tough situations before, and I've been with this since the beginning, so I'm not going to sit on my bum while there's an opportunity for me to bear witness for the record."

Nicholas motioned for us to come up to the table. "Have a look."

Atkinson and I approached and stood next to Nicholas. In front of him was a large, detailed plan of the church complex, which was roughly square in form, with the largest structure being the cross-shaped church that sat almost dead center.

"The Church of the Nativity," Atkinson said to me. She tapped her finger on the other large area. "Just to the side is the Church of Saint Catherine."

The main plaza anchored the eastern end, with two cloistered areas on either side.

"What are these other buildings that look like they connect to the churches?" I asked.

"Two monasteries and a convent," Nicholas said and pointed to the right section drawing. "And that's the crypt and cave system underneath. There are two ways to enter the basilica, via the main plaza and through the northern courtyard. And there are two ways to enter the lower level, one of which is by accessing the grotto network underneath the basilica's sister, the Church of Saint Catherine."

"You think a group of the Black Hand is hiding out in there?" I asked.

"Oh, not hiding. According to a reliable source, they intend to plant a bomb somewhere in the complex. Several busloads of Americans are planning a pilgrimage to the church tomorrow. Included in that group are two of the UN delegates assessing the partition of Palestine."

"Are they still there?"

"Not that we've observed. There was quite a bit of activity earlier, but it has tapered off. Those that we saw go in have now come out. A couple of priests seem to have been the last to leave. Which has just occurred. We wouldn't want a priest wandering into the middle of a firefight, now would we?"

"What about the police?" Atkinson asked. "Are they involved?"

"This is strictly our operation."

"What if they become involved in response to gunfire?" I asked.

"The idea is to get in and out of there quickly and without incident."

"The operatives you encounter just might be police."

Nicholas furrowed his brow at me. "What are you trying to say?"

"Tonight, I picked up the trail of one of the Black Hand members. But before I could follow him to his hideout or pick him up for questioning, the superintendent of the CID drove up to him. They had a friendly conversation, then Wetherbee shot him in the head. Whatever the reason—and I'm thinking he's cleaning house before the big push—there are some big fish involved in this. No telling what they know or who they could take down if the mood strikes them."

Nicholas looked at his men, who returned resolute stares. He then turned back to me. "We trust the source. His information is always reliable. Regardless, we can't ignore the possibility that there is indeed a bomb waiting to go off. We're going in. If you and Mrs. Atkinson decide to stay here or have Dr. Salameh take you back, I won't hold that against you. You weren't invited here in the first place."

I turned to Atkinson and asked her the question with my eyes.

"I'm going in with the rest of you," Atkinson said. "Period."

Nicholas folded the plans and stuffed them into his pocket. "Admittedly, we could use a civilian observer in case there are legal issues. But I would ask you to remain at a safe distance."

"I'll keep an eye on her," I said.

Atkinson backhanded my arm. "You just keep an eye on yourself, partner."

Nicholas held out his hand to indicate the other man at the table. "This is Harry, by the way. My second."

Harry shook our hands with a resolute jerk. He appeared to be in his early thirties, with thick eyebrows and mustache and a hardened face. I could tell by the look in his eyes that he'd seen his fair share of action.

Nicholas nodded toward his companion guarding the door. "That's Sean, and the man out in the corridor is Benjamin." He picked up his STEN gun. "We have someone surveying the area from the roof, if you'd like to join me in a final check on the situation."

Atkinson and I followed Nicholas out of the apartment and to a set of back stairs. A short climb led us to a door that opened out onto the roof. Another one of Nicholas's men stood at the western edge with binoculars in his hand.

A wordless greeting was exchanged between the two men as we joined him.

Keeping his voice down, Nicholas asked him, "Anything?"

The lookout, a young man in his early twenties, shook his head. "No one's gone in or out in the last thirty minutes, sir. Nothing on the streets below. Looks like the town has closed up for the night."

Nicholas scanned the area for himself, then looked up at the dark sky. "A half-moon. I'd prefer it darker." He put his hand on the young man's shoulder. "All right, Charlie, it's time we have a go at the basilica."

38

We moved as a group in silence toward the doorway. I knew the commander was going over the plans in his head; he wouldn't leave anything to chance that he could control, not even if the mission appeared to be a simple one.

When we descended to the third floor, the other commandos were waiting at the top of the main staircase.

Nicholas held out one of the STEN guns to me.

"Thanks, but I prefer my 1911."

"Suit yourself. You and Charlie will go with me. Madam, if you'll remain at least fifty feet behind us."

I nodded. Atkinson raised an eyebrow but said nothing.

Everyone moved down the stairs. We were at the back of the group with Nicholas, and as soon as we exited the building, Harry led his team across the street. Two men would cover while the third moved forward, each taking his turn as they advanced.

Atkinson and I remained at the door with Charlie until Nicholas signaled. We moved out, with Atkinson delaying her start. The city was silent. The only sound was the commandos' boots on the paving stones.

The first team headed down the left side of the rectangular

plaza toward the cloister that provided access to the church from the north. Our group stopped and waited at the church's front entrance that was outlined by three massive stones. I expected the typical set of enormous double doors, but the single entrance was just large enough for a person to squeeze through. The wooden door undulated from centuries of hands pressing on its surface.

Nicholas looked at his watch, presumably counting down the seconds until the second team reached the other entrance. A few tense moments later, he raised his weapon and rushed into the entrance. Charlie and I followed. With quick steps, the three of us entered the confined space of the narthex that had been split into three sections. Immediately in front was another door, which was a single opening cut into a massive wooden door.

Nicholas entered the nave first. He readied his weapon to cover Charlie and me. The cavernous space appeared empty. To the left, the second team rushed in from the cloister. Nicholas gave the order, and both teams advanced, moving between the outer walls and the rows of columns supporting the wood-beamed ceiling. Four hanging electric lights and several oil lamps threw pools of light in an otherwise dark interior.

I was surprised at the poor condition of the interior. Portions of the walls were covered in crumbling plaster. The columns and ceiling were turning black from centuries of smoke and dust. The only bright area was around the intricate Greek Orthodox altar of silver and gold.

The team on the left disappeared down a stone staircase underneath the altar. I braced myself for an outbreak of gunfire or adversaries popping out of the shadows, but neither occurred. No sign of an ambush, at least in the church proper. I looked back and saw Atkinson moving up the north wall. Her mouth and eyes were wide with trepidation, but despite her fear, she kept moving toward us.

Nicholas waited by the altar and the right-side entrance to the caves. A few agonizing minutes passed, then he signaled for us to head down the stairs. We descended the stone steps worn concave by the ages, and we came to a small room of hewn stone walls lit by a forest of oil lamps and decorated with embroidered cloth. A hearth-like altar was at the near end.

Our team held our position while Harry's team methodically searched the underground chambers.

Atkinson hovered about halfway down the steps. Nicholas waved for her to continue, and she came up beside me.

She pointed at the altar. "The traditional spot where Jesus was born."

Nicholas continued to the left. I was tempted to pause and take in the scene, but it wasn't the time for reflection; the tense voices of the commandos demanded my attention. Atkinson and I passed another small altar, then wove around until we came out into a larger grotto with several rooms cut out of the stone. There was another staircase at the far end, which looked more recently built than the ones we had descended.

When one of the commandos put his foot on the first step, a companion jerked him back and pointed. "A booby trap."

A thin, almost imperceptible wire was strung tightly across the second step.

Everyone froze for a moment. It might not be the only one, and we all had bunched up in a small space.

Nicholas pushed Atkinson and me backward. "Get out of here. Now. Go back upstairs until we can defuse the bloody thing and make sure there aren't any others."

The commander ordered two of his men to accompany us, and we all climbed up the stairs to the basilica. Several tense minutes passed. Atkinson held my arm while I continued to survey the church interior in case this was part of the ambush. The two commandos did the same.

"No Black Hand," I said. "No bomb. Just a booby trap. It doesn't make sense."

That statement made Atkinson dig her fingers deeper into my arm. "Do you think Nicholas's source purposely gave him the wrong information?"

I could only shrug a response.

Nicholas popped his head out of the grotto entrance. "All clear."

We headed back down and wove through the grotto network again until we reached the steps that had been booby trapped. The commandos went first, then Nicholas, and Atkinson and I followed. We emerged into another more modern church with square columns and a vaulted ceiling.

"This is the Roman Catholic church, Saint Catherine," Atkinson said.

Despite the church being empty, the commandos had taken up defensive positions, ready for an ambush that never came.

I went up to Nicholas. "Why lay the trap only on the staircase to this church? They could have had us if they'd also rigged the other side."

Nicholas shook his head as he scanned the interior. "Perhaps they expected us to enter via this church. Or they'd planned for us to bunch up in the grottoes—just like we did—for maximum damage."

After a few moments, Nicholas signaled for them to move toward the main entrance to the church. We all moved cautiously and silently, finally exiting into a cloister which consisted of an open center bounded by columns and arches. When it was time to exit the cloister, everyone tensed, with weapons at the ready. As before, the commandos went out first, then the three of us stepped out onto the large plaza. All was quiet.

That silence unnerved me only a little less than the possibility of being caught in a firefight.

Nicholas said something to one of his commandos, who passed on the message. The men moved at double time toward the opposite side of the street.

"It looks like your source isn't as reliable as you thought," I said to him.

"I'll get to the bottom of it. Mark my words."

Atkinson and I walked across the plaza with Nicholas. He pointed to two of his men reentering the two-story building. "Harry and Charlie will stay until morning to keep a watch on things."

"You have more fires to put out?" I asked.

"I'm afraid so. There've been some reports of suspicious activity around the Jewish hospital, the Bikur Cholim."

"That's on the Street of the Prophets," Atkinson said with alarm. She turned to me. "That's near my apartment."

"Then it isn't far from where Wetherbee shot the man I was following," I said. "We'll go with you."

Nicholas shook his head. "Not this time. We're going to set up a surveillance team, which is about all we can do without more information. Go home. Dr. Salameh will take you back."

I was about to object when Nicholas held up his hand to stop me. "I insist."

I let him end the conversation, but I wasn't about to let it stop me from doing a little investigating on my own. We crossed the street and stopped at the entrance of the building. Dr. Salameh came out and met us.

Nicholas pointed to a white panel delivery truck. It had Arabic lettering painted on the side and was parked a block closer to the city center. "This is where I leave you."

Salameh got in front of Nicholas to cut him off. "You want me to take them back? I can't. I wasn't planning on returning to Jerusalem."

"I'm sorry to impose upon you, Doctor," Nicholas said, "but they can't come with us. Please, take them to the safe house, and then you can be on your way."

"My sister needs medical assistance, and you are going back to Jerusalem anyway."

Nicholas peered at the doctor with a stern expression. "I wouldn't ask you to do this if it wasn't important."

Dr. Salameh looked pleadingly at me, as if I might give him a way out. I shrugged, and he returned his attention back to Nicholas. "Very well. Then we must hurry."

"We'll talk tomorrow," Nicholas said to us.

"You know where to find us," Atkinson said.

Nicholas headed toward his men, who were already climbing into the truck.

I watched him go for a moment, then turned back to Atkinson and Dr. Salameh. "Let's get out of here."

The three of us headed for the doctor's car.

A blast of hot wind and the boom of an explosion slammed into us. The force of it pushed the three us almost off our feet. I ducked instinctively, then I turned in shock at the source. The van was engulfed in flames.

We all looked on in horror. Flames licked at a shattered hulk of steel. Bloodied men and parts of men lay scattered around the inferno.

I moved to go to them, but Atkinson and Dr. Salameh held me back. My ears were ringing, and I barely heard their cries for me to stop, urging me to go with them to the car. Reluctantly, I allowed them to pull me along. They were gasping from the shock, and Atkinson began to wail from the trauma. My protective impulses kicked in, and I took her by the elbows and propped her up. Dr. Salameh and I helped her into the car. I got in back with her to give her comfort.

Through the front windshield, I saw the two commandos, Harry and Charlie, rush out of the building.

I hit Dr. Salameh on the shoulder. "We've got to pick them up."

"You want me to go toward the fire?" the doctor said in a panicked voice.

"Go, now, damnit."

He hit the accelerator and raced up to the two commandos.

"Get in," I yelled out the window.

They looked anguished but lucid. Harry waved us on. "Get out of here. We'll take care of things and await further orders. Good luck."

Dr. Salameh hit the accelerator again, made a U-turn in the plaza, and drove away from the carnage.

39

A tkinson had her head on my shoulder. Her shaking had stopped, and her breathing was calm, but she had yet to say anything for the thirty-plus minutes we'd been on the road. We were about halfway between Bethlehem and Jerusalem, in other words in the middle of nowhere. Dr. Salameh was driving the car onto a primitive road, and the car bounced in the ruts and uneven surface.

I was deep in thought, running over everything that had happened in Bethlehem. Was it the Black Hand who had planted the bomb underneath the commandos' panel truck, or some other faction? Was it police officers under Wetherbee's influence? Assuming Charlie had been observing from the roof the entire time before charging into the church, the bomber couldn't have approached the truck without being seen. The only time the truck was out of sight was when we were all in the basilica and church.

I studied Dr. Salameh's eyes in the car's rearview mirror. His concentration was focused on the road, but he must have noticed me staring at him and glanced at me nervously several times.

"Where were you while we searched the basilica?" I asked him.

"I stayed in the bedroom, as Nicholas ordered," the doctor said, his voice rising an octave.

"I'm not accusing you, Doctor. I wanted to know if you happened to see something."

"How could I see something? I was in the bedroom."

"Okay, fine. Forget it."

I meant what I said; I wanted him to forget it. But I wasn't about to. How had he known we had come out of the church to meet us on the street? I intended to ask him, but not at that moment.

We remained silent for the rest of the trip. Dr. Salameh had managed to navigate the web of dirt roads back to Jerusalem, avoiding most of the police checkpoints. I imagined news had reached police headquarters about the bombing in Bethlehem by now, and they would be out in force.

Atkinson recovered enough to sit up. She gave me an embarrassed smile, which I guessed was for using me as a security blanket.

"How are you doing?" I asked.

She searched her purse for a tissue and wiped her eyes. "I'm rattled but fine. Nicholas—if that really is his name—was a good man. The cruelty and injustice cannot go unanswered."

I planned to do the answering, but declaring it out loud would ring hollow, so I said nothing.

We passed through the outskirts of the city. Dr. Salameh had circled around to approach from the west, as the majority of British military installations were in the south end. I kept an eye on the doctor's actions as he picked specific streets to avoid any checkpoints. His eyes were restless, and he kept rubbing his hands of perspiration. He leaned forward as if willing the car to go faster.

When he reached the neighborhood of Nicholas's safe house,

I leaned forward to talk near his ear. "That was impressive, Doctor. Not one security stop."

"I know every inch of Jerusalem. I've lived here all my life. And my family has lived here for generations."

"Then it's a good thing you were driving. But I think it would be smart to avoid going back to the same safe house. If the bombers knew of Nicholas's activities, they could know about the apartment. Take us to another place."

He glanced at me, then snapped his gaze back to the road. "I don't think that's necessary."

"It's better to err on the side of caution. Don't you think?" I snapped my fingers. "I've got an idea. Why don't you take us to your place? We'll just stay the night, and in the morning, we can make other arrangements."

Atkinson leaned forward. "Yes, please, Doctor. I'd certainly feel much better avoiding that safe house altogether."

"If what you say is true," Dr. Salameh said, "then my place might not be safe either."

I put my hand on his shoulder. "You could be right. Take us to Evelyn's car. We'll find somewhere else to go."

Atkinson looked at me like I was crazy. "But where? It's one in the morning."

"We'll figure it out."

Atkinson slumped back in her seat. Dr. Salameh slowed as we approached the safe house.

"Doctor," I said in a threatening tone.

Dr. Salameh let out a big sigh, increased his speed, and we passed the safe house. While I gave him directions to reach the parking lot, I stayed forward with my hand on his shoulder to keep him intimidated. Both Atkinson and I peered at the Bikur Cholim to see if there might be any activity around the hospital. All seemed quiet, but that meant nothing.

In a few moments, Dr. Salameh pulled into the parking lot between Street of the Prophets and Jaffa Road. I pointed to

Atkinson's Vauxhall. Dr. Salameh wove through the lot and rolled up to the rear of the car. I grabbed my backpack off the floorboard, and Atkinson buttoned up her coat.

The doctor turned in his seat to watch us. "Where do you plan to go?"

"We'll figure it out. We might stay in the car, for all I know."

Atkinson shot me a disapproving glance but said nothing.

"But how will I get in touch with you?" the doctor asked.

"About what?"

"Well, anything."

"With Nicholas gone, I figured there wasn't much else to talk about."

Dr. Salameh shifted his gaze between the two of us as if searching for a retort.

I put my hand on the car door handle. "Try here. We'll leave a sign if we need to get in touch. And you can do the same."

Dr. Salameh nodded. Atkinson and I got out and went to her car. She fiddled in her purse, looking for the car keys.

"Hurry, would you?" I said. "I don't want the doc slipping away."

Atkinson continued to rifle through her bag. "Why not?" She found the keys and looked up at me with apprehension in her eyes. "No."

"Yes."

She threw me the keys. "Then you drive."

I climbed behind the wheel, and Atkinson got into the passenger's seat. Dr. Salameh drove away as I started up the Vauxhall.

"What's this all about?" Atkinson asked angrily.

"We're going to see where the doc goes."

I leisurely pulled out of the space, giving Dr. Salameh time to leave the lot. I wanted some time and distance between us and the doctor's Rover 10. After turning out of the lot, I spotted Dr. Salameh's car turn right again onto Jaffa Road. I sped up and did the same. He was two blocks ahead and going at a moderate speed.

"Why do you want to know where Dr. Salameh goes?" Atkinson asked.

"I think the good doctor went over to the other side, if he wasn't already there this whole time."

"What makes you think that?"

"A feeling in my gut."

Atkinson studied me as I followed Dr. Salameh past King George Avenue.

"He was the only one who didn't go to the church," Atkinson said.

I nodded.

"So he was the only one who could have planted the bomb? Nonsense. He's going to take care of his sister. You're seeing conspiracies where there are none."

"That's what I intend to find out."

"That's *we*, since you've decided to include me. And I'm not sure I'm up to this after what happened."

Dr. Salameh made a right turn on the outskirts of town.

"This is the only opportunity. He was pushing hard for us to be somewhere he, or his buddies, could find us. We are the loose ends. I think Salameh has to report the success and the failure."

Atkinson hit her thighs in frustration. "To whom?"

She was still badly shaken, and I felt a twinge of guilt in forcing her to come along. "Looks like we're going to learn who," I said and pointed out the windshield.

Dr. Salameh had parked next to a tract of land surrounded by a chain-link fence and dotted with olive trees. A lone house sat in the middle.

I pulled over and doused the headlights. I turned in my seat, retrieved my backpack, and rifled through it. I pulled out the binoculars and trained them on the house.

It had two stories with a wing jutting out to one side. It was built in stone, with a pseudo turret and architectural accents. It reminded me more of something I'd see in Germany than Palestine. By the dilapidated condition, the house looked abandoned. Boards covered most of the windows, and junk lay about the property. But then I spotted a window almost hidden by an olive tree that had a lowered shade, and it glowed dimly from a light within.

Dr. Salameh got out of his car and walked up to the fence. It didn't appear to have a gate. He just stood facing the house, held up a flashlight, and turned it on and off three times. A moment later, the door opened, and a figure stood at the threshold. His features were lit just enough to see he had white skin and blond hair.

My heartrate shot up. I had to fight the impulse to jump out of the car and run at the house. "How much you want to bet he's Black Hand."

Atkinson sucked in her breath but said nothing. I continued to watch the doctor and the house.

Dr. Salameh fussed with clips in the chain-link and pulled back a section that had been rigged for entry. The movement set off bells along the fence and at the front door. The occupants had set up a primitive alarm.

The man remained at the threshold while Dr. Salameh put the cutout chain-link section back in place and walked up to the porch. Another man moved across the room behind the man at the door.

"There's at least one more in the house," I said.

Dr. Salameh got to the door, and the man pulled him inside.

"Please tell me you're not going to try to take them on yourself," Atkinson said.

I lowered the binoculars and handed them to her. "I'm just going to take a closer look."

Atkinson groaned as I checked my pistol. I stashed it in my

belt, then got my brass knuckles, knife, and lock-picking tools out of the backpack.

Headlights flashed across us. We both ducked, and I peered over the edge as two army sedans peeled out from behind the house. The first car stopped at the cut in the fence. I could make out the silhouettes of five occupants. The driver got out and pulled back the section of chain-link. The man then waved the second sedan through. It turned left on the street and raced away. I counted four in that one. The driver of the first car got back in without bothering to close the fence and turned right, passing me at a fast clip.

Atkinson and I straightened and watched the two vehicles disappear.

"Where do you think they're going?" Atkinson asked.

"Maybe a quick getaway." I grabbed the door handle. "I'll be back. Stay low and out of sight."

"Mason, please—"

40

I got out before Atkinson could say anything else and moved toward the fence. While keeping an eye on the door and windows, I went around to the southern side of the property. I checked for bells or other types of alarms but didn't see any. I grabbed onto the top of the fence and hoisted myself up and over. I hit the ground and waited once more. All appeared quiet. But the house wasn't empty. There was a lone black sedan parked near the back porch.

I crept up to the side of the house and moved toward the back while checking each window. They were either boarded up or the curtains were closed. Just before I reached the corner of the side and back of the house, I came up to a basement window that was hidden by tall weeds.

I knelt and examined it. There was no glass, but there were boards nailed across it. The wood had rotted and shrunk away from the nails. I checked my surroundings, then grabbed the first board. It came loose with little effort. The second board put up more of a fight, but that one finally gave way with a groan. I stopped and waited to see if the noise might bring someone to investigate, but I only heard the wind and distant passing cars.

Feeling sure no one was coming, I crawled through the opening and dropped into the darkness. I used my lighter to find my way. The floor joists were at head height, forcing me to bend at the waist as I moved.

A couple of rats seemed unperturbed at my presence, and they wandered around the scattering of discarded furniture and a stacks of firewood that looked decades old. I reached the stairs leading up to the first floor. Fortunately, they were concrete, making it a silent climb to the door.

I knelt at the lock, doused the lighter, and pulled out my lock-picking tools. The old lock was a simple rim lock. In seconds I got the tumbler to turn, which I did slowly to minimize the noise. The lock slid back with a soft click.

I stood and pocketed the tool, then removed my pistol from the holster and turned the doorknob. I opened it just enough to peek through the gap. Beyond was a long hallway that led to a living room. The space was lit by a single lamp out of view. No one was visible, no noise of walking or talking.

To my left, and from the part of the house still hidden by the door, I heard faint clicking of metal on metal. It came at random intervals, ruling out anything mechanical. I slipped through the gap with my pistol aimed ahead of me. The sound came from the kitchen at the end of the hall. The room was dark except for a pool of light. A man had his back to me and was leaning over a table as he worked on something.

Taking slow steps, I moved down the hallway, toward the kitchen. The tiled flooring masked my footsteps. The light from the living room threw a shadow across the floor ahead of me, and I hoped the shadow wouldn't betray my presence.

I breached the kitchen doorway.

Then I saw the objects surrounding him. A wave of adrenaline coursed through me—detonators, blocks of plastic explosive, wiring, and electronic components. He was building a bomb.

I crept up and put the muzzle of my pistol on the back of his neck. He let out a chirp of surprise and froze.

"Put your hands behind your head," I said in a quiet voice.

The man hesitated, and I pushed the gun's muzzle deeper into his skull.

"I'll be happy to splatter your brains all over the kitchen."

Slowly, the man complied.

"Now, you're going to slide off the chair and lie on your stomach."

The man slid partially off the chair.

Movement blocked light from the living room. I jumped to my left just as a submachine gun opened fire. Rounds ripped into the room, smashing into cabinets, shattering glass, pulverizing plaster. The man making the bomb recoiled as bullets penetrated his torso. He fell to the ground.

I'd fallen on something covered in a blanket. I pulled at a corner. Underneath was Dr. Salameh. His chest was soaked with blood, and he lay still and lifeless. His eyes popped open, and he sputtered blood. With terror in his eyes, he looked at me. "I'm sorry," he said and struggled to breathe. "They have my wife. They—" He sobbed.

The shooter sprayed another burst of rounds into the room.

I crawled to the wall near the door to the hallway. I figured the shooter had about half the ammunition left in the machine gun's magazine. But I only had the eight rounds in my pistol. I cursed myself for not carrying along a spare magazine.

I rose from the floor and listened. No sound from the shooter. Probably waiting for me to make the first move. Charging down the hallway was not an option for either of us.

The bombmaker was still alive. He writhed in pain and tried to crawl out of harm's way. He would be dead soon; he was bleeding too much to survive for long.

If I could get the shooter to expend all the ammo, I might have a chance to run for it while he reloaded.

I slid across the wall, got ready, and stuck my head out. I saw the shooter, and a rage burned through me—

It was the assassin, Nadia.

I fired once and ducked back as she returned fire. Bullets blowing through the wall chased me as I dived for the corner.

Ten more rounds, then silence except for the last of the shell casings hitting the floor. Salameh still sobbed between gasps of air. The bombmaker grunted.

I moved quietly back to the edge of the threshold. With my muscles tensed, I leapt for the opposite side of the doorway. She fired but used fewer rounds.

"Looks as if we're in a Mexican standoff, as you Americans say," Nadia said with a British accent.

"There's one way out of this. Put down your weapon and surrender."

Nadia chuckled. "You know I won't stop until everyone you care about is gone from you. It's the least I could do for killing my lover."

"So you *are* the one behind the bombing at the intersection."

"I intend to finish the job."

Police sirens sounded in the distance.

Nadia said, "As for your friend in the car, she's in terrible need of care at the moment."

Rage and panic exploded in my mind. I growled and stepped out from behind the return wall and fired my pistol three times. There was no return fire. There was no sound from the living room.

I rushed to the back door and kicked it with all my strength. The wood around the door gave way, and it flew open. I jumped down the back portico and ran around the house with my gun up and at the ready. I expected her to take advantage of my panic to ambush me, but as I raced for the front of the house, she was nowhere to be seen.

As I was reaching the opening in the fence, Atkinson's Vauxhall started up, the headlights went on, and the car raced up the street. As it passed, I could see a man behind the wheel. Nadia sat in the passenger's seat, and she stared at me with an evil grin.

I fired at the speeding car until my magazine was empty. The car's rear windows blew out, but it did nothing to stop Nadia.

Grunting came from the shadows on the side of the road where the car had been parked. "Evelyn!" I rushed over to her. She was lying in the dirt. She was choking on her own blood while holding her chest. I removed her hand and pulled away her jacket. Blood oozed from a puncture wound just below the right breast.

I clamped one hand on her wound.

Her eyes were wide with pain and panic. I locked my gaze on her and tried to exude calm.

"She stabbed me," Atkinson said.

"Don't talk. The cops are coming."

"She came out of nowhere."

Two police squad cars, sirens blaring, screeched to a halt in front of the house.

"Help!" I stood and waved my hands like a madman. "Over here. She needs an ambulance."

41

Two policemen came up to me. One of them urged me to move aside, and the other knelt next to Atkinson.

I stood next to the first cop, watching helplessly.

"An ambulance is on the way, sir," the cop said.

I nodded my thanks. The one on the ground was doing what he could for Atkinson, but her breathing had become more labored. The cop standing by me was saying something, but I didn't hear him. I was too busy trying to control my rage, my anguish. My hands shook, and I found it hard to breathe. My thoughts swirled: I wanted to run after the assassin's car, comfort Evelyn, find the next Black Hand killer and gun him down. I thought of Laura, and a wave a guilt turned my stomach; I'd put someone else in danger, and they were paying the price.

"Sir, are you listening to me?" the cop asked with anger in his voice.

The ambulance pulled up, and the cop next to me waved the medics over to Atkinson's aid. Under the beams of the cops' flashlights, the medics went to work on her.

A sergeant approached us. I recognized him. It was Mills, the broad-shouldered cop who had accompanied DCI Gilman the first time I was picked up. There was a flicker of recognition in his eyes.

"You again," Sergeant Mills said. He nodded toward the house. "What's your side of the story?"

I was unsure how much I should reveal. What if he was on Wetherbee's team? Leaving out the events in Bethlehem, I told him about suspecting the Palestinian doctor of being Black Hand and following him here. I then told him about going in the house to investigate and finding a guy in the kitchen with bomb-making materials and then being ambushed by the woman assassin.

"She must have come out here to knife Mrs. Atkinson while I was confronting the bomb maker—"

I stopped when a policeman brought over a stretcher. The medics lifted her and carried her to the ambulance. I followed them over to the back end of the vehicle despite the sergeant's objections.

My chest constricted. Atkinson was lying deathly still while the medics got her ready for transport. The ambulance driver climbed out of the back, closed the doors, and got behind the wheel. I watched through the rear window as the second medic hooked up an IV to Atkinson. The engine started, and the ambulance drove away.

"What?" I asked, realizing Sergeant Mills had said something.

Mills let out an impatient sigh. "We found the bombs. Two were ready to go."

"Yes, and by the looks of the material on the bomber's table, I'm sure there were more. Shortly after I arrived to observe the house, nine members of the group drove away in two army staff cars about thirty minutes ago. Each one took off in a different direction. They were in a hurry, wherever they went."

"Did you get a good look at any of them?"

"They were Black Hand, for sure. Five were in one car and four in the other."

"And you claim that some mysterious assassin shot the bomb maker?"

"Just look at all the bullet holes in the guy's body and the rest of the room. She had a STEN and wasn't too particular about where she aimed it."

"I assume you were the target."

"Of course I was the target," I said, raising my voice. "Look, we're wasting time. There are two teams out there somewhere with bombs."

"I'm sorry, sir, if we neglected to bring our crystal ball. Without information about their destinations, we won't get very far. Come with me into the house and put your skills of observation to good use."

Sergeant Mills walked away from me without looking back. A second ambulance pulled up to the curb, which brought me back to the job at hand. It took all my willpower to move my legs, but finally I managed and followed the sergeant into the house.

As we headed for the hallway, one of the cops was climbing the stairs to the second floor. In the kitchen, another policeman was searching through cabinets, and another was checking the bomb maker, who had curled up and died several feet from the table.

I walked over to Dr. Salameh. The blanket was still pulled back. His eyes were wide and frozen in death. I pondered his last words. He seemed to be full of regret, and I guessed by his truncated message that the Black Hand had kidnapped his wife, and he'd been coerced into betraying his friend to save her.

Mills had me go over the events again, this time physically acting out the sequence as they happened. That done, I examined the bomb-making materials on the table. I had no experience building bombs, but I figured there were enough components and RDX plastic explosive for several large ones.

Someone yelled on the second floor. The words were muffled,

but there was panic in his voice. The boom of two gunshots followed.

The two cops, the sergeant, and I bolted out of the kitchen and down the hallway to the staircase. The two cops led the way. At the top was a broad hallway serving a half dozen rooms.

The third cop was flat against a wall next to the last door. We all stopped halfway down the hall when the third cop waved for us not to come any closer.

Whoever was inside fired two more shots. The rounds blew through the wood and struck the plaster wall on the opposite side of the hallway.

The shooter was trapped. Or maybe not …

I turned and hurried down the stairs.

Sergeant Mills hissed, "Mr. Collins, I'm not done with you." But for whatever reason, he remained where he was.

I headed for the kitchen, stepped over the dead bomb maker, and exited the house by the back entrance.

The trapped man was in a room on the second floor just off the portico. I stepped off and looked up. As I'd figured, the man was already dangling halfway out the single window. I ducked back under the portico roof and waited.

A moment later, the man landed hard on the ground. The twenty-foot drop was enough that he had to roll to keep from breaking any bones. I charged off the portico and was on top of him before he could get to his feet.

He reached for the pistol wedged in his belt, but that left him open. Enraged, I struck him in the face until my knuckles ached. Bloody and stunned, I pressed my knee into his chest and put all my weight on his rib cage. His mouth popped wide as he struggled to breathe. He tried to fight me off. I lifted his head and slammed it hard on the rocky ground several times.

I got in his face. "Where are your friends taking those bombs?"

"I don't know," the man said through gasps for air.

I wrapped my hands around his neck. "You're lying. I'll squeeze the life out of you if you don't tell me." I put pressure on his throat until he tapped my arm.

The man sucked in air through a raspy throat. "I only know one." He took in a deep breath. "Central police station. Because of what he did."

"Who is he?"

Strong hands grabbed me by the shoulders and pulled me off the man. I struggled against the hold of the three cops, but they had me pinned.

"Wait! He's about to tell me something."

Mills got in front of me and pointed a finger at my face. "You will calm down, sir, or I'll have you shackled and gagged."

I stopped fighting. One of the policemen let go of me and went to the prone man.

I pointed at my victim. "He said the central police station is one of the targets. And he claims it was because of someone, but you stopped me before he could say who. Ask him!"

"We'll interrogate him at the station," Sergeant Mills said.

"Didn't you hear me? The man says the station is a target."

The sergeant seemed too flustered for a response.

"I'll take over from here, Sergeant Mills," a man said behind us.

The hairs on the back of my neck stood up. It was CID Superintendent Wetherbee.

"Sir," Mills said in surprise and snapped to attention.

Two policemen came up to flank the superintendent. One of them was Wetherbee's driver, who had been with his boss the night Wetherbee shot the Black Hand member in cold blood.

My thoughts raced through my possible escape options.

The superintendent turned to Mills. "We'll take charge of your prisoner and Mr. Collins."

Maybe the sergeant already had suspicions about Wetherbee, or maybe they were aroused by a high-ranking officer showing up in the middle of the night and trying to take control of suspects. Whatever the reason, the sergeant took a step forward and said in a measured tone, "Sir, we have everything under control here. I assure you."

"I'm sure you do, Sergeant. However, you have your hands full with other pressing matters. Checking out this story of a possible bombing at the central police station, for example. And see what other intelligence you can find in the house. Those duties are far more vital than minding two miscreants."

The two cops accompanying Wetherbee came forward. Wetherbee's driver took my elbow.

I yanked my arm away. "I'm staying here."

The driver pulled out his pistol, held it waist high, and pointed it at my stomach. "Let's not create a fuss, shall we?" He then removed the .45 from my belt and the knife from my ankle sheath and handed them to Wetherbee. He'd missed my brass knuckles, but they wouldn't do me much good against guns.

The sergeant started to move toward me but stopped. He glanced from me to the superintendent, then turned on his heels and marched back into the house.

Wetherbee's other companion lifted the prisoner. The man had a tough time standing and struggled to breathe while holding his bloody jaw. The cop handcuffed the man, then prodded him with his pistol, and they headed for the front.

I locked eyes on Wetherbee. He returned a self-satisfied smile. The driver cuffed me, jammed the gun in my ribs, and pushed me along. Wetherbee followed. At the front of the house, they walked us toward a sedan parked inside the fence with its engine idling.

My mind raced. I knew that if I got in that car, I'd never be heard from again. Trying to fight or flee from three men with guns would be suicide. But so would getting in their car.

Wetherbee and his entourage stopped when they saw DCI Gilman and three plainclothes detectives standing at the gap in the fence. Gilman was talking with Sergeant Mills, but when he saw Wetherbee, he stepped forward.

Gilman and Wetherbee smiled politely at each other, but it felt like a standoff. Any suspicions I had that Gilman was Wetherbee's co-conspirator were gone.

"Superintendent Wetherbee, what a surprise seeing you here," Gilman said.

"This is a serious matter, which I intend to oversee personally."

"Highly irregular, don't you think?"

Wetherbee advanced toward the idling sedan. His two men followed with me and the Black Hand man in tow. "My rank allows me to do whatever I think is necessary."

I turned enough to reveal the driver's gun. "This man has a revolver pointed at my ribs. This is a kidnapping, not an arrest."

Gilman stepped in Wetherbee's way. "I must insist on taking custody of these men."

"Disobey me, and I'll have you put up on charges. I'll see you drummed out of the service."

Sergeant Mills moved in behind Gilman and glanced at the house. Wetherbee turned to look in the same direction. The sergeant's three cops stood on the porch, carefully watching what was happening. The superintendent looked from them to Gilman and his detectives as if weighing his options. Nervousness bled through his defiant façade. There were too many witnesses who might testify against him.

Wetherbee glared at Gilman as if that might intimidate his subordinate, but the chief inspector didn't back down.

Wetherbee nodded at his men. "Release them."

The man behind me holstered his revolver and unlocked my handcuffs. He then pushed me toward Gilman and threw my weapons on the ground near my feet. The other cop did the same with the Black Hand member.

With one last glare, Wetherbee walked past Gilman and

headed for his sedan. The two cops followed. They got in the car and drove off.

While I gathered up my pistol and knife, Gilman told two of the detectives to take the Black Hand member to the station. "Alert the watch commander of a possible bombing at the station." He pointed to the beaten man. "Then stash that pile of excrement where no one else can get to him and stay with him until you hear from me."

The two detectives did as they were ordered.

Gilman turned to Mills and thanked him. "See what you can find here. Anything that might help to track down those bombing locations."

The sergeant headed for the house, and his three uniformed companions entered behind him.

"That was a bold move," I said to Gilman. "You must have something mighty solid on Wetherbee."

"Call it strong conjecture."

"Shouldn't we be in there looking for clues? Especially since one of the targets might be your police station."

"I trust the sergeant to do a thorough job. We are to pursue another avenue."

Gilman tilted his head toward the sedan. I followed him and his remaining detective to the car. Gilman had me get in back with him. The detective got behind the wheel, reversed out of the property, and headed for the main street.

"Are you allowed to tell me what you have on Wetherbee?" I asked.

"Nothing I could use in a court of law."

I told Gilman about spotting a member of the Black Hand coming out of an administration office of the Italian Hospital and following him. "The constable holding a gun on me tonight drove Wetherbee up to the guy. Wetherbee got out of the car and had a chummy conversation with him, then shot him in the head at point-blank range. The guy never knew what hit him."

Gilman's expression became darker and darker with each detail. He stared at me as if trying to determine if I was making it all up. "That's a very serious accusation."

"I saw it with my own eyes."

"Why didn't you come to me immediately?"

"First, I wasn't sure whose side you were on. Not until tonight, anyway. Second, it's my word against a police superintendent."

Gilman thought a moment. "Just about impossible to prove. And a thorny problem if you try to come forward."

"It's gone past thorny. He was taking me and the Black Hand guy out somewhere in the desert to execute us. But you must have suspected that."

Gilman slumped back in his seat as if feeling the weight of everything pressing in on him.

I said, "Wetherbee's getting rid of anyone who might compromise him. Including Black Hand members."

Gilman looked out his window while his fingers drummed his thighs. His face turned resolute as he checked our route out the front windshield. I figured he'd come to some sort of conclusion, one that he wasn't planning on sharing with me. Instead, he changed the subject. "I heard about Mrs. Atkinson. I know you two had become good friends."

"It was that assassin. Nadia. She says she's going after anyone I care about."

Gilman turned to me with a look of confusion. "You talked to her?"

"From opposite sides of the house. She gave Evelyn a life-threatening wound to lure me out and ambush me. It would have worked if it wasn't for the cop cars spooking her."

"How did you find that house?"

I told him about following Dr. Salameh on a hunch.

"And who is Dr. Salameh?"

"He's dead, so it won't matter," I said and told him about

Nicholas, how I met the doctor through him. "I don't know Nicholas's real name—"

"Colonel Nicholas Fellowes. British intelligence. A good man."

"Then you know he died in a car bombing this evening in Bethlehem. Along with most of his team."

Gilman looked stunned, and it took a moment for him to respond. "I heard about the bomb but not the victims."

"Nicholas's source, whoever that was, told him Black Hand would be planting a bomb at the cathedral. It was a trap."

The inspector turned back to the side window and watched the city pass by. "We need to stop those bombers at any cost."

Gilman leaned forward and gave the detective some instructions I couldn't hear. The driver glanced at his commander in disbelief. He then shrugged and made a right turn.

The inspector sat back. "Under the circumstances, it's time we seek out an unorthodox source for assistance."

42

The detective driving Gilman's sedan parked the car in front of a three-story building in the southwest part of town. It appeared to be an office building, though there were no company names or other indications that it was being used as such.

Across the street and sitting in a V-shaped intersection was the military courts building, which despite the late hour was active with military personnel entering or leaving. A handful of soldiers guarded the approach to the entrance and kept a vigilant watch on the area.

I fought the urge to slide lower in my seat. Instead, I pulled my fedora down over my forehead. "The military courts are what you call unorthodox?"

"Not exactly," Gilman said.

The detective flashed the headlights twice, then cut the engine, and we sat there in silence. I found the signal odd and wondered about its purpose. Then a man in a tan suit, with his fedora pulled down in front of his face, came out of an alley while walking a small dog on a leash.

He let the dog explore the sidewalk while slowly making his way to the car. Once he was abreast of us, he leaned down and peered in the back window closest to Gilman. The detective inspector kept his gaze to the front as if he hadn't noticed the man.

The dogwalker tapped twice on the window and walked away. That appeared to be a signal, as Gilman opened the door and got out. He leaned over to look at me. "Come with me, please."

I exited the car and joined him on the sidewalk. We took the same alley that the dogwalker had come from and walked up to a side door of the office building. Gilman stopped and waited. I was about to ask him what was going on when the door opened, and a man stood in the dark hallway. I recognized his large frame. It was Mordechai.

"Okay," I said to Gilman. "This *is* unorthodox."

"Desperate times," the inspector said and stepped inside. I followed, and the three of us moved down the hallway in silence. We mounted a staircase lit by a single ceiling lamp until reaching the third floor. After a short hallway, we entered an open door.

There were eighteen other men and six women in a large space, probably once a conference room but now empty of furniture aside from several desks pushed together. The windows were blacked out. Even with that measure, they still only used small desk lamps for illumination. I recognized Emanuel and the two bodyguards from Ezra's house in Tel Aviv.

Mordechai closed the door behind us. "Welcome to our temporary operations center."

Men and women examined papers and consulted over maps. Someone was on the phone. A woman was talking on a walkie-talkie.

Then I noticed Joshua, Feldman's superior, and to my surprise, Feldman himself examining a set of documents. Nearby, Hazan sat with another man whom I recognized from the time Irgun picked us up in the Palestinian village.

Hazan glanced up at me, gave me a neutral expression, and

went back to his work. Feldman looked to be as surprised as I was when he noticed me. It seemed he wanted to come over to say hello but then glanced at Mordechai and stayed where he was.

"What brings the chief inspector of CID to us?" Mordechai asked Gilman.

The inspector told the man about what we'd found at the Black Hand house and about me witnessing the two cars speeding off in different directions. "We have reason to believe that they plan to set off bombs at two locations. Maybe more."

I said, "We're coming to you because the CID and Brit intelligence are hamstrung by divided loyalties."

"Mordechai is aware of this problem," Gilman said to me. "It's the reason we've formed an alliance of sorts."

Mordechai added, "Your information about the high-level conspiracy is why I approached the inspector."

"We lost one of our most valuable allies this evening," Gilman said to Mordechai. "Colonel Fellowes. The Black Hand is on the move, and Wetherbee has been emboldened. It's time to make an all-out move."

"I managed to get some information out of the Black Hand member," I said. "He thinks the central police station is possibly one of the targets. We don't know the other, but Nicholas—Colonel Fellowes—was going to the Jewish hospital, the Bikur Cholim, on the rumor it was next on the list."

Mordechai thought for a moment. "How do you know it isn't another trap?"

"I don't."

"We can send a team, but it's just one of many rumors we've received. Three of them come from more reliable sources. That's what we've been preparing for this evening. I can give you three people."

"If we come across an armed group, we'll need more than that."

"It's all I can spare."

Mordechai moved to the middle of the room and shouted out orders in Hebrew. The men and women went into action, drawing out STEN submachine guns from a storage box at the back of the room.

Gilman turned to me. "As a policeman, I cannot be a part of this. I will leave you here and go back to interrogate the prisoner."

"Watch out for Wetherbee. He might go gunning for you."

He nodded. "We will both need a bit of luck this evening. If all goes well, we'll meet up later."

The inspector went up to Mordechai and said something I couldn't hear. They shook hands, and the inspector left.

While everyone prepared for an assault, Mordechai walked up and pointed to the three who were assigned to go with me. "Since you've worked closely with Arie and David, they'll go with you. Eliana will be your third."

Feldman, Hazan, and Eliana were preparing their equipment when I approached.

"What about the bomb at your sister's kibbutz?" I asked Feldman. "Is Rachel and everyone else okay?"

Feldman chuckled. "It wasn't a bomb. They thought it was, but it turned out to be a generator in an outbuilding. I tried to convince them to replace it, but they didn't have the money."

Feldman introduced Eliana, and she gave me a curt nod. The woman was in her midtwenties, with long, dark hair and chiseled features. Fierce, determined eyes looked back at me, along with a heavy dose of suspicion. I couldn't blame her. I was an outsider. She didn't know me. My fight was not her fight.

"Together once again," I said to Feldman and Hazan.

"Going out on this operation with you was not my choice," Hazan said.

"Man, you never let up," I said.

Feldman groaned with impatience. "David, please, Mason has proven to be valuable on numerous occasions."

"The mission is the important thing here," Eliana said in a German accent. "Leave your emotions behind and do the job."

I bowed to her. "Well said. If we do run into a gang of Black Hand, we're going to have our hands full."

"We've been in that situation before," Eliana said and headed for the door.

Feldman shrugged. "If she only knew what you and I have been through."

The three of us hoisted our backpacks and followed Eliana. We reached the ground floor and exited the building into a parking lot. Hazan surged ahead and got behind the steering wheel before Eliana had a chance. I got in back with Feldman.

While Hazan navigated a circuitous route north, Feldman told Eliana about our time in Italy and on the *Magen David*. I presumed that was to allay any concerns she had about my presence, but she showed no signs of acknowledging his words. She kept looking out the windshield with a stern expression. I figured, despite any previous experience, she was scared. Grit and determination would be her best weapons.

43

The Bikur Cholim Hospital sat on the corner of Street of the Prophets and Chancellor Avenue, not far from the neighborhood full of cinemas and few blocks from Atkinson's apartment building. Though the building was no more than thirty years old, it reminded me of a Renaissance palace, with its ornate main entrance flanked by columned arches. At three stories high, it sprawled along Chancellor Avenue. Finding the bombers or the bomb in such a large building would be a painstaking job.

Hazan turned onto Chancellor and drove past the hospital. As he reached the southern corner of the building, there was an alleyway. About halfway down, I made out the silhouette of a sedan parked in the shadows. A light by a side entrance lit up the rear fender and part of the roof painted army green.

I hit Feldman's arm and pointed. "I think that's one of the cars I saw leaving the house."

Hazan went a block farther down and parked next to an apartment building. He turned in his seat to face me. "Are you sure?"

"No, but it has the shape of an army staff car—"

"The shape?" Hazan said with skepticism.

"It was dark, but it looked like it was army green to me. What is a car like that doing parked in a dark alley by a side entrance?"

"He has a point," Feldman said.

We looked at Eliana, who nodded her agreement.

"It could be our best shot at getting the gang," I said. "Instead of combing the entire building, we get them as they come out."

"How many, do you think?" Feldman asked.

"The car heading south had five—"

I stopped when a man in a suit with a hat pulled over his eyes emerged from the alley. We all ducked low and watched. The man stood on the sidewalk and looked both ways. He lit a cigarette, took a few puffs, then sauntered back the way he came.

I sat up, as did the others. "Five would be too many to go in unnoticed. I figure one in the car and one keeping watch." I popped open my door. "I'll take care of the watcher. One of you get the driver. And keep at least one of them alive."

Hazan hissed his displeasure for what I figured was me giving orders. Despite that, he, Feldman, and Eliana got out of the car. They hid their submachine guns under their trench coats, and we moved forward.

We crept up to the corner of the alleyway. Hazan and I peered around the corner. The watcher was making his way to the opposite end of the alley. The sedan was parked, facing the other way. The driver's side was in darkness, but I was sure there was someone behind the wheel ready for a quick getaway.

Hazan and I turned to Feldman and Eliana. "We're going to have to do this quick. The guy watching is about to come back this way. Get the driver before he sees me."

We moved out together, staying as low as we could while keeping up a fast pace. The watcher was almost at the other end. I figured he'd do the same thing: stop, check both directions, then head back toward the car and us. I'd be out in the open. I couldn't risk using my pistol and warn his buddies. It would be the knife.

We came up on the car. Remaining low, I ran alongside it. I

pulled out my knife, then accelerated into a sprint. My only hope was that the others would take care of the driver before he had a chance to alert the watcher. If he was on the ball and sounded his horn, I was sunk.

Behind me, I heard the car door open with a creak. A man got out one syllable, then came a muffled shriek.

The watcher turned on his heels, saw me, and jammed his hand in his suitcoat. I collided with him just as he began to pull out his pistol. The impact must have caused him to fire his weapon. He jerked as he landed on his back and cried out in pain as I fell on top of him.

He tried to pull out his gun, but I trapped his hand. Then he began to writhe in pain. I clamped my hand over his mouth to keep him from crying out as he struggled against me.

All the rage burst out, the source of all my loss and pain was focused on him. I wanted to snuff the life out of him, but I repressed the urge and only stared into his eyes as his struggling weakened. In moments, he became still, his face, his eyes, frozen in agony and fear.

"What was that about keeping someone alive?" Hazan said behind me.

I ignored the remark and got to my feet. That was when I noticed my shirt sticking to my stomach. The man had bled profusely, and it had soaked through his clothes and into mine.

I turned to Hazan. The rage and agony still coursed through me. He took a step back. His smug expression was gone, and in its place, one of fear or pity. I didn't care which, and it was the only thing that stopped me from giving him a right cross.

"Eliana got to the driver before we could stop her," he said. "But he's still alive."

I picked up one leg of my victim and started to drag his body around the corner. Hazan grabbed the other leg, and we pulled it up the alley and stuffed it behind a cluster of trashcans.

We were rounding the corner of the alley to head for the car when the side door to the hospital opened. Three men came out and made quick strides for the car. One of them saw Hazan and me. He swung around while bringing up his submachine gun to shoot.

Feldman and Eliana stood up from behind the car and fired their submachine guns.

The sound was deafening in the narrow alley as the three men were gunned down.

Hazan and I ran to the car.

"The bomb!" Feldman said. "We have to find the bomb."

"No, we don't," Eliana said and held up a rotary-style blasting machine. "I found this in the back seat."

We all looked toward the bodies and the side entrance. Wires emerged from a crack in the door and ended near the hands of one of the dead men. They planned to detonate the bomb once they got in the car. Set it off and head for the hills.

"You and I should try to find it," Feldman said to me.

I stopped him from dashing toward the entrance. "It won't go off without the blasting machine. Let the police find it. We've got to get out of here, now."

Hazan tossed me some car keys. "Get the other car. Eliana and I will take this one. Meet us back at the operations center."

Feldman and I ran for the Irgun's car as Hazan and Eliana raced out of the alley.

44

The eastern horizon glowed with the coming of dawn when Feldman parked in the lot behind the office building. We were at least an hour behind Hazan and Eliana, and we were forced to sit tight when the police and army surrounded the hospital. Fortunately, we were parked far enough down the street to avoid being trapped by their vehicles. I figured they'd found the bomb, because the army personnel drove away after about forty minutes. Once their investigation focused on the interior, it was then just a matter of backing down the street until we were clear.

"At least we've eliminated over half the group," Feldman said as we got out of the car.

"If we don't take down the big shots in the conspiracy, they'll just replace them with more."

We headed for the back entrance of the building.

"You're getting as gloomy as David," Feldman said. "We stopped a catastrophic event and saved countless lives. Celebrate that for a second or two."

"I'm not going to do any celebrating until that assassin, Nadia, is dead, and I can get Laura out of here."

"I hear she's out of the coma. Take heart in that."

"Since when did you get so cheery?"

"If you don't release some of that pressure, you're going to explode. I saw you back there with that Black Hand chap, that look in your eyes."

I stopped in my tracks and balled my fists. "I lost a child, I nearly lost the woman I love, and I may lose a good friend. All because of that group of fanatic cutthroats whose only objective is to screw you and your people."

Feldman turned to me, his good humor gone. "Don't talk to me about losing family and friends to wanton murderers. If I counted all the relatives the Nazis killed, the friends in war, or the fighting here, it would eat my insides out. Like it's eating at David. If you let your anger take over your life, you've lost. You'll wind up nothing but a hollow man."

"I see you two finally made it back," someone said behind us.

We turned. Hazan was standing not far from us with a smile on his face, though it looked more bitter than playful. He tilted his head toward the door. "Come on. They're interrogating the driver now."

The three of us mounted the stairs in silence.

When we reached the third floor, I asked, "Get anything out of him yet?"

Hazan's only response was to surge ahead and shove open the door to the operations room. Feldman and I entered a moment later and were treated to a man's muffled screams emanating from behind a door at the far end of the large room.

It sounded like Mordechai and another man were throwing alternating questions at the driver: "Where are they planning to set off the other bomb?" "Where is the rest of the group?" "Who's in charge?" "Where can we find him?"

After each question, the driver let out another cry of agony. Those sounds chilled me to the bone. I had no sympathy for the man, and left alone with him, I might have beat him to a pulp, but his screams inflamed all the scars of my own experience with torture, and the terror that came with it, at the hands of the Nazis. I'd used it a couple of times in the past year or so, but each incident had a cumulative effect on my mind, threatening to push me closer to a breaking point.

Hazan and Feldman stood amid the desks and stared at the door. Several had left, and others tried to do their work. I went to a large map of the city tacked to the wall and feigned interest while a layer of cold sweat dampened my already bloody shirt.

Eliana came over the me and held out a clean shirt. "You should change."

I took it from her. "Thanks. Do you guys always keep extra clothes here in case you get bloodied?"

"This one belonged to Elijah. He always dressed in nice clothes and kept extra shirts and trousers."

"Won't he mind if I'm wearing this one?"

"He was arrested two days ago."

The man gave out a particularly blood-curdling scream, and Eliana flinched. "Are you okay? You look pale."

"That makes two of us."

She gave me a halfhearted smile. "You don't have to stay."

I returned the same weak smile. "I'm fine. Just remembering all the fun I had at the hands of the Gestapo."

I took the shirt. Eliana quietly looked at me. Her facial expression remained neutral, but her eyes lost focus as if deep in thought. She then turned and went back to a desk. I took off my jacket and blood-soaked shirt and changed into the clean one. The jacket's inner lining had a big stain, but there was nothing I could do about it and pulled it on.

The door of the interrogation room opened, and Mordechai and Joshua stepped out—a joint torture effort by Haganah and Irgun. Mordechai nodded to a man stationed nearby, who went into the room and closed the door.

Feldman, Hazan, some of the others, and I gathered around

Mordechai. Joshua blew past us, went to the single telephone, and dialed.

"Did he give up the location of the second bomb?" Feldman asked.

Mordechai shook his head. "The groups were not aware of the other's target."

"And you believe him?" Hazan asked.

An artful smile formed on Mordechai's face. "Only because he gave us something better: the location of Black Hand's headquarters. An old military camp south of Haifa." He pointed at Joshua. "Our Haganah friend is notifying a Palmach unit in the area. They will make the assault tomorrow night. A daylight raid will be too risky." He pointed to me. "You and your companions will come with me, along with Joshua. Emanuel and his group will meet us there. Bring weapons. British paratroopers have a base not far from there. If Palmach fails to make it quickly and quietly, we may run into heavy resistance. In the meantime, everyone should get some rest."

IT WAS PUSHING MIDNIGHT WHEN OUR TWO CARS ROUNDED A BEND in the hills south of Haifa. That day and evening, I'd stayed in the blacked-out room near the military courts with the rest of the Haganah and Irgun people and endured restless naps or paced endlessly. I was in a car with Mordechai, Feldman, and Hazan, while Joshua drove the second car with Eliana and two others as passengers. Nestled in the twists and turns of the hills near Mount Carmel and just south of Haifa, our two cars stopped next to a grove of Aleppo pine trees and got out.

Over the next rise, I saw a column of smoke blotting out the stars. There weren't any signs of military or police vehicles, and there were no sounds of gunfire or explosions. Word was that

Palmach had been forced to make the assault earlier than planned when they were spotted. So either the Palmach assault had failed or the headquarters had already been overrun and silenced.

I was hoping for the latter; I had no desire to get into a firefight with entrenched Black Hand members, which would have surely attracted a company of British paratroopers.

The seven of us regrouped at the edge of the grove. Emanuel and three other Irgun commandos emerged from the trees and greeted Mordechai and the others. Everyone charged their weapons, and we moved out, crossing through the grove as we climbed uphill.

We came across a dirt road and followed it around a sharp curve. The camp's chain-link fence marked the boundary. A gate sat open with two bodies dressed in civilian clothes crumpled next to it. They must have been Black Hand, because no one from our group bothered to check their status.

We passed through the gate. The area was in darkness, though there was a glow of lights beyond an outcropping of rock.

Two men in fatigues and berets with submachine guns slung on their shoulders came out from the shadows. They recognized a few from our group, including Feldman. Handshaking all around and the exchange of friendly banter. Then the two Palmach soldiers motioned us forward.

As we went around the bend, the camp buildings came into sight. They looked to be standard military installations, with one main single-story building and two smaller ones, probably barracks or operations rooms. The smoke I'd seen came from one of the smaller structures.

One of the Palmach commandos pointed to the smoldering building. He spoke in Hebrew, and Feldman translated, "The enemy tried to burn all of their records. The Palmach commandos were only able to save a handful of them."

Four bodies lay on the ground. Two Palmach soldiers were

rifling through their pockets, presumably for IDs or other documents.

I broke off from the group to inspect the dead to see if any of them was Nadia, but they were all males. My impulse was to hurry through the three buildings in hopes of finding her corpse, but I figured it was best to stay with Mordechai's group in case the other Palmach commandos mistook me for Black Hand.

Our group was moving toward the main building, and I caught up with them. An older man came out and stepped up to Mordechai. There were no smiles exchanged, simply cordial nods, a meeting of rivals united by a single cause.

They talked a few moments, then Feldman walked up to them and greeted the man, who I assumed was the Palmach commander. Mordechai called for Hazan, Joshua, Emanuel, and me to follow him, and told the rest to fan out to guard the premises and search for possible Black Hand survivors.

The five of us followed the Palmach commander inside the larger building. The interior was typical army, with bare wood walls and ceiling. To the right was an open space with bunks bookended by several tables and chairs, where two Black Hand commandos lay sprawled on the floor. To the left were three offices. Only one had been occupied, and two more bodies lay motionless among scattered papers and shattered glass.

The commander faced the group and spoke in Hebrew.

Feldman translated for my benefit, "This is the operations and housing building. The one partially burned was for communications and logistics, and the other held weapons, bomb-making material, and supplies, including a quantity of Arab clothing. He says they also found berets we commonly wear, as well as false IDs with Jewish names."

Some of the men talked quietly in urgent tones.

I raised my hand. "Did you find any women fighters?"

The Palmach commander regarded me with curious eyes. "You're the American I've heard about," he said in accented

English. "No, we have not come across your assassin. From what we can tell by the documents we found, there are at least seven or so unaccounted for."

"What about the other splinter groups?" Joshua asked, continuing in English, presumably for my benefit.

"Come with me," the commander said, and he led us to a map laid out on a desk in one of the offices. He tapped on the map. "Besides the one that our American friend here found in Jerusalem, there is one in Jaffa. I telephoned our forces stationed there and told them to take on that group."

Mordechai stepped up to the desk. "Any idea of the intended target of the Jerusalem gang?"

"Unfortunately, there's only a list of possible locations: the Jewish Agency, the central police station, and the Rothschild-Hadassah University Hospital on Mount Scopus."

"Another hospital," I said. "We stopped them planting a bomb at the Bikur Cholim. They're hoping for maximum casualties."

"It's also the easiest target of the three," Feldman said.

Joshua picked up the telephone and dialed.

Mordechai turned to Emanuel. "Find another phone and get a squad over there, too. And tell them to watch out for the Haganah unit. We wouldn't want them shooting at each other."

As Emanuel left the building, he passed a Palmach commando rushing in. He went up to the commander and said something to him. The commander then announced to us, "The Tel Aviv detachment successfully assaulted the Black Hand in Jaffa. The Black Hand unit was eliminated, though apparently, they put up a strong defense. Heavy casualties, but no figures yet."

The room fell silent. The only sounds came from the activity outside. The commander dismissed the messenger and said to the room, "At least, gentlemen, we can say that the Black Hand is effectively put out of action."

"Let us hope the seven remaining members aren't aware of

the attacks on their headquarters and the Jaffa contingent," Mordechai said.

"If they know, they'll be desperate," I said.

"And these assaults will not go unanswered by the police and army," Hazan said.

"Agreed," the commander said. "I suggest we take as much material and weapons as we can, as quickly as we can, and go underground."

The group broke up and began exiting the building in twos and threes, while the Palmach commander ordered his commandos to gather up what they could. I took one last look at the dead Black Hand members and noticed something odd about one man's cheeks. They were puffed out slightly, and there was something white in his mouth.

No one paid attention as I squatted next to the victim and pushed down on his jaw. The man had stuffed a piece of paper in his mouth. He must have tried to swallow it but was stopped by a bullet. I plucked out the wad of half-chewed paper and stretched it out. The man had pulverized most of the paper, and the words in ink had blurred. There was only a portion of one word distinguishable: "Oper …"

I joined Feldman and Joshua. "I found this piece of paper in one of the dead men's mouths."

Feldman and Joshua looked at the chewed mess.

"Oper," Feldman said. "Not much to go on."

"Did you show it to Mordechai?" Joshua asked.

I shook my head. "There's not enough here to bother him with it."

Joshua nodded, and we headed out of the camp with the others.

"I'd like to be on the team going to the university hospital," I said.

"Mason, we're two hours away from Jerusalem," Feldman said. "We won't make it in time. And they're not going to wait for us."

"We'll be fortunate enough to get back without being held up by the Brits," Joshua said.

"Get me to Jerusalem, and I'll take it from there. I'm not going to rest until I know that Black Hand is wiped out of existence. And that includes the ones at the top."

45

I t was dawn as we approached Jerusalem from the north. The sun had yet to rise above the mountains to the east, but it still lit up the gold dome of the mosque on the Temple Mount. The trip back from Haifa had taken three hours, with Feldman using back roads to avoid patrols. Joshua sat up front, with me in back. Mordechai and the others had gone to Tel Aviv, leaving the three of us to make it back to Jerusalem on our own.

Between brief periods of dozing—I couldn't remember the last time I'd slept—we debated our next move and the possible meaning of the word "Oper" on the chewed note. Mount Scopus and the university hospital lay off to our left, and we half expected to see smoke on the horizon from the bomb we were unable to prevent, but the mount and the city to the south looked deceivingly peaceful. That led us to hope Haganah had found the remainder of the Black Hand and put them out of action.

We descended the hill and pierced the outskirts of the city dotted by houses and fields with patchworks of olive trees until reaching a densely packed neighborhoods with single-story houses.

Feldman took several turns to avoid major intersections. I

held on to the back of his seat when he took a sweeping curve a little too fast. I was about to suggest he slow down when a man stepped out of his car and waved at us.

Feldman slammed on the brakes. I put my hand on my pistol, but neither of my companions reacted.

The young man rushed up with a look of urgency, and Feldman rolled down the window.

"You just missed a military patrol," the young man said in English with a British accent. "They keep coming back and forth, and they've blocked the next intersection. You've got to get off the streets right now." He pointed to a house not much bigger than a single-car garage. "Park behind there and wait inside. I will let you know when it's clear."

Feldman did as the young man directed. The yard was nothing but dirt and rocks. The car kicked up a lot of dust, and I hoped we hadn't attracted any attention. The young man met us as we jumped out of the car, then went to the back door and unlocked it. We entered the house, but he stayed on the porch.

"The Haganah unit found nothing at the university hospital," the kid said.

"No Black Hand and no bomb?" Joshua asked.

The young man shook his head. He must have heard something we didn't, because his ears pricked up, and he rushed toward the front of the house.

We entered the ramshackle house. The interior consisted of a corner kitchen and cramped living room, a bathroom, and one bedroom. The heat of the previous day still lingered in the space, along with the odor of old frying oil.

I went to the front window and peeked through a gap in the burgundy curtains. The kid jumped back into his car and sat low in an attempt to conceal himself. The street was quiet, no pedestrians, no vehicles on the road.

Then I saw why the kid had run to his car. A three-vehicle

convoy of soldiers slowly rolled past. The floor vibrated from the heavy armored cars, and I stepped back from the window.

"We should be able to move out once the curfew lifts," Feldman said and looked at his watch. "About an hour and a half from now."

I turned back to the room. "The police know who you two are. As far as they and the army are concerned, those Black Hand members we killed at the Bikur Cholim Hospital were Brits. It's risky to go out there while they're looking for suspects."

"Let us worry about that," Feldman said as he dropped to the dusty sofa and leaned back. "In the meantime, why don't you try to get some rest."

Joshua took his advice and sat in one of the chairs, laying his head back and closing his eyes.

I couldn't sleep or even sit down. Something was gnawing at me, and I wouldn't rest until I figured out what it was. I pulled out the ball of paper and flattened it out. It had to be part of an important message, important enough for the guy to try to swallow it during an assault.

I held it up to the sunlight filtering through the curtains. It was still a blurry mess, but a few words started to resolve on closer inspection. The "at" after the word fragment "Oper," had to mean "Operation." The next word was faint and indistinct, but the letters were clearer in the light. But the combination of letters made little sense to me.

I stepped over to Feldman. He opened his sleepy eyes and gave me a look of annoyance. "What?"

"Look at this," I said and handed him the chewed paper.

"It looks just the same as last time."

"Hold it up to the light."

He did so, and I leaned over to point out the few letters that were discernable.

I said, "Add the *at* to *oper* and you have *operation*. The next word seems readable, but I can't make out the meaning."

Feldman sat up as he stared at the word. "Hinnom."

Joshua pushed himself out of the chair and ambled over to us. He took the message and looked at it as we did.

"What is Hinnom?" I asked.

Joshua handed the paper back to Feldman. "It's a valley south-west of Jerusalem's Old City."

"It's more than just a valley," Feldman said. "Using that name for an operation makes my flesh crawl."

Joshua gave him a quizzical look.

"You should know the *Tanakh* better than that," Feldman said, referring to the Hebrew Bible. "It is said that the valley is where some of the kings of Judah sacrificed children by fire to the ancient gods. It was then considered cursed."

The idea of an operation referring to burning children sent a chill down my spine.

Joshua gave Feldman a dismissive wave and returned to his chair. "Do you seriously believe that someone in British intelligence made up the name of an operation based on ancient writings about Judean kings?"

"What other reason would they have for doing such a thing?" Feldman asked.

"Don't dismiss British intelligence," I said. "They came up with this name on purpose, and it has two elements: a location and an objective. It's not something we can afford to ignore. If we assume they're referring to the real valley, and it has to do with children, then what can that be? What children's activities takes place there?"

"Sports fields, playgrounds, schools," Feldman said, and he studied the rumpled piece of paper more intently.

The idea of a school being the target sent another chill through me. "When I interrogated a Black Hand member in Evelyn's apartment, he said their plan was to cause the greatest pain for the Jews. That sounds like a school to me. You guys know the city. What kinds of schools are located in the valley?"

"There's the Arab College," Joshua said. "It's not far from the British governor's mansion."

Feldman shot to his feet, a look of alarm spread across his face. "The Hebrew School for Girls. It's at the base of Mount Zion and right next to the Valley of Hinnom."

I hurried over to the window, opened it, and waved for the young man in the car to come. He cracked open his door, looked both ways, then dashed out of the car and headed for the back of the house.

All three of us met him at the rear door.

"Did any bombs go off in Jerusalem last night?" Feldman asked.

The young man didn't know me from Adam and shifted his look between Feldman and Joshua. "I don't think so."

"South of the Old City," I said. "Nothing? Are you sure?"

The kid continued to look to my companions. I snapped my fingers in his face to urge him to speak.

"We thought it would be at the university hospital on Mount Scopus. But nothing happened. The city was quiet. I guess because the police and soldiers are everywhere."

Joshua dismissed him, and the young man headed back to the front.

"Maybe we were wrong," Joshua said.

"Are there any dorms at the school?" I asked.

Feldman shook his head.

"Then setting off a bomb there in the middle of the night wouldn't do much."

Feldman looked at his watch. "They have to wait until classes are in session. It's almost seven. Classes should start in an hour."

"Call your friends and get them down there, now," I said.

The three of us searched through the house for a telephone, but there wasn't one.

"How far is it from here?" I asked.

"Two and a half to three miles."

"You're not suggesting we go there on our own," Feldman said to me.

"It'll take longer to track down your friends than it would to go ourselves."

"You forget that the city is crawling with cops and soldiers," Joshua said. "We won't get a mile before they pick us up."

"We've got an hour," I said. "Find some back ways and get us there."

Feldman looked to Joshua, who bit his lip as he thought. Finally, he said, "Worth a try."

We gathered our weapons and packs and ran out of the house. Joshua got behind the wheel. Feldman got in the front passenger's seat, and I got in back. The kid in the car sat up and stared at us wide-eyed as Joshua raced out of the lot and fishtailed up next to him.

I rolled down the window and said, "Find whoever you can and tell them to get to the Hebrew School for Girls in Hinnom valley as soon as they can."

Joshua hit the accelerator.

46

I had to hold on to the back of Feldman's seat each time Joshua took another crazy turn on the twisted streets. He was taking the hilly roads east of the Old City, climbing up and over Mount of Olives. The sun was high enough in the sky to spill its orange light onto the city and throw long shadows in the valleys.

Feldman pointed out Mount Zion south of the Old City walls. Just beyond that and still hidden from view was the Valley of Hinnom. Urban sprawl had not reached that area, and it was dotted with churches and smaller structures amid swathes of olive trees and Aleppo pines.

We began to descend toward a road that swept around Mount Zion. The far side of the valley was in sight and not more than five hundred feet across as the crow flies, but we still had to navigate a winding road to get us to the bottom. Joshua used the slope to increase his speed, but when we came around a hairpin turn, he let off on the gas.

A police checkpoint was up ahead with wooden barriers blocking the road. Three police stood near the barrier, and two squad cars and an army Jeep were parked nearby. The other policemen and soldiers were leaning on their vehicles, talking and smoking. There were no side roads, and the land rose steeply on the right and dropped on the left. We had no way to escape short of hitting the brakes and reversing uphill. And that was out of the question because several cars had already come up from behind us.

"What do we do, lads?" Joshua said.

I leaned forward to get a better look. There was one car stopped at the checkpoint. If we could time it right ... "Come up to the barricade nice and easy so they don't start shooting, then crash through at the last moment."

Joshua did as I'd suggested, rolling toward the cops and the barricades as if planning to stop. It took longer than I'd hoped for the car in front of us to move on. Both Joshua and Feldman stiffened in their seats, and my fingers dug into the back of the driver's seat.

Not fifty feet from the checkpoint, one of the cops moved the barrier to let the car through, and it drove off. Then the same cop waved his arms at us to stop.

"Brace yourselves," Joshua said and hit the gas pedal.

Our car surged forward. The three cops dived out of the way, and Joshua slammed into the wooden barriers. The wood shattered, and the pieces flew out of the way or clattered on the car's hood.

We came up fast on the car that had been waved on before us. Joshua had to swerve out of the way and barely avoided a head-on collision with a delivery truck. Cars honked at our recklessness and excessive speed.

Behind us, the two police cars and the Jeep were in pursuit.

"Step on it," I said. "We've got the cops and army on our tail."

Joshua sped around another slow-moving vehicle. "I can see them."

The car's tires and brakes strained in the brutal turns. Fortunately, the same could be said for our pursuers. We took another curve in the descent, bringing the cops and army vehicles above us.

"There," Feldman said, pointing to the opposite side of the narrow valley. "The school. If we can just stay ahead of them—"

The Jeep that was behind us had bypassed the curve and now bounced down the rocky slope. It hit the pavement right in front of us. Joshua swerved left. The Jeep impacted the road and bounced onto the shoulder, narrowly avoiding a tumble down the next slope.

Joshua flew past the Jeep while the driver got control of his vehicle. It had failed to cut us off or ram us, but I had to congratulate the bold move.

It was now just behind us, giving one of the soldiers a clear shot. He fired his pistol. Rounds hit the trunk. One pierced the back windshield and exited through the roof.

Joshua zigzagged the car to make it harder to hit us. He steered around other cars, men riding donkeys, a horse-drawn cart. That slowed us down, allowing our pursuers to catch up. We quickly encountered dense traffic, causing the soldier to refrain from further gunfire, but what they would do once we stopped was something I couldn't answer.

We got to the valley floor and made one last turn. The school came up fast. It sat on a flat, open area near the summit of the southern edge of the valley. Several cars were parked on the side of the road. School kids were still filtering into the front entrance.

Joshua slammed on the brakes. Even before the car came to a stop, I launched out of the back seat and turned to the police cars and the Jeep screeching to a stop only yards away. Cops got out with their pistols up. The three soldiers in the Jeep jumped out and brandished their rifles.

I held up my hands and yelled, "American. I'm an American. There is a bomb inside the schoolhouse."

The cops moved forward. No one listened to my warning. I

heard car doors shut behind me, and two of the cops altered their aim away from me and toward Feldman and Joshua.

"Get on the ground, now," the police sergeant said as he continued to aim his pistol at me.

"You have to believe me, Sergeant," I said. "We only did this to stop a violent gang from setting off a bomb. You've got to send your men in there and get the students out before it's too late."

The sergeant waved his pistol toward the car. "Put your hands on the roof and don't move."

As I complied, I pleaded, "You have to listen to me. Get them out, now!"

Feldman and Joshua protested as well, but the two cops shoved us against the car and started to search us for weapons. I glared at the sergeant while they were doing it, then I noticed Sergeant Mills step forward from the second squad car.

He looked at me, then went up to the other sergeant. "I know this man. He's on our side. I can vouch for him. If he says there's a bomb inside, then it's the truth." He turned to the soldiers and his two companions. "Get everyone out."

The sergeant guarding me nodded to his two constables. "Let him go, but restrain the other two."

The constable holding me removed his hand from my back, and I turned to watch the other constables and soldiers rush toward the school. They yelled at the students and teachers who were still outside to run for the street.

Shots erupted from the east side of the school building. One soldier went down. Rounds from a machine gun whizzed past my head.

I spun around and saw four men with submachine guns firing their weapons as they raced for a sedan parked on the side of the building with the driver waiting behind the wheel. I recognized the sedan as one that drove away from the Black Hand safe house east of Jerusalem.

The three policemen near the car ducked and opened fire, as did the cops and soldiers running for the school. One of the Black Hand shooters tumbled to the ground, while the other three managed to get in their car. The driver peeled out of the dirt space and raced for the street. All the while the cops and soldiers fired at them.

The car hit pavement and started to turn on the road to get away.

Sergeant Mills brought up a Bren machine gun from the Jeep, propped it on our car, and pulled the trigger. The gun jerked on its bipod and spewed out bullets.

Rounds pierced the car's trunk and smashed the back window. The escaping car looked like it might make a clean getaway, but then it slowed and veered for the ledge and the valley floor below. It careened off the cliff and rolled down the steep hill until it rammed into a boulder.

Most of the policemen sprinted for the getaway car.

"No, wait," I yelled. "The children. The bomb!"

The sergeant and his two constables holding us went for the getaway car, leaving the three of us alone. Mills and his team sprinted into the school. Joshua, Feldman, and I looked at each other, half surprised to be left unguarded.

I dashed toward the school. Joshua and Feldman followed me. We yelled at the girls and teachers outside to get far away, and then ran inside the school. The vestibule led to three hallways that formed a T. Girls and the adult teachers were already running in panic and bypassing us.

Two soldiers were in the front hallway, going from door to door. At the junction of the hallways, we saw constables to the left.

Feldman, Joshua, and I hurried down the right hallway. We checked each room and worked our way down. Most of the classrooms were empty, but in the last one, a teacher and a handful of six- and seven-year-old girls were huddled together in a corner, seemingly too frightened to move. The woman had her arms wrapped around the girls, her eyes wide in panic.

The three of us rushed up to the group. The woman curled into a ball when she saw us. The three of us shouting for her to move made it worse. Finally, Feldman and Joshua picked up the woman while she cried out and flailed her arms and legs. They ignored her while speaking Hebrew in reassuring tones.

I enveloped the girls in my arms and pushed them to the door. "Go, go, go!" I didn't care if they understood English or not, but it didn't matter. They got the message and raced for the hallway.

The bomb might go off any minute. I held my breath as we corralled the group down the hallway.

We encountered the policemen and soldiers all urging small groups of girls and adults in the vestibule.

"Is that the last of them?" I asked one of the constables.

"Think so."

We all filed out of the front doors. Once our group of girls saw the other teachers and students on the other side of the street, they ran to them. The rescuers and I headed for the line of vehicles.

A rumble coursed through the ground. A smaller explosive set off the main charge. Most of us dived to the ground, but some didn't react fast enough, and the force of the blast knocked them off their feet. Bricks, chunks of concrete, and burning debris rained down around us.

I got up and checked on a cop who had failed to hit the ground. He was stunned but unhurt. Feldman did the same for another constable and helped him to stand. A soldier and a constable were bleeding from falling debris. I looked toward the sixty or so students and teachers. Most were traumatized but appeared unhurt.

I raced across the grounds and the street, then descended the hill. Three constables and two soldiers were already there inspecting the wreckage. The car was riddled with bullet holes, and half the windows were blown out.

Two of the occupants had been extracted by the cops and lay dead on the rocky slope. Both men. I ignored one of the cops trying to stop me from approaching and slid to a stop by the side of the vehicle. The two in front were still in their seats. Both had been hit several times by bullets and lay slumped on the dashboard.

Neither was Nadia. She wasn't there. Frustration and disappointment enraged me, and when one of the constables tried to pull me away from the car, I shoved him against the car before walking back to the street.

Sergeant Mills was waiting for me at the top of the hill. "I don't want to see you ever behave like that around my men again. Is that understood?"

I stopped beside him, apologized, and pointed toward the wreck. "There are only four of them."

"And?"

"By my count that leaves at least two more. And one of them is a woman assassin named Nadia al-Katib. She's responsible for several bombs and murders."

"Was she the one who stabbed your friend at the house?"

"Yes, and set off the bomb that killed my unborn child and put my fiancée in the hospital."

"And you have no idea where she might be?"

"The best I can figure is that she's still in Jerusalem somewhere. I'm betting she and her cohort are planning another bomb. This isn't over yet."

"You and your two friends saved many girls' lives today. Their parents will be eternally grateful, but I still have to take the three of you in."

"Sergeant, you take us in, and you'll put us at the mercy of Wetherbee. You saw what happened with him and DCI Gilman the other night."

"That's not for me to decide, and you know it," Sergeant Mills said.

He started to walk away, but I stood in his path. "There are still two bombers out there. We don't know where or when they'll strike next. The best way to find them is to let me go. That assassin is hell-bent on seeing me suffer. I'm the bait."

Mills responded by turning to the three cops standing near the crowd of teachers and students. "Take this man and his companions and put them in a car until we can get them to the station."

Two of the constables came up to me and took my arms. As they led me away, I continued to stare at Mills.

"No good deed goes unpunished, right, Sergeant?"

47

The irony was not lost on me: an ex-cop being an old hand at spending time behind bars. And this one was like so many others: dark, windowless, and cold despite the heat outside. Feldman paced the ten-by-ten holding cell while Joshua leaned against the bars separating our cell from a neighboring one. He talked quietly to another arrestee, who mirrored Joshua's posture.

I sat on the concrete bench, leaning back against the wall. I'd dozed off and had no idea how long I'd been out or what time it was. My cellmate's constant footsteps on the gritty floor had finally woken me up, and it was beginning to bug me. "You're going to wear out your shoes if you keep doing that."

Feldman ignored the comment. As much as I needed a good night's sleep, further dozing was now out of the question. I got up and moved over to the front of the cage and grasped the bars.

He came up next to me and got in my face. He kept his voice low and hissed his words. "If they want to charge Joshua and me for being members of Haganah, they could throw us in prison."

"Are you saying that saving those kids was a mistake?"

"No, but I don't trust the British. They lock up Jews for less. And they arrested us despite what we did."

"Relax," Joshua said as he walked up to us. "We'll be taken care of if that happens. We all did some good work." He thrust a thumb at the man in the other cell. "And word is, the assault on the Black Hand in Jaffa was a success."

"There are at least two still out there," Feldman said.

Joshua put a hand on Feldman's shoulder. "But we've managed to cripple the group."

"The ones pulling the strings are just going to turn around and form another one," I said.

"That will take time. We use that time to expose the leaders."

Feldman pounded the bars. "And how are we supposed to do that from prison?"

"Stop worrying about things that haven't happened yet," Joshua said. "Focus on what needs to be done to cut off the head."

I squeezed the bars harder and jerked them in my frustration. "They have to let us out of here. Nadia will carry out her orders. Hell or high water."

"You're hoping she doesn't leave before you can get your hands on her," Joshua said.

"Truer words have never been spoken."

The door at the end of the corridor opened, and a constable headed for the holding cells. He stopped in front of us. "Mason Collins, you're to come with me."

I glanced at my companions, who returned looks of trepidation. "Looks like they're going to put the screws to me first."

The guard opened the cell door, and I stepped out. Once he locked the door again, I followed him down the corridor and through the reinforced door. We went down an equally dim corridor until coming to a room at the end. The guard stepped aside to let me enter.

I was expecting a couple of detective constables getting ready to grill me, but instead Gilman was sitting on the edge of a square table.

"Thank you, Corporal, that will be all. And close the door."

The corporal did as he was told. Gilman lit a cigarette while waiting for the guard to move out of listening range. He offered me one.

I took it and used his lighter. "Any news on Mrs. Atkinson?"

Gilman hesitated by taking a drag on his cigarette. I braced myself.

"I understand there were some complications. They took her in for a second surgery, but I'm afraid she didn't make it."

My gut clenched with guilt and anger. I wanted to punch something, cry out in rage. Instead I turned away from him and took several puffs off the cigarette. Gilman remained silent, which I figured was to give me time to absorb the news.

I had to change the subject, or I would explode. "Why are you down here? It's more than just telling me about Evelyn."

"I've said it before, you've been a busy man, but I think the last couple of days have exceeded my expectations."

"Am I supposed to take that as a compliment?"

"I approve of your results, but not your methods. What do you know about the assaults on a military camp outside of Haifa and an installation in Jaffa?"

"What kind of assaults?"

The detective constable raised an eyebrow, then threw his cigarette on the floor and stomped it out. "The men in the Black Hand were operating illegally, but many were still active military intelligence personnel, not to mention all of them being British citizens. Their killings will be met with a swift response."

"Don't tell me you're defending them."

"Not at all, but my concern at the moment is that you and members of Haganah and Irgun may have taken the law into your own hands. If you are withholding information about your friends' involvement, I will be forced to charge you with accessory to murder."

"I don't know anything about what Haganah or Irgun did or plans to do."

Gilman looked me in the eye as if deciding how far to press that line of questioning. He didn't seem angry or frustrated, calm really. "While I'm sympathetic to your motives and applaud the loyalty to your friends, I'm still a policeman. I won't look the other way when it comes to murder, regardless of sides."

"What about the murder of children?" I growled. "Or innocent people who just happen to be in the radius of a bomb blast? Me and my *friends*, as you call them, stopped those bastards when the police couldn't. Or wouldn't."

The inspector's face turned red, but his expression remained neutral. "How did you know about the bomb at the international school?"

"I put certain clues together. I still don't know who on the police force is friend or foe, so we took it upon ourselves to deal with the situation."

"But you've so far failed to capture Nadia."

"That's right."

"Do you have any leads to follow in that regard?"

"Nothing. And I'd brace myself for another bomb. She's a soldier and a fanatic and won't stop until she's carried out her mission."

"Which includes you."

"You're the one who wanted to use me as bait, so yeah, I hope so."

Gilman turned his focus to the wall and lit another cigarette. I got the feeling he was torn between duty and conviction.

Finally, he said, "I'll help when and where I can. In the meantime, I'm having you released. Under the circumstances, you're not what I would consider a flight risk."

"You know I'm going to be looking into police involvement in the Black Hand."

Gilman turned his gaze to me and nodded.

"What about Feldman and Klein?" I asked.

"They'll be interviewed—"

"You mean interrogated."

"Call it what you like. If those go well, and since they're heroes—for a day, at least—they'll be released on their own recognizance."

Gilman got up off the table and opened the door. He leaned out, called for the corporal, and then turned back to me. "You're free to go."

The corporal arrived at the door.

I started to exit when Gilman said, "See that you're always somewhere I can reach you. Just make sure it isn't the morgue."

48

A crush of people formed a semicircle at the front entrance of the Italian Hospital. Concerned family members peppered questions at the four guards at the doors, while walk-in patients with bandages or doubled over from pain—alone or with companions—clamored to be admitted quickly.

I had to wait patiently while the guards briefly interviewed people and let them in one at a time. Others arrived as the crowd shuffled forward. I asked a couple of people around me the reason for the chaotic scene, but no one seemed to know except that they were redirected to the Italian Hospital from the Bikur Cholim and Rothschild hospitals. The guards at the entrance didn't know or weren't saying.

Inside, I excuse-me'd my way through the lobby and checked in at the guard's desk. I handed over my backpack and pistol. I'd done this with him so many times before that he took them without questions.

"What's going on?" I asked.

"We're getting most of the ambulatory patients from Bikur Cholim because of the bomb they found. And Rothschild because of a power failure of some kind. They've had problems with the electrical system for months."

I wished him luck with the crowds and left.

Seeing a woman on a gurney with blood on her blouse conjured up images of Atkinson in my arms and bleeding from the chest. Her dying words, and my part in her murder. As I climbed the staircase, those thoughts made my legs feel heavy and my chest throb. The fatigue and hunger made my emotions worse, and I found it hard to keep them under control.

The only way to shake off those feelings was by focusing on Nadia. What was her next move? Was she in hiding until things blew over, or out there stalking the streets looking for me? Unfortunately, my only real option was to hang out on the city streets, baiting her to come out of the shadows.

But first, I needed time with Laura. She was my salve, my light in the fog. She never tolerated my brooding, chiding me anytime I went to those dark places in my mind. And this time those thoughts were particularly bad.

Her mother had found Laura a private room a floor above the old one. After asking around, I was directed to the last door on the left and knocked. I entered without waiting for a response.

The space was large enough for two beds, but there was only Laura's. She was sleeping with a pained look on her face. Mrs. McKinnon sat in a chair near the bed and glared at me over the top of a fashion magazine.

She got up and cut me off before I could get any closer. "What kind of man leaves the woman he professes to love while she's recuperating in the hospital?"

"The one trying to find the killer of our child."

"A life for a life. Is that how you see it?"

I clamped my mouth shut before I said something I'd regret later.

"Mother, let him be," Laura said.

Mrs. McKinnon rushed over to her bedside in another

blocking maneuver. "I'm sorry, pumpkin, for waking you. How are you feeling?"

Laura waited until I was at her side. She smiled at me. "Better now."

Most of her bandages were still in place, though the bruising and swelling had reduced somewhat. Still, the sight made my stomach clench. She could barely keep her eyes open, but she found enough strength to raise her arms to me. I bent over and let her embrace me. I tried to keep a gap between us; I was terrified of pressing her in the wrong place.

I could feel her mother's cold, hard stare on my back. Laura gave me a peck on the cheek and held me in place. She said in my ear, "Did you get them?"

I stood up straight and nodded. The words clogged in my throat, but I finally said, "We got them."

Her eyebrows bent, which I knew meant that she didn't believe me. "Good."

Mrs. McKinnon hissed her displeasure and backed away. "I'm going to get a cup of coffee." She stuck out a finger in my direction. "And you should get a bath. You stink."

"Mother. Stop it."

Mrs. McKinnon shot me another icy glare before leaving the room.

"I think your mom and I are getting along great."

Laura returned a look of exasperation. She took my hand and squeezed. "I was so scared you'd be hurt or worse. Or that you'd be put in prison or expelled from the country."

"I'm here, so no worries."

"I'm sure it'd take both my hands to count the number times your life was on the line. But I can't think about that right now."

She was trying to put on a brave face, but the pall of loss hung like a dark shadow in the room.

She didn't seem to know about Atkinson's death, and I did my best to hide the weight of my sadness. She could usually decipher my emotions with just a glance, but she was probably too weak and distracted to pick up on them. I debated in those seconds whether to tell her ...

"My father is due in tomorrow," Laura said with little excitement behind it.

I muttered a "That's good," and I took off my jacket.

"I want you to meet him. He'll like you, I'm sure."

"I look forward to it," I said flatly.

"Well, that sounded sincere." She knotted her eyebrows again. "There's something on your mind that you're not telling me. And if I had to guess, it's that the Black Hand isn't really gone."

"Oh, they're gone."

She peered into my eyes. A touch of fear crossed her face. "But that woman assassin is still out there, isn't she?"

"Laura—"

"Tell me."

"Yes. She and one other man are the only members to have survived."

Laura unconsciously glanced at the door, prompting me to do the same. The noise from the chaos in the hallway had gotten louder.

"They've had to admit patients from two other hospitals," I said. "It's getting crazy out there."

She turned back to me. "The doctors said I'm well enough to travel in a day or so. My parents are insisting that I go back with them. My mother drives me crazy, but perhaps that's for the best." She paused and looked at me expectantly.

I said nothing. I could have blamed it on the lump in my throat, but the reality was that I didn't have a good counteroffer; I had no money and nowhere to go that ensured she'd be safe and able to recover.

She said, "If I'm leaving, I want you to get away from here too. Forget going after that woman. It's not worth it."

"I think it is."

"Damnit, Mason. Killing her is not going put things back the way they were."

"That bomb is not the only reason."

"What do you mean?"

"She murdered Evelyn."

"She what? Evelyn's dead?"

Tears formed in Laura's eyes, and I found it hard to look at her. I told her that Atkinson had come with me while I followed a suspect to a house. That when I went in, she stayed in the car, thinking she'd be safe, but that the assassin wounded her in the chest purposely to get at me. "She died here, at this hospital, sometime today."

"You get her, Mason. Do you hear me?"

She started crying. I bent down, and we held each other. We stayed that way for a long while until Mrs. McKinnon came back in the room.

She waltzed over to Laura with her cup of coffee. "I met the sweetest woman in the cafeteria. She seemed very interested in what I was doing in Jerusalem. She heard my American accent and said she was always curious about America and Americans. She hoped my stay in Jerusalem was not too troublesome since I was in a hospital."

I was only half listening to her as I continued to look at Laura. But when she said that the woman kept asking questions about her daughter and if she could meet her, alarm buzzed through me.

"What did she look like," I asked, interrupting her.

"What do you care?" Mrs. McKinnon said.

Laura must have picked up on my train of thought because she squeezed my hand in a tight grip. "Mother, it might be important."

Mrs. McKinnon looked confused as she shifted her gaze between her daughter and me. "Well ... she spoke in a British accent. Though she looked like a light-skinned Arab, if I had to guess. Quite pretty. Maybe in her late twenties, but as you get older people start looking younger, you know—"

"Did you tell her what room Laura is in?" I said with urgency in my voice.

"Don't take that tone with me, young man."

"Mother!" Laura said.

She turned to her daughter, her face twisted in confusion. "She said she wanted to visit. I didn't see the harm."

I thought of the Black Hand commando I spotted around the hospital, the Black Hand guy in Atkinson's apartment saying they were going to cause a maximum amount of pain, Nadia promising to harm anyone important to me. I rushed for the door. "She could be coming for Laura. She could have planted a bomb. Block the door with whatever you can find."

"But I—" Mrs. McKinnon said.

"Do it now!" I said as I exited and slammed the door behind me.

49

I took long strides down the hallway, scanning faces I passed. The chaos I encountered in the lobby was filtering to the upper floors. The influx of patients transferred from the other hospitals had overloaded the Italian Hospital's capacity.

A perfect scenario for a bomb. Maximum casualties.

And if Nadia's mission was to cause me the most pain, killing Laura in a devastating explosion was her obvious and best option. I went from room to room, searching for signs of a bomb. I disturbed patients and elicited the wrath of nurses, pushed past anyone trying to stop me. One nurse followed me while yelling for me to stop, that I was violating patient privacy and that she'd call security. I Ignored her and searched the storage rooms, the nurses' stations, and lounges.

In minutes, I'd searched the entire floor. Nothing. No sign of a bomb.

I stood at the end of the corridor and ran through the possibilities. If the bomb wasn't here, then where else would it do the greatest amount of damage and still have a good chance of hurting Laura? Someplace they could plant the bomb undetected.

The King David Hotel was heavily damaged when Irgun

stacked milk churns full of explosives in the basement. That blast took down an entire wing.

The nurse who had threatened me with security was now coming down the hall with an oversized cop in tow. She pointed like she was siccing a dog on me.

As the cop surged forward, I did the same. He tensed, ready for a fight, but I held up my hands in a peace offering. That gesture didn't work. He grabbed me by the arms to drag me away.

I spun out of his grasp, trapped his right arm behind his back, and pushed him against the wall. "I don't want any trouble, sir, but we have an emergency."

He tried to squirm out of my grasp, but I held him firm. I lowered my voice and said in his ear, "Look, I don't want to create panic, but there could be a bomb in this hospital."

"Don't want to create panic? Too late for that. Now unhand me and get out of here before I have you arrested."

I let him go and held up my hands in another gesture of peace. Which he again ignored and went for his truncheon. I had no choice, and with three strategic blows, I put him on the floor.

I raced for the stairs and took the steps three at a time. On the ground floor, I raced up to the first soldier I could find.

"Private, I believe there's a bomb planted in the basement of this hospital."

He gave me the same look as the big cop, like I was a raving lunatic. "Sir—"

"Soldier, I don't have time to argue. You need to come with me now to the basement."

"I'm not going anywhere without the sergeant's okay."

"Then get him."

"Sir, I'm not leaving my post."

I was about to curse at him when someone said, "I'll go."

I turned to see a young redheaded corporal standing behind me.

He said, "Private, go tell the sergeant I'm going with this man. Ask him to send a few others, if he can spare them."

The private went off to find the sergeant.

"I'd have your pistol ready," I said. "One is a skilled assassin, and the other is former special forces."

The corporal removed the Webley from its holster. "Shall we?"

We went down the corridor leading away from the lobby and then turned down the same administrative hallway I'd used a few days earlier after entering through the garage. The corporal stopped at the last door on the left before the exit to the kitchen. He opened it and flicked a light switch.

A bare lightbulb illuminated the concrete steps leading to the basement. The corporal led the way. The thrum of the ventilation system grew louder as we descended. The air was cooler and permeated with the faint odor of fuel oil.

We reached the bottom and took cautious steps down a long corridor. My ears were alert for any unusual sounds. The corporal had his Webley out in front.

There were several openings off to the left before the corridor took a turn in the same direction. We came up to the first one. I tapped on the corporal's shoulder and signaled that I would take a position on the opposite side. I did so, and we peeked around the edges at the same time. It was a sizeable tool room and lit well enough to see that it was empty.

We moved on to the next opening. It accessed a short hallway of ten feet, and beyond was a large space with furnaces and turbines. Portions of the main support columns were visible and stood like a pine forest. The lights were on but sparsely placed, creating small pools of illumination with the rest going into shadow.

I figured we were in the structural heart of the wing. If I wanted to bring down a building, this would have been the place to do it. Despite any sign of life, I signaled for us to enter.

We hugged opposite sides of the hallway and moved to the end. We peeked around as before but saw nothing. The ventilation fans were loud and echoed off the stone walls, but a faint click of metal on metal reached my ears.

The corporal must have heard it too, because he raised his gun and aimed it at the sound. I figured they were behind one of the columns or off to one side, not visible from where we stood.

I counted down with my fingers—three, two, one—and we both surged forward.

Nadia and her companion came into view. They were both kneeling and adding wires to blasting caps embedded in three fifty-five-gallon drums.

"Stop right there!" the corporal yelled as he brought his pistol to bear on them.

Nadia sprang from her coiled position and threw a tool at the lightbulb above her head. The bulb burst. The area fell into darkness.

The corporal shot at Nadia, but she was too fast. The flash and explosion of a gun came from where the companion had been squatting. The corporal and I ducked, and the man fired again. Above the ringing in my ears, I heard running footsteps on the concrete floor.

Fortunately, we were in the dark as well, foiling the shooter's accuracy. I launched from my prone position and sprinted toward the sound, stopping behind one of the support columns. Nadia's companion had stopped as well. The sound came from the ventilation fans.

I surveyed the pools of light in the near distance and quickly spotted a sliver of the shooter's jacket peeking out from a column fifteen feet away. The corporal had stayed where he was and fired one shot into the shadows. Nadia's companion fully revealed himself when he returned fire at the corporal.

I moved slowly, keeping to the shadows, and hooked around to get behind him.

The corporal must have seen what I was doing and fired once more.

I slinked across the space, one slow step at a time. I ducked behind the last column between me and him, tensed my muscles, then rushed him.

The man spun around, but I was on him before he could bring his gun around. I pushed his gun arm up to the ceiling just as the gun went off.

The man was too fixated on his gun and left himself open. I kneed him in the groin and struck his neck at the same time.

The gun clattered to the floor. He tried to strike me, but I blocked his swing. Grabbing him by the neck, I slammed his head against the column multiple times. His eyes rolled back into his head. I let go of him, and he crumpled to the concrete.

I immediately grabbed the gun and went into a defensive position. I knew Nadia would charge. I peered into the darkness all around me.

I heard rustling but couldn't tell from which direction. The corporal cried out, then grunted. I swung around with the gun pointed. The corporal was on the ground. Blood was pooling around his head. But no Nadia.

I pivoted toward the shadows, my senses on high alert. A clank of metal hit the floor off to my left. I turned.

A zip of fabric was the only warning, and I spun around. Nadia burst out of the darkness. She lunged with her knife and sliced it across my gun arm. I recoiled from the searing pain and lost control of the pistol.

To stop was to die, and I kept moving to avoid another swing of her blade.

She did a pirouette and slashed. Instincts took over, and I was ready this time. I blocked her arm and tried to trap her, but she was too fast.

She twisted out of my grasp and pivoted, sweeping her knife at me.

I ducked, then threw a roundhouse punch. My fist slammed into her jaw, but it barely fazed her.

Like an acrobat, she spun away from the blow and came back with more fury, slashing and lunging.

Blood poured down my arm. I kept backing up as she advanced, watching for an opportunity. I knew if I backed up anymore, I'd step out of the light.

I stopped and feigned a weak stance and waited. She was so crazed that it interfered with her judgment, charging, leaving herself open. It was just for second, but I took it and struck her in the chin.

She recoiled and slashed at me, forcing me to jump to the side. Blood ran from her mouth, and her swings had less accuracy.

She growled with rage and lunged. A bad move.

I grabbed her wrist with my left and clamped onto her throat with my right.

She kicked at me and tried twisting out of my grasp, but I had her, and my fury matched hers.

I kept squeezing her neck. I could feel her windpipe collapsing under my fingers.

She backed up to pull away and collided with one of the columns.

Her face was turning from red to blue. She fought with less power. She dropped her knife, and I kicked it into the blackness.

She attempted to yell, but it came out as a gurgle. Her eyes widened in a crazed, wild glare. Like a cat, she bent her legs, knees to her chest, and kicked me with such force that it propelled me backward.

The wind was knocked out of me, and I staggered back on my heels. I tripped over Nadia's unconscious companion and fell onto my back. The back of my skull struck the concrete, and my head spun.

Nadia came at me with a metal pipe and brought it down on my chest.

I tried to get some distance by pushing my back along the floor.

The pipe came down again. I turned, and it hit me in the hip. Still gasping for air and disoriented from the fall, I got to my knees and retreated for the shadows.

With a sickening swoosh, the pipe slammed onto my back. One more blow, and I would be done.

In crawling in the darkness, my hand landed on the companion's pistol.

Nadia let out a wild growl. I spun onto my back with the gun raised. She was in midswing when I emptied the pistol into her chest.

She was dead before she hit the ground.

I forced myself to stand and staggered over to the corporal. His throat was open from ear to ear. He was gone.

Nadia's companion was stirring to consciousness. In two strides, I was on him and jammed the muzzle of the pistol against his neck.

"Who is behind the Black Hand? I want names."

The man was still coming out of a stupor. I'd opened up the back of his skull, and blood pooled on the concrete. His eyes focused on me, and his face twisted in fear. He stiffened and tried to move his head away from the gun.

I repeated the questions with my face in his. I wanted to pull the trigger, and he seemed to sense this.

"I don't know," he said with panic in his voice. "I'm just a squaddie."

"You took orders from someone."

"Colonel Blaine. He's the highest I know."

"You had a handler. Someone who gave your group direct orders."

His fear grew. His eyes bounced around in their sockets as if answering me was more dangerous than the pistol I had at his throat.

I jammed the barrel under his chin and pressed.

"The CID superintendent. Wetherbee."

"Did he order the bombing on Julian's Way?"

"Yes."

"The killing of those Palestinian villagers?"

"Yes. Everything else we've done in Jerusalem. He said he was following orders and that we should do our duty for king and country."

My rage overcame me, and I struck the man in the side of the head with the pistol grip.

I knew Wetherbee was involved, but I'd assumed he was more of a facilitator, not that he was calling the shots. I was sure the superintendent answered to higher-ups, but him being in control of the intelligence branch of the police meant he would be a formidable target to bring down. And that meant his bosses were even more powerful and untouchable. The only chance was to create a scandal.

"Hands in the air!" someone yelled to my left.

Two soldiers had their guns aimed in my direction. One of them was the private I'd tried to convince to accompany me.

I stood with my hands up but kept one foot on Nadia's companion.

A sergeant stepped between the two privates, his eyes fixed on me. Then his gaze went from the dead corporal to the oil drums of explosives behind me. "Get the bomb squad down here as quickly as you can," he said to the privates.

He pointed his chin at me and asked the remaining private, "Is this the man you spoke of?"

"Yes, sir. Corporal Williams went with him instead."

I wobbled in place as I tilted my head toward the man under my foot. "The corporal and I found this man planting the bomb."

I glanced at Nadia. "Along with that woman. She's a known assassin. They were both Black Hand."

"Restrain the man on the floor," the sergeant said.

While the private did as ordered, the other soldier returned with a five-man bomb disposal team with their tools.

"They got here quick," I said to the sergeant.

"We called them after your warning of a bomb."

The squad went to work, and the two privates dragged Nadia's companion out of the room.

"You're going to have to be debriefed about all this," the sergeant said.

"I've been in frequent contact with DCI Gilman. He can vouch for me."

He pointed to my bleeding arm. "Why don't you see about getting that patched up. In the meantime, I'll send word to Inspector Gilman. You're not to leave this hospital until we're done with you."

"That's okay by me. You'll find me in room 407."

By the time I made it back to Laura's room, I could hardly hold myself up. My hands were shaking, my legs had turned to rubber. A nurse had stitched up my arm, but she could do nothing for the broken ribs or massive bruises on my hip and back. She let me take a shower, which sapped whatever adrenaline I had left in my system, and I nearly passed out under the warm water.

I knocked softly on the door and expected Mrs. McKinnon to yank it open and tell me to go take a hike. But no one came. I entered and saw Laura was alone and asleep.

I shuffled over to the chair near the bed and sat. I took her hand and laid my head on her thigh. She stirred and began stroking my hair.

"Where's your mom?"

"Once we got the all clear for the bomb, she said her nerves were too rattled to spend another hour in this place. She went back to her hotel room. So you can ravage me if you like."

"Take a rain check? I don't think I can move."

"Pity. We won't get another chance for a while. My dad's

arriving in the morning, and I got approval to travel. They'll be taking me home tomorrow."

I said nothing. It hurt too much to think about her out of my life once again.

"You could come," she said.

"That'd go over well with your mom."

We lay there in silence for a moment.

She lifted her head. "You're hurt."

"You should see Nadia. On a cold slab in some morgue by now."

Laura smiled, put her head back on the pillow, and let out a long sigh of relief.

"The only surviving member of the Black Hand is behind bars. The gang is no more."

She stroked my face. "Thank you."

"The pleasure was all mine, ma'am. But it's not completely over. I got the man to talk."

"I would have liked to have been there for that."

I was glad she wasn't anywhere near that scene. I didn't want her to ever witness the rage that came out in me. The urge to kill.

"What did he say?" she asked.

I hesitated. I was unsure how much to tell her. But I decided she deserved to know, and I needed to share it. "He said Wetherbee was calling the shots."

That name seemed to focus her attention, and her eyes blazed with anger. "You didn't find all my documents, did you?"

"Evelyn and I got everything that we could find."

"Look behind a panel in the wall. North side of the room."

I started to make a move to get up, but she grabbed my hair and pulled me back down onto her thigh. "Hold your horses, cowboy. You're staying with me tonight. Get the bastard in the morning."

I wasn't about to argue. For a few moments I was going to

enjoy being with the woman I loved, feel her warmth, and simply listen to her heartbeat.

Then and there, I decided to leave Palestine with Laura. To hell with Wetherbee and his co-conspirators.

For too brief a moment, I could calm the storm raging inside me.

~

LAURA'S FORMER HOTEL ROOM HAD BEEN SEARCHED SEVERAL TIMES after Atkinson and I had gathered up all the documents we could find. The mattress lay on its side with long gashes cut into the fabric. The bed frame sat askew, and the bedside table was in pieces. I knew that Hazan had been here, certainly the police, and more than likely other parties.

I stood for a moment in the debris strewn on the floor. Being in that room again unleashed a flood of emotion, from the of joy at seeing Laura once again to the loss and pain.

It was around 6:40 a.m. I woke up in the same position, sitting in the chair and lying half on Laura's hospital bed. I ached all over and found it hard to stand. I managed to write her a note, telling her where I was going and that I'd be back. Then I slipped out of Laura's room without waking her. For some reason I felt lying in a note was not as bad as looking her in the eye and saying it.

I went over to the north wall of the room and scanned the space between the bed and the west wall. There was a slight bulge a foot square just above the baseboard. I squatted near the spot and ran my hands along the area. On closer examination I noticed a fine seam in the wallpaper. Laura had done a great job of making it almost invisible.

I pulled at one edge and peeled back the paper. Underneath was a thin piece of wood covering a cutout recess in the plaster.

The board popped off easily. Inside the hole sat several file folders bundled together by strips of cotton.

I removed the bundle, placed it on the ravaged bedside table, and untied the ribbon. Inside were a handful of black-and-white photographs, several carbon copies of documents, and around fifty typewritten pages.

I leafed through everything, photographs of Wetherbee with Black Hand members in the Palestinian village and in cafés or bars. The typewritten pages looked to be Laura's interviews with five eyewitnesses to Wetherbee's complicity.

But the real kicker was the set of carbon-copied pages. It was an official British Army document with "Top Secret" stamped on the top, and it outlined the strategic need to keep the oil pipelines from Iraq to the Mediterranean open. That Mandatory Palestine was too important to leave, that the group feared the British government would bend under international pressure to give up the territory and weaken the empire. The authors proposed a scheme to create chaos by terror, blaming the Jews and Arabs and justifying a severe crackdown, taking over cities and expelling thousands of Jews in the process.

"I see you found what you came for," someone said from the door.

I spun on my heels. Gilman stood just inside the door and was flanked by two other detective inspectors. He had a grim expression and stood with his arms folded.

I tried to discern his intentions, especially showing up with two brawny inspectors.

"I went by the hospital this morning to pick you up," Gilman said. "Imagine my surprise when I found you weren't there. Miss McKinnon was most helpful in showing me your note." He held out his hand. "I'll take those."

"What are you planning to do with them?"

"If they're what I think they are, then it can only help."

"Help how?"

Gilman's solemn look transformed into a sly smile. "You're always ready for a fight, aren't you?"

"A life of hard knocks."

"The man you captured in the Italian Hospital basement has talked. Quite a bit, I must say. He confessed and implicated Superintendent Wetherbee as the leader of the Jerusalem cell." He pointed to the bundle on the bedside table. "If those documents corroborate his statement, then we have a very good case. It's a good thing you didn't kill him. I'm sure you were tempted."

"In that case," I said. I picked up the bundle and held it out to him. One of the inspectors came over and took it from me. "Does that mean I'm off the hook?"

"Not with Mrs. Talbot. She expected you to return. But with me? Yes. However, I can't speak for some high-ranking individuals. I'm going to escort you to the military airport and make sure you get on the next flight out of here. It's going to Gibraltar. From there you can go wherever you like."

"My plans don't include Gibraltar."

"I'm afraid you don't have a choice. Stay here and risk jail or assassination. Plus, I want you gone so you don't stir up any more trouble."

I picked up my backpack and hoisted it on my shoulders. "In that case, I have a favor to ask."

Gilman and his two inspectors waited in the car while I walked toward a single-propellor five-seat airplane at the civil airfield outside Jerusalem. The late morning sun already pressed down on my shoulders. The scent of aviation gas was heavy in the air. The airplane's crew was loading luggage and prepping the interior for a bed to accommodate Laura.

Before heading out, Gilman agreed to take me to the morgue to view Atkinson's body. I had to say good-bye even though it was painful to see her like that. Her remains were scheduled to be shipped back to her home in Bath. With my last words, I promised her I'd visit her when I got a chance. I never did get to say good-bye to Feldman or Hazan, but I was sure they would understand. At least, that way, I didn't have to promise to look them up one day when my intention was to never step foot in this land again.

Mrs. McKinnon stood by the plane, pointing and shouting at the hapless crew. As I got closer, she spotted me and sent an icy glare in my direction.

A man, who I assumed was Laura's father, was pushing Laura in a wheelchair from the terminal. Her glum expression brightened when she saw me. My heartbeat jumped into high gear from the flood of bittersweet emotions. Smiling was a chore, but I did it anyway and walked up to them.

"You must be Mason," the man said. He smiled and moved toward me with his hand out.

"Mason, this I my father," Laura said over the noise of another aircraft taxiing on the runway.

The man's smile seemed genuine as we shook hands.

"I've heard a lot about you, son. Good, mostly," he said and winked. He moved in closer. "And I'm glad you got the sons of bitches who did this to my girl and grandchild."

I thanked him. I was too full of emotion to say more.

He glanced at Laura and then turned back to me. "Well, I'll go see how the crew is doing." He said to Laura, "We'll be leaving in a few minutes, honey."

When he headed toward the airplane, I kissed her on the cheek. She grasped my cheeks and pulled my mouth to hers. The kiss was gentle and brief.

"I'd try to convince you to stow away on board, but there's only enough room for the three of us." She shifted her gaze to Gilman standing by his sedan. "They're not arresting you, are they?"

"Kicking me out, more like. There's a transport at an airbase near Tel Aviv with my name on it."

"Then you're coming to Boston," Laura said matter-of-factly.

"As soon as I can," I said after a moment's pause.

She must have seen the uncertainty on my face, because she frowned. "If I don't see you there, I'm going to track you down and box your ears bloody. Do you hear me?" She patted the arms of the wheelchair. "Well, as soon as I can get on my feet." Then her look turned serious. "I need you, Mason."

I became aware of my empty pockets and a backpack with nothing but weapons, a pair of binoculars, one change of clothes, and a second pair of shoes. "I promise, I'll be there."

The airplane's engine coughed a couple of times, then burst to life. Her father approached. Laura stared into my eyes. She knew our future was uncertain and seemed to understand my reluctance in giving her any more than I could.

"Don't give up on us," she said.

"I could never do that."

Her father shook my hand, said good-bye, and wished me luck. He then wheeled Laura to the plane.

I watched as her parents and a crewmember hoisted Laura into the cabin. She glanced back at me. There was strength and certainty in her look, and it gave me hope I'd find a way to see her again.

As I watched the airplane taxi on the runway, I knew one thing for certain: I was nervous, and that surprised me.

I'd be going back the U.S. after five years. I had no idea what to expect once I returned.

What I expected from the place, or more to the point, from myself.

THE END

ALSO BY JOHN A. CONNELL

The Mason Collins Series

Madness in the Ruins (Book #1)

A mutilated body. No witnesses. The only clue, a message, "Those who I have made suffer will become saints and they shall lift me up from hell."

Winter, 1945. Munich is in ruins, and a savage killer is stalking the city.

U.S. Army investigator Mason Collins enforces the law in the American Zone of Occupation. This post is his last chance to do what he loves most—being a homicide detective.

But he gets more than he's bargained for when the bodies start piling up, the city devolves into panic, and the army brass start breathing down his neck.

Then the murderer makes him a target. Now it's a high-stakes duel, and to win it Mason must bring into deadly play all that he values: his partner, his career—even his life.

Haven of Vipers (Book #2)

A fairytale town with gingerbread houses has become the Dodge City of post-WW2 Germany. And the gang running things are ex-Nazis and crooked U.S. Army officers.

Not the best place for U.S. Army detective Mason Collins to keep his head down, serve out his time, so he can go home.

While investigating a rash of murders, Mason discovers a web of coconspirators more dangerous than anything he's ever encountered.

Witnesses and evidence disappear, someone on high is stifling the investigation, and Mason must feel his way in the darkness if he is going to find out who in town has the most to gain—and the most to lose...

Bones of the Innocent (Book #3)

Summer, 1946. Just as assassins from a shadowy organization close in for the kill, a flamboyant stranger offers Mason a way out: He must accompany the stranger to Morocco to investigate the abductions of teenage girls. Girls that vanished without a trace.

Once Mason lands in Tangier, he discovers that nothing—or no one—is what it seems. This playground for the super rich is called the wickedest city in the world, and he realizes those who could help him the most harbor a terrible secret.

But just as Mason begins to unravel the mystery, the assassins have once again picked up his trail. Now, Mason must put his life on the line to find the girls before it's too late. If he lives that long…

To Kill A Devil (Book #4)

1946, Vienna. When a shadowy organization fails to assassinate Mason Collins, they go after his colleagues, his friends, and the love of his life. Mason knows the only way to stop the killings is to cut off the head of the snake.

Armed only with the alias, Valerius, Mason treks across Franco's Spain to war-torn Vienna to eliminate the man ordering the hits. But tracking him down seems to be an unsurmountable task; everyone speaks his name with awe and fear, but no one knows if he's real or a gangland myth.

Mason, desperate for answers, abandons his strict moral code, leading him down a very dark path, and to succeed in hunting one devil, he makes a pact with another.

But what Mason doesn't know is that, even if he does find his way in the darkness, the man they call Valerius has something special in store for him.

Where the Wicked Tread (Book #5)

It is 1947. Mason is on the hunt for the Gestapo commander who, during the war, executed a little girl Mason had sworn to protect. He's tracked the man to the notorious Italian route for escaping Nazi war criminals. The problem is the man is fleeing justice with several other Nazi fugitives, who are bent on abducting a mysterious woman and her young son.

Mason's troubles escalate when he agrees to escort the woman and her son to safety, while helping to smuggle a convoy of Jewish refugees down through Italy to a ship awaiting in Naples. Like a pack of wolves, the Nazis nip at the heels of the convoy in order to capture the woman and child. It finally becomes clear that the only way to stop them and get his man is through one final showdown.

Mason is ready to make the ultimate sacrifice for retribution, for forgiveness, to exorcise his demons. But first he has to survive.

A standalone historical crime thriller

Good Night, Sweet Daddy-O

1958 San Francisco

Struggling jazz musician, Frank Valentine, suffers a midnight beating, leaving his left hand paralyzed. Jobless, penniless, and desperate, Frank agrees to join his best friend, George, and three other buddies to distribute a gangster's heroin for quick money.

What he doesn't know is that George has far more dangerous plans...

Inexperienced in the ways of crime, Frank quickly slips deeper and deeper into the dark vortex of San Francisco gangsters, junkies, and murderers for hire. To make things worse, Frank's newfound love, a mysterious, dark-haired beauty, is somehow connected to it all.

And when it becomes clear that a crime syndicate is bent on his destruction, Frank realizes that the easy road out of purgatory often leads to hell.

AUTHOR'S NOTES

Like all the Mason Collins adventures, this is foremost a work of fiction. The people and incidents in the book are solely my invention. However, I endeavored to stick as close as possible to the historical reality of that region in 1947. My decision to have Mason in Palestine was more of a challenge than I'd first imagined. Trying to get a handle on all the competing factions and personalities had me poring over a pile of books and articles to get the historical backdrop accurate.

Needless to say, the region at that time (as it is now) was a hotbed of passionate views, conflicting truths, and political agendas—no one was in the right, and everyone was in the right. As a writer, my desire is to tell a good story and not get mired in politics or philosophical arguments. I didn't want to distract readers with any political agendas, and I tried to look at each side of the conflict, the British, Jewish, and Arab perspectives to understand their motives. Creating a compelling thriller, while respecting the history of the region, demanded a delicate balance.

The names of the Jewish agencies and militant organizations, and the clandestine Palestinian Arab groups, did exist as portrayed in the book, and the British police and military situation is as close to accurate as possible. As you might imagine, Jerusalem, and Israel in general, were vastly different in 1947. Jerusalem was a small town compared to its urban sprawl of today, and Tel Aviv was still in its relative infancy. I was fortunate to find several maps and photographs of Jerusalem and other cities of that time, providing me with street names (most street names were changed once Israel came into being), the locations of the hotels, hospitals, police stations, and British military installations. Those aided me greatly in having an accurate lay of the land. A militant group of Palestinian Arabs called the Black Hand did exist, though it ceased to be a viable organization by the mid-1930s. The history of the group and its leader, as laid out in Mason's story, is a matter or record. However, the Black Hand group in the book is fictitious, though I did find some historical sources alluding to the fictitious group's conspiracy that was planned but never hatched.

The Palestinian village Alal, while modeled after real villages, exists only in the book. The Black Hand's military camp, too, sprang from my imagination. The same applies to the refugee ship and Mason's experiences on the voyage; those were an amalgam of the real ships and the refugees' experiences in attempts to reach Mandatory Palestine from war-torn Europe. The bombing incidents in the book are also fiction, though the actual violence occurred on an almost daily basis in 1946 and 1947. On the other hand, the hospitals, churches, police stations were real, as is the kibbutz, Kiryat Anavim, which was settled by Ukrainian Jews in the 1920s.

The books, articles, and websites about this era are exhaustive. There are so many sources, both in print and on the web, that it was impossible to include them all. Below is a list of the resources I relied upon the most:

Underground to Palestine and Reflections Thirty Years Later by I. F. Stone

Anonymous Soldiers: The Struggle for Israel, 1917-1947 by Bruce Hoffman

The Making of the Arab-Israeli Conflict 1947-1951 by Ilan Pappé

Righteous Victims: A History of the Zionist-Arab Conflict by Benny Morris

Irgun: Revisionist Zionism, 1931-1948 by Gerry Van Tonder

I truly learned a lot when researching for this book and enjoyed writing it immensely. Like any writer, my greatest wish is for you to enjoy the adventure while being transported back in time. And if you're a fan of history, like me, you'll revel in living through a tiny slice of this complicated and emotionally charged place and time.

ABOUT THE AUTHOR

John A. Connell writes spellbinding crime thrillers with a historical twist. His Mason Collins series follows the ex-military policeman to some of the most dangerous and turbulent places in the post-World War Two world. The series has garnered praise from such bestselling authors as Lee Child and Steve Berry. *Where the Wicked Tread* has been nominated for best e-book 2022 by International Thriller Writers, and *Madness in the Ruins* was a 2016 Barry Award nominee, and. Atlanta-born, John spends his time between the U.S. and France.

You can visit John online at: http://johnaconnell.com

 facebook.com/johnconnellauthor1
 twitter.com/johnaconnell
 bookbub.com/profile/john-a-connell

Made in the USA
Monee, IL
17 January 2023

25448616R10218